KATHERINE KEMPF

Copyright © 2023 Katherine Kempf.

All rights reserved. No part of this publication may be reproduced, distributed, or transmitted in any form or by any means, including photocopying, recording, or other electronic or mechanical methods, without the prior written permission of the publisher, except in the case of brief quotations embodied in critical reviews and certain other noncommercial uses permitted by copyright law.

For more information, email: katherine.kempf@posteo.de

This is a work of fiction. Any references to historical events, real people, or real places are used fictitiously. Names, characters, and places are products of the author's imagination and any resemblance to actual persons, living or dead, organizations, events or locales is entirely coincidental.

ISBN: 978-1-960477-00-2 (Digital)

ISBN: 978-1-960477-01-9 (Paperback)

Book design and front cover image by Joseph Dente.

Edited by Alexandra Vasilyevna and Ziva Larson

First printing edition 2023

Katherine Kempf Books

Germany

www.katherinekempfbooks.com

For my parents, who fostered my love of writing
For my husband, who coaxed that love back out of me
And for my daughter, who gave me a reason to write again

PROLOGUE

She watched the glowing embers rise up into the moon-lit sky. The ash from the atmosphere had been falling a little more every day, revealing the silver beams that she remembered from The Time Before. Tilting her head to the side, she watched the way the milky light wove through the clouds, trying to trace them back - through the ash - to the moon itself, but it had been so long since there'd been an illuminated night that, she no longer knew where to look to find the moon in the darkness.

She followed the trail of smoke in the sky back down to where the flames were rising from the bonfire and thought of the ash that would be left behind when the flames had died.

When she was young, her father had called the ash fairy dust. He told her the fire was important because the ash it produced would help new things to grow.

Her mother, however - never one to mince words - told her that the fire was a warning to the other tribes not to challenge the Celts or risk their eradication. She'd definitely preferred her father's version as a kid.

So, when the Earth spit up fire and covered all the world in ash, she called it fairy dust and knew her tribe - so steeped in the lore of the fire - had been blessed with a new beginning.

Her she-wolf mother and her Druid-father rallied the remaining Celts to them, from all across the Old Kingdom. Together, her parents unified the people of the isles, painted their bodies with the ashes of the Old World, and, like their ancestors of old, warred naked against the rebels.

When their islands were swallowed up by the sea, her mother brought the Celts across the water and found them a new land. She bound them to their unified tribe, offering them food, shelter, and protection in exchange for their loyalty. And they gave it to her willingly.

But, the land was hard won and littered with natives, so she led the Celtic people on a crusade along the crumbling city roads and through the ports of the fjords. They had left each place smoldering so that whomever came after them would have fertile ground to cultivate.

Smoldering, indeed, she thought to herself. She scoffed thinking of how her mother's face had looked after her match today in the ring. She was glad she'd been assigned a scouting mission, glad to be leaving camp for a few days.

"Oi! Quit mucking about!" A voice called out to her from beyond the tent as a hand hit its side. An eager smile crept onto her face when she heard the lilting in the voice. It made her feel even more eager to be headed out on the scouting mission since he would be going too. "I don't care whose daughter you are, we need to get a move on!" he shouted.

She lifted up her hunting knife and weighed it in her hands tossing it from left to right and back to left. She paused, her right hand instinctively reaching up to her neck and sweeping her thick, raven hair aside. Her fingertips traced the scar at the base of her neck, following the sideways "T" down her vertebrae, carved there the day she was born with the very knife she held in her hand.

It had been her mother's gift to her, the scar of her birth. Her welcome into the tribe. She'd been celebrated as their next leader, her fate sealed. The "T" was taken from the language of the Old World. It symbolized the birch tree - stark and white - and the birch tree was the promise of the tribe's new beginning. It had been her birth that launched the ships across the water in search of their new homeland.

So, all this is my fault, she reminded herself, though she pursed her lips in defiance. It had been a necessary sacrifice for their survival. Just like her newborn blood. She had, after all, caused her mother so much pain that day, and pain was meant to be shared. It was collective.

A blonde head appeared in the doorway of her tent. "Let's go!" he said, exasperated. She shook herself free of the reverie, her fingers closing around the worn-leather hilt of the knife. She sheathed it, the scrape of metal ringing in her ears, and swung her fur-lined jacket over her shoulders as she followed him out.

1

LYSANDER

FOOTFALLS SHOOK ASH FROM the floorboards above. Residual heat from the fire that had blazed through the village pushed water from the concrete walls of the basement around them, making them sweat black, sticky charcoal. The room still radiated with a warmth that briefly made him hesitant to remain. However, they would be hard-pressed to find another place to stay for the night, let alone one that was heated.

Gruff voices overlapped with the sound of several pairs of heavy boots entering the house. A table was overturned with a violent thud and he heard the kitchen cabinets slamming. It sounded like it was only a raiding party, but Lysander ran his hands through his hair nervously, trying to clear his head. If they were looking for food or supplies, they would venture down to the basement eventually. He needed to think of a way for them to get out.

He looked from Magdelena, with ash settling in the long, corn-silk braid trailing over her shoulder, down to Linnaea, whose usually inquisitive, cinnamon eyes were squeezed shut and whose cheeks were streaked with silent tears and soot. Her long, white-blonde hair was tangled in the braided ends of the earflaps that trailed from the woolen hat on her head. The girl's fingers were spread out on the basement floor, rooted like tendrils, absorbing the vibrations from above. Lysander's eyes drifted to a pile of extension cables in the corner and his mind whirled.

Clicking his tongue at Magdelena, he jerked his head toward the cables. She unwrapped her arm from around Linnaea as she slid the pile across the floor towards him. The movement made Linnaea's eyes snap open, and she watched as her mother signed in the dim light from the narrow, sooty basement window above them.

"Why don't we just wait them out?" she suggested. Lysander shook his head.

"It's too late for them to make camp anywhere else," he signed back before beginning to untangle the pile of cables. Magdelena's eyebrows furrowed over her warm, moss-green eyes.

"Well isn't it too late for us then?" she pressed him, her signs strong and determined. He sighed and put down the cables to reply.

"We can't stay here with them," he asserted.

"But we'll freeze out there alone. At least here it's warm," she protested, zipping up the neck of the fleece under her parka with a grimace on her face. He knew she was trying to forget that the reason it was so comfortable in the basement was the burnt village and its charred occupants just above them.

"I can rewire the heat lamp to give us enough energy for a big burnout tonight and we'll just have to figure out something else for tomorrow," he informed her, nervously running one hand through his hair again, causing ash to fall to his shoulders. "Just help me with these." Magdelena raised a skeptical, ashy eyebrow but picked up the cables and started untangling them.

"What are we going to do with these?" Linnaea signed to Lysander before picking up a particularly grimy-looking cable to help.

Lysander followed the length of the soot-stained wall until he found the pipe he was looking for and pointed to it.

"This runs into the gas tank through that plastic pipe," he signed to her, then indicated the pipe in question. He smiled to himself in the darkness as his hand touched it, the plastic sticky with ash from the walls. "*If* there's enough heat, I can use the cables to create a distraction to mask our escape." Linnaea nodded, slowly in understanding. Magdelena paused in the process of untangling cables.

"Your engineering professors would be proud of you," she signed, her weather-beaten face solemn.

"Haha. You're hilarious," Lysander retorted, but he knew she meant the comment earnestly. Crouching, he unzipped his pack, pulled out a worn multimeter, and connected it to an electrical outlet. They were in luck. The house must still have a generator running somewhere because the meter was hovering at 230 volts, just like it should be. He stood up and rummaged through the shelving units around them until he found a rusty pair of cable rippers.

"At least you picked a profession that's useful for the end of the world," she replied to him, her face only slightly bitter as she signed. Returning to her and Linnaea, he started stripping down one end of a cable.

"I have a feeling we'll need your expertise before this is all over," he reassured her.

"Kind of hard to need a botanist when all the trees are dead and there are only four hours of sunlight a day, L," she signed his nickname fondly - an 'L' coming down like a hammer - then tucked a lock of hair that had fallen out of her loose braid behind her ear. Lysander looked to Linnaea, hoping for her help to bolster her mother's ego a bit, but the girl had stopped paying attention to them and was lost in the cables she was untangling.

"I'd argue that's when you need a botanist most, Mag," Lysander replied. "We just need to get you to your lab." He saw Magdelena's shoulders tense as she pulled aggressively at a tricky knot. Linnaea looked at her mother's face in response to the change in her body language and put down the cables she was untangling.

"What was that about?" she signed, and Magdelena shook her head.

"Svalbard." She spelled the word with her fingers, longingly and meaningfully. Linnaea's eyes glowed in the dim light the way they had the first time she and Magdelena had told Lysander about the island and who was waiting for them there. She was nervous, he knew, about what would happen when they got there. *If* they got there.

The three of them worked quickly, Magdelena and Linnaea silently untangling and coiling the cables on the basement floor, Lysander stripping and splaying the exposed copper wiring.

When they had finished, he made sure to place the cable rippers into his backpack, nestled between his spare water and his sleeping mat. They were a valuable find.

Magdelena helped him move several old filing cabinets as quietly as possible into a barrier to protect them from the blast that would come from his distraction.

When the heat from the live copper wires had melted the plastic pipe, the gas tank would be exposed to air and could combust - he had essentially assembled a makeshift bomb in the same room they were in - and that would be their chance to escape. It would take some time for the plastic to melt, but that would give them time to prepare for departure. Lysander's fingers, raw from stripping the wires, ached as he gripped the rough edges of the filing cabinets and slid them into position.

He had plugged one end of the cable into the outlet across from the gas tank, run the cables along the wall to the pipe, and was carefully wrapping the exposed copper around it when the noises upstairs changed abruptly.

Voices picked up outside the building. There were indiscernible shouts, and a gun went off - automatic gunfire - followed by a loud crash. The fragile frame of the house shivered, and ash shook loose from the boards above their heads. The commotion of the fight moved indoors and something pounded against the basement door over and over until a powerful crack rang out with finality. There was a moan and a squelch of blood.

Lysander looked over at Magdelena and Linnaea, frozen where they stood. Blood started to seep through the bottom of the basement door onto the steps, and Linnaea pushed herself back against the wall as she let out an involuntary whimper. Magdelena's hand went to cover the girl's mouth, but it was too late. There were a few careful footfalls above them and then a long, burning silence. Lysander held his breath.

All at once, bullets began spilling into the basement.

Magdelena instinctively shot her body over Linnaea, enveloping her as they rolled behind the file cabinet barrier. Lysander retreated behind a shelf, metal and glass exploding in the air around him.

There was a pause and Lysander could make out foreign insults being shouted from above as the shooter reloaded. He chanced a glance up through the bullet-riddled ceiling and saw a wild-eyed woman click a second mag into place as she barked orders in a language he realized he could almost understand. And in the momentary stillness he heard it – she didn't speak like a Celt. His brain accelerated, eyes darting to Magdelena, then back up to a gun barrel pointing down into the basement, just as the woman cocked it. He stepped out from behind the shelf as the woman raised her weapon.

"*Ohittaa ruuvimeisselin.*" His voice rang in the ashen air. It meant 'pass me the screwdriver,' and was hardly an appropriate phrase for the situation, but it was one of the few things he knew how to say in her language, although he definitely wasn't pronouncing it right.

The wild-eyed woman kicked in the disintegrating remains of the basement door, then stopped and cocked her head, confused. She had a tangle of long, copper-colored curls and a face splattered with freckles. Her tawny eyes shone so brightly they had something feral about them. Her jacket, pants, and boots were all black, making her hair and eyes shine that much more dangerously in the darkness, like the last embers of a dying fire.

The woman's mouth turned into an amused half-smile as she murmured something down the hall to a partner who Lysander couldn't see.

"...*Opps.*" He caught her saying, and the other person answered in a hushed voice, a male voice.

"...can't be...are you sure?" he asked dubiously. The woman nodded to her companion. "Then, it's clear what we have to do," Lysander heard the man say, his voice now at full volume. The barrel of the woman's gun still aimed at him, Lysander made a move towards the stairs.

"*Hitaasti,*" the woman warned, and Lysander nodded, cautiously stepping one boot onto the first step. "Who are you?" she continued.

"Please, there's a child down here." Lysander didn't shift his glance from the woman, her face unchanging, like an insect trapped in amber. She used the gun to gesture for Linnaea to come out. Magdelena hesitantly unfolded herself from around Linnaea, and the two of them moved slowly toward the base of the stairs.

"She's hardly a child," the woman growled. "What is she, thirteen? That's no child. Not in this world. Now, who are you?" the woman repeated.

"Lysander, Magdelena, and Linnaea." Lysander pointed as he introduced them.

"Your wife and daughter?" the woman demanded.

"No. Friends." The woman let out a sniff at his reply.

"Are you armed?" she asked him, and Lysander pulled his multi-tool from his belt loop and held it in his hand where the woman could see it. With an irritated sigh, Magdelena pulled out her hunting knife as well.

"We gave you our names, we've shown you our weapons. Your turn now. Who are you? Why are you here?" Lysander prompted, but the woman scoffed and spat at him.

"I'm asking the questions here. Don't you see the gun? Why do you speak Finnish?" Lysander shook his head.

"No. If you want us to trust you, we're going to need a little more from you." The woman raised the barrel of her gun, and her grip on the trigger flexed. Lysander looked straight into her eyes, his heart thudding loudly. The woman's eyes flashed, almost gold with anger.

"You're not a Celt." It wasn't a question so much as a statement. Lysander shook his head.

"No. None of us are." Magdelena's voice was resolute.

"No," the woman sighed. There was a pause and she lowered her weapon. "I'm Petra." She gestured to the person in the hallway. "This is Lasse. You will come with us."

"Where are we going?" Lysander asked as he climbed up the basement stairs, glass crunching under his boots on the blackened floor. He helped Linnaea up out of the basement and over the blood on the steps, trying to block the dead Celt lying in the hallway from view as he did. Presumably, this was the guy they had heard Petra kill.

They were greeted at the top of the ladder by a friendly grin from a man with ginger stubble and long, blonde hair tied up into a knot on his head. He towered over them, not only in height but also with broad shoulders that might have been intimidating but for the laughter in his pale eyes, which put them immediately at ease. *This must be the Lasse person Petra introduced*, Lysander thought.

Lysander reached around to help Magdelena navigate around the blood as she climbed out of the basement.

A rustling noise caused Petra to snap her head around to check that the back entrance was clear.

"We know a place you will be safe," she said, her eyes still searching for the source of the rustling, like a fox searching for prey in the dark. "That's where we're going." Lysander nodded his thanks in reply, and Petra returned the gesture. Lasse held a finger to his lips and beckoned to them, guiding them past the blackened living room and down the hall to the front door.

The door itself was charred and hanging precariously off its hinges as if it had been kicked in after the blaze. Lasse paused at the door frame, looking both directions for Celts before waving them over the threshold. The sky was heavy and dark, like always. The buildings that lined the street had been emptied, their contents piled up outside each structure and burned after being picked over by the Celts - vultures feeding off the dead. The houses, too, were scorched, their darkened structures stark against the backdrop of snow that had begun to fall. The tree line at the edge of the village that led into the hills was ashy and barren. Lysander felt Linnaea's hand slide into his own as they descended the front steps. He squeezed it reassuringly, watching Lasse nod to a third soldier as he joined their party.

This one was slighter than Lasse, with a cropped, blonde beard and a long ponytail that was braided down his back from the top of his otherwise-shaven head. The side of the man's head sported a long, bright scar. Out of the neck of his parka poked the top of a bright red and true-blue sweater. The man looked over, taking stock of the newcomers with dark eyes as he sheathed an unusual knife.

"*Opps?*" the man asked and Lasse gave a curt nod in reply. The man bent to adjust the laces on his worn, leather hiking boots.

"*Opps?*" Lysander repeated, puzzled, while Magdelena shrugged.

"Short for *opptenningsved*," Lasse explained, zipping up his grey-green jacket to his chin, the discolored collar of a *lusakofte* peeking out. "You guys are firewood. You know, for the Celts. Not anymore, of course, now that you're with us," he grinned, adjusting his pack. Petra gave him a withering look. *Clearly, she was in command here,* Lysander thought.

With the grey light of day having faded and the chill of night rolling in, Lysander had a better gauge for how long they had been in the basement. It had been more than a few hours. The dark afternoon snowfall drifted through the air, mixing with the ash from the Celtic fire.

As they moved down the road in the premature twilight, snow crunching under their boots, Petra and her men checked the bodies strewn about for supplies. Lysander watched them pocket ammunition, medicine bottles, and old, faded papers. Beside him, Linnaea tugged on his hand, her eyes hollow with hunger. She didn't have to sign for him to know what she needed. He considered asking Petra for help. It was worth a shot, at least.

"Excuse me?" Lysander asked tentatively, reaching out to Petra and cautiously tapping her on the shoulder.

"What?" she groaned irritably as if she was already regretting taking them with her.

"Look, I realize we don't have much time, but do you guys happen to have any food? We haven't eaten in two days." He translated his question into sign language as he spoke so Linnaea could follow the conversation.

"You're right. We don't have time," Petra replied shortly.

"Just five minutes?" Lysander exchanged a hopeful look with Linnaea as he asked. Petra dropped her head in her hand and sighed. She raised her other hand to show all five fingers.

"Five minutes," she huffed. Lasse immediately dug into a pocket and pulled out an old tin of tuna fish. He peeled back the metal lid and bent it into a makeshift spoon before handing both it and the tin to Linnaea.

"Thank you," Linnaea signed, looking up gratefully at the large, viking-man before digging into the food. Lasse crossed his arms, watching her, amusement still dancing in his eyes.

Lysander dropped his pack onto the ground, rooting around for a water bottle and drinking deeply before handing the bottle along to Magdelena. She passed the bottle further onto Linnaea, then began unbraiding her hair. The long, corn-silk strands flew back in the gentle wind and snow, as she shook ash and soot from them. Lysander's hands absentmindedly made their way to the *logr* carving strung around his neck that had belonged to his little sister, tracing the notches and twists in the wood as he watched Petra clean residual powder from her gun. The soldier with the braid and the scar pulled out his knife and started sharpening the blade. Both of them avoided eye contact with anyone else, instead keeping their gazes fixed beyond the group, on the perimeter.

"What's up with the girl? Why doesn't she use her voice?" Petra asked, her eyes still focused away from them.

"Nothing's up with her," Magdelena bristled, the pitch of her voice rising as she instinctively became defensive. Lysander was quick to interpret for Linnaea. Magdelena turned to look her daughter in the eyes as she continued. "She's deaf." As Lysander continued to sign, he could see out of the corner of his eye that the soldiers were entranced by the movements of his hands. "She was born that way," Magdelena explained, sitting up straighter as she said it, her voice now melodic with pride. Linnaea matched her mother's expression, the flush on her face accentuating the freckles across her nose. There was a moment when their energy hung in the air, and then Lasse spoke up.

"How do you sign 'Will you teach me some sign language?'" he asked Magdelena, and she looked sideways at Linnaea, whose mouth curled into a smile as soon as her mother had interpreted for her.

"I'd like that," Linnaea signed, and Magdelena translated her reply on for the burly man.

"Thank you," said Lasse, then inclined his head. Magdelena interpreted and Linnaea showed him how to sign 'thank you'. Lasse's blonde eyebrows lifted in concentration as he copied her gesture.

Magdelena cleared her throat, smiling slightly, and started plaiting her hair again as a silence settled back over the group. After a moment, Lysander spoke up, changing the subject with a question that had been gnawing at him.

"Can any of you tell us where exactly we are? It's been a long time since we knew for sure," Lysander asked. "My um…well, my compass is a few degrees off. Water damage," he explained. He saw Petra open her mouth to speak, but Lasse, hands still raised as he practiced the gesture for 'thank you,' chimed in first.

"On the edge of Saltfjellet." He reached into his pocket with his free hand and pulled out a worn map - one of the papers he had lifted off a dead soldier just a few minutes earlier - unfolding it to show them. Magdelena leaned over to look and let out a long breath.

"That far, really?" she gasped and Lasse nodded. "Wow." Magdelena shook her head in disbelief, then showed the map to Linnaea, the girl nodding as she gulped down some water. "We've gone a long way, Sprout," Magdelena put down the map and signed the girl's nickname in the chilly air.

"Where did you start out?" Petra asked, without looking away from the tree line. Magdelena's eyes narrowed at Petra, but she answered, and Lysander continued to interpret for Linnaea.

"Old Stockholm, before it flooded. My husband was a researcher at the university. But we had to leave along with all the other refugees."

"I remember watching those floods on the news," Lasse commented. "Old Stockholm was one of the first Scandinavian cities to go under, after Old

Copenhagen, of course. You guys are a long way from home." Magdelena nodded and tied off the bottom of her braid before she spoke.

"It's a long way, but it was never home. We were headed back to Old Norway, back to my home, when everything started. I had amends to make, you know, before the end of the world." Her words fell harshly, but everyone was familiar with the grief woven into them. Everyone had lost someone.

"When did you meet up with him?" Petra asked, her eyes glowing golden again as she jerked her head towards Lysander. It made him uncomfortable.

"Not until the Lillehammer refugee camp," he replied, and her gaze shifted to Lysander.

"You don't sound like you're from Old Oslo," Petra said, raising an unkempt eyebrow and he shook his head.

"No, I'm not."

"So then, where did you start out? And how did you end up at the biggest camp for Oslo refugees?" She inquired. He could tell she was trying to sound disinterested, but her eyes betrayed her.

"When the volcanoes erupted, I had already been deported," he replied, sitting up straighter and scratching his head, "so I was on a refugee boat in the sea of Old Denmark, trying to get back to my parents and sister." His heart clenched as he spoke of them. Even after all the time that had passed, he could still see Judit's, his little sister's, obstinance and determination to prove the world wrong in Linnaea. He felt his hand jump again to the charm around his neck, his fingertips tracing the notches Judit had carved into it. He heard the gentle tinkling of her fingertips over the rickety old piano keys and saw the red paint on its sides peeling in the sunlight that streamed in through their apartment windows. "They'd also been evacuated from Old Stockholm, like Magdelena and Linnaea," Lysander explained. Magdelena signed for Linnaea, even though it was a story the girl knew all too well.

"Why were you deported?" Petra's voice was challenging, provocative. Lysander nervously ran his fingers through his hair. *Did she think he was a criminal?* He sighed.

"For being Norse. What else?" He answered. "I was studying engineering on foreign soil. If you had a screen or a radio then you know what happened to people who didn't go back to their homelands after the deportations were ordered. The beatings, the lynchings." He saw the gold in Petra's eyes flicker and worried he had given too much away.

"You seem a bit young, yeah? To have been studying in a university when Ragnarök came?" she pressed.

Ragnarök? Lysander thought, confused. It was such an arcane word to be using to describe what had happened to them. He wondered if they had stumbled upon some religious zealots with their own militia or something. He exchanged an uncomfortable look with Linnaea and her mother as Magdelena interpreted for her, their mutual puzzlement over the word shared in the glances they exchanged.

"I was considered, well, gifted is what they called it," Lysander continued, awkwardly. "I started university when I was fifteen years old." Petra's shoulders tightened and she looked down at her weapon, rubbing at some invisible speck of dirt or ash.

"So, engineering, huh? What can you fix?" she asked. *Ah, so this was the reason she was interrogating them,* Lysander realized. *They needed help with something. She wasn't doing a very good job of trying to appear indifferent.*

"Enough," he replied, deciding quickly that if they wanted his help then he was going to try to use that to his advantage. "I tried to help out as much as possible in the refugee camps I stayed at, you know, with power or water. That's where I picked up my Finnish."

"Your Finnish is terrible," Petra told him flatly.

"Maybe so," he shrugged. "But it helped me out in the camps to try to learn a little Finnish or a little Danish. Helped me talk to the other engineers."

"You met a Finnish engineer in one of the camps? What was his name?" The words tumbled abruptly out of the other soldier, the one who had been outside when they'd exited the house. Lysander looked over at him, startled. "Sorry – it's just. I'm looking for someone -" the man stumbled over his words. "We were separated when I got called to active duty, right before Ragnarök," he explained, fingering the ivory blade of the knife Lysander had seen him sheath earlier.

"He was called Gunnár. Good guy," Lysander answered, and he saw the man's face fall at the sound of the unfamiliar name. The ashen snow continued to fall quietly around them. Magdelena was still interpreting for Linnaea, and Lysander could tell from their faces that they, too remembered the old Finn. But he was just one of the many people they'd crossed paths with over the years. "I'm sorry -" Lysander hesitated, unsure of the soldier's name.

"Benjáme." The man spoke his name quietly.

"I'm sorry, Benjáme," Lysander finished, watching the man turn the curious knife over and over in his hands. The cream-colored blade bore carvings of what looked like three pine trees close to the hilt, but the handle was what struck him - smooth and sandy brown - it branched out in several different directions and appeared to be made of some kind of antler.

"That's an interesting knife." Lysander nodded to the piece in Benjáme's hands. He felt the man tense up as he said it, but when Benjáme looked up at him, his face was tender.

"Thanks," he said.

"May I see it?" Linnaea signed, and Lysander interpreted for her. Benjáme stood up and handed the knife across to Linnaea.

"It's made from reindeer bone," he explained as the girl ran her fingers over it, tracing the carvings carefully.

Suddenly, Linnaea jumped up, the empty tin of tuna falling from her lap into the snow, the blade sliding into her small hand a bit too naturally for Lysander's liking. Down and across the street, a motion-sensor light had clicked on in the twilight. A shadow just outside of the beam quivered. Following Linnaea's gaze, Petra snapped her fingers at her men, signaling for Lasse and Benjáme to cover her. Linnaea handed Benjáme back the knife and he sheathed it as silently as possible. Petra caught Lysander's eyes and, with a jerk of her head, indicated that he should stay close to protect Magdelena and Linnaea. Lysander swung his pack onto his back and moved towards them.

The three of them watched Petra side-step lightly, cat-like, through the snow. She gestured to her men and they doubled back, rushing around the side of the building to flush out whatever Celt straggler was lurking on the far side.

Lysander positioned himself in front of Magdelena and Linnaea, a few paces behind Petra, as they all crossed the street towards the opposite side of the building behind which Lasse and Benjáme had disappeared.

A muffled gunshot rang out through the falling snow as a scrappy mess of unruly, black hair came bounding around the corner of the building.

Lysander watched the dark, elfin creature skid to a halt in front of Petra, whipping a knife from her boot and dodging Petra's first swing at her with ethereal agility. The young woman ducked under Petra's gun, elbowing it up into her nose, hard. Blood splattered the snow as Petra kicked the woman's feet out from under her.

Sprawling, Petra grabbed the woman by her long tangle of dark hair and pulled her close enough to twist the knife blade back against the woman's own throat.

Where are Lasse and Benjáme? Lysander thought frantically, searching for some sign of the soldiers. Unable to see them, he sprinted forward to help. Though the strange, raven-haired young woman looked barely of age, the fire of the Celts blazed in her flame-blue eyes.

She struggled against Petra for only a split second before slamming her forearm into the soldier's trachea. Petra stumbled backward, losing her grip on the knife as she gasped for air. Before Lysander could reach her, the woman caught the knife in midair and dove after Petra, slicing open her thigh, then darting off into the ashen night. Petra collapsed.

Lysander took off after the young woman, but she was much faster than he was. As she disappeared into the tree line, the knife came whizzing back past his face. He felt a sting as it nicked his ear before landing in the snow, a bright spot of red melting into the mucky grey. He bent, wiped the blade on his pant leg, and pocketed the knife, before stumbling back towards the others. It was certainly more practical than the Swiss army knife he'd been making do with until now.

The other soldiers finally appeared, hobbling around the corner of the house. Benjáme was supporting Lasse's weight while the latter clutched at a wound in his side, blood soaking his jacket and shirt. Petra lay in the snow, one bloody hand pressed on her thigh, the other massaging her throat where she'd been punched.

"That little *tispe* of a Celt -" Benjáme began, a small cut bleeding down his forehead. Petra groaned in agreement and began unhooking her belt with one hand. Magdelena rushed to help Benjáme lower Lasse to the ground, then dabbed at the cut on Benjame's face with the sleeve of her parka.

"One Celt against the three of you? Who was that?" Lysander's voice had more admiration in it than he had anticipated. He dropped to his knees beside Petra, helping her slide the well-worn, leather belt under her leg and pull it tight, securing a makeshift tourniquet above the wound in her thigh.

"Does it matter?" she replied, her voice raspy and annoyed as she struggled to rise. "If we don't get out of here, she'll be back with more *Saatana* Celts." Magdelena and Linnaea both rushed forward to help Petra stand, but with a groan of frustration, she collapsed back to the ground. She muttered, "*Perkele*," and then the sky lit up brighter than it had since the world hardened.

His copper wiring. His bomb.

Lysander opened his eyes, still half-blinded by the flash of light. His ears rang, and fire and snowflakes swirled in the air around him.

"Status!" Petra screamed hoarsely into the mix of ash and snow falling around them, peering anxiously around for the rest of the group. Lysander saw Linnaea crawl into view, coughing. Her big, brown eyes met his, and she signed that she was okay. He nodded back at her as Magdelena's voice emanated from somewhere within the dense cloud of debris.

"Lasse's losing a lot of blood!"

"How bad is it?" Petra's voice was ragged.

"I can't tell where it's coming from, but I think the blast caused the bullet to move!" Magdelena shouted back through the ash and smoke, her voice trembling. Lysander peered through the smoke and found her willowy silhouette a few meters away, kneeling beside both Benjáme and Lasse's bodies in the shadow of the building. Behind them, a figure was stumbling out of the tree line, coughing and spluttering. *The raven-haired woman must be back to finish us off,* Lysander guessed. He yanked the knife she'd thrown at him from his pocket and jumped to his feet.

However, to his surprise, instead of attacking, the mysterious figure dropped to their knees beside Benjáme and Lasse, a bag falling from their shoulder to the ground beside them.

Lysander slipped through the ash and snow towards the stranger just as they put their fingers to Benjáme's throat and pressed. Lysander reached for the stranger's hands, intending to pull them away until he realized the stranger was looking for a pulse. There was blood in the stranger's dirty-blonde hair as he made eye contact with Lysander, staring him down with steady, midnight-blue eyes. This man could have passed for a Norseman by his looks, but when he spoke, his voice betrayed him.

"Don't worry, I'm a doctor." The timbre of his voice was unmistakably Celt, though there was something unusual about it. The stranger nodded when he found Benjáme's pulse and turned his unwavering gaze to Lasse, who was wheezing in the night air.

Magdelena had her ash-streaked hands pressed against his gunshot wound, but the cream-colored sweater under his jacket was darkening with blood.

"Keep pressure on that wound, but ease up just a bit," the Celtic doctor instructed Magdelena, who nodded. He guided her hands as he pulled up Lasse's sweater and base layer, exposing his chest. "His lung is collapsing. He's going to stop breathing soon unless I help him," the doctor pronounced. Without looking up from Lasse, the Celt unzipped the bag beside him. Benjáme, regaining consciousness beside Magdelena, abruptly sat up, startled by the stranger bending over Lasse, and snapped the blade of his reindeer bone knife to the Celtic doctor's throat.

The Celt carefully pulled his hands out of his bag and put them up in the air. "I'm just getting my med kit."

"Show me," Benjáme spat. The doctor reached down slowly with one hand, lifting the open kit up and emptying the contents into the snow. Lysander could see vials, syringes, scissors, and bandages among the pile of medical supplies.

Benjáme, the blade still raised in one hand, rifled through the medical supplies with his free hand. On the ground, Lasse sucked in a ragged breath before wheeling again as he exhaled, his chest falling still for far too long. Blood pounded in Lysander's ears. "If I don't do something soon, he *is* going to die. I'm just trying to save your friend," the Celt growled.

Magdelena let out a shuddering breath, still pressing her hands against Lasse's belly. Linnaea placed her hands slowly on top of her mother's fingers, locking eyes with her, and Magdelena's breath steadied. Benjáme nodded curtly, lowering his blade and wiping congealed blood from his eyebrow.

"Thank you," the Celt replied tersely. He pulled a flashlight out, clicked it on, and handed it to Benjáme, who sheathed his knife and took it. In the beam of light, the Celt slipped on a pair of gloves that, although they appeared used, were, at the very least, not covered with ash. He slid gauze under Magdelena's hand; it absorbed the oozing blood quickly.

"Does anyone have any alcohol?" the Celt asked as he pulled a syringe from his medical bag. Benjáme immediately turned,

"Lysander," he said gruffly, "Lasse's bag." Lysander hurriedly overturned Lasse's pack, emptying the contents onto the snowy ground. All the bottles were stamped with some sort of insignia. He looked to Benjáme for guidance.

"The unmarked one," Benjáme said, jerking his head unhelpfully. Lysander scanned the pile, turning the bottles over until he found a plain one. He cracked the lid, grimacing at the smell.

"Will this do?" he asked, handing the Celt the bottle.

"Home-brewed?" the Celt asked Benjáme, an amused smile playing on his lips as he gave it a whiff. "Yeah, it'll do."

He poured the liquid on his gloved hands and Lasse's nearly-motionless torso. "He's got air trapped between his lung and the chest cavity," the Celt explained as he ripped open the plastic seal of the syringe. "The extra air is stopping his lungs from fully expanding, so he can't breathe." He tore off the needle cap with his teeth and spit it into the snow. "I need to relieve the pressure, to let the air out." The Celt ran his fingers along Lasse's side, counting two ribs down.

In one steady motion, he pushed the needle into the space between the second and third ribs, then unscrewed the barrel and plunger of the syringe. As soon as the barrel detached from the needle, Lasse gasped in a deep breath.

Without skipping a heartbeat, the Celt shifted his attention to the wound where Magdelena and Linnaea were still applying pressure. He moved their hands gently, nodding his thanks as he took over for them and pressed down with one hand. They watched him clean around the wound with more alcohol and gauze before taping it closed. His gloved fingers checked Lasse's pulse.

"Will he be okay?" Linnaea signed, her hands moving tensely, her eyes dark with concern. She liked this kind, viking-man they had just met. Seeing the incomprehension on the Celt's face, Lysander interpreted for him.

The Celt's face cleared in understanding. He returned his gaze to Linnaea, nodding to her and arranging his features in an attempt to appear reassuring.

"Good," Petra responded before anyone else could. She had managed to drag herself over to them through the snow. "We've got to get out of here before more of you come and try to kill us." The Celt looked over to her as she spoke, and Lysander watched Petra's eyes flash gold at the Celt in a mix of rage and pain as she tried to stand on her wounded leg.

"There's no more of 'us' around here," the Celt replied coolly.

"You're telling me the Celts just leave their doctors behind, unprotected?" Petra countered. The Celt raised an eyebrow as he watched her struggling to stand. Lysander knelt beside Magdelena and Linnaea, helping them clean their bloodied hands in the snow and trying to distance himself from Petra and the Celt as they sparred with one another.

"Trust me, they won't be making that mistake again, now that they know you guys are blowing up buildings with innocent people inside," he retorted bitterly. "Let me take a look at your leg." Petra hesitated briefly before growling and reluctantly giving up trying to stand. The Celt took the flashlight from Benjáme and moved the beam to Petra's belted leg.

"You think we caused that explosion?" she spat as the Celt knelt beside her and pulled back the bloody pant leg sticking to her wound. "We don't do that. Norse don't burn things that don't need to be burned." She glared at him, accusation on her lips. "That's a Celtic calling card." The Celt said nothing but cleared his throat as he poured what little remained of the spirits over her leg. Petra let out an anguished hiss while he used gauze to clean the blood away. "Besides, why would I blow up my own men?" Distrust darkened her face as he cut into her pant leg to get a better look at the wound.

Lysander and Magdelena exchanged a glance, silently weighing the decision to tell them about Lysander's copper wire coil. Finally, with a nod, they agreed that they needed a better idea of who these Ragnarök people truly were before owning up to something like that.

The Celtic doctor grimaced and looked around at them. He sighed, and Petra's eyes blazed.

"What is it?" she demanded, her fingers digging into the snow.

"I need to cauterize the wound," the doctor said, and Lysander felt the Celtic knife grow heavy in his hand. "We need to get a fire going so the blade will be hot enough." Petra's jaw tightened as the Celt spoke.

"We can't do that out here in the open," she said through gritted teeth and she began to push herself up to a seated position.

Lysander looked around at the ashen remains of the village. The building that Benjáme and Lasse had been thrown against by the blast was charred but looked solid enough. Part of it was built into the earth, as the ancient houses had been, which Lysander hoped would help insulate them and keep them warm. The silhouette of the turf house was dark against the night sky, which was now sprouting stars like tiny blossoms. It felt an odd moment to notice it, but he realized it was the first time in years he had been able to see any stars through the volcanic ash in the atmosphere.

"We can make camp in there," he gestured to the turf house, and Magdelena translated the plan for Linnaea. The Celt nodded in agreement.

Benjáme rose to help Petra as she attempted to stand again, but the Celt was faster, swooping her into his arms before she had the breath to protest. Linnaea grabbed the Celt's bag, lifting it onto her scraggy shoulder.

Magdelena and Benjáme each supported one side of Lasse, helping him to his feet, while Lysander gathered everyone's packs together, threw them onto his back, and followed the rest of the group into the building.

Once inside, they realized it had been used as a storage barn. One wall was lined with the last of some old kindling. The floor was littered with shattered glass and rusted metal, the remains of some jars of canned goods. A part of the ceiling above them had collapsed, and starlight spilled in as the snow slowly piled on the edge of the sagging roof.

Quickly, Lysander moved to clear a place on the floor with his boot. Linnaea dropped the Celt's bag and joined in, collecting the larger pieces of glass carefully with her hands. When they had cleaned a large enough area, the doctor set Petra gingerly down, while Benjáme and Magdelena did the same to Lasse, both of them propped against the back wall of the barn. Lysander and Benjáme exchanged a look and headed outside to collect enough stones for a fire ring. Magdelena rummaged around in the backpacks for sleeping bags, unrolling them and helping Linnaea ease Lasse onto the faded nylon sack. Meanwhile, the Celt helped Petra slide onto hers with a grimace.

When Lysander and Benjáme had gathered enough stones to make a perimeter for the fire, they piled the old kindling in the middle and the Celt tossed them a lighter from his bag. Lysander took it and knelt by the pile of kindling. His heart was pounding so loudly, it felt like it took an eternity to get the fire going. He could feel how low the lighter was on fluid. Luckily, the kindling was already good and dry, so when it finally did light, it burned hot.

"Can I borrow that?" the Celt asked him, gesturing to the knife in his belt. Lysander nodded, handing it to him. The doctor laid it on the stones, the blade extending into the flames, the worn leather grip facing out. Lysander watched the way the flames licked the blade and noticed an etching that looked like a sideways "T" springing to life in the heat, glowing blue like the Celtic woman's eyes. Tearing his gaze away from the fire, he looked over at the others.

Lasse was resting, his chest rising and falling steadily in the firelight. Linnaea's knees were pulled up to her chest, as she watched Lasse's breathing. Petra's eyes were wild as they bored into the flames, and her leg was beginning to turn purple from the belted tourniquet.

When the blade of the knife was so hot that the Celtic rune etched into the side glowed, the doctor gave Petra an apologetic look. He produced from his bag the remains of the alcohol and handed it to her. She took the bottle and downed all but the last gulp before handing it back to him, her face grim as she wiped her mouth with her free hand and coughed.

"Doc, you look like you could use a little liquid courage." He took the bottle in his hand and finished it off. He coughed enough to make Petra's face twitch in amusement.

"That is *not* like anything I am used to drinking." He stuck his tongue out in disgust, and Petra laughed a little. The doctor nodded his thanks to her and tossed the bottle aside. Picking up the flashlight, he handed it to Magdelena, motioning her to come closer to Petra. Then, the Celt placed his hand on her thigh with the same tenderness he had used with the others, but Lysander saw Petra react to his touch. She lifted her face to the fair-haired doctor, her eyes alight with that golden fire of determination.

"Just give me something to bite on," Petra rasped. The doctor unhooked his belt deftly with one hand and eased Petra into a fully prone position before placing the leather between her teeth. Petra bit down hard, her entire body tense in anticipation.

"Ready?" He asked and she nodded. Magdelena steadied the light over the Celt's shoulder. He lifted the blade of the knife, and as he pressed it against Petra's skin, it released a sickening, searing sound. Petra let out a hoarse, agonized scream through the leather belt in her mouth.

It seemed to Lysander to go on far too long. The smell of burning flesh filled the room - reminding him of the odor that had permeated the basement of the house in which he, Magdelena, and Linnaea had hidden - and floated up and out through the hole in the ceiling. Linnaea backed against the wall, her hands pressed against the barn floor, eyes closed, steadying her breathing after what she'd just seen. Benjáme put a hand on Lasse, as if to calm him, his gaze on Magdelena as she kept the flashlight's beam steady in the dark.

By the time it was over, Petra was unconscious. The Celt dabbed the wound with a salve from his bag, then covered it meticulously with gauze.

"Will she be okay?" Lysander asked the doctor as he bound a bandage loosely around her thigh.

"She needs rest, but she will be okay," he replied quietly.

The doctor zipped Petra into the sleeping bag which was closest to the fire. After a quick examination of Lasse, the doctor packed him into his sleeping bag as well. Benjáme pulled out dark, knitted hats with the same strange insignia as the water bottles and slipped them under Lasse and Petra's heads as makeshift pillows. Lysander unrolled his own sleeping bag, then took out their heat lamp and clicked it on, positioning it near Linnaea and Magdelena.

"It'll be critical for them, the next few hours," the doctor said as he carefully packed his supplies back into his bag. "And he," the Celt gestured to Lasse, "will need someone to remove the bullet as soon as possible, or it'll get infected."

The doctor stood, throwing his bag over his shoulder. Lysander cleared his throat.

"Thank you for all your help. You saved their lives." Lysander heard the guilt in his voice and hoped no one else could.

"Well, we don't know that yet," the Celt said, "but I'm happy to help." He adjusted his jacket and turned towards the door.

"You won't make it through the night out there on your own." Benjáme's voice was gruff as he spoke grudgingly. "And anyways, one of them might need a doctor again," he added quickly.

The Celt nodded, understanding. "Thanks. I appreciate it." He slowly lowered himself back to the ground, situating himself directly across from his two patients.

Magdelena looked sideways at Lysander, intention lighting up across her rosy cheeks. He nodded and scooted closer to her in the darkness.

She pulled up her fur-lined hood and gazed into the flames. Though the flames caused flickering patches of shadow and light to dance across her face, the curve of her cheekbones and her dark lashes bore a steadiness, a resilience. Her long, plaited blonde hair seemed to glow in the firelight. As Lysander watched, it made him think of the dark-haired Celtic woman from earlier. How lithely she had cut right through their group, not as if she were running from something, but rather as if she were dancing. Magdelena's gentle touch on his shoulder brought him back from his musings.

"What do we do, L?" she signed. "If we say we caused the explosion, they might be less inclined to take us to wherever this safe place is." The fire crackled and sparked a thick log broke in two slightly obscuring the view the others had of their conversation.

"But what if it's not as good of a place as they are letting on? What if, once we get there we can't leave again?" Lysander countered. Magdelena frowned in consideration.

"I have to do what's best for Linnaea, even if that means trusting these people for now." Lysander looked over at the others and noticed Benjáme watching them curiously from across the fire. He returned his attention to Magdelena.

"These strangers, you mean," Lysander signed back.

"You were once a stranger, too, you know. And I trusted you," Magdelena responded. "Even after you fainted in the medical tent." Her face displayed her amusement at the memory.

"I could not have faced what was waiting for me in Lillehammer without you both, you know that." His expression tightened as the cold faces of his family flashed in his mind. Judit's face. Magdelena reached out and squeezed Lysander's hand sympathetically before continuing to sign.

"But I agree with you. We should try to find out as much as we can about this place they want to take us to before we make any decisions."

"Agreed," Lysander signed and nodded. He fed the fire with a little more wood, the image of his little sister's pale face still lingering behind in his mind's eye.

"And what about the doctor?" Magdelena asked.

"Oh, I'm sure he'll be gone by morning," Lysander responded, his gestures and expression conveying nonchalance.

"No, I mean - he's a Celt. You don't think he'll tell them anything about us? Like who we are and where we are headed?" She chewed her bottom lip anxiously as she signed.

"Svalbard? It won't come up."

"You're sure enough about that to bet our lives on it?" she asked him, trying to angle her body further away from their new companions.

"There's something different about him. Different than what people tell us about the Celts." Lysander assured her. He had watched the way the Celt tended to Petra and he somehow felt that the doctor wouldn't betray them. He had a look in his eyes that Lysander hadn't seen in a long time. A look that Lysander had thought, until today, was gone from this world.

As the hours passed, the members of their small group sat huddled together in weary silence. Petra and Lasse were both sleeping in their sleeping bags. Linnaea rested against Lysander's shoulder. Lysander eventually shrugged off his parka and pushed the sleeves up of his boiled wool sweater, sufficiently warmed by the heat from the fire, the heat lamp, and the bodies of his companions. Linnaea resumed dozing against his shoulder, and he could feel her jolt each time she reawakened in the glow of firelight.

Lysander looked across the flames to where Benjáme sat beside Petra, appearing lost in his thoughts.

"Benjáme?" Lysander called softly, and the soldier looked up.

"Uh, yeah?" Benjáme replied, shifting his body to face Lysander.

"What is your engineer friend like?" Lysander asked and Benjáme's mouth curved into a surprised smile. It was an unguarded expression of young love, and it revealed a yearning that Lysander could only assume came from the fact that Benjáme didn't get to speak about his engineer friend as much as he would like.

"Taavi? Oh, he's actually my husband," Benjáme told him. "He's the smartest person I've ever met. Sometimes too smart for his own good. But, he could always bring me back to myself, especially after a tour or something." His smile fell, his now-bittersweet expression reflecting some memory that was surfacing.

"When was the last time you saw him?" Lysander asked quietly. Benjáme hesitated, glancing across Petra's sleeping form at the Celtic doctor.

"The Celts had launched an attack on the village that took us in after our home flooded. I got called up to defend the village, but the Celts split their forces and circled back around when we were out fighting. They either killed or imprisoned everyone left behind in the village. That was before Mimameid found me." Lysander didn't quite catch the strange word Benjáme had uttered. Was it a person? Their leader, maybe?

"When who found you?"

"Mimameid," Benjáme repeated.

"Who's Mimameid?" Lysander asked. In response, Benjáme reached up and tapped an insignia on the sleeve of his jacket, the same symbol that Lysander had seen on the water bottles earlier, and the knitted hats. He looked over at the jackets that Petra and Lasse were wearing as they slept next to Benjáme. They, too, bore the same insignia - a tree within a circular border. "Is it your organization?" Benjáme shrugged, looking down at Petra as he answered.

"It's a group of believers that takes in strays like us. Some believe more than others do, but no matter how you slice it, they saved us. Humanity, I mean."

The doctor snorted quietly, with suppressed laughter, the unexpected, jarring sound interrupting their conversation. Benjáme's eyes glowed with anger at the doctor's casual dismissal. Lysander raised an eyebrow as he and Magdelena exchanged a wary look. She moved to shift a now deeply sleeping Linnaea from her position against Lysander's shoulder, draping Linnaea across her lap and stroking her daughter's hair as she stirred briefly before continuing to sleep. The doctor turned to Benjáme, an incredulous look painted on his pale face.

"Mimameid saved humanity? Is that what they tell you?" the Celt asked, his midnight-blue eyes searching for some hint of irony in the soldier's expression.

"Well, yeah. The number of people they have down there-" Benjáme stopped himself. "Forget it. I'm not about to waste my breath on a Celt," he muttered. The doctor shifted his weight, irritated.

"That's right, I wouldn't understand," He retorted. "I'm just a bloodthirsty barbarian." He turned to Petra, lifting her wrist to take her pulse. "That's why I saved your friends, I guess," he continued. "Because I'm out for Nordic blood."

"Tell that to the families left behind after the Celts slaughtered that village." Benjáme pointed to the door, "Or any other town in Scandinavia south of the Arctic Circle, for that matter." Benjáme's voice had become savage, his deep-set eyes flashing furiously. The doctor shook his head as he cleaned and re-bandaged Petra's wound.

"You have no idea," he muttered, his eyes flashing with some unknown rage.

"So, then, why did you save us?" Benjáme challenged.

Lysander watched the Celt's hands move tenderly, brushing Petra's copper curls from her forehead as he checked her for a fever.

"I'm a doctor, that's what my job is," the Celt replied without hesitation. He tucked a lock of Petra's hair behind her ear, hand lingering for a moment before he turned to Lasse to check him for infection and fever. Benjáme's dark brown eyes shifted as he watched the doctor warily, his hand instinctively finding its way to the reindeer knife at his waist. Lysander, however, wanted to know more about Mimameid.

"So, you don't know what happened to Taavi?" he prompted gently. Benjáme slowly took his gaze from the doctor and shook his head at Lysander.

"Some of the villagers were burned pretty badly, but I didn't recognize any of the bodies," Lysander closed his eyes, his own family's burnt corpses seared into his memory. "He either escaped or was taken prisoner," Benjáme finished. Magdelena spoke up when Lysander didn't reply.

"If he is out there somewhere, I'm sure he's looking for you, too." Her green eyes were warm, like a sunny day in late spring as she gently ran her fingers through Linnaea's tangled locks. Benjáme nodded his thanks, and Magdelena continued, looking down at her daughter as she spoke. "Benjáme, if Taavi found you, would you stay with Mimameid?" The new word still sounded strange to Lysander as Magdelena said it aloud, but she had phrased her question exactly right for the young soldier. Benjáme shrugged.

"Honestly, I don't know. They protected me, they gave me a sense of purpose again, but I don't know." He paused, then turned to face Magdelena squarely, lowering his voice. "I'll tell you this because you have a child, but-" he paused again, looking first over at the doctor, then down to the sleeping Petra. "Don't say anything. Petra wouldn't understand." Magdelena nodded. He leaned in and whispered. "If Taavi was here, I think I'd want more than Mimameid has to offer." Benjáme sat back, and his hand made its way up to the scar on the side of his head, tracing it as he looked up at the part of the roof that had collapsed. Lysander followed his gaze and saw that the snow outside had stopped.

2
PETRA

SHE FELT THE WARMTH of the fire on her cheeks before she opened her eyes. Above her, an arctic black sky swirled with smog, some twinkling stars peeking through. She let out a hot exhale that lifted into the night sky like a cloud and in it, she thought she saw the face of Madderakka, the Sámi all-mother her father used to tell her stories about. Before her *babushka* would scold him for filling her head with nonsense.

    She blinked and turned her head, the fire coming into focus, amber in the dark night. Benjáme was asleep against the back wall next to Lasse, both their chests rising and falling and it eased her, to see her men alive and peaceful.

    Lysander was sitting up on his sleeping bag, having taken his feet out she could see the many places where his woolen socks had been darned and the beginning of his big toe was starting to peak out on the left foot. His head was heavy, his chestnut hair loose around his face, hiding those trusting, brown eyes from view. He was slumped against a backpack, large paws-for-hands splayed out as he slept beside Magdelena. She was a woman like Petra had never seen. Even in sleep, she looked like some gossamer Norse queen of old, her cornsilk-blonde hair spilling like a waterfall onto the earthen ground.

Linnaea was barely visible between the two of them, buried in her faded nylon sleeping bag.

The quiet was petrifying. There were no air purifiers humming or water tanks bubbling in the walls. There were no lock pads or bands beeping instructions at them. She lowered her head down to her right wrist, where her band was still strapped into place. To the strangers around her, it would just look like a watch.

Petra's heart skipped as she became aware of the feeling of being watched. It twisted around in her and she tried to breathe, to lower her heart rate. She turned to see the Celtic doctor's face across the fire. He had his knees drawn up to his chest, and the firelight flickering against his fair skin. His soft, blue eyes were alight like a warm August day in The Time Before.

He reached out for her hand gently, squeezing it in his reassuringly.

"How are you feeling?" he whispered, as he took her pulse. He brushed his shaggy blonde hair - blood and ash still in it - from his face and she felt her heart skip another beat. She tried to answer but groaned instead, her thigh throbbing where it had been seared shut. "It will get better," the doctor reassured her. "The wound is healing, but you have to keep it clean, it can't get infected."

She averted her gaze up to the starlight pouring in through the collapsed roof. She felt a cool hand on her cheek and closed her eyes, breathing in his musky scent. Petra didn't know why, but she felt some strange, creeping trust in him. Like her trust in Sigrid, but somehow different; this felt innate, intuitive, maybe even primal. Or maybe she was just too bone weary to know the difference between trust and resignation.

When she opened her eyes again he had a kind expression on his face. "No Valkyries will be coming for you tonight," he whispered. Confused, she wanted to ask him how he knew about the shield maidens of the Aesir, but she found when she opened her mouth that she had no voice. "Rest now," the doctor responded gently. She nodded, drunk with the wave of exhaustion that was washing over her. His eyes warmed to a shining, wild blue as he saw her starting to slip.

"But, just before you go, I wanted you to know my name. I'm Arthur." She reached for his hand and felt the electricity pass from her arm into his as their fingertips touched before she sunk into sleep.

Arthur.

The name spiraled her into a series of strange Camelotian dreams fueled by the bedtime story Petra's *baba* had read to her over and over.

Of a good king, wearing the doctor's face, pulling Excalibur from Magdelena, the Lady of the Lake, then returning to wrap a Celtic Guinevere in a triumphant embrace, while the land around them burns. Linnaea was a little Morgan le Fey, planting a bomb in the earth like a sapling and it exploding into the dark sky, shattering the blanket of stars. She took the shards of the glittering sky in her hands and threw them down into a river of beautiful golden hair, looking back at Petra and signing thank you over and over, as the stars burned like embers in the shape of a "T"...

A hazy light shone through the skylight, ushering in the day. Petra, stiff and aching, opened her tired eyes to the morning.

She pushed herself to her elbows and looked around. In the fireplace smoked the remnants of a fire that could have only recently gone out. Lysander, back inside his sleeping bag, held one end of a charred piece of kindling in his hand, presumably having taken on the task of keeping the fire alight. Magdelena was wrapped around Linnaea's sleeping bag. Lasse was restless, sweat beading his hairline, but still asleep, and Benjáme was slumped beside him. Only Petra had been roused by an odd stirring.

And then it dawned on her that the doctor wasn't there. *Arthur.*

As quick and quiet as a spirit, he had evaporated into the morning mist. He must be truly gone, as his medical bag was nowhere in sight, but in place of his hand in Petra's was a roll of fresh bandages. Ignoring the pulsing in her leg, she pulled herself up to sitting.

If Arthur was supposed to be reporting to anyone, he'd certainly get in trouble for giving his medical supplies away to strangers, let alone enemy

Norse. And maybe he should be punished; they were enemies, after all. Just because he said one thing didn't mean he wasn't going to use what he had learned from them for his own ends. She felt her stomach knot up.

Lysander stirred, his kind, brown-bear eyes fluttered open and he saw that Petra was awake.

"You okay?" he asked, his voice low and soft, not wanting to wake anyone. Petra nodded, tightening her grip on the bandages.

"Yeah. Yeah, I'm good. The doc fixed me up real nice."

"Strange guy," he said, rubbing his eyes. "I mean, don't misunderstand me, he did good work, patching you guys up right. But running off without a word in the middle of the night? What does he think we would do to him?"

Petra tried not to show it on her face, that he had spoken to her in the safety of the night. She repeated his name softly in her head: *Arthur. Arthur.*

But then the memories of the dream she had, of the Celtic Guinevere and the explosion started flooding her, bubbling up, hot and uncomfortable.

Petra turned away from Lysander, retching beside herself. He scrambled up immediately, all sleep gone from his face.

"All right, there. All right." He peeled her sweaty mess of red tangles off of her neck, searching for a water bottle with his other hand. When she felt everything had left her stomach, she accepted the bottle from his hand, gulping back water, her throat still hot with vomit and some strange jealousy. Benjáme raised his head, looking around, groggily.

She shook her head, trying to clear it, and pulled her tangle of hair up into a ponytail. Magdelena and Linnaea were both stirring now, roused by the sudden movements around them, with looks of concern clouding their barely-rested faces.

The fogginess started to dissipate. With the vomit out of her system, Petra felt stronger and more clear-headed. She clenched the bandages in her fist, pushing them into her jacket pocket and zipping it up.

Lasse's eyes fluttered open, whispering through cracked lips, "Water," and immediately Petra passed the bottle across to Benjáme, who tipped it into

Lasse's mouth. He coughed as he drank, the water spilling onto his chin, almost like tears.

Lasse pushed himself up, glancing over at Petra and breathing deeply.

"How're you doing there, Sergeant?" She tried to lighten her tone for him, but he didn't look good. Lasse nodded, replying.

"I've been better, sir. But I've also been worse," he groaned as he adjusted himself.

"Take it easy, there." Magdelena's voice was maternal from across the fire and she paused untangling Linnaea's stringy blonde mess of hair to sign the conversation.

"We are in no rush, Sarge. Take it easy, soldier," Petra ordered him as kindly as she could muster through her usual bracing temper. She knew Milla would kill her if she didn't get Lasse back to Mimameid in one piece.

"You too, sir," Lasse joked, wincing and then sighing into a more comfortable position.

Having spoken to Lasse now, her mind was turning, reeling, and planning. They wouldn't be moving as fast with the two of them injured and they now had three more mouths to feed to boot. They certainly weren't going to make it back to Mimameid for the planned rendezvous. She looked down at her band and tapped it. The relief map opened to where she had had it before, just inland of Mimameid. She tracked eastward until she got to Saltfjallet. The path home took them over dangerous terrain - rock scrambles and frigid, high-altitude temperatures. They were out of range for any real help, but at least they still had navigation functionality. She looked up to see the three Opps watching her operate the navigational map with awe. Awkwardly, she closed the map and pulled her sleeve over her band.

She looked over at Benjáme. "What have we got for food and supplies?" His face was already grave, having done the same math as Petra.

"We need to find a mountain spring sometime soon because we will run out of water before the end of the day," he said as he unpacked his food rations: Two cans of tuna, a helping of dehydrated apple, four rolls of seaweed and a parchment paper of dried haddock. They had that amount of food times three, counting hers and Lasse's. For the six of them. She looked at the rations with disappointment.

"What's the problem?" Lysander asked and Magdelena perked up beside him. To them, Petra realized, he was probably looking at the largest pile of food they'd seen in months.

"The problem is, we have two full days ahead of us before we're within range of Mimameid. If we manage good time over the mountains, that is." Her voice was solemn, thinking of Lasse. Lysander seemed to figure out the problem the quickest and interpreted for Linnaea.

"Okay," Benjáme began. "Haddock for breakfast, tuna for lunch, apples and seaweed for dinner." He stood up resolutely. Linnaea stood up too, shoving her matted hair into her woolen hat.

"How can I help?" she signed and Lysander interpreted. Petra sighed, impressed but also saddened at how quickly the girl had been able to come to terms with their situation. This girl, she was a child of Ragnarök.

"Divide up the haddock for breakfast while we pack," Petra instructed while her mother interpreted. The girl nodded without question, taking the haddock from Benjáme's outstretched hands.

They were hasty as they packed the bags, eating their haddock in silence only broken by the rustling of nylon and scraping of zippers. Though her leg still throbbed, Petra rolled the sleeping bags up, shoving them into their packs, and trying to think to herself if there was an easier way to get home, now that they had injured. They would need to stay near fresh water, not only for drinking but for keeping her's and Lasse's wounds clean, which made the mountain pass still their best shot.

"It's good we're moving on." Lysander's voice cut into the silence. "We don't want to linger here too long. The doctor is a good man, but he is still a Celt who knows where we are." Petra's jaw flexed at the mention of Arthur, as she nodded curtly at Lysander.

When they had all finished eating, they heaved their packs on their backs. Helping Lasse to his feet turned out to be more difficult than she'd hoped, requiring both Lysander and Benjáme. Petra was glad they had divided up the weight of his pack among themselves.

She, however, was determined to stand up on her own two legs. She tested her weight out on her injured leg and though it sent a dull stabbing pain up her thigh, she found she was strong enough to stumble around unassisted. Steadying herself on the door frame of the building, she searched for a sign of sunlight behind the ashy clouds, looking for a way to orient herself.

"Where to?" Lysander asked her.

"We head north until we hit the river and then we follow it upstream."

"Upstream how long?" He helped Linnaea adjust the smaller pack onto her back.

"Until we hit a lake, and then we follow it until we hit another lake," she replied, showing him on the relief map from her band.

"And that's our destination?"

"No, then we keep going until we hit the coastline." She scrolled across the mountains until she reached the water.

"We're going all the way to the coast?"

Petra didn't respond, instead closing the map, throwing him a brazen look and hobbling forward to lead them into the wilderness.

Once they made it deep enough into the forest, Petra picked up the path that took them over the mountains. They broke through the naked trees gradually, until only bright mosses, arctic juniper, and blue mountain heath blanketed the rocky trail in front of them.

This trail was her favorite way back to Mimameid. As they continued on, she fell into a rhythm. The path was so familiar to her that even with the dull searing in her leg, she could cut through it without much thought. And because today they moved slower than usual across the terrain, she had time to soak it up in a way she never had been able to before.

The river followed the twists and turns of a solid granite ribbon in the earth. When they stopped to fill their bottles, she watched the way the water rippled over it, dancing in the grey light of the muted morning.

Over the last five years, she had seen this path in every season, even the darkest and coldest of days. When ash littered the ground and when snow had completely covered the landscape. When the ice had crept in, swallowing up the valleys between the peaks. When the lakes became solid and the only fish to eat were frozen through.

It had been a while since those days, and even though there were no summers up here anymore, the snow had begun to melt again, bringing new life to the little valleys that had been carved out by the melting glaciers.

But today she could tell something was different. The mosses were more luminescent than she could remember and the heath felt soft to the touch. The juniper was lifting a tangy scent into the air and the dawn had a misty sort of weightlessness to it, which she hadn't seen the landscape bathed in before.

The granite glittered as a few precious beams of sun cut through the ashen sky and reflected off its surface. The rushing water danced in the light.

Petra was reminded of the stars that had flickered above her the night before and she realized, all at once, that it hadn't been some pain-induced dream, but that the river and the heath - just like the stars - were coming back to life.

Could it be that the sun was returning? Could it be that the worst was behind them?

She glanced over her shoulder, looking at the others. While Lysander, Benjáme, and Magdelena wore the weight of survival in the lines on their faces, Petra's eyes were drawn to Linnaea. Radiant with curiosity, she would stop, bend and feel the heat of the sunlight on the rocks with the palms of her hands. She stuck her freckled cheeks into the juniper bushes and let the icy river water run across her fingertips, something like joy warming her face. Petra looked at Linnaea and could feel the earth healing, even if the people were still sick.

At midday, they stopped to refill their bottles in the glacier-river and to adjust the weight of everyone's packs. Petra found the break soothing on her leg, her thigh still sore and raw. She could feel her body pulling the muscle back together and slowly rebuilding itself, but when she looked over at Lasse, he was much worse than she had anticipated.

Sweat beaded his forehead as he lay on a bed of moss, eyes closed, breathing heavy. Magdelena went over to him, pulling off her hat and laying it under his head. He opened his eyes and nodded a weary thanks. With careful hands, she lifted his sweater up, waving Petra over to Lasse.

They peeled back the bandages the doctor had bound him with and saw the red, raw skin of Lasse's wound. It was crusted with a thick, yellow puss that was giving off a putrid smell. The infection flared in the heat of his skin and the tenderness of his belly.

"That Celtic *vittu*." Petra swore under her breath. Magdelena poured some water on the edge of her undershirt and tried to clean the infected wound. Lasse let out a whimper of pain as she touched him and Petra thought again of Milla. Whatever Lasse was to her as a friend, he was much, much more to Milla.

Feeling helpless, Petra watched Magdelena bind the wound back up and they exchanged a look over his tired body.

"What about those medicine bottles I saw him pocketing back in town?" Lysander asked and Benjáme dug in Lasse's pack for a second before producing them.

"*Bergalaga Biru*," he cursed, "They're just prenatal vitamins." He threw them back into the bag with frustration.

He dug out their lunch, passing them a tin of tuna to share as they leaned back against the rocky bank and Magdelena closed her eyes in exasperation, letting her head fall into her hands.

Petra didn't understand why Magdelena was so upset. Lasse was her soldier, her's and Benjáme's friend. And they had only just met, even if Lasse had been particularly nice to Linnaea. The wiry girl rose to her feet and walked across the granite riverbed to her mother. She knelt and tapped her on the shoulder, signing something Petra didn't understand. The mother and daughter conversed for a moment, and after what looked like Magdelena explaining what was going on, Linnaea pointed back down at the path they had come from and asked a question.

Magdelena's eyes lit up at whatever the girl was saying, a brilliant light in them that Petra hadn't seen before. She sat straight up, her voice alight with anticipation.

"Yes, of course." Magdelena's mind looked to be racing. "You're absolutely right!" The girl smiled, satisfied. "Do you think you could find it again?" her mother signed, excitedly, "Not too far, though." Linnaea nodded and started retracing their steps back down the path.

Petra was confused. She looked from Magdelena to Lysander, trying to figure out what had just happened. Recognizing the confusion, Lysander jumped in to interpret the conversation.

"Linnaea remembered a moss that grew around a pond at her *amma* and *afi's* mountain house. They used to collect it and dry it to use on cuts and scrapes."

Magdelena turned to Lysander. "Make a fire, quick as you can. I can't believe I didn't think of it earlier." Petra and Benjáme exchanged a glance and watched them work. It only took a few minutes before Linnaea was back, her hands filled with a dainty star-shaped moss. In the meantime, Lysander's small fire was flickering to life. Once the flames had burned down, Magdelena and Linnaea laid the bright green plant out on the heated stones to dry. They worked in synch with one another, as though they had done it all before, many times.

As they waited, Petra unwrapped her own leg wound to inspect how it was healing. The cold air stung against the burn as she exposed it. The skin was still red, particularly around the small "T" that had been branded onto her flesh from the blade of the knife, but she was contented that it didn't look like it was headed for infection. She quickly redressed her leg and pulled her jacket back around her shoulders.

When Magdelena was satisfied with the dryness of the moss, she went over and peeled the pus-encrusted bandage from Lasse's wound.

Petra stuck her hand deep into her pack and produced the clean bandage that Arthur had left with her. Nodding her thanks, Magdelena wrapped the dried moss in the bandage and gingerly redressed the wound.

"Sphagnum peat moss has anti-inflammatory properties," she explained as she worked, finally having noticed Petra and Benjáme's confused faces at her bizarre plant witchcraft. She had no way of knowing it, of course, but Petra and Benjáme were used to more advanced and scientifically forward medicine in Mimameid. It was scavenged from their Above Ground missions, yes, but it felt state-of-the-art compared to this. Magdelena continued to explain.

"It hasn't grown for so many years, I'd almost forgotten. But here we are in the middle of a heath, one of the only places on earth sphagnum grows." She smiled to herself, signaling for Linnaea to come over, so the girl could tie the knot at the end of the bandage. She looked up at them when they were finished.

"It won't work indefinitely, but it will buy him some time and it should help ease the pain a bit." Petra looked at both of the women, surprised. Maybe she had underestimated them, and their plant witchcraft.

"Thank you." Lasse's eyes fluttered open and he reached for Linnaea, hands moving as she'd taught him. A soft blush crept up under her wide, brown eyes.

"You guys aren't like any *Opps* I've ever met," Benjáme sighed and stood up, throwing his long blonde braid over his shoulder. He seemed to be genuinely impressed there was anything they could do at all to help Lasse. "Well, let's get some more then. Show me what the moss looks like. We can gather some more and take it with us." He joined the spirited Linnaea and together they trotted back down the path back to where she had found the moss before. Lysander added more juniper brush to the fire and the air around them filled with smoke.

Petra couldn't stand feeling unhelpful and in the way when Magdelena instructed her to stay where she was and rest her injury. She watched the woman rinse the old bandage in the mountain stream and lay it out to dry on the heated rocks. The elegant woman was quiet as she worked, which suited Petra just fine. She was just grateful that, of all the people they could have stumbled upon in the wilderness they had happened upon an engineer and a healer.

The next day, as they set out into another misty morning, Petra watched Linnaea running her hands across the mountain heath. Whenever she came across a patch of the star-shaped moss, Linnaea would bend down and stuff her jacket pockets with as much of it as she could find.

Magdelena signed for her to come back after a half hour or so. Linnaea returned to her mother and produced the moss from her pockets.

Magdelena smiled kindly at her daughter and thanked her for looking out for Lasse.

"But don't forget *skatten min*. The plants have only just begun healing, so we should let them grow, too. We don't need as much moss as the earth does," Magdelena signed and bent down to pluck a twig from a juniper bush next to her feet. She brushed it under her nose, inhaling its sweet scent and placed it behind Linnaea's ear, held in place by her woolen hat, and the two of them continued walking on together. Petra watched as Magdelena signed to her daughter. As if he'd seen her curiosity, Lysander joined Petra and interpreted for her.

"Do you know why we named you Linnaea?" Magdelena asked and the girl shook her head.

"I don't think you ever told me. Only that *pabbi* decided on the name," Linnaea replied.

"Linnaea borealis is a plant that can survive each winter beneath periglacial ice. It's one of the most resilient." The girl looked sideways at her mother, a few of the day's precious few sunbeams catching in her white-blonde hair.

"But why did you choose it as a name?" Linnaea signed the question Petra also wanted to ask.

"Your *pabbi* and I knew something was coming. We knew it was only a matter of time. The earth told all of us - the biologists, the geologists, the meteorologists - that it was hurting. We knew there would come a time when the earth would say enough, and we would have to start again. And we hoped you would be the one to survive what was coming, Linnaea. That your generation would be strong enough to start anew and do things right this time." Petra was enraptured by the words as they reminded her of everything they believed in Mimameid.

Linnaea paused, thinking about what her mother had told her.

"So, this is something *pabbi* decided, too?" Linnaea signed.

"Yes. It was your *pabbi*'s idea. He believed in you. That's part of why he had to go away to Svalbard." Magdelena spelled out the last word with her hands and it got caught in Lysander's throat - like maybe he hadn't meant for her to know the name. Petra wondered what *Svalbard* was and why it mattered so much to them.

"Then I think *pabbi* would want you to teach me what you know," Linnaea signed, looking up at her mother, brown eyes shining. Magdelena nodded slowly, a smile creeping onto her elfin face.

"I think you're probably right," she replied.

As they continued on the path, Petra watched with interest as Magdelena and Linnaea conversed, pointing to various plants from time to time as they passed them along the trail.

"Are you talking about how the plants are back?" Lasse asked them, his face sunken and weary, but his eyes bright.

"I'm helping her identify the plants, actually. Now that they are starting to come back," Magdelena explained to him, then interpreted for Linnaea. Lasse smiled - a pained smile - but a smile nonetheless and tried out some of his sign language, stumbling through the signs.

"I owe the plants a 'thank you,'" He signed and the girls smiled at him cheerily. "Would it be okay if you spoke a little too, so I could learn a bit as well? My sign language obviously isn't quite up to scratch," He joked, but then the laugh made him groan and he clutched at his side. Magdelena inclined her head and reached out for him. "I'd be happy to," She said and with a smile from her daughter, glowing with pride, Lysander began interpreting.

When she started telling them about the medicinal properties of the plants as well as identifying them, Petra was intrigued, but when she started to talk about the chemical breakdown of all the different types of plants and how they interacted with each other in the ecosystem, Petra realized that Magdelena's understanding of plants was far more than she'd expected.

"What did you do before all of this?" Petra asked as they hobbled along.

"Sorry?" Magdelena had been guiding Lasse along a particularly uneven part of the trail while telling them about the golden lichen on the granite and she seemed thrown by the question from Petra.

"Well, you seem to know a lot about plants and biology and stuff." Petra didn't want to be too direct or offensive, but she wanted to make sure Magdelena wasn't some kind of lunatic who had covered herself in ash at environmental protests or something in The Time Before.

Not that Petra had anything against protecting the environment - but she hadn't understood how some people had time for things like that. She always assumed they were really rich and didn't need to work. Plus, they all lived in cities, so what did they know about the environment, really? Not like she and her family up north. She tried to form her question politely. "What did you do in The Time Before? Were you a scientist or something?" Magdelena blushed a little.

"I, well, something like that. I - my husband was a researcher. So I learned a lot from talking to him." She stumbled over the words, keeping her gaze fixed on Lasse and the path in front of them. Petra raised an eyebrow, unconvinced. She looked around for Linnaea, trying to discern what they could be hiding from the girl instead, but she had already run ahead and was bent over something on the path.

Linnaea turned and signed something at them that Petra didn't recognize. Maybe she should take a hint from Lasse and try learning a few more signs.

"What is it?" Lysander signed back and he hurried along. "She found something on the path," He explained to Petra. The girl bent down to pick something up off the path in front of her. Lysander caught up to Linnaea first, pausing to examine it in his palm before passing it onto Magdelena. Petra's heart skipped a beat when she stumbled up and saw what it was.

A small bit of red nylon cord - as if from a tent or a backpack - had been twisted into an intricate knot, looping over and over in a circle about as big as a face of a watch. If it weren't for the bright color, they might not have even noticed it on the path.

"I know this knot," Benjáme said grimly, helping Lasse to the ground while they paused. "This is a Celtic love knot." Of course, now Petra could see the interlocking hearts in the pattern. "They know we are here." Benjáme's voice was low, afraid. She saw his hand move instinctively to his reindeer knife.

"But if it's a love knot, surely that can't be a sign of aggression," Lysander replied, taking the knot again from Magdelena's hands and examining it more closely.

"It's not the shape that disturbs me, but the color. The Celts use red to symbolize bad luck. It's meant to be anything connected to the fairy world, like how they believe red-haired people are descended from fairies." As Benjáme said it, Petra knew who had left the knot. *Arthur.* She reached out and took it from Lysander's hands, tracing the delicate handiwork with her fingers.

"It is not a good omen, then," Magdelena said, looking over at Linnaea, bent over, slurping water from the stream with her hands.

Petra chose not to contradict the woman, whose green eyes flashed dangerously as she scanned the misty wilderness around them. Instead, Petra shoved the knot deep into her jacket pocket and zipped the pocket shut.

She could feel that though Arthur was long gone, he was looking out for them. And even if the others didn't believe it, he wouldn't betray them.

By the end of the day they had made it to the glacier-lake that was Petra's favorite among these mountains. It was a brilliant turquoise of an old summer melt, and it reminded Petra that she was nearly home.

They made camp in a dilapidated, old fishing hut by the water's edge, watching the dark clouds in the night sky as they searched for old twigs so they could start a fire inside.

Once the fire was burning, smoke billowing up out of the chimney, they settled around it, leaning back against the birch bunks build into the side of the hut. Their faded, silver bark reminded Petra of a lullaby her *baba* used to sing to her about a birch tree in a meadow. She couldn't remember the words anymore, as it had been ages since she'd used her Russian, but the memory was still there.

Benjáme passed around the apples and seaweed. Petra took small bites to make the meal last as long as she could. Her bottle now full of fresh water, she gulped it back greedily and the icy water made her sigh. She poured it on her leg, where the burn was starting to blister. The water stung at first, but as it drizzled down the side of her thigh, she felt relief and her muscles relaxed. She reached into her jacket pocket and wove her fingers into the cord of the love knot.

Maybe it was a combination of feeling Arthur close while they all shared food and fire. Or maybe it was just light-headedness from her wound, but Petra was reminded of winters from The Time Before.

It was one of the few memories she had of them all being together as a family, their sacred winter solstices. She and *Baba* would make *pryaniki* while they waited for her parents to come home from the long workday and then they would all nibble the precious honey-and-clove biscuits bit by bit, to make them last as long as possible.

Huddled around a roaring fire, *Baba* would tell them stories of the splendor of an old Russian winter. Of eggshells painted in deep shades of blue and real gold inlay, of dresses adorned in hand-made lace that spun while women danced like delicate scraps of tissue paper under glittering chandeliers. *Baba's* strong fingers would comb through Petra's copper-colored plaits over and over until she slept, still waiting for Grandfather Frost, *Ded Moroz*, to appear.

And now, in the barn, with their dried apples, seaweed, and glacier water, it felt as if time was turned back and stood still. It felt as if her men and these *Opps* were - for a moment - family. Even Lasse's sallow face shone from the food and cheer as the fire blazed long into the premature darkness.

Lysander and Benjáme traded stories of engineering and refugee camps like they were lifelong friends, catching up after an extended time apart. Magdelena stroked Linnaea's blonde hair just as Petra's *baba* had, until she slept. Lysander helped her lift Linnaea and tuck her into the sleeping bag on the bunk closest to the fire. Carefully, she rose and placed a hand on a sleeping Lasse's now-flushed cheek. He flinched in his drowsiness at the coolness of her hand in the warm hut.

Confirming Lasse and Linnaea were both asleep, Magdelena jerked her head for the rest of them to follow her out into the cold. They zipped up their jackets, squashed the hats down on their heads, and followed her out, huddling together in the crisp, clear darkness, their breath circling up and up into the atmosphere. They listened to the growling and the thumping of the ice, thick across the surface of the lake and to the trees, cracking like gunshots in the stillness.

"How much longer until we get to this Mimameid place?" the blonde woman asked, rubbing her arms up and down with her hands as she bounced in the cold.

"He isn't going to make it back if we keep up at this pace," Petra confirmed, pulling out her band and opening up the relief map, scrolling along to the coastline with her freezing, red fingers. The grim look on everyone's faces reflected her own conclusion back at her.

"Should we split up? Some stay with Lasse and others go for help?" Lysander offered, uncrossing his arms to blow on his hands and warm them, but Magdelena shook her head in response.

"He's got an infection, the peat moss slows the process, but it can't stop the inevitable." She adjusted her fur-lined hood, pulling it closer around her face. "The only thing that is sure to save him is proper medicine in a proper medical facility." Petra felt a soft twang in her ribcage, wishing the doctor hadn't left them. Was this how it was to be tethered to someone, even when you were separated by such a great distance? She dismissed the thought. He was practically a stranger. A stranger who had branded her, but a stranger nonetheless. Benjáme, who had been unusually quiet for most of the day, spoke up.

"We have to get him through one more day. If we can do that, then our signal will be strong enough to get a medical evacuation for him." Petra nodded, not even caring that they had just revealed their plan to the refugees.

"Signal?" Lysander asked, but before Benjáme could respond, Petra shook her head. She had shown them the bands, but she didn't think they needed to know just how much the bands could do, not yet, at least. Surprisingly, there was no resistance to their withholding information. It seemed that even Lysander was too tired to press them further tonight.

Her eyes were drawn up to the clear sky. The clouds had moved on and there was no moon out tonight. But the darkness didn't feel so heavy. The black felt like giant, understanding eyes of the universe looking down on them. Her hands were already in her pocket and felt the small, rowan-red chord in between her fingers again, tasting his name on her lips.

For just a space of a second Petra thought she caught a wisp of wild green and purple ripple through the sky. But then she blinked and it was gone.

"Did you all see that?" she asked faintly into the night.

"See what?" Benjáme chattered in the cold, following her gaze up to the empty sky.

"Never mind. Nothing." She squinted, but the night was as dark as it had been before.

"Well come on then, it's freezing out here." Benjáme's voice was gruff, as she followed him back into the hut, feeling something safe wash over her. A whisper of a future she hadn't known was possible for her.

Looking around at it all, the warm glow of the fire, and the people drifting to sleep around her, here, on the edge of her favorite lake, Petra found she could barely feel the pain in her leg. She let herself, rosy from the heat of the fire, slip into the dream-world of night, her thoughts swimming with the image of the good King Arthur.

When the faint morning light broke through between the wooden beams of the fishing hut, Petra's eyes snapped open, where they were and what they had to accomplish today rushing back to her all at once. Lysander had already shoved his feet into his muddy boots and had the bottles in hand to collect fresh water from the lake. She sat up slowly and the two of them nodded wearily at each other as he headed out into the cold, lumbering like a massive brown bear in his thick winter coat. Petra swung her legs around the edge of the bunk, grabbing a stick to stoke the embers of the fire. The day had started, but it was foggy and the dampness in the air had a chill that made her feel almost feverish. Petra watched the embers kick back to a small, hot flame and she thought of home. What would she say during their debrief? How would she explain this shift that she was beginning to feel? She couldn't see it being well-received. Not by Sigrid. Not by anyone.

By the time Lysander returned, Benjáme was awake and lacing his boots up. Petra massaged her leg muscles lightly. They were still sore, but she could feel the strength returning to her leg and her burn was healing nicely.

After waking Lasse, Benjáme divided up the last of the haddock. Magdelena roused Linnaea, who although she said nothing, looked none too pleased to be eating dried fish again. *Better than nothing, kid,* Petra thought.

"So what did you all eat before us, anyways?" Lasse was apparently also watching Linnaea's face. Lysander signed for her and Petra laughed a little at the look the young girl threw Lasse in response. Lysander laughed too and he patted her on the shoulder.

"Poor Linnaea. You miss my grilled rat, after all?" he signed and Lasse couldn't help but let out a weak chuckle. "It goes best with canned potatoes, right?" Lysander signed, then teasingly tugged on the ear flap of the girl's hat.

"Only potatoes that are older than I am," she signed shrewdly and Lysander let out a snort of laughter while Magdelena explained for the rest of them. The woman took the opportunity after breakfast to teach Benjáme how to redress Lasse's wound with fresh moss while Lysander redistributed food and Linnaea worked with Lasse on a few more signs. Petra watched at the periphery, trying not to let the others see her curiosity. Before it became too light out, they finished packing and left the fishing hut behind them.

They hiked onward around the edge of the lake, where, after half an hour or so, Petra turned around and gave one last wistful look back at the hut. It was a little sanctuary, and if they didn't make it to the coastline, then this was their last haven before they were at the mercy of more than just the elements.

With a squeeze of the knot in her pocket, she resumed walking - reminded of her duty to Mimameid, regardless of the cost, through a valley boxed in by snow-capped mountains.

The heath here had a crusty sheen of ice on top of it. Magdelena picked up pieces of the thin ice, offering them to Linnaea. After a taste, Linnaea broke the piece she had in half and handed it to Petra. Petra felt the ice melt on the warmth of her tongue and slip cooly down the back of her throat. It was a small gesture, but it helped keep them hydrated without dipping into their precious water supply. Petra wasn't sure if Linnaea realized how helpful she was actually being.

Lasse's pace started to wane after the sun hit its midpoint, though it wasn't until the clouds were pink with the two o'clock twilight that Petra doubted he would make it to the coast.

The trail pulled back in towards the roots of the surrounding mountains and they decided to stop for lunch and a rest. There among a grove of thick, old trees that had long since lost their leaves, they peeled open their last cans of tuna as the twilight melted into dark.

Petra sat down between Benjáme and Lasse, taking her portion from Benjáme and passing it on. Lasse accepted the can, turning to her, his voice weak.

"What do you think, Sir?"

"Soldier?" Petra responded, confused.

"Am I going to make it back? We still got a long enough way to go," he croaked. Petra gave him a hard look.

"You're going home, soldier." It wasn't a request. It wasn't even a command from a superior officer, so much as a prayer whispered out to the All-Father. The can of tuna still in his hands, Lasse closed his eyes and leaned his head back against a tree trunk.

"Yes, sir," he replied and Petra wondered what he was thinking of to keep himself going. Was it a warm bed? A hot meal? Milla?

Petra looked across to see Magdelena and Lysander signing back and forth, eyes darting, heads huddled together. Her eyes narrowed as she watched them, aware that they were talking intentionally so that she and Benjáme couldn't follow along.

After lunch, they left the valley and climbed into a fold of snowy mountains. It was a slow-going ascent and made her leg ache more than she cared to admit, but Lasse's time was running out. To make matters worse, it was bitterly cold and dark along this part of the trail, especially after spending yesterday beside the jewel-toned lake. But the way the snow glistened in the dark was so serene, that Petra was again reminded of why she loved this trail so much. That, and the quiet as they trudged onward through the snowdrifts.

Thankfully, as they broke through the pass over the mountain, they began their descent into a grove sprawling with the trunks of young, dead evergreens.

The ground crunched with the sound of long-fallen pine needles and ice-covered snow, but the trees about them stood stark like jagged headstones in a grey cemetery of a world destroyed. Petra smiled as she began her descent. She knew this cemetery. It meant that they had, at last, reached the coast.

3

LYSANDER

Lysander caught his breath at the reflection of faint moonlight against the misty waters of the fjord. It was beautiful, but it was also desolate.

He wasn't sure what exactly he had expected, a log cabin with a fire already blazing or maybe just some remnants of the people of Old. Maybe a military unit waiting to escort them to wherever this Mimameid was. They glanced left and right, as if they were still in The Time Before and they expected traffic to come barreling around the curve of the old, cracked highway. The three of them followed the soldiers across the road and down the side of the barren coast, the faded bronze of long-dead grasses and fallen pine needles peeking out from in between the patches of snow.

Once they were down the hill far enough to be out of sight from the road, Benjáme and Petra dropped their bags and lowered Lasse to the ground. They started to gather together some of the dead wood for fire and set up a temporary camp.

As they made their way past the naked pine trees and towards the shoreline, Lysander felt the pull to keep walking, onward into the water. To just keep walking, as he had been since the start of this 'Ragnarök'. He'd come so far, only to end up back at the water's edge again. Without a second thought, he continued on.

He fell to his knees on the rocky beach, his head heavy. Tears brimming in his eyes, his hand found Judit's charm, still hanging by an old leather band. The last time he had been at the coast - the last time he had heard the sound of the waves - he had been pulling himself out of the water, to what he thought was towards his family. He was lucky the charm had stayed around his neck that day.

But here, the fjord water was frosted over with a layer of thick ice, broken up into chunks by some unseen force below. The glacial melt clunked lazily against one another as the rhythmic waves drummed upon the shoreline, like the base line of a song Judit was playing on their old family piano. The fog still sat in the air, making it impossible to see beyond a few meters onto the water, but for the sunbeams desperately trying to make their way through the ashen clouds above.

A hand on his shoulder startled him and the brimming tears spilled over onto his cheeks. He sniffed, hastily wiping them from his stubble, and tucked the salty strands of hair that were being whipped around by the wind behind his ears, hoping whoever had tapped him wouldn't notice.

His face warmed when he saw Linnaea's stringy, blonde hair, tossed and sticking to her cheeks in the damp, cold air. Her brown eyes were luminous as she looked down at him, crouched on the beach. He reached up to take her hand and squeezed it in wordless gratitude. He imagined how things would be different if Judit had been there when he had landed back in Old Sweden. She had been the same age Linnaea was now. He tried to banish the thought from his mind. It wasn't helpful to think like that.

"You okay, L?" Linnaea signed, the gloves hanging from her jacket sleeves floating in the wind as she moved her hands.

"Yeah Sprout," Lysander signed back, trying to compose himself. "yeah, I will be." He couldn't help feeling like he'd gone in a big circle, but in truth, the very fact that Linnaea was there reminded him that, at least this time he wasn't alone. He stood back up and took a step towards the water, letting the weary waves lap over the toes of his well-worn boots. Even though they were waterproof he could feel the cold of the water through his boot, especially in the spot where his big toe had rubbed a hole in his sock.

"Are you thinking of your family?" she asked, her fingers pink with the cold wind coming off the coast. He nodded and squinted out at the fog, clenching his jaw, trying to figure out what exactly was bothering him. He turned back to her.

"With my parents, it's a little easier. You know, my *pabbi* and I didn't get on so well and my *mamma*, at least she got to live a relatively comfortable life. But I can't help imagining who my sister might have become. If she'd gotten the chance," he signed.

"It's okay to miss them sometimes," Linnaea signed. She bent down to pick up a rock and tossed it toward the water. It skidded over the ice before sliding off into the water below. He could see from the dimples in her cheeks that she'd felt the vibrations of the rock hitting the ice. A curious smile slipped onto her face. He squatted down and gathered a handful of rocks into a pile on the shore.

"At least I have you," he signed. Linnaea knelt beside him.

"I know. And you're completely stuck with me," Linnaea signed cheekily at him, then stuck her tongue out as she stole a rock from his pile and threw it into the water. It skidded across a chunk of ice and slide sideways into the fjord.

After a few minutes of tossing them into the water, the two of them turned and paced back up the steep slope towards the others, who were finishing up their makeshift camp on an outcropping of a rock at the edge of the dead evergreen forest.

"And now?" Lysander asked Petra as she leaned back, her thigh propped up, looking swollen compared to her other leg.

"And now we wait," she told him, and Benjáme looked up, beckoning them over for some seaweed and apples.

"It shouldn't be too long," he promised Lysander, a hopeful smile working its way into his dark eyes, confidence in whatever signal he had mentioned the night before. Lysander raised an eyebrow as he took his dinner from Benjáme's outstretched hands.

An engine revved - no, two engines - whipping Lysander from sleep. After eating the last of their rations, they had settled into their sleeping bags for what he hoped would only be a few hours. But based on how far the temperature had dropped, it was now deep into the night.

In the black, the peeling bark of the pine trees shone a pearly white. The long beams of light cut through the night high up along the road above them. Someone had stamped out their fire, but the smoke still rose into the dark night air, pale grey against the black.

Petra looked back at Lysander, her eyes glinting dangerously in the darkness. She was poised, ready to jump if it was the Celts. But the glimmer of gold in her eyes told him she was hopeful this was the medical evacuation. Benjáme was crouching protectively over a sleeping Lasse.

Lysander reached over Linnaea and placed a hand on Magdelena, shaking her ever so slightly to wake her. He put a hand over her mouth as she rolled over, her eyes immediately alert, luminous in the dark, pine needles stuck in her long braid.

The cars above came to a stop with the loud crank of the hand breaks - one after the other. Doors opened and voices spilled out into the night.

Lysander held his breath. They were too far away for him to make out what language they were speaking with one another, friend or foe, but Petra was leaning far over trying to make out their faces.

There was nowhere to hide if they made it down to the outcropping of rock. He hadn't been thinking of what they would do if the Celts found them there first. They pressed together as a group, waiting, their heartbeats thumping in their ears.

Magdelena reached over and woke Linnaea gently, her eyes wide as two harvest moons hanging low in the sky as searchlights from the new arrivals combed the hillside. The sound of loaded guns cocking joined the footfalls and the voices Lysander felt his heart drop into his stomach as his hand raised to his logr charm. He thought about reaching into his bag to try to use the cable rippers as a weapon.

The headlights on the cars flashed three times and all at once, an expression of recognition melted onto Petra's face. She looked heartily at Benjáme, whose face mirrored her own. It could mean only one thing. Friend.

Benjáme stood up in the darkness and called out something undecipherable to Lysander.

There was a response to Benjáme's greeting and then the chatter lifted as Swedish mixed with Norwegian and Finnish, overlapping into one joyful noise.

The large group of soldiers stumbled down the slope and onto the rocks where they were camped out, wide smiles visible, even in the dark. They leaped forward to embrace their comrades, Benjáme launching into the story of their journey and explaining what had happened to Lasse, while Petra pointed down towards the three of them, huddled away from the rest. Lysander instinctively drew closer to Magdelena and Linnaea, painfully aware of how very foreign they appeared to these war-bonded soldiers.

They watched speechlessly as the soldiers called up to their transport for a stretcher to carry out Lasse.

Meanwhile, an incredibly tall, but young soldier with a laughing face followed Petra's finger down and approached them. He had a loose, carefree gait and a shock of cropped, blonde hair brilliant enough to see in the dark. He strutted forward past Petra, who was tiny by comparison, and stuck out his hand to the three of them.

"I'm Anders. You guys must be the new *Opps*. Let's get you three loaded up." Lysander felt Magdelena frozen beside him and put an arm out to accept Anders's greeting. As he did, he saw the splatters of scar tissue that wound their way up Anders's arms, neck, and into his hairline. They were the kind of scars you only got from one thing: fire. Celtic fire.

"Thanks," Lysander said, trying not to stare at the burns, but Anders flashed a big smile when he noticed Lysander's gaze.

"Ah, don't worry. You should see the Celts who gave me these," he joked. "These your things?" He asked gesturing at the sleeping bags and the heat lamp. Lysander nodded and they all bent down together, shoving their belongings haphazardly into their backpacks. "We want to get a move on. Lasse's in a bad way, you know. Well, of course, you know." Anders laughed lightheartedly and threw Magdelena's bulging pack over his shoulder. They followed him quietly, while Lysander's mind raced.

"You guys do this a lot? Picking up strays like us?" he probed as Anders led them further up towards the road. He saw Benjáme helping Petra up the hillside just ahead, the two of them trailing behind Lasse's stretcher.

"Not as much as we used to, you know, in the early days. But I was a stray once myself, until Mimameid." Lysander cocked his head, urging him on.

"You'll see." Anders waved them on, encouraging them up the hill. There, parked in the middle of the desolate street were two enormous Humvees. Lysander couldn't believe it. Cars. Running cars - not ones abandoned in the middle of the highway trying to flee a sinking city with everyone else. No, these looked like they were fresh out of the shop.

Even more surprising was that they weren't Celtic. As far as he knew, every vehicle still kicking had been absconded by the enemy. But these were Norse. Was this what Mimameid was? Lysander adjusted his pack and saw that Magdelena was just as overwhelmed as he was. Linnaea, however, looked poised for adventure.

"Here goes nothing," the girl signed and they followed Anders' lead in throwing their pack into the back of the vehicle. Petra and Benjáme jumped in behind the backpacks to ride beside Lasse's stretcher while the other driver started the engine. Anders beckoned them around to the front and helped boost them into the passenger seats of the second Humvee. Then he jumped into the driver's seat, slammed the door shut, and revved the vehicle back to life with a monumental force.

Lysander rolled the window down as they drove along the road and let the freezing air rush over his face, numbing his ears and tousling his tawny, unwashed hair.

Ashy clouds hung in the sky as they had for so long, but it seemed like the waning moon was trying to reach back down toward them. He followed the coastline with his eyes and tried to imagine what Mimameid would look like, this paradise they all spoke of. Next to him, Linnaea was fighting against sleep, her head bobbing against his shoulder. He reached up and put his arm around her. She adjusted, snuggling closer as her blonde wisps tangled up in the open night air.

He kept the window down as night gave way to dawn with a faint gold over the horizon and let it warm his cheeks.

After a few hours following the road along the winding granite coast, when the sun was settling into its place in the ashy sky, they passed a city limits sign that had been blacked out with spray paint and replaced by the white Mimameid insignia. Lysander sat up a little straighter.

They entered a town that, as he looked around, Lysander saw still had people living in it. It was strange to see somewhere that hadn't yet been burnt, that didn't echo with death. Most had been raided by the Celts or deserted out of fear. The crumbling buildings had been crushed under the weight of snow and ash. Shaken to the core by earthquakes. They were creeping shadows of what used to be - graveyards, really - you held your breath while you were there and moved on as quickly as you could without disturbing the dead. But this place wasn't like that.

He pulled his hands back inside the window of the Humvee, wary of the people walking around as casually as if they were headed to work in the early morning of The Time Before as if nothing had changed at all.

He was still watching the people curiously from the car window when they turned abruptly down the street and headed for the water. Beside him, Linnaea jerked awake, groggily looking around and squinting in the light.

"Are we there yet?" she signed, glancing from her mother to Lysander. Anders watched with intrigue in the rearview mirror.

"Looks like we could be?" Lysander signed in reply, shrugging his shoulders and making space for her to peer out the window at the glassy water. It looked alive, yes. But it didn't look like paradise.

After a few more minutes of navigating the streets, Anders pulled over and the soldiers piled out of the back, unloading their various equipment as well as their belongings. Anders helped them climb out, while a few others lowered Lasse carefully out of the back of the vehicle. Benjáme grabbed their packs and directed the group towards what looked like an old marina down the narrow street. Petra, however, waved the three of them over to her.

"You guys are coming with me," she said brusquely, and led them off the main road, away from the others.

"Where are they going?" Lysander asked her, jogging to keep up with Petra's surprisingly brisk pace. Her leg was obviously feeling better. He wondered if maybe they'd given her a shot of something in the back of the vehicle for the pain.

"They're taking The Back Door," she replied. "A sort of service entrance. It's closer to The Infirmary, so they'll be able to treat Lasse faster."

"And they're taking our packs?" He looked back as the group of soldiers moved further and further away. Petra didn't answer him right away, leading them to the waterfront and following along a row of colorful houses with peaked roofs and crisp paint lining the shoreline. They passed a plum purple one, then a deep forest green.

"They will make sure your belongings get safely to Mimameid. There just isn't much space in the sub." Petra had a wicked excitement coming off of her as they passed a coral-colored house, then a cherry-red one, then a warm goldenrod.

"So then if they're going in The Back Door, how are we getting in?" Lysander grumbled a little as he asked, a little impatient that he wasn't getting more information.

"Well." Petra stopped abruptly in front of a cornflower blue house and threw him a roguish look. "We're going through The Front Door."

She knocked a rhythm on the wooden door and they heard the sound of several latches unhooking from the other side. A giant of a man, with long, grey hair and skin that looked like leather from the long-forgotten sun opened up.

"In the boughs of Mimir's tree, Fiske." Petra had a smile on her face as she raised her right hand to her brow, palm down to greet him. It was the same greeting Benjáme had used back at their campsite with the other soldiers. "Nice to see you again," Petra said as she stepped inside. He made a mental note of the strange gesture and followed Petra over the threshold.

It was a boathouse. Small, cold, and dimly lit. Inside, Lysander could hear the lapping of the water beneath them and smell the salt of the sea blending with the freshness of the pine wood. It occurred to him, maybe these buildings weren't from The Time Before, they were just built to look like the Old World. Maybe he'd been wrong - this place had burned and they'd just rebuilt on top of the ashes. With a crack and a sizzle, a safelight came on inside the boathouse: an eerie, red glow. The man called Fiske raised his hand to his brow in greeting.

"In the boughs of Mimir's tree." His voice creaked like an old wooden boat as he spoke. Lysander awkwardly mirrored the motion. Magdelena interpreted the odd phrase for Linnaea. The girls turned to the old man and repeated the greeting with equal hesitancy.

"Interesting name, Fiske. Like, fish?" Lysander asked, trying to alleviate the discomfort he felt at the strange greeting.

"Fiske is his family name, if you can believe it. He's old enough to still have one," Petra explained and Fiske nodded.

"My dad and my grandad and all my family back and back were fishermen. Couldn't see myself doing something that didn't send me out on a boat every day." The old man was definitely missing some teeth.

Lysander didn't know that anyone with a family name was still alive, it had been so long since they'd been given. At some point before Lysander had been born, the number of ecological refugees and orphans had rendered them virtually obsolete. Only the really old or ultra-wealthy had still used them as far as he knew. And who could he have known who was that wealthy? Magdelena interpreted for Linnaea and her face changed into a smile.

"My mother has a family name, too," Linnaea signed to Lysander's surprise. He turned to look at Fiske as Magdelena interpreted for her daughter. The old man smiled his nearly-toothless grin even wider.

"Is that so?" the old man chuffed, absolutely delighted. "And what is it?"

Magdelena looked sheepish. It took Lysander a second to realize why - he didn't know much about her past - but he did know she didn't get on with her parents much and her family name was probably the last real connection she had to them.

"Ellefsdötter," she replied, modestly, spelling the name out with her hands with care.

"Well, it's a pleasure to meet you." Fiske gave a sort of funny bow to her and Lysander repeated the name back to himself.

As his eyes tracked the row of drysuits that hung along the wall, Lysander felt a pit developing in his stomach. Ever since the boat capsized off the coast of Old Sweden he had been more wary of water, avoided it really, but here he was, water lapping just beneath his feet.

"Ready?" Petra's eyes shimmered in the darkness as she said it.

"For what?" A mildly panicked glance passed between him and Magdelena, who interpreted for Linnaea. The three of them had been in a lot of strange situations over the past few years together, but this seemed like the weirdest.

"Suit up." Petra sized Lysander up and tossed a suit in his direction, before unzipping her jacket and stepping into her own. Fiske unhooked a smaller size and handed it over to Linnaea, who signed 'thank you' back with wide eyes. Magdelena pulled a suit off the hook.

"Our lore prepared us for Ragnarök. And Ragnarök was predicted to consume all the earth in water," Petra explained to them, Magdelena interpreting, though her wince told Lysander that she wasn't quite used to the word 'Ragnarök' yet. Lysander considered what they were about to do. Flooding had become so common that diving was a skill everyone grew up with, but it didn't mean he liked it. "So, what did we Norsemen do to protect ourselves from Ragnarök?" Petra asked them. "We built a place to live on an earth consumed by water." She zipped up her suit. "Look, I promised to take you somewhere safe, and there's no place safer than Mimameid." Petra stuffed her tangled, copper hair into the cap.

Still confused about where exactly they were going, Lysander climbed into his own drysuit - socks with holes into the footed bottoms first - and zipped it up. He was glad, at least, that the suits were thick. If they were really doing what he thought they were doing, the water would be cold, very cold.

Lying under where his suit had been hanging, on a bench that ran along the wall, was a pair of diving fins, a helmet, and a weight. He picked up the helmet, examining it. It looked like a motorcycle helmet, but the glass panel had a soft pink tint to it.

"It's a special design by the Swedes," Petra answered his unasked question as he turned it over in his hands. "The Mimameid military bought them out so they could divert all production toward getting survivors safely to Mimameid. It's pressure-resistant and made of a crystal that stores oxygen from the environment around it, so no bulky tank on your back. Oh, and there are integrated monitors for temperature and depth." Lysander glanced over at Magdelena and Linnaea, half suited up and wearing similar looks of apprehension on their faces. He interpreted what Petra was saying and they nodded, the apprehension melting from Linnaea's face somewhat faster than her mother's. He was privately proud that they needed no further explanation of the more technical terms. They'd certainly spent enough time together over the last years for them to have picked up a thing or two from him.

Petra was so at ease here in the boathouse, it was obvious that this was simply old habit to her. She threw open a trapdoor in the floor and sat down on the edge of a ladder, her legs hanging into the frigid water below. As she strapped her fins on, she looked up at the boathouse keeper, smiling in a way Lysander had not seen before. When her fins were on, she put on her helmet and looked over at them, bidding them to follow suit.

"The important thing is to keep breathing normally in the helmet," she explained, taking care to look at Linnaea and enunciate clearly, as they wiggled their helmets into place. "You'll feel two buttons over your right ear. The top one seals the base of the helmet - pressurizes it, essentially - and the lower button activates your comm." She indicated each of the buttons as she spoke, "Any questions?" She looked around at them.

"How many times have you done this?" Linnaea signed and Lysander was grateful to see her face was filled more with anticipation than fear. He had more than enough fear for the both of them.

"So many, I've lost count," Petra told her, reassuringly and held up all her fingers at once. She was trying to string together a few signs she had picked up from watching them the last few days. "Ready to go?" They all nodded - Lysander still hesitantly - and Petra clapped her hands together. "Okay. Let's do it. Good to see you again, Fiske." She raised a hand to her brow through the glass.

"Always a pleasure, Petra." Lysander noticed the informality between them - he didn't call her by her title as he returned the gesture to her - his eyes sparkling with kindness, affection even, as she went underwater. Petra was home.

Lysander grabbed his fins and weight and walked over toward the trap door. After strapping on the fins and belting on the weight, he took a steadying breath as he slid into the icy water. He tried not to think of the last time he was in open water, swimming to shore through torrential currents and away from the sunken refugee boat. The weight of the water against his chest had been enough to stop his heart. In earnest, he didn't know why it hadn't. He focused now on the silence in his helmet, the feeling of the fins on his feet and breathing deep into his belly - the water here was calm.

When he opened his eyes everything around him was dark, except for the faint beams of light cutting through the surface. His heart skipped a beat and he stopped breathing as he watched the floor of the little wooden boat house shrink above him and he sank deeper into the fjord.

A light switched on in his diving mask and he remembered Petra's instructions in the diving helmet. He took in a deep breath. Looking around, he saw the girls' faces, bathed in the pink glow of the crystal and his heartbeat began to level out. At the same time, the monitors activated and a small screen in the upper left corner of the glass told him the water was 3.3 degrees Celsius and dropping.

Petra glanced around at them, making sure they had adjusted to breathing in the helmets before she spoke.

"Everyone still doing okay?" she asked into the comm, and Lysander stuck a thumbs up at Linnaea, who nodded and smiled in the dim light from the mask. The girl's eyes were so wide with wonder, he needn't have bothered. She was completely enamored.

"Where to next?" Linnaea signed and Petra smirked, not needing a translation to see the enthusiasm on the girl's face.

"First, we drop the weight," she explained and gestured to her belt. Lysander saw on his display that they had reached the optimal thirty feet, so he unclipped his weight and let it drop. The girls did the same, watching the belts fall.

"What happens to the weights now?" Linnaea looked at Petra and signed. Magdelena asked Linnaea's question over her comm.

"Fiske and his team will come and get them," Petra assured, again fumbling through a few signs. She'd picked up how they'd signed Fiske's name, for one. Lysander was warmed by her trying to learn for Linnaea. "Come on, there's more to see." She beckoned them to follow her onwards.

Petra turned and took a fearless nosedive further into the depths, Linnaea following in her wake. Lysander and Magdelena exchanged a nervous look before swimming after them. Lysander was clumsy about it at first, as he got used to the movement of the fins but, he found after some experimentation that the less resistance he put up against the water, the more natural it became to glide in placid waters.

They passed deep water corals, spotted with anemones and grasses that swayed wistfully in the current. Starfish crawled across the coral, seemingly in slow motion, wiggling their tiny suction cups in the water.

"The fjord used to look a lot worse." Petra's voice echoed over the comm and this time Lysander saw Magdelena pause to interpret. They hovered in the water, looking at the life around them. "Right after the volcanoes, everything died. The water was black with ash and what little sunlight got through perpetuated an explosion of algae growth that caused most of the coral to die and the animals to suffocate," Petra explained, flipping around to face them. "They really thought the ecosystem would never recover."

"But it did," Linnaea signed and Petra nodded, a small smile creeping onto her face.

"It did," Petra echoed, mirroring Linnaea's hands in the water. "It's still got a ways to go to getting completely healthy again. Every day, ash still falls, but without so many humans, it's easier." Her voice was momentarily somber over the comm.

Lysander was genuinely awestruck. There wasn't anywhere in the Scandinavian backcountry they had seen that looked this alive anymore. Underwater plants were not her specialty, but Lysander saw Magdelena transform into the curious, young scientist she was in this aquatic orchard. It had been a long time since either of them had seen anything this green.

They swam deeper, watching the fish get bigger, thoroughly unperturbed by the people passing them. He felt small knowing that all the destruction above the surface had brought a sense of peace under the waves. The fish did not fear their cohabitants here in the fjord. They had been allowed to heal, to rebuild.

A series of clicks and pops echoed out across the water, and a forceful roll of waves left Lysander in a wake of bubbles. He spun in the water, regaining control. Above, below, and between them, was a pod of chittering black and white orcas.

He hovered, not sure how they would react to him, blood thumping in his ears. The huge whales coasted beside them, a few brave youths weaving in and out of the stunned humans. But in seeing the softness on Petra's face, his breath leveled.

Lysander felt a nudge as one of the largest orcas in the pod bumped his leg. His heart stopped for a second, looking deep into its dark eyes, glittering with discernment.

"It's a female," Petra told him, her voice more tender than usual. "Judging by how she's interacting with the others, I'd guess she's a grandma." The orca rubbed her snout against his leg like a giant cat. It twisted around him, letting out a cheery, pulsating call. Her tail wrapped up around Lysander and he could feel the power beneath the creature's skin before it pushed him onwards in the water with a giant sweeping motion.

They had all been following what seemed to be an underwater ridge line when Petra beckoned them around a curve in the fjord. The pod kept swimming straight and Lysander watched with longing as the magnificent creatures pressed on. He couldn't remember the last time he had seen wildlife, let alone interacted with it. Had he ever, or had they all been in heavily guarded protection zones? He thought he could remember a trip to something called an 'aquarium' from when he was very small, before even Judit had been born. But it was so long ago, all he had of the memory were flashes of exotic, unidentifiable fish and the feeling of the cool glass against his sticky cheeks. His mother had been feeding him knäck toffees all day long as a special treat...

A hand tapped his shoulder and he jerked around in the water, clinging to the wistful memories for a fraction of a second longer before following to where the hand was pointing. He let out a soft gasp.

He wouldn't have noticed it if Petra hadn't shown him where to look.

There, built into the rocky side of the fjord, was a massive bunker. A construct of immense hexagonal pillars - as dark as basalt stone and clustered together - all rising to different heights but all reaching down into the depths of the fjord below. The murky, green waters trembled around the structure, as though suspending the fortress in time and space.

He found himself looking at Petra, mouth ajar inside the helmet. She smiled at him, the freckles on her face illuminated pink from the crystal.

Something compelled him forward towards the bunker. He was hypnotized by the bolts and screws holding the giant columns together. The steel was coated and crawling with algae and little sea creatures, telling him it had been underwater for some time now. Longer than 'Ragnarök,' certainly.

But as he followed the columns down, he noticed that approximately two-thirds of the way to the base the structure appeared older. The grooves in the metal showed signs of having been reformed and the scattered portico windows - which on the upper levels were consistently hexagonal - were round, like on a submarine from The Time Before. It looked to him, that at least some parts of the bunker were recycled, which only intrigued him further.

Illuminated by a faint blue glow to the right of the bunker spread an expansive, multi-tiered series of metal frames dripping with thick, lush seaweed. There - like tiny worker ants - were people, clad in similar diving suits to theirs, weaving in and out of the frames. Lysander thought of the seaweed the soldiers had had in their packs and realized this must be where it had come from. The divers grabbed onto the metal frames and the seaweed fluttered as a rush of current swelled and Lysander looked up to see where it was coming from.

Overhead was a small submarine pod, dull with age and bubbles spitting out the back. They watched as it disappeared around the back side of the structure, seemingly into the rocks below. The Back Door, Lysander thought. As the last of the bubbles floated away, Lysander's eyes tracked to several loops of glass stacked like a spiral staircase on top of one another, rising around the side of one of the columns.

"What's that down there?" he asked Petra, her face still verging on delight as she watched them take in the bunker.

"That would be the fresh-water fish farm, for spawning trout and salmon; it's meant to simulate the current of the rivers as much as possible," Petra explained. "And down there," she pointed to a black netting encasing a larger part of the rocky bottom Lysander hadn't noticed yet, "is one of the places where we raise and harvest the saltwater populations. We have a few places netted off along the coast for various other fish. We get haddock, redfish, shark. Cod for caviar from time to time. Sometimes we get halibut or plaice." He exchanged a look of surprise with Magdelena. "The bottom feeders and the fish that live deeper down, they tended to do better when it came to surviving. But we never take more than we need and we always release them back into the wild if we can. It's as much about rebuilding a healthy population of fish as it is about sustaining the people of Mimameid." Lysander saw a group of people dressed like them, sinking down toward the fish farms and thought it must be a diving class. "Come on," Petra encouraged, "we can get closer, you know."

As they approached the bunker, he noticed the hexagonal panels forming a massive geodesic dome ceiling over the top of the largest basalt-like column. It was the only column with a dome and though it was darkened, Lysander could see the reflection of the glass and he wondered. He realized Magdelena was watching him with a knowing smile on her face.

"How do you power it all?" Lysander finally asked the question behind all his awe at the entire structure.

"I could try and explain, but I think you'll get better answers from the lead engineer, don't you?" Petra chuckled heartily through her comm. Fair enough. Lysander thought and he shrugged. "Ready to see how to get in?" Petra asked.

"Get in?" He had almost forgotten there was an inside to see.

"Honestly, I don't know how you guys have gone all these years without hearing about Mimameid," Petra told them. "We tried as much as possible to get the word out. It's the safest place for a Norseman to be."

Shadowed by the vastness of it, he suddenly felt a twinge of hesitation. This bunker was an engineering playground, and it was true Lysander ached to explore every facet of its design, but he and Magdelena had set out with a plan. This wasn't a part of that plan. A knot formed in his throat, the feeling that somehow, this bunker would cost him this family he had found. That he had made for himself. He looked over at the girls.

It was hard to make out their faces. Linnaea had never experienced anything even close to this. Her life of scavenging for food and trying to stay one step ahead of the Celts while she searched for a way to Svalbard could be over. Magdelena was the one who had more to lose by staying here and giving up the search.

He resolved to gather as much information as possible about the bunker - before deciding what to do - together with Magdelena and Linnaea.

Petra gestured for them to follow and took a sharp dip into a grotto that under different circumstances might have looked too foreboding to enter. He braced himself with one last glance up at the surface of the water, before following behind Magdelena and Linnaea.

"Just have to knock to let them know we are here." Petra swam forward to a scanner, sticking her arm up and extending the band she'd used to show them the map towards it in the dark, green waters. Lysander was briefly grateful they'd come to the end of the swimming portion of their journey - not only because of the water, but his pants were beginning to chafe against the loose diving suit.

"Grab onto something." Petra tapped Linnaea on the shoulder as she warned them over the comms and gestured to the handlebars that protruded from the bunker's exterior walls. Linnaea nodded and grabbed hold with both hands.

A light switched on, luminescent green, as the scan was completed and from the belly of the metal bunker, a hexagonal door groaned open, like a shark's jaw, wide and willing.

The water rushed into the bunker with such force, Lysander understood why Petra had warned them to hold on tight. He wrapped his hands together and braced his feet against the side of the door, as the water washed over him.

When the door was fully opened and the antechamber had filled with water, Petra guided them inside. She slammed a large red button on the wall, triggering the door to close behind them.

When it had shut completely, the room went red and a chirpy woman's voice echoed throughout.

"Antechamber has been breached. Please wait to remove your helmet until the room has been secured." The water around them drained from the chamber like bathwater from a tub being sucked out through the industrial-sized drain in the far corner as the woman's voice continued to replay.

When the water had emptied, both sides of the chamber erupted, blasting air and drying their suits. Petra took off her helmet and let her mane of copper hair out of her diving cap, the forced air sending the tangles into a frenzy. When the air shut off abruptly, so did the red light and the woman's voice informed them that the room was now "secured."

Lysander stepped forward to peer through the hexagonal portico window just as the door opened with a hiss and he felt the rush of fresh, filtered air wash over him.

The dome, which from the outside had appeared to be opaque, was designed to be one-way glass, displaying a peaceful view out into the fjord for the people scattered about the room. They mingled, drinking cocktails being dispensed from machines against the far wall that they were accessing with bands like the one Petra had used. The floor was made up of honeycomb-shaped concrete tiling with a large, hexagonal glass cutout in the center, artfully decorated with spotted sealskin rugs, soft leather couches, and beautifully handcrafted driftwood tables. Descending into the center of the room from seemingly nowhere was a sleek, rounded fire pit that crackled and popped artificially, the fake wood in the hearth keeping the flames at bay.

It could have been the reception at an exclusive ski chalet, aside from the view of the underwater world, through the spectacular glass dome. Everyone was dressed in clothing different from Petra and her men, but with the same insignia emblazoned on their sleeves. In place of the jumpsuit and jacket that Petra donned, they were draped in what looked like soft silks and finely-knit cashmere in muted, neutral colors. Leisure clothing that matched the atmosphere he saw as he looked around.

Lysander noticed people lounging on the sofas and wearing tinted VR glasses and earpieces, like the ones he used to see commercials for splashed across billboards in the city in The Time Before. The smart-glass technology was always considered such a luxury though, he'd only ever had access to it through his university equipment, and that was always secondhand so the glitches from being mishandled or not properly updated made for some interesting workarounds in the engineering department. Other people in the room were reading books on projections from their bands or playing games with their children, tiles of vintage strategy games spread out on the polished concrete floor and the driftwood tables.

Approaching from the other end of the room was a silver-haired woman with steely, grey eyes. She wore the same jumpsuit as Petra, the insignia embroidered on her sleeve. Her hair was pulled tightly back into a bun, lifting her ears so it looked as if she could hear every noise, every tap, and every word echoing in the room.

A young woman with blonde hair that fell to her waist kept pace beside the silver-haired woman, her face was buried in a tablet as she spoke rapid-fire in a chirpy voice - the same chirpy voice that had been on the intercom. Lysander could tell that the silver-haired woman's focus wasn't on what the blonde girl was saying, but rather, on them - the '*Opps*' who had just walked through The Front Door.

She halted abruptly in front of them. Lysander glanced over at Petra, who had already removed her diving fins, to see what the protocol dictated. Precariously, Lysander began unstrapping his own fins before turning to help Magdelena and Linnaea with theirs.

When Petra had stripped back down to her clothes, she stepped over the threshold into the lounge, grabbed a robe from a hook on the wall which also bore the tree insignia on the back, and embraced the woman. They pulled apart and the older woman left her hand lingering gently on Petra's cheek. It was a gesture of fondness, but Lysander felt the hairs on his neck prickle, it was a calculated decision to pause for that moment with Petra. When she lowered her hand, Petra's own went to her brow.

"In the boughs of Mimir's tree." She spoke reverently and the woman inclined her head in response, repeating the words back, but not raising her hand to her brow as Fiske had done to Petra. That, it seemed, was a gesture made between equals.

"In the boughs of Mimir's tree," the silver-haired woman said to them. Lysander felt the cold from the naked concrete floor seep up through his socks, into his feet and crawl up his legs, leaving an icy knot in his stomach. "Welcome to Mimameid. I'm Sigrid." The smile she wore sat on her lips like an old habit.

"Thank you for having us here." Magdelena inclined her head slightly before interpreting. "This is my daughter, Linnaea." She gestured.

"In the boughs of Mimir's tree," Sigrid replied. "Oh, your daughter is deaf, is that correct?" she asked and Magdelena nodded. "Very well. Welcome, Linnaea," Sigrid responded, surprising them as she signed her response alongside her words. Lysander saw Magdelena's face was wary of the individual greeting. This was a lot to take in.

"Can you tell us what exactly Mimameid is?" Lysander blurted out, tearing his face away from Magdelena's. There was a moment of silence as Sigrid stared at him, her eyes shining like polished silver.

"A community of survivors," Sigrid finally replied didactically, lifting her arm to invite them in and over towards the robes. "I apologize for the somewhat informality of our welcome," she continued and Lysander had to stifle a laugh as he reached for a robe. He hoped she was joking. It hadn't even been this formal when he was deported from the mainland. "We used to have quite the welcome and reception staff at the desk here, but since the influx of survivors has declined, we've repurposed it into our Virtual Reality station,"

Sigrid finished signing and gestured to a long, white desk over to her right with a cleanly manicured finger.

The young woman's long blonde hair spilled onto the top of the desk as she bent over it, feeling around the other side of the desk blindly for something, her other hand clutching the tablet to her chest and her face scrunched up in frustration.

"What's the VR for?" Lysander asked as the young woman leaned further over, head upside down now as she searched.

"To experience the world as it once was. We find it has helped immensely in adjusting to life underwater," Sigrid explained, her hands moving lazily as she spoke and her voice soft and slow, like honey dripping from a spoon.

"There must still be a few processing kits up here," the young woman sighed, exasperated as she came back up, empty, her face still scrunched up in frustration, even though her voice somehow managed to maintain its chirp. She picked her tablet back up and began tapping it, ferociously.

"It's no matter, Yvonne," Sigrid said, waving her hand gracefully at the young woman, her eyes still shining. "We can process them downstairs."

Sigrid lifted her wrist to a pad to the right of a hexagonal, rusting door with a large wheel lock on it that Lysander had only seen the like of on ships before. The pad flickered from red light to green and the large lock on the door clicked, swinging it open. As they followed her through the doorway, Lysander realized it was the band itself which had unlocked the door, like Petra's had. If people were getting drinks with the bands and opening doors with them, the entire bunker system must be accessed through the bands.

Once they had crossed over the threshold, Sigrid pointed to a large metal handle on the wall beside a shelf.

"You can deposit your drysuits and fins here," Sigrid told them, continuing to sign. Lysander pulled back on the handle, revealing a deep, metal chute, into which Magdelena deposited her and Linnaea's diving gear, it squelching on the way down. They set their helmets on the shelf.

"And what if we want to go swimming again? Or go back up to the surface?" Lysander asked quickly, letting go of the handle and gripping his helmet a bit tighter. The door to the chute slammed shut, echoing loudly. The corner of Sigrid's mouth twitched. But having diving gear was the only way to get out of the bunker he knew of, except maybe the pod, and Lysander didn't fancy the idea of giving up his only chance at freedom just yet. Not when he didn't know this Sigrid character. The silvery woman raised an eyebrow above a thin smirk that made him glad he had asked.

"Well, I can't imagine why you'd need to go back up to the surface once you've seen what we have to offer here - but, once you are processed, you will be issued a suit personal to you for recreational use," she replied calmly, opening the chute back up and offering it to him. Petra tossed hers down and reluctantly, Lysander loosened the grip on his suit releasing it to the darkness below. The metal opening closed again behind him, resonating along the concrete walls.

Wordlessly, they followed Sigrid and Yvonne down the hall into a large rusty service elevator with a grill door and when she spoke again, it was over the sound of the grinding chains. The sound set Lysander's teeth on edge.

"So, tell me a little bit about yourselves. What do you two do best?" Gulping nervously, he saw the top was open above them and as they descended he could still see the shimmering of the fjord. "It will help us - and improve your quality of life in Mimameid - if we can place you all in work assignments where you will be most fulfilled," Sigrid continued, her voice had a honied sweetness to it, some half-hearted attempt at making small talk perhaps, but Lysander thought that the rickety elevator was probably not the best place to try to make them feel at ease, at least not him. "I bet you're an excellent mother. Bringing your daughter so far under such dangerous circumstances," Sigrid said to Magdelena. Before she could respond, Sigrid continued signing as she spoke. "Caring for the next generation, that's the most important job we can have these days, I think. I certainly couldn't do it." Lysander felt a lurch in his stomach at yet another calculated decision, this time to not let Magdelena speak for herself.

"Oh, do you have children?" Magdelena replied, a flash of defiance in her eyes as she interjected. She put her arm around Linnaea, who was preoccupied with the whirrs and vibrations of the elevator, her hands wrapped around the metal bars.

"Not personally, no," Sigrid faltered, her hands fumbling with the signing. Maybe there was a history behind the curtness of her reply. "But I prefer to think of every citizen of Mimameid as my child," the silver-tongued woman replied. "And what about you?" Sigrid turned to Lysander.

"Do I have children?" he stuttered, unprepared.

"No. What do you do?" The woman's eyes flashed with annoyance at having to repeat herself. The blonde woman, Yvonne, looked up and sucked in her breath before quickly burying her face awkwardly even further in her tablet. "Do you have any special skills?" Sigrid probed.

He looked over at Petra. She urged him on with her eyes, a docile, tawny color like a fawn in the forest, neutered, almost, and it unsteadied him, but he knew what she wanted him to say. He tripped over the words.

"Uhh...well, I'm an engineer. Or I was. Student of electrical engineering. Ma'am," he managed. She clasped her hands together.

"Ah! Engineer. How serendipitous," she exclaimed without explanation but gave Petra a look as if she was a dog who had performed a trick admirably. "Excellent."

The elevator shuddered to a halt and Sigrid yanked the grill doors open with long, spidery fingers. She exited, Petra falling in closely behind her. Yvonne, bubbling with energy and the tablet pressed against her chest, stepped up to the front of the exit before the rest of them could debark. Sigrid looked at them squarely while Petra melted into the shadows behind her.

"Yvonne will show you around and get you processed and settled in. We'll be seeing one other again very soon. Once more, we welcome you into the boughs of Mimir's tree." Nodding, as if confirming to herself that her performance for them had ended, she spun on her heel. She had disappeared before Yvonne had finished wrenching the rusted grill doors closed again. The elevator hummed back to life. She looked at them with eyes alight with greens and browns that seemed to already be speaking before the words came out of her mouth, but the spirited voice came tumbling out, nonetheless.

"In the boughs of Mimir's tree. Nice to formally meet you all, as you heard, I'm Yvonne." She spoke without breath or pause in that uncanny chirpy voice. "You've been on the road a long time, so I'm just here to make sure you guys are properly processed and get settled in without any lingering questions. You can ask me anything about Mimameid. Anything at all." She seemed harmless enough, but maybe her friendliness was why she had been assigned this position. Magdelena stretched out her hand and Yvonne looked at it amusedly before taking it and shaking it. The gesture seemed to be almost foreign to her.

"*Hej* Yvonne. I'm Magdelena and this is Linnaea." All three of them glanced over at him.

"Lysander," he grunted, uncomfortably.

"Pleasure." The elevator thudded to a halt and the doors jerked open again, shaking the frame of the elevator. Yvonne, utterly unperturbed by the unsteadiness, led them, to Lysander's great relief, out of the elevator.

"I'm sorry," Magdelena began. "but, are you the voice in the wall we heard coming into Mimameid?" She felt rude for asking, Lysander could tell, but it had been bothering him, too. The young woman's face broke out into a bright smile as she continued to lead them down a series of concrete hallways, spotted with unmarked doors made of rusting iron.

"Yes," she confirmed, "an excellent observation. And I never have gotten used to it." She laughed, lightly. They took another turn down a concrete hallway. "Look, It's normal to get a little lost at first," she explained as they moved through the hallways briskly and skidded around a few turns, "but, once you know where everything is in Mimameid, it'll really feel like home. And everyone's quite friendly, so if you ever get turned around, just ask for someone to point you in the right direction. Shall we get you all processed?"

Lysander was still wondering what exactly she meant by 'processed' while Yvonne explained that she was taking them to where they could get a much-needed change of fresh clothes. Compared to the clothing they had seen in the lounge upstairs and the freshly pressed jumpsuits that Sigrid and Yvonne were in, their tattered, crunchy clothes made them look like they'd been wandering the wilderness for years. Lysander had to remind himself that that was because they actually had been wandering the wilderness for years.

The hexagonal door opened before them to a small room with a few chairs pulled up against the walls and a smaller sealskin rug greeting them like a welcome mat. There was a wall mounting that had a few fluffy plants hanging in a hydroponic planter under a grow light. Besides the plants, the room looked like it wasn't used very much anymore.

"The Closet is our storehouse of clothing. You step on up to one of the screens here and tap your band into the port." She demonstrated and the screen lit up. "Your unique bio-signature appears - or well, usually - because you would have been processed upstairs already." She pointed to the screen at a series of lines Lysander assumed was her bio-signature. "Then the options of cataloged clothing available in your size are shown and you can select the options you'd like to try on. They get deposited here." She put her hand on a belt embedded in the wall below the screens.

"What do you mean, cataloged clothes?" Lysander asked as Magdelena scrolled through the options that were listed in Yvonne's size. She scooted aside to share the screen with Linnaea, who continued to scroll in bewilderment at the options while Magdelena interpreted Yvonne's rapid-fire dialogue for her.

"When you get processed, any extra clothing is donated to The Closet for the good of the collective. We have a handful of seamstresses who work to produce Mimameid-issue clothing from old material and repair old clothes, but clothing and skilled seamstresses are both valuable resources, so we recycle everything we can." Yvonne took a breath. "That's something you'll notice about Mimameid in general, though. We don't let a single precious resource go to waste. Everything, down to your waste products, will be reused. I'm sure you can understand." She smiled, warmly. He did understand. How could you not, having seen what the greediness of The Time Before had done to them?

"Okay. Since you guys haven't been processed yet, let's plug in your sizes manually and see if we can't find at least one other complete set of clothes for each of you." She looked them up and down critically, still in their robes and sweat-stained, ashen clothing. before typing in their dimensions into three respective machines.

"You are welcome to launder your existing clothing and keep them with your personal belongings if you would like since, of course, we already know those clothes will fit you." The machine took a minute to process and sort through the catalog before it beeped at them and deposited a vacuum-sealed package to the conveyor in the wall.

"The plastic they are packed in is recycled from seaweed, so make sure to dispose of it correctly - that is - into the organic waste."

Yvonne ripped open the bag and placed the 'plastic' into a chute on the wall marked 'BIO' to demonstrate. She handed Lysander a dark pair of pants that looked like what he had seen the soldiers wearing Above Ground with a small Mimameid insignia embroidered on the front pocket, a rusty-red thermal shirt that had been repaired around the cuffs and a pair of candy-striped, clearly hand-knit wool socks that had no holes in them. He curled his toes up, suddenly self-conscious about his old, hole-torn socks as she handed the new ones to him. "But anything that isn't being worn under your jumpsuit, please refrain from wearing outside of your personal quarters. Everyone here has suffered a great deal. We can't know each person's degree of trauma, but we find it is easier to respect their individual sufferings by not walking around wearing relics of our painful past." She watched with curiosity as Magdelena interpreted for her daughter and then after a quizzical expression came over her face, Linnaea signed,

"What about those people up under the glass dome?" and Lysander had to agree, although it hadn't occurred to him until just then.

"Yeah, they weren't all wearing jumpsuits, were they?"

"Ah well. First of all, good attention to detail." Yvonne crouched down to eye level as she addressed Linnaea, condescendingly. Lysander hoped she simply didn't realize what she was doing. Most people didn't understand that Linnaea had already lived more at thirteen than most people did in their entire life. "Those are the people in Level A. They have special privileges because they are the people and families of those who funded the creation of Mimameid. We owe them all a great deal since they saved us." The girl's voice was starting to grate at Lysander's nerves.

Yvonne handed Magdelena a cream-colored lopi sweater, a style Lysander knew originally came from Old Iceland. Lasse had also been wearing one. Magdelena seemed to recognize the pattern as well, hesitant, as she took it from Yvonne's outstretched hand. She looked up at him, her eyes shining. He wanted to say something, comfort her, but the way Magdelena was biting her lip, he felt it was better to keep quiet, for now. "But you'll notice even the A-levels have to play by the rules. They submit every article of clothing to be approved and embroidered with the symbol of Mimameid."

Yvonne stood back up and handed Linnaea a lopi sweater, this one sage green with bright reds, purples, and oranges knit into the yoke pattern across the top. "So, it's really not that different from the rest of us at all." She smiled her ear-to-ear grin. Lysander stepped in to interpret while Magdelena pulled the sweater over her head. When he had finished, Linnaea arranged her face into a pleasant smile back at Yvonne, but it shot a raised-eyebrow look to Lysander. "Look! You guys are lucky!" Yvonne kept talking, oblivious. "You get matching sweaters!"

The fact that the lopi sweaters were in The Closet meant that there had to be, or at least at some point had been, some Icelanders here. As far as he knew though, when the island erupted, there had been no survivors. How could there have been? They had all seen the aerial footage of the island in the aftermath of the eruptions. Or at least what remained, covered in rivers of lava. Yvonne's bubbly voice barreled on and Lysander tried not to roll his eyes.

"You also get two new freshly laundered jumpsuits. Every six days you'll get a new delivery, along with your laundered clothing to be worn underneath, delivered to your housing assignment. You dispose of your used laundry through the chutes in your housing assignments, so it stays sorted. I'll show you when we get there." Yvonne swiped to another screen where the jumpsuits were listed and ordered a handful more in their respective sizes. They arrived on the conveyor belt sealed in their vacuum-packed seaweed-plastic bags.

The grey-green jumpsuits bore the tree insignia embroidered on the sleeves just like Petra and her men's clothes, the survivors in the reception hall, and Sigrid's own uniform. They were also issued the drysuits Sigrid had promised them, each embroidered with the tree.

Yvonne explained that they were allowed to swim as a recreational activity, as long as they logged it and they would be issued a second suit if they were assigned to work in the seaweed farms or fisheries outside in the fjord.

They followed her, dressed in their new jumpsuits and clutching their fresh clothes tightly in their arms, out of The Closet and down another hall to a set of stairs. Through another honeycomb portico window, this time fogged, Lysander saw what looked to be their next stop. Yvonne held up her wrist to the door and with the flash of a green light, they parted for her, ushering a cloud of steam into the concrete hallway.

They stepped into a high, hexagonal room. It was damp and warm. There was steel scaffolding built up which spiraled its way around the room upwards into the mist. On the bottom floor where they were, rows of steel closets lined the wall and a large steel table was set up across from several industrial sinks with drying racks filled with glass beakers and pipets. What was this place?

Through the hazy air, Lysander saw Yvonne reach out to a woman donned in a sealskin apron and thick rubber boots. She took the woman's gloved hand and led her forward to where the three of them stood.

"This is Runa, she's one of our workers here."

Framing the woman's striking face was soft, dirty-blonde hair pulled back from her face and curling at the nape of her neck from the humidity in the room. On her lips was a gracious smile with freckled, pink cheeks. She raised her hand to a pair of smoky grey eyes and greeted them.

"In the boughs." It must be a less formal version of the greeting, Lysander thought. "Just through those doors," Runa pointed to some plastic sheeting at the end of the room, "is our 'cold' room for the plants that like it a little cooler." Plants, of course. Lysander looked up and noticed the leaves spilling over the edges of the scaffolding above them. He would never have been able to guess. Runa continued to explain what they did there for work, her voice gentle, like a cup of warm milk before bed, as she pulled off her gloves and gestured them forward. Lysander saw that her fingernails were tinted green from the plants. What a delicious little luxury to have. Plants that were so healthy, your fingernails were green.

Though she was hospitable and welcoming, Lysander could tell Runa wasn't someone who sought out the company of others, probably preferring the company of the plants to that of people. "Feel free to roam around. I'm happy to answer any questions you might have." Yvonne thanked her and led them to the edge of a grated metal ramp that led up to the first level in the room, while Runa walked through to the cold room. Eager to explore, Magdelena already had one foot on the steel ramp as Yvonne pushed past her to lead the way.

"The Gardens aren't open to the public for recreational use, but I thought you all might like to see it." Yvonne turned her head so they could hear her as they ascended.

"The Gardens?" Magdelena mouthed down to Lysander excitedly, and he just smiled at her glowing face, the thick scent of pollen tickling his nose.

He examined the setup, bushy, plump plants of various shapes and sizes suspended in white piping that hung, mounted to the hexagonal walls. Lysander looked down at Linnaea, knowing she would have little memory of something like this, a garden. Her eyes were wide as she soaked it all in and she signed in awe and wonder, to no one in particular, but to all of them.

"What is this place?" Magdelena reached out and hugged her daughter before she signed back.

"Live plants. A garden." How long it had been since she had seen so many in one place? He wondered. Yvonne was smiling at them as they continued on the snaking path that wrapped around, plants descending on them from either side.

"Everything is grown hydroponically here in The Gardens - spinach, chard, ginger, herbs, potatoes, strawberries, roses, oranges, oats, hops, mushrooms even. It's a better use of our resources and energy. Oh and of course," she swatted at something, absentmindedly, "we have our own bee colonies."

"No way," Magdelena said, unable to control herself. Lysander raised an eyebrow skeptically. It sounded too good to be true, like some marketing ploy to entice them into staying on. "Bees have been extinct since before I was born," Magdelena breathed. She would do just about anything to study the bees, Lysander knew. Yvonne shook her head.

"Not in Mimameid." And sure enough, as she spoke, her back to them, a little black-and-gold-bellied bee floated down to a strawberry flower. Linnaea looked up at her mother in awe and they watched the bee land tenderly on the petals of the blossom.

"Well, they're bot-bees," Yvonne admitted, a little pink tinting her cheeks, "producing synthetic honey. Still edible, of course. But you have to admit, it's pretty impressive technology." The young woman's initial embarrassment had risen into pride.

"It is impressive," Lysander admitted.

The girls still distracted by the bees, Lysander turned his face upwards. He leaned out over the edge of the railing and he caught his breath. The room went on and on, up and up into the hazy cloud, level after level. It was so tall, he couldn't see where it ended. He went to tap Magdelena on the shoulder, but she had already followed his gaze.

"I see it," she whispered with reverence.

Once they had left The Gardens, though with much reluctance, Yvonne took them down a flight of concrete stairs that led to a long hall. As they stepped off the stairwell, Yvonne pointed down.

"If you keep going down here a few more levels, you get to The Engine Room. Just in case, you know, anyone was wondering," she said playfully to Lysander. He could feel his fingers twitch even as she said it, eager to be useful, but Yvonne kept going. "It's in the oldest part of Mimameid, the original bit that was constructed out of disused submarines. Built before any of this was actually sanctioned," She explained gesturing around them, "A revolutionary experiment. Thankfully, the military stepped in to help fund the final stages of the project, or else none of us would be here."

With a flick of her wrist, Yvonne opened the doors ahead of them. They walked under the sign labeled "B," superimposed onto a Mimameid insignia and hanging above the door as Yvonne explained it was one of four canteens within the complex and that they would be assigned to a canteen based on what housing block they live in.

The room was smooth and clean if perhaps a little impersonal. The furniture - tables, benches, couches - were all made out of concrete with thick, fatigue-green cushions on them, like the grey-green of the Mimameid jumpsuits.

"Interesting decor," Magdelena commented, her eyes tracking down to the hexagonal concrete flooring before landing on Lysander. He raised his eyebrows at her and then followed the sounds of electricity buzzing up to the paneled lights above them, also arranged in a hexagonal pattern.

"The concrete resists the wear and tear of the brackish air much better than any metal we tested," Yvonne stated academically.

The far wall was decorated from floor to ceiling with backlit wooden honeycomb shelving that displayed cascading, leafy house plants artfully spotted among a mass of books ranging from children's stories to philosophy. A little girl, around seven or eight, with skinny, blonde braids and a pair of round glasses too big for her face, likely salvaged from The Closet, had her button nose pressed up to a book as she lay sprawled across the sealskin rug.

Lysander recognized the book from his childhood about a girl with red hair who lived in a rainbow house. His gaze wandered to the people around them. Different heads of hair from charcoal black to white blonde dotted with soft russet and warm browns among the crowd. Skin of every shade and soft, dulcet eyes - every one of them. Their jumpsuits were neat and pressed, their nails trimmed and clean. No one had ash in their hair from running from the Celts, everyone here had showered, probably even a hot shower, in the last week. They didn't have the feral look of people who had spent the last few years trying not to freeze to death.

But they seemed subdued, reading alone while sipping a coffee and adjusting their glasses on their noses or talking in hushed voices, polite and polished movements as they ate their meal. He caught drifts of the different languages being spoken, the melodic inflections of Swedish, the warbled, sing-song lilt of Norwegian, even the lax drawl of Danish. Although it was a soft and humble space, he found the unity of it made him proud. Proud to be Norse.

Yvonne held her wrist up again, to a machine mounted on the wall by the door that looked like the one in the reception hall which had dispensed drinks. It identified her as Yvonne - 18 years old, 49.8 kilograms, and 163 centimeters tall - as the machine in The Closet had. The screen listed her the available options for a snack.

"All the food is packaged and delivered in one-hundred percent recyclables, so make sure you separate your trash when you are finished eating. Bio-waste goes to gas production first and then becomes compost where as the seaweed-based paper products we use get incinerated before they can become fertilizer. And always separate your fish waste, too - that becomes a separate fertilizer for The Gardens." She led them past the machines and along the counter where people were disposing of their garbage so they could see the separation process.

"We have optimized how we feed, condition, and house each survivor in Mimameid, so you can live your most effective, most fulfilling life here. Each survivor has a meal plan, exercise, and sleep regime tailored to their own body's needs, as well as work that is derived from algorithms designed to indicate where you will feel the most sense of accomplishment and satisfaction." Yvonne lifted her wrist up to show them her band alongside the big smile on her face.

"When you're fully processed, you each get your own personal band. They are responsible for taking the readings which provide us with the data we need to be able to exist down here without overextending our resources. It also gives you access to the bunker, just as an added security measure. That should make you feel safe from the Celts running around up there." She pointed to where presumably the surface of the water was, with a comically tense expression on her face. Lysander exchanged a glance with Magdelena which told him she was also wondering exactly how long it had been since this girl was Above Ground. "We started out as a military facility, so security has always been one of the foremost concerns of Mimameid," Yvonne finished.

Since Lysander could finally look critically at the bands, he began disassembling the mechanics of the hardware with his eyes. He could find no indication of how the device could take biological readings - perhaps there was some micro needle implanted in the bands which took readings periodically throughout the day?

They exited the other end of the B Canteen and continued onwards down a hallway. On one side was a handrail protecting them from a steep fall into the hollowed-out middle of the complex. They watched the rusty elevator as it creaked down into the metal belly of the bunker.

Lysander walked slowly, observing the structure as a whole for the first time from the inside. There were four elevators in total, just like the four canteens, all equally rusted, and he thought absentmindedly that perhaps that was from the salt water. Lysander had noticed that even down here the smell of the brackish fjord water lingered in the air. The elevators themselves seemed all to lead into other wings of the bunker, into various other basalt-like column structures. Looking up, he could see the glass cutout in the floor of the dome and the bottoms of A-levelers feet as they crossed over, blocking his view out into the fjord. Leaving something to aspire to, he supposed, the life of an A-leveler.

Yvonne turned sharply into a dimly lit hallway that led up to another hexagonal door. Again the green light flashed at the flick of her wrist and they passed over the threshold. Linnaea's feet froze and he saw her eyes were wide as she looked out at the room before her. Lysander followed inside.

They stepped onto a glass floor, but this time the murky green fjord was illuminated below their feet. All three looked up in astonishment at Yvonne.

"I thought you guys might be interested in this." Her face was alight with pleasure at their surprise. "This is The Observation Deck for the seaweed farms."

The room was large - not as big as the A-level lounge or The Gardens per se - but glass spanned the entire, massive floor and the outer wall, making it feel bigger than it was. Fish swam beneath their feet, weaving between the careful rows of seaweed. They moved like scraps of silk swirling in the water, beautiful pieces of color, listless in the sea, pulsing with the rhythmic humming of the tide.

As they stepped carefully forward, the glass lit up beneath their feet, an icy blue glow left behind by each footprint. Linnaea's mouth hung open in silent awe as she walked forward, tiptoeing across the glowing floor to the observation window, the soft blue fading again as quickly and wondrously as it appeared.

"It started out as a functional room, to observe and better optimize the seaweed growing process. As you may have gathered, it's one of our main crops. But as the farmers have become more familiar with their work, the room has transitioned more to a recreational space. A peaceful place."

Magdelena was entranced. Her mouth open as wide as her eyes, she sank to the floor, looking out into the mix of blue and green, her body haloed by the luminous floor. Linnaea joined her, wandering to the center of the room, face flooded by the fish-world beyond. Lysander continued to walk, slowly around the room, following his own glowing footprints. He turned to Yvonne, who smiled at the reverence on his face.

"It's piezo crystal," she told him, answering his silent question. "It reacts to pressure, causing the fluorescent light."

"I might have guessed," he responded. "It's just - I've never seen anything like it in person. I didn't know something like this could still exist."

"Well, everyone is given access to the room here. It's purely for your enjoyment, so you are welcome to come back any time you like. We only keep it locked for safety." Lysander noticed that even Yvonne's voice had become quieter here. Magdelena looked softly at her.

"Thank you for showing us this." Yvonne inclined her head, beaming. She let them linger among the soundless seaweed for a moment longer before speaking again.

"Shall we continue?" she suggested politely.

"Oh, yes. I suppose we should." Magdelena ran her fingers through the end of her braid absentmindedly. Linnaea lingered behind as long as possible, signing her protests at leaving, at not being able to stay and watch the creepy, crawly sea creatures. Lysander reluctantly followed them out of a second door at the other end of the room.

They stepped together back out into the grey, dim hall passage, leaving behind the magic of The Observation Deck behind them.

4
PETRA

"Dismissed."

Petra nodded and stood up, heading towards the door.

"Oh, and Lieutenant." Petra turned, hand poised in front of the pad. Sigrid's eyes glistened as she spoke, "Very good work." She paused, a smile on her lips. Then in one swift motion, Sigrid's silver hair whirled back around to face her desk. Petra stepped out into the hallway and the hexagon door rotated shut behind her.

When the lock clicked she let out a deep sigh. All the tension she had been holding inside was released, a sense of relief rising in her. She didn't think she'd said anything that Benjáme and Lasse wouldn't have mentioned, too. But, she knew the band would record her heart rate as irregular. Hopefully, Sigrid would read her stress as exhaustion from her injury rather than what it actually was. She had, after all, ordered Petra to The Infirmary before going anywhere else.

She paused briefly in front of the rusted elevator, considering whether she wanted to ride it down to The Infirmary. But instead, Petra placed her fingertips on the cool concrete wall, following it to the edge of the main stairwell and descending the steps. She wondered what would happen to

Lysander, Magdelena, and Linnaea, but was looking forward to seeing her men again when she got to The Infirmary. Maybe seeing them would help her find her footing again back down here in Mimameid; something felt off-kilter.

It had been a long time since they had gone out on a routine mission and come back with *Opps*. Sure, in the first few years that had been their primary directive when leaving Mimameid. Bring people home. Save as many Norse as possible so that the human race could live on. But five years on, Petra was out of practice in processing *Opps*. The standard debrief questions from Sigrid had felt more like an interrogation. She'd never noticed before how much the questions seemed to twist the *Opps'* stories into a narrative that assessed their worthiness of being saved by Mimameid. Sigrid had asked her what kind of deals the *Opps* might have made in order to survive for so long Above Ground when Petra herself was honestly just impressed that they had. They certainly had no love of the Celts, if that was what Sigrid had been implying. But of course, that was exactly what she had been implying.

These people were just trying to survive like anyone else post-Ragnarök. Why did it matter so much where they had been, who they had been in The Time Before, and what they had done to survive? Had the debrief only seemed more rigorous because of how exhausted she was?

Petra had generally considered her instincts pretty good and these new people did not seem to her like the kind to be looking for trouble. They were just as scared of what the Celts might do to them as any other ordinary Norse.

Back when the Celtic islands flooded, they had sailed east to find a new place to live. There was so much tension between the islands and the mainland in the years leading up to Ragnarök that when the Celts arrived on their shores, both sides were bristling for a fight. Millennia ago, the Norse had been fierce warriors and adventurers, just as the Celts had. But in the world that had existed before Ragnarök, the Norse had grown into nations of peacemakers, advocating for unity, pacifism, and acceptance. Only on the fringes of the Nordic lands, where borderlands still needed defending, did they still train to fight like those Nordic warriors of old.

The Celts, however, had not had those decades of peace. They lived in a militarized state where every man, woman, and child was trained to raise a weapon against their enemies. Petra could remember watching the deterioration of their state on the news when she was a child. And most people could remember the historic massacre that had truly changed everything.

As the ice melted, the flooding had pushed people closer and closer together. Food shortages led to famine, medical supplies became more precious than gold and the government - buried beneath bureaucracy and greedy lawmakers unwilling to share resources - was overrun. But, of course, it had been like that all over. Petra had just grown up so far removed from the rest of civilization that the fall of the Finnish government hadn't affected her that much.

The new regime of the Celts had begun with the northern Irish. Accustomed to life under martial law, they'd seized their chance when the Republic deteriorated, their Irish brothers grateful for the relief of the northern Irish military aid. With the Irish peoples united and their land and resources diminishing, they turned to their next-closest neighbors. They'd forged a pact with the Scots, promising food and aid if they helped them overturn their long-time oppressors, the English. The Welsh, too small on their own to stand against the Irish and Scots together, had conceded and pledged allegiance to the reformed Celtic tribe.

It was summer when they'd launched their attack on the English. Those who didn't fall in the swift and heady battles were given a chance to renounce and join the Celtic tribe. Every public trial and execution was televised. Celtic tribe members were called as character witnesses to testify as to whether the captives would make loyal citizens of the Celts and whether their skill sets were valuable. But Petra remembered that there were not many willing to renounce their heritage.

Such was the English massacre. And it made the inflection of Arthur's voice that much more dangerous. A traitor to his own people, he couldn't be trusted and she knew that. Her head knew that. But Arthur had treated them as equals, not as the enemy. He hadn't needed to step out of the woods to help them, but he had done so anyways.

Petra herself had grown up on the fringes of the Nordic empire, one of the militant borderlands, the ones trained to be like the Nordic warriors of old. She was a Sámi, a shieldmaiden; half-Norse, half-Rus. Pacifism and unity had not been options for her. They had spent centuries fighting their Russian cousins over resources and territories. And she wore the betrayal of her heritage on her head. A Finn by birth, her flaming, Russian-red curls were a symbol of the dirty blood that flowed in her veins, passed down by her mother and her grandmother before her.

It had not made life easy, but it had made her stronger. Her parents - two fated lovers from different worlds - hadn't been clever and they hadn't been wealthy. But they'd done the best they could for her - hugged her often and encouraged her curiosity. They were unremarkable mechanics stationed as far north as you could go without freezing on a military base. Working constantly on round-the-clock shifts, Petra had grown up under the care of her *baba* and the two dozen other soldiers stationed with them. She had known the feel of different plants in her hand and could smell it in the air when the enemy was nearby. They had taught Petra tactics, planning, combat, wilderness, strategy - everything they knew. That is, until during a ceasefire, the Russians bombed their base. Petra had just turned thirteen years old. She and her grandmother had stayed for two more months, alone on the abandoned base, lone survivors, snowed in and waiting for help that never came.

The night before she died, *Baba* had held her in her arms, as an ashen, mid-winter snow fell quietly outside, and whispered a sweet Russian lullaby in her ear.

No, the Norse had not been prepared for the brutality of the Celts. But Petra had been. The Norse wanted to defend their homeland, some even to share it with the homeless, wandering nation of Celts. But the Celts arrived and they took no survivors, killing anyone who got in their way, pillaging anything they found, and burning the remains to the ground.

Sigrid was the person who had seen Petra's pain and encouraged her to use it. She, too, wanted the Celts to suffer for the slaughter of the Norse. It hadn't been the Celts that were responsible for the deaths of her parents or grandmother, but their cruelty had provided an outlet for her revenge and Sigrid had been the one to help refine her into the perfect tool against them. Forging her in the fires of battle, Petra had faced more than her fair share of guerrilla fighters as they searched for *Opps*, sometimes entire companies of them. So there was a flicker of guilt that refused to die as she silently questioned Sigrid and her aggression towards the new *Opps* and their supposed ties to the Celts.

The invasion had, of course, been what drove the remaining *Opps* to the bunker. The military, who had survived Ragnarök by waiting it out beneath the waves, rose to the surface, spreading word of its safety and seclusion. Their mission became the survivors and, little by little, the bunker became Mimameid - the legendary hall where the survivors of Ragnarök would live out their days.

And here were more survivors come to Mimameid. Just as she had so many years ago, and yet now, Sigrid didn't trust them. Was it only because they had survived longer than five years out there alone instead of only a couple of months? In all the time that Petra had known Sigrid, she had displayed sound judgment, guided by a drive to preserve humanity. So was it Petra and not Sigrid, who had somehow changed?

Her thoughts had wandered so far, Petra had lost track of where she was headed in the bunker.

A pain shot into her thigh and it brought her back to the staircase. She realized she had descended a level too deep for The Infirmary. As she let out a wince and turned around, she saw the subtle side glances from the other people on the stairs. To them, she was just some useless refugee with barely enough Norse blood in her to justify being kept alive. She had grown accustomed to the looks, and to brushing them aside.

She shook her head to clear it as she climbed back up. Her men's familiar voices bounced off the concrete walls as she reached The Infirmary's door.

There, sitting up in bed near the end of the ward, was Lasse. The color had restored to his cheeks and a smile on his face as he laughed with Benjáme, seated in a chair beside him. Their hands raised to their brows in greeting, as she entered.

"Lieutenant." Lasse inclined his head and Benjáme jumped to his feet. Never one to remain serious for long, Lasse's face broke back into a smile so wide Petra couldn't help but smile back.

"Glad you made it down," Benjáme said, pulling Petra into a solid embrace that she ordinarily wouldn't have tolerated, but her leg felt weak after the stairs. The adrenaline which had gotten her over the mountains back to Mimameid and through the interrogation must have finally begun to wear off.

"Well, I gotta get checked out like everyone else," she responded, gruffly.

"Sir?" Lasse prompted, still smiling.

"Yes?"

"I just wanted to say thanks for getting me home." Petra nodded to him curtly, feeling her cheeks flush with embarrassment.

"Just doing the job, soldier, you know that." But Lasse refused to accept her excuse.

"Tell that to Milla," he laughed, though his shining blue eyes were earnest. "No, sir. The job was a routine border check. You brought all of us home after a surprise assault, as well as the *Opps*. You definitely went above and beyond the job, Lieutenant." Petra looked at him for a second, then with a small smile of gratitude, leaned over and hugged Lasse. She buried her head in his shoulder, covering up her face and hiding how much she really did appreciate the comfort.

A voice she didn't recognize rang out from behind her.

"Are you the Lieutenant?" Petra released Lasse and she saw a nurse addressing her. He was bulky and dark circles ringed his fatigued grey-blue eyes. Her first impression of him was that the man was overworked and under-appreciated. Petra nodded. "If you'll just follow me, we're holding a bed for you. Sigrid called down ahead, said we should be expecting you."

She followed the nurse through, past the other beds, some empty, some with curtains drawn. From a room off to the left, Petra heard a set of familiar voices. She peered through the doorway and saw Lysander, Magdelena, and Linnaea with Yvonne in the room where people usually went when they had trouble with their bands. Something about their expressions made her stop.

"Just one second," she said to the nurse and hobbled into the other room.

As she entered, Yvonne was holding their blood samples in her hand, chittering away.

"We have survived in the bunker for so long because we don't waste any resources. And we can focus our energy not only on protecting the survivors here but by looking towards the future and rebuilding the Nordic population that was lost in Ragnarök." Petra tried not to roll her eyes at Yvonne's word-for-word-out-of-the-Mimameid-handbook statement as she came in. These poor *Opps*, to be stuck with Yvonne of all people for their tour. "Oh! *Hej*, Lieutenant. In the boughs of Mimir's tree." Yvonne greeted her with an indifference that Petra was accustomed to from her. She didn't know why, but the girl had never really warmed to her. Maybe it was the same as all the others - she wasn't Norse enough for her. She got along well enough with Petra's men, after all. Based on some of the looks she'd seen, Petra wondered if she got along with them *too well* with them - something she'd chosen to keep to herself and not report to Sigrid. In any case, Lysander and Magdelena had visibly relaxed at seeing Petra enter the room, sitting down on some of the stainless steel stools as Yvonne deposited their vials in the lab fridge and continued speaking.

"Now that we've tested your blood for damage from the ash in the atmosphere and harmful antigens, the next thing we can do is get you guys fitted for bands." She paused briefly, accommodating for Magdelena to interpret for Linnaea, who had her hand on her arm where her blood sample would have been taken from and was frowning. It occurred to Petra that perhaps the girl had never had her blood taken before. "The bands collect the data that we need in order to create the algorithms to determine your meals, sleep, recreation, and work schedules. We just insert a small bio-implant into your wrist - which sends the data it collects into the system - and then you put on your personalized band and you're all set to go. Once you get your band, you'll be assigned your housing block, canteen, and so on."

"Excuse me, bio-implant?" Lysander's voice cut into her monologue. Petra recognized the skepticism in his voice, he'd sounded exactly like that when they'd been discussing how to get Lasse back.

"It's non-invasive, there's no danger to the body." Yvonne was quick with her answer, almost defensively so. "And the implant can also detect any change in body temperature of course, or infection in your bloodstream before symptoms even begin, so we can stay on top of your health," Yvonne continued cheerily, but Petra could see the newcomers remained unconvinced. She cleared her throat, hoping she could help. Sigrid would not be pleased if their engineer decided against staying in Mimameid.

"The implants are how they found us in the woods," she pointed out. "They're the reason Lasse is still alive. When we got within a certain radius of the bunker, they were able to pinpoint our location and send us help."

"And I'm grateful, truly," Lysander began, "but I have a hard time trusting a piece of equipment I don't understand." Petra slid a glance across the floor to Yvonne, whose smile didn't waver as she replied.

"Well, that's easily remedied." She opened a drawer and pulled out one of the bio-implants sealed in sterile packaging. The implant itself was as small as a single grain of rice. Realizing she may not actually have the authority to sanction such an action, Yvonne looked to Petra for confirmation.

"Some rules are allowed to be bent, on occasion." Petra allowed this, hoping secretly that her glancing over this small infraction might earn her some points with the young girl. A silly thought, she knew, but she couldn't help it sometimes - the desire to be liked, accepted. "I think that would be permissible." Petra knew what lengths Sigrid would be willing to go to in order to keep useful survivors here, so this small act of rebellion would be worth it. Yvonne handed the bio-implant to Lysander. It wasn't as if they had anything to hide anyways, Mimameid was paradise on earth. Or as close to it as you could find these days.

"Why don't you take that and you can examine it," Yvonne offered. "It's important you feel at home here. In the meantime, I can escort you all back up to Sigrid and then we can get you all something to eat. How does that sound?"

Lysander looked at Petra and she felt him study her. His brown eyes were alight; he was calculating something. She felt a bit vulnerable as he did whatever math he was doing. He broke his gaze and signed something to Magdelena and Linnaea, who had stopped fiddling with the bandage over her needle prick now.

"I think we'd prefer to eat first," Lysander concluded. "Lieutenant?" He asked Petra, those chestnut eyes unflinching.

"Yes?"

"Would you accompany us to the canteen for some food, by any chance? I think we'd feel most at ease with you as our escort." Petra saw Magdelena raise an eyebrow out of the corner of her eye.

Petra was also impressed by Lysander's sudden offensive play, but she managed to hide her surprise better than Magdelena.

"I think we can manage that," Yvonne replied stiffly, looking at Petra. Poor Yvonne, she wasn't used to people questioning her so much.

But Petra wasn't phased, it worked in her favor, as hours in The Infirmary resting and running tests were not what she wanted to spend her first day back home doing anyways.

"Yes. Just give me one minute." Petra raised a finger and slipped out of the room quickly, tapping the nurse from earlier on the shoulder.

"Turns out I won't be staying after all, but I'll monitor myself and report back if anything seems like it isn't healing properly. Is there anything else you need from me?" The nurse pursed his lips in annoyance but nodded. Petra was, after all, the nurse's superior.

"Very well. I have in your file that you should be issued some medication for pain management over the next seven days." Petra raised an eyebrow and scanned The Infirmary briefly, eyes landing on an old Finn she had seen Milla with a few weeks back, arguing with another nurse about medication that was supposed to be delivered for his wife.

"I think we'd better save those for someone who really needs them, don't you?" Petra forced a smile as she shifted her weight off her injured leg. Despite the pain, she was determined not to take medicine that could be better used on someone else. Petra thought she saw a hint of fear in the nurse's eyes at disobeying Sigrid's specific instructions on her care.

"Why don't we just say that I'm taking the medicine so there are no questions from the *pomo* upstairs about the quality of your work here, yeah?" Petra herself didn't like the idea of lying to Sigrid, but she felt in her gut that it was the right thing to do, just like she had about Arthur. The nurse nodded reluctantly, his dogged exhaustion working in Petra's favor. "I can just sign that saying I released myself," she interjected. The nurse started to object, but Petra took the pad from his hands and held her band up to scan her bio-signature into the file. "Thanks so much."

She walked as evenly as possible back into the processing room where the others were. Taking Lysander by the arm, Magdelena and Linnaea following closely in tow, they paused only to bid Lasse and Benjáme a brief farewell before stepping back out into the bunker.

"So, something to eat, then?" Petra asked them, feeling weightless at the freedom of having disobeyed a direct order from Sigrid. Lysander nodded in response, watching her surge of adrenaline curiously. "Have you all been given your bunk assignments then?" she asked them as they started down the hall.

"Well, no, since we don't have our bands yet, I don't think we've been fully 'processed'." Although he seemed a little unsure about what had happened, there was a glint in Lysander's eye that told her he had also enjoyed running out on Yvonne and the nurse.

"They aren't so bad you know, the bands," she replied, examining Lysander's smirk beneath the chestnut eyes that had been so alive and calculating in The Infirmary. "But it makes sense, being an engineer and all, you want to check out the machine first."

"Yes, well, they seem *accommodating* here." Lysander chose his words carefully as they continued walking. "They took our blood though, is that normal?" he asked her. She felt a smile twitching on her lips. They really *hadn't* seen many people in the last few years.

"Yeah. It's part of the standard medical exam. You know, to see if you have any antigens that could be harmful to the population if they got into the air filtration system or the water. Our medical facilities are substantial, as you can see, but not equipped for containing an outbreak. And some people have more delicate immune systems than others, so we have to be *accommodating* to them here as well." She winked, using his words back at him, trying not to think of the time they actually had had an outbreak. "And, of course, to check how Ragnarök affected your lung function and blood oxygen levels. Didn't you say you were in a big refugee camp? I thought they did that stuff in the camps, too." He scoffed, looking at the ground and instead, Magdelena answered.

"I think they would have loved to be able to screen people like that, but the Lillehammer camp definitely didn't have the resources for that," she said while Lysander signed. Linnaea's face twisted up bitterly at the response.

"I would have been able to learn so much more from them if they had been able to do something like that," she signed, and Lysander gave the girl a snarky smile while he interpreted for Petra. She felt her cheeks warm a little with embarrassment and she lowered her eyes, momentarily humbled by the fact that she'd forgotten just how bad life had been Above Ground.

Even Mimameid had had its struggles at the beginning. She had done her best to forget about the outbreak in D the winter after she'd arrived. So many had died. The family she'd been placed with temporarily had gotten sick. She remembered that she hadn't been able to go see them because of quarantine restrictions once she was moved to C for training. They were the reason she knew a handful of signs - the granddaughter and grandfather had been deaf. But, of course, the outbreak had spread, even through the quarantine and the medicine that had gone to A and B first. The military had needed it, too. By the time the 'spring' had come, many of the old and vulnerable in D had died, including her entire foster family. She knew it had sewn a lot of discord between the levels, the aftermath of which Sigrid was still dealing with.

"Well," Petra started to reply, an idea forming, "then we will just have to take advantage of the resources we *do* have here in Mimameid. See if we can't get you an apprenticeship in The Infirmary, perhaps," she offered, spelling out the word 'apprenticeship' since she hadn't seen them use a sign for it yet.

"Would you like that?" Magdelena asked and Linnaea's hands lit up with energy in response.

"Would I like that? That would be amazing if you could do that," she signed and Petra's shoulders lifted a little at the idea. She saw Lysander nod gratefully to her.

"If you don't have your bunk assignments, then you don't have an assigned canteen either." Petra changed the subject, though inside she was still glowing proudly at her idea. Just another small act of defiance that felt deliciously good. What was happening to her?

"Nope," Lysander confirmed.

"No problem, you guys can eat with me, then." Petra gestured for them to follow her, plowing ahead as fast as her leg would allow her. At the doors to Canteen C, Petra's band lit up green and they swung open with the familiar gush of air, the roar of C crashing into them like a tsunami.

"Who usually eats here, in Canteen C?" Lysander shouted at her, as they moved forward, through the crowd. Petra led them to the automats and lifted her band to the scanner. She caught Lysander's eyes scouring the diverse mass of people. Everything from Northern Sámi to Trøndersk dialect bounced off the walls.

Although she was fond of it, she could see how C looked chaotic to an outsider. The tables were mismatched, wobbly, and old, a combination of leftovers from upstairs and the salvaged remains of the old submarines below. The chairs were anything they could find that wasn't nailed down, and sometimes seating that had been, and they'd pried off the floor. A handful of swiveling stools and old supply crates had been dragged in as seating to accommodate the growing military unit. The cracked and faded polyester canteen chairs from the original submarines were used for the eating area, while they had ripped out and retrofitted the old navigation seats into a grungy lounge area with some pub games that had inevitably lost key pieces over time to the bowels of the bunker.

She saw him scan over the dart boards at the far end with pictures of Celts ripped from old briefing books pinned to the bulls-eyes with an eyebrow raised. The faint glow of the pool table they'd crafted from the old tactical touch table and pool cues they had fashioned from disused carbon fiber rods gave the room a little bit of a dive bar feel. She couldn't help but smile.

"C is for military and their families," she explained and watched Magdelena interpret for Linnaea with increasing wonder. "It's a lot of people who have been here from the very beginning, and anyone who has enlisted since. They get moved into the barracks that are attached to C. The cooks work on different schedules here in C, as to accommodate the military routine. That's why it's always kind of full. But you get used to it. It's better than it being too quiet."

The machine whirred for a couple of seconds and Petra had to bang the side before it deposited her meal on a tray in front of her. Linnaea's eyes fixated on the little brown box in disbelief. The girl had undoubtedly never seen an automat dispense food before either. Amused, she chuckled at the girl's wonder.

"How will we get food without our bands?" Lysander asked her, his face ragged with hunger.

"Yvonne will have put you guys into the system already." Petra walked over to the greasy counter that led back into the kitchens. She knew all the cooks in C, having trained a few of them in their mandatory defense classes, but Milla was her bunkmate. She saw her hazel eyes and hair as dark as chocolate *kolbasa* and waved her over.

"Milla!"

"Petra! You're back!" Milla greeted her from a distance, waving a massive knife around in her one hand. Petra couldn't help but smile. Milla always had something going on. "You got an *Opps* order in the system?" she asked, knowing it sounded like a weird request given how long it had been since they had had newcomers in Mimameid.

"*Opps*?" Her eyebrows shot up her forehead. "Let me check." She pulled off her gloves and tapped a tablet she pulled out of her apron pocket. It took a minute. "How many is it for?" she asked as she swiped the screen.

"Three. They haven't been processed yet, hence the '*Opps*' status." Milla's eyes continued moving across the screen as she responded.

"Wild. How long has it been since we had *Opps*?"

"An age, at least," Petra responded.

"Well, looks like it's all taken care of. Say what you want about Yvonne, but she gets it done, doesn't she? Standard issue meals - I'll pull something out from the back." Milla disappeared into the kitchens and Petra tapped the counter once.

"See? No problem." She watched Linnaea wet her lips in anticipation while they waited for Milla to return.

"Do you know everyone in here?" Lysander asked lightly. Petra looked around at C, humming with activity. They were all she had left by way of a family.

"I know a lot. C is pretty tight." Milla returned with their meals, passing the brown boxes over the counter into their eager hands.

"I'll see you over there," Milla told Petra, wiping her hands on her apron and pulling it over her head. "I just have to finish one thing in the back." Petra turned to lead the three of them to her usual table in the corner.

"Sir!" Petra was greeted by Anders standing up to offer her his seat at the table filled with her men.

"Anders." She grinned, "Nice to see you again."

"Glad you made it back in one piece." He was grinning from ear to ear.

"Glad you were able to bring Lasse back in one piece," Petra replied. "And I know I'm not the only one." She winked at Anders as Milla came around the side of the table to join them.

"Ah, that guy? He wouldn't have died if the gods came down and picked him up personally for the trip to Valhalla." Milla raised an eyebrow, slyly.

"He's not going out until he has my permission anyways," she assured the table as Petra gestured to some empty chairs at the next table over with her elbow. Two of the men, Aksel and a younger one she didn't recognize, jumped to their feet and pulled over a crate and a chair for Linnaea and Magdelena, respectively.

Petra put her tray down and slowly lowered herself into the chair, a groan escaping her as she eased her injured leg out from under the table. Luckily no one could hear it over the ruckus of the canteen.

5
LYSANDER

Lysander grabbed a wobbly chair with his ankle and dragged it to the table in between Benjáme and where the soldiers had put Magdelena and Linnaea. The three of them sat down stiffly, feeling wildly exposed as people chattered around them in the canteen. Lysander dropped his bundle from The Closet beside his chair and kicked it under the table.

"Sorry I took so long," the cook named Milla said as she sat down, "just had to water the herb garden."

"You and your little plants," Anders' laugh was jolly.

"Just be grateful I even have it. It's the reason your food is edible, quite frankly," she teased him, but her tone had a depth to it that Lysander didn't quite understand and it hinted at something uncomfortable.

"Oh, I thought they grew herbs in The Gardens?" Magdelena inquired and everyone at the table adjusted themselves awkwardly, no one daring to explain. Finally, Anders cleared his throat. His jaw flexed and Lysander noticed how thick and veined his arms were despite the burn scars, under the rolled-up sleeves of his jumpsuit. It looked like it would be quite easy for him to snap any one of them in two.

"They do," he explained, the scarring on his neck shining in the fluorescent lighting, "they just don't always make it down here to C."

"Much less D," muttered the small, dark soldier Petra had called Aksel. He shot a look in Petra's direction while the others changed the subject. Lysander could only guess that he came from D originally.

Exchanging a tense look with Magdelena, Lysander thought about the last time he was this close to so many people. It must have been the day he'd stumbled into the Lillehammer camp. He remembered being so relieved to have found people again, other refugees like him. But he couldn't say the same about the canteen at the moment.

It was overpowering, the sound of cutlery and chairs scraping and banging against each other all around. The different languages drumming together, which at first had felt so musical, was now simply too much. The mix of smells was something he hadn't experienced in so long that it made him nauseous. The lights here were dimmer than in B, but still far brighter than they were used to, having been Above Ground so long. They buzzed loudly as if they'd been patched together by someone who didn't know what they were doing and could explode at any moment.

He watched Benjáme picking at his food, Petra reclining into her chair as she popped open the small brown box of food in front of her. They were certainly at home here, and it did make him relax slightly to see them so at ease.

Linnaea, who Lysander had thought would be just as overwhelmed by the people here as he was, seemed to be focused on just one thing. She had ripped off the top of her box, eyes gleaming ravenously. He decided the food might make him feel better, so he did the same.

Inside was a generous piece of salmon, salted, with a portion of roast potatoes. Besides the salmon and potatoes on the tray was a small container of red jam. He dipped his finger in tentatively - as if it wasn't quite real - and his tongue melted at the tartness of a rose hip jam, just like his mother used to make from the roses in the greenhouse when he was a small child. Wrapped in paper was a roll of seaweed and beside it sat a fragrant, plump orange, he held it up to his nose, hardly daring to believe it was real. Finally, he opened up a metal thermos and smelled to his delight a ginger-green tea, steaming up into his face. Petra raised her glass to him,

"*Skol*," she toasted him. He returned the gesture, something setting inside him as he did.

Lifting a forkful of the salmon up and spearing a potato on the end, he took the first bite. The oil and salt and starch of fresh-cooked food warmed him from the inside. He leaned over the cup of tea and let the spicy ginger aroma waft into his sinuses. He closed his eyes and felt a sense of calmness start to simmer inside of him. He had completely forgotten the effect a proper meal could have.

When he opened his eyes again, Petra was looking at him, clearly pleased.

"Enjoying yourself, engineer?" she asked him, bemused. "They will have given you some extra portions of food since you guys are a little on the scrawny side." Her voice was matter-of-fact, but Lysander felt suddenly a little self-conscious, like they were all watching him. The others did indeed have smaller portions of food on their plates. He nodded tentatively to Petra in response, shoveling in another mouthful of food. Rather than being jealous though, they all seemed amused at his lack of restraint, joking around and kicking their heads back with such ease. But he exchanged a look with Linnaea, who was also shoveling food in her mouth with equal lack of restraint, a grin of satisfaction on her face, complete with rose hip jam smeared across her cheek and he decided he didn't care what they thought.

"It gets old after a while," Aksel promised them, his voice flatter than the rest at the table. It had a guttural undertone to it that Lysander recognized as Danish. He was slighter than the others, with dark eyes and dark curls. "Fish, potatoes, and seaweed... seaweed, potatoes, and fish." Magdelena interpreted before continuing her meal. "But I suppose if you haven't had anything warm or fresh in a while, it's pretty good. You know what I could use? *Myseost*," he sighed and Lysander lifted his head in interest. Just the mention of it made his mouth water.

"Brown cheese? Do they really have that here?" He hadn't seen or tasted the sweet, creamy cheese since - well, he couldn't actually remember. It had used to be so normal, so commonplace, but when the milk became contaminated because of all the eruptions, they couldn't make the cheese like they used to.

"I wish," Aksel said wistfully. "Maybe next time they build a life-saving bunker for the apocalypse they will remember to bring livestock with them."

"As I have explained to you before," Milla said to Aksel in exasperation, "we tried to make some from the oats when we first got here, but it just didn't work right and no one wanted to eat it." She saw Lysander's eager expression and pursed her lips together. "Look, if you guys decide to stay I'll do my best to try to recreate it, but I'm telling you, it's not the same as the real thing."

"What else is there to eat?" Linnaea dropped her utensils excitedly, her mouth full of food, and signed. Lysander looked to Aksel and Anders let out a light laugh, like Aksel maybe wasn't so good with kids. Magdelena was quick to interpret and Milla answered, much to Aksel's visible relief.

"Ah well. Sometimes we get white fish, like haddock or cod, from the fisheries and I make a nice mushroom sauce with the herbs I grow. We get a lot of greens from The Gardens, too, like chard and kale and spinach, so I sauté those." Lysander interpreted as Magdelena raised a few forkfuls of fish into her mouth, "And for breakfast, I always make a good porridge." Linnaea shrugged in response and Milla looked over at Lysander for direction. He nodded his head in thanks to Milla as Linnaea continued eating. The menu probably wasn't quite what she'd had been hoping to hear - maybe honey or rosehip candies. He remembered how mind-blowing it had been for her the only time they had found some old candies in a cupboard at one of the houses they had squatted in for a week or so. He was pretty sure it was one of the few times she'd ever had something that sweet.

The unit talked among themselves as they ate. Petra allowed Benjáme to recount their journey from the village back to Mimameid. He was very clinical and didn't embellish, but Lysander noticed that when he mentioned the doctor, an absentminded rosiness crept onto Petra's freckled cheeks. Magdelena continued to sign for Linnaea, and Lysander saw that Anders and the younger boy at the table were watching with curiosity, trying to internalize the signs as best they could.

Since he already knew the story of what had happened and had more interest in his new environment, he allowed his gaze to wander around to the others in the crowded canteen.

There were many tables packed with enormous descendants of Odin himself. The room echoed with the sounds of their heavy combat boots drumming on the floor as they cheered for whomever was playing darts or lining up a shot at pool. At the table next to them, two men were locked in an arm wrestling contest.

Most of the soldiers were built, their jumpsuits rolled down to their waists and their arms and shoulders rippling with muscles under the t-shirts they were sporting. Some looked younger than others, and some looked spindlier, but Lysander had a feeling they could all take him down without too much thought. It looked like Mimameid took their security pretty seriously. Although they had skin and hair colors of all shades, some had grown their hair and beards out, braided and beaded like the sagas of old had described the Viking warriors.

Walking around in a way that almost felt like patrolling, was a group of soldiers with hair that was clipped into short, military crew cut style, displaying runic tattoos down their necks, chests, and arms.

Dotted among the others were a few tables of brazen-looking women, their hair braided out of their faces in complex knots and twists like the shieldmaidens he had read about in the sagas. One of the women had a long scar running down her cheekbone and was whittling a pair of wings with a short, tapered blade. The woman beside her tossed long, dreaded braids over her shoulder and raised a baby up to breastfeed. They seemed insular and protective of one another, glaring at the group of men with the runic tattoos as they paced.

On the outer edge of the canteen, he saw a few tables pushed together where a group of quiet soldiers, both men, and women, were sitting and whispering in a language that sounded like Old Slavic, but he couldn't make it out from across the room. A petite, blonde woman at the table had her arm around the waist of a burly man with a thin, banded tattoo around his bulging neck, like a collar of red, blue, green, and yellow.

"Oi, hands off her you stinking *Fenni*!" one of the biggest of the men with the runic tattoos said and started approaching the group.

Another woman at the table with flashing, hazel eyes stood up to face the instigators, but the man with the banded necklace tattoo waved her down.

The tattooed soldiers stalked up to the table and kicked out the chair from under the man. The Sámi soldier's nose slammed into the table in front of him, spouting blood immediately, the blonde woman beside him let out a gasp of surprise before standing up and hissing at them. He felt Magdelena tense up beside him. The aggressor glared at the two women, then spat on the man and walked away. While no one else at the table retaliated, Lysander saw their faces, cheeks glowing with anger and their narrowed eyes fixed on one another, the bleeding soldier mopping at his face on the sleeve of his jumpsuit.

Lysander wanted to jump up and run over, to at least try and help, but as he looked around the canteen, none of the other soldiers even seemed to take notice. In fact, it looked like they were ignoring it on purpose. He saw a glance exchanged between Milla and Benjáme and Anders cleared his throat uncomfortably, but other than that, nothing. Linnaea put her silverware down in her box and glanced over at Lysander. She didn't seem afraid like her mother, but she was certainly puzzled.

"What was that?" Linnaea signed to him, sensing the tension and trying to be discreet.

"I'm not exactly sure, Sprout," he signed back hesitantly. As inconspicuously as possible, he took another swig of his ginger tea and turned back to the group they were seated with, confused. He scraped at the last few potato crumbs on his tray, letting the food settle in his stomach and starting to feel like they had overstayed their welcome in C.

He felt the weight of the bio-implant in his pocket and the soft pull of curiosity to go examine it. But a whisper in the back of his mind told him to stay and take in as much of the canteen as possible. He and Magdelena had, after all, decided to figure this place out, and there was more at work here than what Yvonne had shown them. He took a deep breath.

"So, what are you guys, the Lieutenant's unit?" He decided to start small. Anders threw him a cheeky grin.

"Ha! She wishes. We trained together, we eat together. But no way she's *my* commanding officer." It had taken some time but he realized now that Anders' voice was laced with an inflection that he couldn't quite place.

"Oh?" Lysander prompted him, but Petra jumped in.

"He's just scared of me, is all. He knows he'd never make it under my command. He's too soft to be one of my men anyhow." They were inflammatory words, but they didn't seem to ruffle Anders.

"Oooff," Benjáme chuckled and punched Aksel in the arm.

"Nah, don't bet against a man who's the last of his kind." Anders crossed his scarred arms as he said it and then Lysander knew why Anders' voice sounded so foreign. He was one of the last of his kind. It could mean only one thing.

"Hang on," Lysander stopped him. "Anders, are you Icelandic?" The giant-of-a-man broke into the biggest grin Lysander had seen from him yet.

"Clever lad," he laughed, clapping Lysander so hard on the back that it made him cough.

"Really?" Magdelena's voice slipped out. It was the first time she had spoken since they left The Infirmary. "You really survived?" And Lysander knew Magdelena was thinking of Helgi and of Svalbard.

Anders nodded, gulping down his own ginger tea. "How?" Magdelena asked him, incredulously. He gave a reluctant half-smile, as if he'd told the story a thousand times already. But he saw the hope that shone in the lines on her face, so he continued.

"I lived up in the western fjords. Not many people lived up there, but it wasn't in the path of the volcanoes, so when they started going off, people started driving north." Magdelena was quick to interpret, to make sure she and Linnaea didn't miss a single detail. "My *pabbi* owned a commercial fishing boat, so we loaded up the neighbors, anyone who would fit and we took off. One couple who had left Old Reykjavik got to us before we raised anchor. We hit some powerful waves though, when we made it south. Reverb from the eruptions they told me here. That they had been like that all over."

It had been. Lysander sucked in a shuddering breath thinking again of the refugee boat and the water that had engulfed him. Anders continued. "My *pabbi* tossed the lifeboat into the water right before the boat flipped. I watched the waves take him and my brother. I thought I was done for, too. But then there was air. And when I looked around I saw the lifeboat and it was still intact and everything. I swam over, climbed in and I spent I don't know how long looking for the others, but I was it. The only one that made it. There was a kit in the side of the lifeboat, with one of those silver heat blankets and a thermos of fresh water and a light. The oars were strapped in, so I just started rowing. The sky went black after that and I couldn't tell you exactly how long I rowed for, but it must have been a couple of days. I tried to follow the birds since the sun and stars were covered by ash. Eventually, I ended up in Old Norway. I foraged for a long time, jumping from freshwater to freshwater, following the coastline and eventually I got picked up by Mimameid people. But not before a few run-ins with the Celts, of course." He cracked his knuckles and stretched his neck out, the scars shining in the light as he said the last sentence, and the men around him grunted with admiration.

Even though Lysander could see that there were pieces of the story, details, that Anders didn't want to share or maybe didn't want to relive, they could all fill in the blanks with their own version of the day of Ragnarök.

"And is there anyone else here? Anyone else Icelandic?" Lysander heard the hope in Magdelena's voice, the brightness in her fingers as she signed.

"There are a few actually, yeah. Most of them were already on the continent when it happened. One ship of survivors made it though, from Iceland. It brought a couple of families." Magdelena sighed, disappointedly, and interpreted for Linnaea, although somewhat lackluster. It hadn't been what they'd hoped for.

"No one from...further north?" She didn't dare ask her question in full. Anders shook his head.

"Sorry, I don't think so. But we all tend to stick together, so it'll be easy to check. Since I enlisted, I live in the military bunks, but everyone else is together down in the housing block adjacent to canteen D. You can go down there and ask around. Maybe someone knows something." Magdelena gave him a grateful look and nodded her thanks.

"What about other people?" There was no hope for his family of course, but if there were Icelanders still alive then he thought maybe someone from back home had made it to safety.

"What do you mean?" Anders asked him.

"Like Swedes? Is there somewhere I can look or ask?" The others all let out a light laugh. Lysander looked at them blankly, uncomprehending. "What?" Petra answered him.

"There's plenty of places to look for Swedes. There's a lot of them here. There's so many, I think there's even a registrar around somewhere you can look through to see if they are here or anyone here knows whomever you're looking for."

"Oh?"

"Yeah, most of the people in Mimameid are Swedes actually. That, or Norwegians. A couple of Danes. They got evacuated so early on during the flooding that a lot of them made it to the bunker. Then us Finns, of course. Too many of us were slaughtered by the Rus before Ragnarök for us to have a majority, but there are a couple of us here. Most of us Finns that are left are Sámi too, so we tend to keep to the other Sámi, regardless of where they were born." She threw a glance over at Milla as she explained and Lysander realized that Milla must also be a Sámi. "And then, as we said, your Icelanders, rare as a bird in the sky these days."

"Yeah that's why the city Swedes and the city Norges get to tell everyone else what to do," Aksel grumbled under his breath. Anders hit him in the chest, harder than he probably meant to. The blow knocked the wind out of the man.

"Come on, Aksel," he said to him.

"What?" The man choked on his drink as he replied, massaging the spot where Anders had struck him. "It's the truth. Everyone else gets treated like they owe them an eternal debt or something. And we do just as much, if not more, keeping Mimameid operational these days." Lysander watched Aksel's words ripple through the group of men. Benjáme and Anders averted their gazes, the younger boy, who hadn't spoken up getting a spirited look in his eyes. Milla picked at a frayed edge of the old upholstered stool she was sitting on.

Petra's face, however, did not change. Only her eyes betrayed some momentary golden flash of truth. Lysander wanted to know more but he didn't press the issue. He made up his mind to ask someone about it later. Maybe Benjáme or Lasse.

"And here? In Canteen C?" Lysander asked.

"Well we're military, so commanding officers are in charge. Like the Lieutenant here." Anders clapped Petra on the back.

"But even our top commanders are exclusively Swedish and Norwegian military," Aksel countered.

"They are good commanders. They take care of us. And there are more Danes, Sámi and Finns enlisted than there ever have been before." Petra interjected sternly before the conversation could turn again.

"Anyone you know from back home?" As soon as Lysander said it, he knew he'd gone too far. There was an awkward shuffle as Petra adjusted herself in her seat.

"I think we should probably get you all back up to Sigrid, she'll be expecting you guys," Petra offered, flexing her jaw tensely. There was so much more he wanted to know, but it seemed like their time was up. As she pushed her tray away to stand, a deep voice spoke behind her.

"Yeah, that's right. Run back upstairs to the boss and tell her what kind of *skit* these *drittsekk* friends of yours are spouting. You filthy Rus. You're as bad as the rest. You don't belong here." The tattooed man that had assaulted the Sámi had now made his way over to their table, reaching out and fingering a lock of Petra's copper hair as he spoke. He bent down, so as to speak the last words directly into her ear. Lysander felt the back of his neck bristle and glancing from side to side, he saw Anders and Benjáme both on their feet. Milla's eyes were narrowed dangerously.

Petra raised her hand to settle her men. Their shoulders relaxed, but they didn't sit back down.

"You want to say that, again?" Petra asked the man without looking at him and Lysander saw the man's hand close around her hair, pulling her neck back and exposing her throat like a wounded deer in the woods.

Surprisingly, however, Petra's eyes betrayed no fear, but the canteen had gone silent this time. The man had crossed a line by disrespecting a superior officer.

"I said: There is no place for you in Valhalla. You don't belong here," he spat, enunciating every syllable.

She exhaled evenly and if Lysander had blinked he would have missed it. She slammed the back of her head into the man's nose, and the crack as it broke turned the fish in Lysander's stomach. The man let go of her hair as his hand went to his nose and he howled. Petra shot up, grabbing and twisting the thick, tattooed arm around the man's back. He cried out in pain as she pushed against it.

"Come on, guys." She looked at Lysander and Magdelena and jerked her head towards the door. "This piece of *perkele* isn't worth the time." Petra dropped his arm like it was a piece of meat and turned to go.

"Yeah, okay." Lysander stood up slowly, gathering his clothing from The Closet up to his chest while Magdelena and Linnaea fell in behind him. They looked around at Petra's men who all nodded curtly. They would take care of this.

Hurrying to follow Petra out of C and still shocked by the situation, Lysander figured at least he'd be able to examine the bio-implant sooner rather than later.

The elevator ride up to Sigrid's office was unsettling for Lysander. Petra was silent and the creaking of the rusty, old machine shot his pulse into erratic nervousness. He exhaled deeply when they finally stepped back onto solid concrete.

Yvonne was there again to greet them at the landing.

"In the boughs of Mimir's tree," she greeted them and they gave their best attempt at the awkward gesture. "Sigrid is looking forward to getting to know you all a little better. Lieutenant?" She turned stiffly, Petra raised her hand to her brow informally in response, nothing awkward about it at all. "Your presence is no longer required. You are dismissed. Thank you so much for taking care of our guests." She looked over at Lysander for confirmation before she answered. He nodded.

"Very well." Petra raised her hand again, then boarded the elevator. Her face was apologetic to be leaving them alone with Yvonne.

"Follow me!" Yvonne's vivacious voice instructed them when Petra's red hair had disappeared from view, down into the open elevator shaft.

Lysander ushered Magdelena and Linnaea in front of him, following them down the hall to Sigrid's office.

The hexagonal door was already open, as though Sigrid had been expecting them. As though she had been watching them. Was it possible she had seen what had taken place in the canteen? They shuffled into the room and heard the seal of the door closing as Yvonne slipped out behind them.

Sigrid looked up as they entered, her eyes glinting like freshly polished silver.

"Welcome! Welcome again to Mimameid." She stood up as she greeted from across her desk with her hand to her brow. "In the boughs of Mimir's tree." Lysander raised his hand halfheartedly in reply, while Magdelena attempted to mumble the words. Sigrid shot him a look of disapproval that dissolved into her practiced smile as quickly as it had come. But he could tell she had interpreted his attempt as being rude. But he didn't care much about being rude or not. He wanted to know what was going on.

Lysander took in the ample sealskin rugs overlaid on the floor, the massive, concrete desk, and the wide window-wall out into the fjord above it. He watched as little crustaceans gobbled up the algae building on the edge of the glass pane. Their tiny legs were moving at lightning speed in the water as they floated along, briefly eclipsed by a shadow and then swallowed up into the drooping mouth of a grey, ugly fish, its eyes bulging oddly as it swam onward.

"I was wondering," Magdelena began, her voice diplomatic, as they sat down in the three minimalist chairs laid out before her desk, "why is it called Mimameid?"

"Oh!" Sigrid let out, a didactic note slipping into her silvery voice as she moved the tablet in front of her to the side of the near-empty desktop and began signing. "Well, you all seem like intelligent people, so you must know the sagas of our people." She paused, waiting for them to agree. Her lips twitched uncomfortably. Unsure where the conversation was going, Lysander bit down on the inside of his cheek. He had a working knowledge of the old mythology of course, but they had always been just that to him, mythology. He knew Magdelena had read the stories too, but she was a scientist and didn't take much stock in them either.

"The history of our Norse ancestors. Of Ragnarök and the time thereafter." Sigrid tried to read the blankness of their faces as she signed, the glimmer in her eyes remaining steady. Linnaea shifted in her seat, uncomfortably. She knew even less of the stories than Lysander and Magdelena did. It had been some time since they had entertained notions of fantasy. Life Above Ground simply didn't have room for it anymore.

"I mean. We know the basics of course," Lysander began, "Ragnarök is the end of times, the apocalypse. And -" he stuttered when Sigrid raised one coy eyebrow, "and we have heard the volcano eruptions referred to as Ragnarök by some of the people here. But, we haven't interacted with any other people in several years, so our knowledge" - he took care with his words not wanting to offend a potential religious fanatic - "may be a bit lacking in the proper terminology and understanding of what actually took place." Sigrid's expression tightened.

"Of course," she signed and then rapped her fingers on the desk, channeling some annoyance at them that Lysander couldn't understand. Magdelena tensed a little in the chair next to him as Sigrid leaned back in her chair and crossed her arms.

"Perhaps you could explain to us," Lysander offered, trying to give Sigrid whatever it was she wanted to hear. The response was immediate, alarmingly so.

"It would be my pleasure." Sigrid's voice was grandiose, prepared. Her gestures equally so, as she signed alongside this well-rehearsed performance.

"The gods predicted that the earth would end in fire and water." Lysander nodded - this much he remember from Petra. "And we broke our world. We stopped caring for the innocent ones - the children and the animals and the dying forests. We turned the world into what it became - a place of division and strangers only concerned with putting up walls and exploiting the weak and helpless for profit.

You all are still young," she reminisced, "but you will remember how the governments were in the chaos, dissolved one by one. The borders to countries melted away and the very nationalism that had broken us apart was the only place you could find mercy. With your own kind, your own people, your own tribe. And the gods watched all of it in anguish.

So they called us a danger to earth and declared war. Yggdrasil World Tree squeezed the forests dry till they shriveled, burning up to ash. The great snake *Jormungandr* shivered in the melted glaciers and ice caps, churning great tsunami waves to rise from the sea. Earthquakes cracked open our earth's crust, waking the volcanoes once more. And the innocent we had failed to protect - they were lost to the fire, to the sea, and to the earth." How zealous Sigrid's language was becoming as she told her story. But, Lysander and Magdelena needed to know what it was they believed here in Mimameid, and this story was their scripture. Sigrid continued,

"But we *Nordmenn*, we had our sagas that warned us how the gods would punish us. So we prepared for the coming of Ragnarök, for the day when the veil between worlds would dissolve and the protection of the gods would disappear. The day when fire and water would consume the world and the sun would darken in the ash and smoke.

We built a place fire couldn't touch, a place beneath the rising tide. And gathered to us, those Norse who would protect the innocent. We gathered those who still believed in the will of the gods.

We wait here in the hall of the survivors of Ragnarök - in the foretold Mimameid - for the time when the earth is ready for us, fertile and new and we can begin again. We wait for the sign of Yggdrasil to beckon us forth to the new world." Sigrid's words echoed against the concrete walls. So this was their creed, their manifesto.

"And that is where the bunker gets its name." Sigrid gestured to Magdelena as though she had just answered a simple question over a coffee. "As foretold by the gods there would be a great hall for the survivors. And we have built it - a haven where the future can begin." The last bit she signed more to Linnaea than anyone else.

"I think we can agree this is a very impressive operation you have going on here," Lysander started and again her eyebrow shot up her forehead, as Sigrid turned to look at him.

"Thank you." She inclined her head in calculated gratitude. "But I see you haven't gotten your bands yet," she noted, the slightest flash of provocation in her eyes. Lysander was quick in response.

"I think you can understand that, ever the engineer, I prefer to understand a machine that will be implanted into my body." Sigrid's jaw flexed, but her tone was even.

"Naturally."

"Is it still possible for us to spend the night here in Mimameid without the bands?" he asked her, leaning back and crossing his arms.

"It is an unorthodox request," she paused, "but I think we can find something temporary for you all, given the circumstances." She tapped her band twice and the door behind them opened abruptly. Yvonne's blonde head appeared in the doorway.

"Yes, ma'am?" she asked, long hair falling to the side as she leaned over.

"Yvonne," Sigrid smiled warmly, "would you be so good as to find bunks for our guests this evening?" The question sounded normal, but of course, Lysander had to remind himself that here, 'evening' could be whenever Sigrid wanted it to be. Yvonne's face scrunched up, fighting the urge to ask why they wouldn't simply receive their bands to get housing, but she swallowed her words. The young woman nodded and Lysander watched her face disappear and the door close.

"Anything else we can do for you all?" Sigrid's matronly smile returned to her face and she signed as she spoke.

"Actually, yes." Lysander leaned forward, spreading his arms out on the armrests. "I've been given one of the bio-implants to examine and I'd like a few tools to help with that." Sigrid nodded, sliding him a small notepad from across the desk.

"Make a list for us and we will see what we have. Whatever tools we can find will be delivered to your accommodations."

"Thank you." He was glad to see just how desperately they wanted an engineer, and to what lengths they were willing to bend their Mimameid rules to get one.

"If that puts your minds at ease?" Sigrid continued gently, but firmly, "I'd like to discuss possible work assignments here. If you all decide to stay with us, that is." She enunciated deeply, heavily.

Lysander was scribbling on the notepad as he answered for them. Magdelena made sure to continue signing for Linnaea.

"That would be in order."

"Excellent." Sigrid leaned back in her chair. "What profession did you hold before Ragnarök?"

"Electrical engineering student - as you already know." Lysander continued scribbling.

"Specializing in?" Sigrid prompted, her hands poised above her tablet to take notes as she paused in her signing.

"At the time - robotics, but I ended up getting more experience in energy and power through my work in the camps. Turns out that's a more useful skill set post-apocalypse, er-Ragnarök," Lysander's responded, dryly.

"So, you would be suited to having a look at our power systems here?" He stopped writing on the notepad and looked at Sigrid, suddenly his hand jumping to his logr charm, excitedly. He caught himself and lowered it back to the table, trying to curb his enthusiasm as he signed his answer.

"Yes. I'd be happy to take a look," Lysander replied. "Is there something in particular that you're concerned about?"

"I think that is something you should be able to determine after having a look," Sigrid responded evasively. Lysander smirked slightly at her but nodded. He didn't mind solving puzzles and he wasn't afraid of her little test. "Excellent." She finished with him and turned to Magdelena.

"And what about you?" she asked, still signing as she spoke. "We place a very high value on being a mother, as our very survival as a species is dependent on the children. But we need to put your other skills to good use. We are a small community and take all the help we can get. So, is there something else you have a talent in?" Lysander was surprised at how quickly Sigrid had written off Magdelena's potential at being anything other than a mother as her primary occupation. He thought this place was supposed to be progressive.

"I'm fairly good with plants," Magdelena offered, a little smugly, but it would have been tricky to pick up if Lysander didn't know her so well.

"You were a gardener in The Time Before?" Sigrid picked up a tablet and began scrolling through a schedule, forgetting to sign for Linnaea now that she had the tablet in her hand, so Lysander jumped in.

"Something like that, yes." Lysander noticed how Magdelena left out the part about being a world-renowned botanist. The way she was chewing her lower lip told him it was an intentional omission.

"Well, then I think we can give you some regular rotations in The Gardens." Magdelena nodded. "Some hours that will mix well with Linnaea's schooling so as not to interfere with your parental duties," Sigrid said all this while swiping on the tablet. When she seemed satisfied, she set the screen back down on her desk, looking at Lysander.

"We can, of course, make those accommodations for your schedule as well, so you can attend to your parental duties." Magdelena cast her gaze down and Lysander shifted in his seat. Sigrid pursed her lips, irritated at their silence. Magdelena decided to answer the unspoken question.

"Lysander and I aren't - " She paused. "I can see how it would look, but -"

"I'm not Linnaea's father," he said, flatly.

"Oh. I'm sorry, I just assumed," Sigrid began, her signing becoming somewhat flustered.

"No, her father is from The Time Before," Magdelena explained.

"I see. And you two are not -" Sigrid looked down at Linnaea as she asked the question, signing again after realizing her blunder, "together?" Linnaea shook her head, her hands moving with purpose as she signed,

"Definitely not." An amused smile crept onto her face.

"No," he confirmed.

"Ah, well then that will mean some changes to our planned housing arrangements for you all. I apologize for the misunderstanding." She immediately double-tapped her band again.

"Oh!" Magdelena was surprised, "Well, to be perfectly honest, we've grown rather used to having Lysander with us, so I think staying somewhere together with him would be our preference, actually." Yvonne appeared in the doorway behind them, but Sigrid was shaking her head.

"No. I'm afraid such arrangements are available for officially registered pairings only." This time it was Lysander who was surprised. He thought Mimameid was all about maximizing their efficiency of resources - putting them together in a room would certainly fall under that category. It felt somehow more like a power move from Sigrid.

"Somewhere nearby, then?" Magdelena prompted, hopeful.

"I'll see what I can do, but I'm afraid I can make no such promises." Sigrid stood up abruptly and turned her gaze to Yvonne.

"I take it you heard that dear? We need to make some changes to our housing arrangements for the guests." Yvonne exchanged a severe look with Sigrid which made the room get a little colder.

"Yes ma'am, immediately." She started to close the door but Sigrid, still standing, spoke up.

"And dear, I think our guests are ready to leave now, if you could accompany them to their housing assignments." They all rose to their feet as Sigrid turned back to them.

"Thank you very much, I look forward to seeing more of you all." She tried to smile warmly down at Linnaea, coming around the side on the concrete desk and kneeling down to look the girl in the face, but Linnaea recoiled at the woman's approach. There was something penetrative about it, invasive. Sigrid brushed the offense off as Magdelena's melodic voice broke the silence.

"A question - before we go, if you don't mind." Magdelena's directness caught Sigrid off guard, but Magdelena was all manners.

"Yes?"

"What's the sign you are waiting for?" she asked, politely, but pointedly.

"I'm sorry, sign?" Lysander was just as confused as Sigrid by Magdelena's question.

"Earlier you said you were waiting for a sign from Yggdrasil. A sign that the earth was healed."

"Uh-huh." The woman's eyes flashed like a sword in sunlight. Her performance had ended.

"What's the sign?" Though Magdelena's eyes were bright with innocence, Lysander knew her better than that. The woman was not afraid of anything and certainly not of a religious fanatic.

"We will know it when we see it," Sigrid replied, cooly. "Off you go." She waved them from the room and the door hissed shut. Lysander gave Magdelena's shoulder a grateful squeeze as they followed Yvonne down the hall and back into the rickety elevator for what he sincerely hoped would be the last time for a long time.

"Here you are, then." The door opened with a gush as Yvonne unlocked it with her band and let him in.

He stepped onto the spotted sealskin rug. The walls were the sleek grey, which elongated the already narrow room, and a small portico window at the far end overlooking the fjord. As the door clicked shut behind them, warm lighting along the wall jumped to life revealing his belongings from his pack evenly spaced out on two levels of shelves. Someone had brought them in from the pod. Yvonne fiddled with a panel on the wall to the left of the door as Lysander walked the length of the room. The floor on the back end of the room was one step up and had a shower head, a ribbed glass panel for privacy, and a drain in it. He turned to the opposite wall and tapped a panel as he had seen Yvonne do in Magdelena and Linnaea's room. A toilet descended from the wall. He tapped again at the narrow rectangular panel above the toilet and a small sink pushed out like a drawer under the mounted mirror, foggy from saltwater stains.

Yvonne turned to him as he stepped back down from the bathroom section of the room.

"You seem to have the hang of how the rooms here work." She pushed on the top panel under the shelving unit and a table rolled out into the middle of the room. Sliding one of the opaque covers to the lower shelving back, she pulled out a lamp, positioning it so that a concentrated pool of light fell on the center of the table. "There are two chairs for a unit this size," she explained. "Your bed is the second panel from the bottom. And the closet is over here." She slid open the panel on the opposite wall with one hand and set his folded pile of clothes from The Closet inside. "This unit also belongs to Canteen B, so you and the girls will be able to eat together, assuming your schedules allow."

"Thanks," he said as he reached into his pocket and pulled out the bio-implant, placing it gently on the metal table. It wobbled for a second and he wondered if the room was completely level. Or maybe just the roll-out table was off.

"One more thing." Yvonne waved him over to where she was next to the panel. She lifted her band up to its screen and it illuminated with her details, just as it had in the canteen. "Look in the retinal scanner for me?" She pointed to a red light. When it was finished scanning, a question confirming the temporary transfer of authority to him appeared and Yvonne tapped it to accept. "There you go. You should be all set now. It's on a 24-hour lock so only you will have access to this unit for that time period. That way you have some time to acclimate to life here in Mimameid before you need to get a band." He nodded, but his curiosity heightened.

"If you have the capacity for retinal scanning, why don't you all just secure the place using that? Why bother with the bands at all? It seems like a lot of extra effort. And resources." Yvonne paused and sighed as if debating how much to tell him.

"In the beginning, it was all done through retinal scanning, but then, there were some incidents-" A knot tightened in his stomach as he looked at Yvonne's darkened face. Like she had an image in her head she couldn't erase. "The bio-implants are designed to function only with one unique set of DNA, so it makes it a much more *secure system*." She seemed to choose her words carefully.

"Ah. I see." There was an uncomfortable silence and Lysander tried to forget he had asked.

"If there's nothing else, then?" she concluded, politely. The chipper tone was a little undercut with whatever lingering discomfort she had from the retinal incident.

"Oh, no. And thank you." Lysander moved to open the door for her since the lock in the pad was now tied to his retina.

"Of course. Do let me know if there is anything else you need." Lysander smiled, grateful both for her guidance and for the fact that she was finally leaving. She flashed him her bright smile as she exited the room, the door closing automatically behind her.

It was the first time he'd been alone in a very long time. Longer than he could remember. And the first thing that struck him was the maddening silence. He shook his head as if trying to rid his ears of water and started looking for the chairs Yvonne had mentioned.

Once he had found them, attached to the bottom of the table, he unstrapped the Celtic knife on his hip, set it on the table, and sat down. The chair creaked but held firm. He lifted the bio-implant up and set it in the center of the pool of light coming from the lamp. He reached down to peel back the paper seal around it when an alarm beeped in the room. Startled, he dropped what he was doing. The bio-implant rolled across the metal and he caught it in his hand, placing it carefully back on the table.

He looked up to see a small red light blinking on the panel by the door. When he got close enough, it read his retina again and the door opened with the gush of the pressure lock that he was starting to get used to, revealing a small, unmarked parcel wrapped in brown paper on the floor.

Inside the parcel was the tool kit he had requested from Sigrid.

He was pleased to see they had been able to find a large magnifying glass with a long adjustable arm which he could use by attaching it to the lamp. The rest of the tools were relatively rudimentary, essentially an antique eyeglass repair kit, with pincers, what looked like two types of eyeglass screwdrivers, and a cleaning cloth.

He set the implant on top of the cloth and busied himself fastening the magnifying glass to the lamp and adjusting the angle. When he was satisfied, he finished ripping off the paper packaging around the bio-implant and sat down again to examine it.

Using his pincers, he peeled back a soft, squishy layer of silicon, revealing the mechanical innards. It was a relatively uncomplicated device. He saw two tiny batteries alongside the implant's storage device - where the information on their blood levels and other bio-data would be saved. The implant's Central Processing Unit was in the center, next to a transmitter chip that interacted with the wristband via the antenna wrapped around the other small pieces of the device.

With pincers in each hand, he lifted the device out by the antenna, slowly uncurling it. The antenna out of the way, he could see underneath two small metal capsules attached in the middle by what looked like a microscopic valve. He squinted his eyes to read through the magnifying glass if there was anything etched onto the side of the metal capsules.

Abruptly, there was a knock on his door. He jumped, nearly dropping the implant for a second time. Taking a deep breath, he set the pincers down on the cloth and rose to answer the door.

He looked for a moment for the door handle, before remembering that it was controlled by the screen on the wall. *Stupid Mimameid door,* he thought as he moved to the screen. The retinal scanner beeped and the door whooshed open before him.

Magdelena stood there, her nose a little red and her eyes a little sad. He reached out to her as she stepped over the threshold and into his room. She leaned into his embrace and he felt a little sob escape her before she sighed and pulled back out of the hug.

He offered her the chair and she sank into it, as he pulled out the other one and sat down across from her.

"You want to talk, Mag?" he asked, hesitantly. She nodded and gulped back tears. It took a minute before she could begin.

"After we got settled into our quarters, I took Linnaea down to see the school, to see how she would get on with the other children."

"Is she okay?" he asked, worried, but Magdelena waved her hand, reassuringly.

"No, no, she's fine. A group of kids went over to her right away and the teacher even knows some sign language from a previous student," she soothed him. "I mean, she was a little overwhelmed by it all, but, in general, a good kind of overwhelmed. The teacher said she'd send someone to find me if anything went amiss." She finished her tangent and then seemed to find her thoughts again. "So, anyways, I decided to go down to the Icelandic quarters, you know, the ones Anders told us about?"

Lysander nodded.

"Well, Anders didn't mention there's actually a Celt that lives down there."

"Wait, what?" Lysander felt the words fall out of his mouth, harshly. After everything they had gone through to get away from those Celtic barbarians over the years, and then there was one living here, among them? In Mimameid?

"Yeah." The way she breathed the word he knew there was more. Her jaw flexed.

"Wait a second. You know him, don't you," Lysander realized, and Magdelena nodded with a sniff, now in control of her tears.

"Yeah."

"But Mag, how?" he asked.

"His name is Ned. He worked with Helgi up on Svalbard. He's this crusty, old, whiskey-soaked Scot, from up near Inverness, but he'd lived on the island for nearly fifteen years by the time Helgi started working there. God, he always spoke about what a betrayal it was to the world that the Scots participated in the English Massacre. He was so ashamed of them for it. I met him a few times when they would have funding events down in Oslo and he'd be forced to come down from the island and socialize. They'd always tried to get him into a suit, but he looked so odd in a necktie that they let him wear his kilt. He'd stand there out in the middle of winter in Norway - bare legs, whiskey in hand, and the wind in his hair." Lysander watched her mind wander back to a time when life must have seemed so much simpler.

"I remember the last one, too. It was right before they got sent back up there. I was pregnant with Linnaea, but I hadn't told Helgi yet, I wanted to wait until the first trimester was finished. But I was wearing this long silver dress that night that I had bought especially for the occasion and it felt so strange on my body, so naked now that I was growing another person inside of me. Helgi was preoccupied, running around talking with all of his colleagues about the end of the world, he didn't notice." She waved her hand, as though she was back at the party, excusing his absentmindedness all over again.

"But Ned," she continued, "he saw me sulking in the background, drinking my seltzer with a slice of lime, so as not to arouse any suspicion, and he knew. He took me out on the balcony, to the fresh air, and he congratulated me. He promised to keep my secret. And then he and I talked about what herbal teas I had been making to help me with the morning sickness. It was such a relief to talk about it with someone. And someone who had such knowledge of plants. He was the team geologist, but he really knows his plants - sort of his hobby he had told me. They both left for Svalbard three days later. " Lysander saw her eyes glazing over with tears so he decided to redirect her.

"And this Ned - he's here?" Magdelena nodded.

"Yeah, I guess the Norse let him stay. He's lived for so long among us, maybe they thought he was too dangerous to send back. But in any case, he's here. He's living with the Icelanders."

"But then, if he's here and not on Svalbard -" Magdelena's eyes shimmered like green ice caught in the sunlight.

"They were told to abandon Svalbard. Everyone was supposed to leave because ice melt had compromised the compound. But a few of them stayed behind to try to save the samples."

"Helgi," Lysander sighed and Magdelena nodded, hanging her head.

"I should have told him. I should have told him about Linnaea that night. Then he never would have gone in the first place. He would never have gotten involved." Lysander reached his hands across the table towards her.

"You always say that. But you couldn't have known. No one could have known what was going to happen." Magdelena looked up at him, her mossy eyes magnified with fresh tears.

"That's just it, L. If anyone could have known, it should have been us. We were the scientists - biologists, geologists, meteorologists - Stockholm and Copenhagen were under water and what were we doing? Having a party to celebrate our new billionaire donors months before the world went belly-up. In any case, he shouldn't have been so stupid as to try to save the seeds instead of coming back to find us." There was hurt in her voice and Lysander gave her a sideways look.

"From what you've told me about him, knowing that you all were alive wouldn't have made any difference. He believed in the work he was doing." Magdelena laughed a little at that and wiped her red nose with her hand.

"Ned said the same thing." She took a deep breath and straightened herself up. She looked around the room as if she had only just remembered where she was. "Your room looks different than ours," she commented, looking slowly around.

"You think?" he asked, ashamed to admit he had also noticed it.

"I can't quite put my finger on it though," Magdelena continued. Lysander knew though. His room was bigger, despite being only for one person. He had more closet space, and a larger shower and he couldn't be totally sure, but he thought the bed was also ten centimeters wider. He hoped his getting a better room was simply a coincidence, but he had a sneaking suspicion it had to do with his coveted position as an engineer.

"Well, anyways. I guess I should go pick up Linnaea. Otherwise, she'll think I just abandoned her there." Now it was Lysander's turn to laugh.

"You don't know that, Mag. Maybe she's having a really good time being around other kids for the first time." But they both knew Linnaea better than that. Magdelena gave him a skeptical glance, her eyes still shining a bit.

"You're sure you're okay?" Lysander asked her as she stood up.

"Yeah." She sighed and patted her hair down, fixed her braid, and smoothed out her jumpsuit. "I mean, I will be."

"Okay. If you say so. You want me to come get Linnaea with you?" Magdelena shook her head, gratefully.

"I think this is a conversation I should have with her on my own," she assured him, "but tomorrow morning, you want to meet us in the canteen for some breakfast?" She headed for the door and he went to the pad to let her out with the retinal scanner.

"I'd love to," he said and she smiled at him as the door whooshed open.

"Good. Then we will see you then." It felt weirdly rehearsed and formal, the way Magdelena was speaking, but Lysander played along as the door shut and he sat back down at the table, windswept.

When morning came, the lights gradually came on, imitating the sunrises from The Time Before, followed by a gentle alarm filling his room. He groaned as he rolled over, eyes still as heavy as the night before. He had been jolted awake throughout the night by the sounds of the bunker creaking in the flow of the fjord. Each time, he'd turned over, momentarily forgetting where he was and in a panic, looking around for Linnaea and Magdelena.

Now with the gentle alarm music drifting in the air, he did not feel any more rested than he had Above Ground, and his back ached from the foreign softness of the mattress.

But he rose anyway and turned the alarm off. When he tapped the panel by the door, it listed off a schedule that had been curated for him for that day. First on the list was a rotation for breakfast, followed by a meeting in The Engine Room and later on another meeting with Sigrid. But it was Petra who he really wanted to talk with.

All night as he'd been tossing and turning, he'd mulled over his perception of Mimameid. If he was to stay, he had a favor to ask of her. He had a feeling that the meetings today were meant to entice him into staying with whatever engineering problems they had that needed solving. So he pulled his bunker jumpsuit on over a fresh thermal undershirt they'd provided, rolled up his sleeves, and resolved to find Petra before anything else.

6
PETRA

She felt the light spread in her room before her alarm went off. She tapped her band to turn it back off before it woke Milla up. Floor lights clicked on quietly, illuminating the bare concrete floor in a soft, blue light.

Sighing as she sat up on her bed, she swung her legs over the side. Her thigh still ached as she put weight onto it and stood up. She shook the healing muscle loose as she ambled over to the sink. The water purification tank gurgled in the wall as she turned the faucet on and splashed some water on her face.

When she opened the cabinet mirror to pull out the tooth tabs, the plant that Milla had brought back from the kitchens to help ease the strain on their air purifier nearly tumbled to the floor. Petra caught it with one hand and carefully eased it back up, balancing the hydroponic planter precariously atop the mirror, squashed in between the rattling bottles of home-brewed liquor that Milla bartered off when she needed favors. Petra's roommate groaned and rolled over on her bed, eyes cracking open in the dim light.

"You trying to kill my rosemary plant, again?" she asked, her voice groggy.

"Not on purpose." Petra threw her an apologetic smile.

"No worries," Milla told her, sitting up on her bed and looking down at her band with a yawn. "I should be getting up, anyways." She slide down from the top bunk and opened up the closet, browsing her options.

Petra's band beeped at her while she was still chewing the tooth tabs. Pausing, she tapped the red light blinking up at her. The message was for a briefing for her next Above Ground mission. She stopped chewing and spit into the sink.

"What's wrong?" Milla asked, giving her a quizzical look as she zipped up her jumpsuit.

"Oh, nothing. It's just odd." She paused. "I got assigned another Above Ground mission." She waved her band in Milla's general direction, indicating the message.

Normally, she'd be on rotational training exercises and combat simulations for the next few weeks before cycling back out for an Above Ground. Back-to-back missions were uncommon under ordinary circumstances, but the fact that their last one had been so irregular made the order for another Above Ground seem even more out of place. Her injuries had barely had time to heal and it wasn't as if they were in open war.

"That seems a little soon, doesn't it?" Milla pulled a red *korsnäs* sweater over her head as she replied and Petra pursed her lips inadvertently. "What?" Milla asked, pulling her dark curls out from the frayed neck of the sweater.

"You aren't supposed to be wearing that around outside the bunk, are you?" Petra wrangled her tangle of red hair up into a messy ponytail. She knew Milla played by her own rules sometimes, but she felt that her loyalty to Sigrid required her to at least question the act.

"It's fine," Milla said dismissively and Petra gave her a skeptical look. "Come on." She threw a combat boot across the room at Petra playfully. "I'm just in the kitchens all day, anyways. It's not like anyone sees me."

Petra rolled her eyes and tried not to take it too seriously as she walked over to the closet, trading places with Milla. She cornered off her bedsheets and blanket, pulling them tight, and then opened her neatly organized side of the closet. Choosing a ribbed black turtleneck, she stretched it over her head and considered the timing of her new assignment. Did they suspect her after the debrief yesterday or was it just that she was the only one qualified for whatever the job was? She stepped into her standard-issue jumpsuit, zipped it up, and sat down on the bed, slipping her warm, wool socks onto her feet, one by one.

An alarm went off on the panel next to the door and Milla shrugged her shoulders, confused. Petra stood up, shoving her hands into the pockets of her jumpsuit and straightening them out. She felt electricity shoot up her arm as her fingers brushed up against Arthur's love knot, scrunched up into the crease. She'd completely forgotten that it was still there.

"You aren't expecting anyone, right?" Milla asked, her head over the sink, tooth tab gunk coming out of her mouth as she spoke. Petra shook her head but clicked on the camera view on the screen anyways. Lysander was standing outside, looking nervous.

Confused as to how he managed to get into the Canteen C quarters - he hadn't been here long enough to learn the shortcuts yet - she tapped the open button and shoved her feet into her boots as he entered.

"Funny. Yours looks just like mine, but the lights definitely have more blue in them." He looked around. "I bet they do that to keep them more on edge," he muttered under his breath. "Oh *hej*, Milla." They exchanged a quick wave, Milla's head still hanging over the sink.

"Well, good morning to you, too." Petra raised an eyebrow at his mutterings and pulled the laces of her boots tight as she replied to him. "The um...the Mimameid look-" she indicated his jumpsuit with one hand, "it suits you." Lysander shook himself from whatever his thoughts about the lights were.

"Oh, thanks." He looked around, eyes suspiciously combing the walls.

"Did you sleep okay?" she asked, following his eyes around the room.

"Yeah, yeah. I mean. It was weird sleeping on a mattress again." He seemed to be pandering, unsure of how to start.

"Can I help you with something?" Petra asked him, straightening her jumpsuit collar. She moved towards the door, her band vibrating gently at her. It was time for breakfast before the mission briefing.

"Yes, yes sorry. I wanted to-" Petra ushered him out the door, and it sealed behind them.

"Walk with me?" she interrupted quickly and he nodded.

"Well, the thing is..." he started as they walked. They passed a pair of soldiers who saluted Petra, and Lysander cut off.

"Yes?" She prompted him again.

"Well, I was hoping you could give me some self-defense training." The words came tumbling out of Lysander's mouth, wild and uncertain. Petra turned to him, her eyebrows shooting up her forehead in disbelief.

"Really?" He nodded and a little smirk crept onto her lips. "Uh. Yeah. I can do that." She straightened up a bit as she said it.

"Good, good." They walked a few more paces towards the canteen and another pair of soldiers making their way to the canteen passed them, raising their hand in the Mimameid greeting. "Could we get started right away, then?" He asked her and she gave him a sideways look. "Well, after breakfast." He conceded and she sighed wistfully. Didn't he have somewhere to be? As much as she would love to stay behind and train him with a group of new recruits, that wasn't her call to make.

"I can't. I'm getting rotated back in. I've got another mission Above Ground."

"What, already?" Even Lysander was shocked. "But what about your leg?" She shrugged in response. "I thought, at least I'd have an even shot if you trained me while you were injured," Lysander said, halfheartedly. That made Petra laugh lightly.

"You wouldn't have a shot even if I was paralyzed from the waist down," she told him. "But, we'll start as soon as I get back." He clapped his hands together triumphantly and reached up, running his hand through his hair. The muscles in his lower arm flexed and caught her eye. It wasn't anything she wouldn't have seen in training with her men, but since Arthur...she caught her mind wandering to how it had felt when the doctor had carried her into the house - how instantly secure she had felt cocooned in his arms. She cast her eyes to the ground to hide the blush, but Lysander didn't seem to notice or care.

"Deal," he said gratefully, and she raised her face to Lysander, trying to figure him out. He wasn't like anyone she had known before. He wasn't like the soldiers she'd grown up with or who she worked with. Sure, he was annoyingly persistent with his hundreds of questions and his inability to react without overthinking things first. But, he was something she hadn't seen in a long time, he was kind. She had only ever known one other man like that in her life before - her own father. And most of the people he had worked with had considered it a flaw. Only Petra and her mother had seen how his kindness had held their family together all those years. And now she had met two men like that in the course of just a few days. They walked in silence for a few minutes before either of them spoke again.

"You remember the doctor that helped us back in the village?" Petra blurted out. She felt that, of all the people who had been on the mission with her, she could trust him the most with this little secret. And she was bursting to talk about him. Lysander nodded. "He made it back to wherever he was going, right?" she asked, speaking her own uncertainty away. She saw Lysander's face wash over with comprehension.

"Yes. I think so," he said, looking sideways at her and putting his hands in his pockets.

"Yeah. Me too." She exhaled. As they continued walking, she watched Lysander's eyes darting around the hallway, thinking something through, deciding something. She wasn't surprised when he opened his mouth to speak.

"You know the bomb that went off in the village?" Petra's mouth twitched into a smile as he asked the question.

"Mm-hm."

"That was mine. I built it," he said with a hint of pride. Petra nodded, her lips involuntarily curling into a smile.

"Genius move, letting everyone think it was the Celts," she acknowledged. "I'm very impressed."

"Well -" he added quickly. "Don't tell anyone." And she let herself feel the warmth of her smile, a kind of feeling in her belly at this small act of trust. This exchange of secrets.

"I won't," she promised as they arrived at Canteen C and ground to a halt.

"Me either," he promised with a wink. How was it, that she could share a secret so close to her heart with this person she'd just met, but not with her own men? Before she could speculate, Lysander added, "Well, if we can't train together yet, then I guess I should get going to my breakfast. Too bad we can't eat in here with you guys, again." He shrugged, but Petra knew enough rules had already been bent on their account. Sigrid's patience with the rule-breaking wasn't infinite.

"No, sorry. Rules are rules. And rules are why this place works." She thought back to Milla this morning with a sinking feeling. She should have tried harder. "Besides, why would you want to eat with us when you can get a better breakfast in B and sit on an actual chair?" She laughed a little.

"Yeah, I was wondering about that, actually," Lysander probed, but Petra shrugged it off.

"The military has always been willing to make certain accommodations for the collective good of Mimameid." There was a pause. "We're happy to," she added.

"I see." He was more relaxed than when he'd arrived, but he still hadn't settled. "Guess I better get going, before I mess up my schedule on the first day," he hesitated. "But Petra," It was the first time he had used her name, looking her full in the face, "good luck on your mission. Come back safe." Petra wanted to reach out, to thank him for keeping her secret about Arthur.

"I'll contact you when I'm back," she assured him and reached out her hand as if they were going to shake, but Lysander took it and pulled her into an embrace. She was so shocked she almost pulled back, but it felt good to be hugged again, in a way she hadn't been since her *baba*, wrapped up tight. Almost like having a family again.

She leaned into the hug and closed her eyes. No one in C ever hugged her like that. Not even Milla. Milla knew her better than to try. She tried to recall the last time Sigrid had genuinely hugged her. She certainly must have at some point.

The canteen doors whooshed open and they broke away from one another as several soldiers shuffled passed them. Petra cleared her throat and stepped towards the door.

"See you on the other side." Lysander smiled again and he turned to leave, trudging back down the way they had come.

"Hey, engineer?" she called out and he stopped to turn back to her, "*Ohittaa ruuvimeisselin*," she said with a grin and she saw his face light up before the doors whooshed open again and the smell of food and din from C washed over her.

When she had scarfed down her morning ration of clumpy porridge and tea, Petra's band beeped to let her know which room to report to for the morning briefing. She kicked out the crate she'd been sitting on and replaced it against the wall.

As she walked back across the hall, she nodded to Anders and Aksel. They'd arrived later than usual and were now huddled in a corner together, talking in hushed voices beside Benjáme, who jumped up as she passed them.

"You headed to the briefing?" he asked her in a low, tempered voice, keeping pace.

"What? You too?" Petra looked sideways at him incredulously and dodged a handful of darts being shucked across the room by some angry soldier who'd just lost a bet.

"Yeah, I got the message this morning when I was visiting Lasse, before breakfast. I guess he gets a pass since he's still in The Infirmary, but when I saw your name on the list..." His voice trailed off. "Let's just say it seems like they're in kind of a hurry to get us back out there."

"Seems so," she replied, her mind buzzing. They exited C, climbing the stairs up to the briefing room. The room they'd been ordered to wasn't in C like the usual military briefings. So as they climbed, the window above them looking out into the fjord swirled as they climbed around the spiraling perimeter of the column.

Today they'd been summoned to a room that jutted off between levels A and B. Petra had only been here a handful of times before. It was where the more sensitive military missions were generally planned before they made their way down to C. They exited the stairs and turned off into a darker hallway lined with honeycomb doors with antique wheel locks retrofitted to interact with their bands. Benjáme extended his arm to the door panel when they arrived and it opened to a thick walnut table surrounded by a few people sitting in plush, leather chairs. There was paneled lighting along the walls that gave the room a homey, upscale feel.

Petra was startled to find she didn't recognize the other three military personnel sitting at the table. All three were women, huddled relatively close together, as though they were part of the same unit, and they were staring up at her with sharp, critical eyes. Even if she didn't know them, they knew who she was, and their faces told her there were expectations.

She hadn't known there were soldiers in Mimameid she wasn't acquainted with, let alone three that were high enough ranks to be on a classified mission. Whatever this mission was, Petra was already more intrigued. Sigrid stood up and smiled as they entered, gesturing to Petra to take the seat to her right. She made her way around the table, rising onto her tiptoes to squeeze behind the heads of the other women seated at the table. When she passed Sigrid, the women touched her arm and gave it an affectionate squeeze, or what was meant to be perceived as affectionate, but felt more like a choke-hold to Petra. She released her arm and Petra took her seat. Benjáme sank into a spot at the other end of the table and immediately crossed his arms and legs in the leather chair.

"Good." Sigrid looked around at everyone in the briefing, a practiced warmth emanating from her. "So, everyone is here now." She glanced down at her band, her mouth twitching amusedly, then raised her silver eyes to the group and lifted her hand to her brow in greeting.

"In the boughs of Mimir's tree." They all lifted their hands in response, repeating the words back to her. Petra tried to mask the unsteadiness of her voice among the others. The words felt tinny today, somehow false.

"This mission, as with all you do on behalf of Mimameid, is extremely confidential. But this one, in particular, requires more discretion than most." Sigrid turned and threw the briefing documents from her band up to the viewer above the table. Petra scanned them, seeing a terrain map flash beside a tactical plan.

"We have received intel that Mimameid itself has been compromised. The information alone wasn't enough to confirm that we are in danger, but coupled with the fact that the Celtic raids have started to form a pattern and are systematically closing in around the perimeter of Mimameid means it is time to take this threat seriously." Sigrid's face grew stern as Petra's stomach turned. Was this why she was being rotated out again so soon? "We need to find out what the Celts know, so we are sending you all out to infiltrate their camp and evaluate the sensitivity of the information they have. That is your objective."

Though her stomach was uneasy at the thought of Mimameid and her men being compromised, she could close her eyes and feel the cool of Arthur's hand upon her cheek. She felt the possibility of seeing him again rising in her.

"Does this have anything to do with the Celt that's living here?" Benjáme spat, a little too aggressively from the other end of the table. "The one that fancies himself Icelandic?" Sigrid raised her hand to Benjáme and shook her head.

"Ned Wallace is above reproach. So much so in fact, he was asked to join this mission." Sigrid spoke the words as a finality. Petra had forgotten there was a Celt in Mimameid at all, much less that he was one of the ones old enough to still have a family name.

"But, conveniently couldn't be bothered to lift a finger, as usual," Benjáme mumbled scornfully under his breath. He sank back into his plush chair as Sigrid's eyes flashed briefly ice-cold at him. Petra was surprised by the coldness in them but decided to focus instead on the maps in front of her and on how Arthur was out there somewhere.

"Their camp has been gradually moving up the coastline since they landed off the coast of Old Bergen, we know this. But these are approximations of their location. We need you to actually go into the enemy's camp and bring back what information you can." Sigrid was watching their faces. "Which means you have to find the camp first." She stood with arms akimbo.

"Mimameid wasn't built to keep people out. It was built to keep people in. It was built to be a fortress, to keep our people safe behind our walls, but The Celts have changed that. They threaten the innocent lives we protect here and we have a responsibility to the generation we are raising in Mimameid to make sure that they have a future." Petra found herself being swept up by Sigrid's words. "You all are the best we have and we are depending on you."

She felt the swell of loyalty to Sigrid rising in conflict with her anticipation of Arthur. Sigrid took a swig of some brown liquid from a glass, an actual tumbler glass, on the table in front of her. It landed on the hardwood with a thud and left a ring on the table.

The day Sigrid had brought her back to the bunker, she had come to see her in The Infirmary to make sure she was doing okay. She had nearly lost the toes on her left foot to hypothermia and Sigrid had dragged her on the sled most of the way back from where they found her in the snow. She would never forget what Sigrid had said to the men who had been with her when they wanted to leave Petra behind. *We are Norse. We are Mimameid. We are the ones the gods have chosen to lead humanity into the future and we will not leave anyone behind.*

Norse don't leave anyone behind. The words had stuck with her over the years and it was part of why she was having such a difficult time understanding Sigrid's suspicions of the newcomers now. She wondered if maybe Sigrid's behavior had something to do with the changes in the Celts' movements. Something maybe beyond what Petra knew.

"Wouldn't you agree, Lieutenant?" The woman at the far end of the table, bearing the mark of a Captain asked.

Pulling herself out of her thoughts and back into the room, she nodded in agreement, as she watched Sigrid wipe the ring of condensation from the table with the sleeve of her jumpsuit discretely.

"I'll leave you all to it and be back later for an update on your plans," Sigrid announced and made her way out of the room, leaving the glass behind on the table.

They dug into their strategy over the next couple of hours as a team and Petra started to understand why the three strangers at the table with her were on this mission.

Mimameid's patrols had collected spotty records of the Celts' movements over the years, but being nomads, the Celts moved frequently enough that the information they got was usually outdated by the time they received it. It made finding their exact location the first step in the plan, as the captain called Maike explained.

Maike had been beyond the borders before, like Petra and Benjáme. Missions beyond the borders were always for survivors and those had virtually ceased, until a few days ago, that was. But, Maike was older than Petra so she had likely been on those types of missions before Petra herself was even in Mimameid. The woman looked weather-beaten and tough, with her steely blue eyes. Her hair was braided high on her head, with twists and knots like a Valkyrie warrior of old, the end hanging long and loose down her back. She stood as though she was carrying a weight on her shoulders, but with a stride that told Petra she was proud to be carrying it.

"They never venture far from the villages they are pillaging, so their access to food and fuel can't be cut off. But they aren't amateurs. Wherever they are, it will only have one access point, and it will be heavily protected."

"But we can make that work to our advantage. It will be easy to monitor what is getting in and out of camp as well as who is getting in and out," the small, dark woman named Onni added. She was a specialist in Celtic battle strategy and had honest, olive eyes. Maike had been in charge of Celtic movement operations at the beginning of Mimameid, right after the volcanoes and the invasion, when they had been a more active threat, but

Onni understood how they thought and how they chose their more long-term locations.

"Their raiding parties are always small and separated too, so while it makes them less predictable, it also means they will be easy to overcome."

"How exactly does that help us?" Benjáme interjected snidely. Petra looked sideways at him. Did he want to give Sigrid more reasons to kick them out? "Besides racking us up a few kills, that is."

"*Because* our mission is to infiltrate." Onni swiveled around in her chair to look at him, an amused look on her face at Benjáme's attitude. "Overpowering and then impersonating a raiding party could be a way in," she explained, turning to the third woman at the table, "and that is where Anja will come in." She gestured warmly at the woman beside her, who had been quiet up until then.

Anja was soft-spoken as she introduced her role in the operation, running thin, clammy fingers through her mousy, blonde hair, her pale blue eyes darting around the room. She was their linguist and she was there to train them in how to speak with the timbre of a Celt, so their voices wouldn't give them away under cover.

Petra couldn't help but let her mind wander back to what Benjáme had said - why were he and Petra being rotated out so soon again? Everyone else on the team had some special Celtic skill, but she and Benjáme, they were just soldiers. Good soldiers, of course, with records that were known within the ranks of the Mimameid military. Sigrid had made sure of that when she had taken Petra under her wing all those years ago but was that really the only reason she was here - to be Sigrid's eyes and ears in the camp? Or was Benjáme right and they were trying to get rid of them? Or did it have to do with Arthur somehow?

When they had outlined a plan for the mission, they were dismissed for a late lunch and to gather what belongings they needed to take with them. They would reassemble for departure at 1500hr to begin their mission under cover of darkness. The long nights would provide the camouflage they needed to travel undetected as they searched for the Celts. As Benjáme made for the door, Petra saw him catch Onni's arm and say,

"Onni, right? Is that name by any chance Sámi?" The woman's face lit up as they stepped over the threshold together.

Petra stood up to follow them and someone reached out for her shoulder. Sigrid's eyes speared her as she signaled for Petra to hang behind. She obeyed, stepping back into the room, the wheel lock grinding shut. Sigrid sat back down in one of the empty leather chairs and gestured for Petra to do the same.

Now that the room was empty, Petra could see how luxurious it really was. A sealskin rug was rolled out under the table. There was a highboard with a mirrored tray displaying water in a carafe, some more of the brown liquid Sigrid had drunk and antique glasses. It all felt weirdly like it was trying to be too 'Above Ground' to Petra. Like war room out of an old film from The Time Before, when frivolities like that were still possible. But it was a war room made by someone who had never been in an actual war room, only read about them or seen staged models of one.

"I was wondering if I could ask something in particular of you on the mission." Sigrid placed her hands on the table, wrapping the wood with her fingernails as Petra sat back down. This had to be it, the reason why she had been chosen. She exhaled.

"Of course. Anything I can do to protect Mimameid, you know that." Petra kept her voice steady.

"Good. I'm glad to hear that." Sigrid's thin smile glinted like silver in the sunlight as she leaned forward and grabbed hold of Petra's hands. She cradled them in her own cold, clean fingers. "I understand you formed a connection with the young Celt that aided you all on your last mission." Petra felt her pulse jump to her ears. Her cheeks grew warm. She didn't know if she'd been caught or not. How much did Sigrid know? "First of all, well done. I should have told you that during the debrief, but I admit I could hardly believe our luck. So, well done indeed, Lieutenant."

Though she could not deny the flush in her cheeks, her voice refused to choke out any words. She just nodded her thanks. "Your quick strategic thinking in forming that attachment could be the thing that saves us all," Sigrid continued. "Now, I know there's not much to work with - I mean he didn't even give you all a *name* - but I want to ask you to try to find him in the camp. You alone have a way into the camp which your team will need. Mimameid's safety depends on the quality of information we will get from your mission, so we must use every available asset." Sigrid's words slipped through her lips like a toxin. Petra's happiness at seeing Arthur again turning rancid at being ordered to use him. "I hope we can count on you," her commander finished. Petra's stomach turned over. She tried to hide her discomfort in her next question.

"What if he doesn't remember me?" She felt too much vulnerability lacing her words as she spoke and wished she could take the question back. Sigrid's eyes twinkled, mischievously. So, she knew.

"Make sure that he does," Sigrid whispered, squeezing Petra's hands so tight she could feel the freshly clipped nails digging into her skin. "Make sure that he does," she repeated, and when she let go, Petra could see the marks where her nails had cut her.

And then Sigrid stood and left Petra alone in the room, looking out at the empty doorway. Her fingers stayed twisted, white-knuckled, on the arms of the chair until she shoved her hand into her pocket and felt feverishly for the buried love knot.

Petra walked slowly back to her housing unit after lunch, drinking in Mimameid. She had missed it, especially on the last mission, and breathed in its salty smell and cool concrete against her fingertips. Above Ground was quiet, it was true. There were no more birds or animals or leaves to rustle in the trees. But there was something different about the quiet in the bunker. Under the water, she felt protected, safe. It was similar to how the world would get on the base in the north after a long snowfall late into the night, when Petra would be alone at home with her *Baba*, and they would wrap up under one of her faded, hand-knit blankets, all the world standing still. For her, that stillness had become the feeling of home.

In a moment of longing, she decided to stop by The Observation Deck before going back to pack for the mission. When the door whooshed open, the room was empty. She let herself be drawn to the window, the glass illuminated by that ever-so-gentle blue at the touch of her fingertips. She sighed, feeling the muffled silence of the room surround her. Here, her grief for her mother, father, grandmother stopped. Her grieving had been so deep, so fundamental, but being in Mimameid dimmed the sound of that loss.

She was so grateful to Mimameid and to Sigrid for the way they had rescued her. She had been a broken person when the Norse troops had found her, stumbling through the backcountry of northern Sweden. After she had buried her grandmother in the cold, hard, winter earth, she had set out to find someone, anyone. And she remembered with perfect clarity every moment of the first people she found. Men. Men ravenous for a young girl.

They hadn't expected a girl that could fight - a young shieldmaiden bred from both the wild northern Sámi and the whipping Rus winds. And yet, the fight in her seemed to make them thirst for her that much more, until the fight was gone from her. And they took their turns, leaving behind a hollowed-out shadow of a girl, crumpled in the ash and snow.

Sigrid had picked up the pieces of her that were left and stacked them up again into the form of a woman. They had trained together, both body and mind, in the solace of Mimameid, until Petra felt the rush of air that is life fill her lungs once more. And for that, she knew she owed everything to Sigrid and the people of Mimameid. They'd given her a home again, a purpose.

She wished she had more time to soak in the peacefulness of the bunker before heading back Above Ground. She wished she had time to go to Sigrid and talk like they used to. But even as she leaned against the cool glass and said the words to herself, she could feel the little flame inside her that burned for Arthur.

It was small, but it was a compassion she hadn't known since she was a child.

With a breath, she steadied herself and turned, back towards Mimameid. As the door whooshed back open, the pressurized air washed over her face. She was ready to head back out into Celtic country.

7

LYSANDER

He was energized as he entered Canteen B. Scanning the room, he saw Linnaea stand up and wave him over.

"She's been eyeing the door for you," Magdelena signed as she reached out to hug him and he smiled. "Come on, let's try this breakfast thing out." She indicated the door leading back into the kitchen and together they all walked over to ask for their "Opp" meals. It wasn't like in C where the kitchen flowed right into the canteen. Here, the cooking space had to be separated from the eating space - the citizens of B didn't like the canteen smelling like the kitchen - so they quietly slipped through the door trying not to draw too much attention to themselves.

"I talked to Petra on the way over here and she's being rotated back out to the surface," he informed the girls as the ornery cook shooed them back out into the canteen, the door flopping back and forth behind them.

"Is that so?" Magdelena answered, one watchful eye on Linnaea's precariously balanced tray while they made their way back to the empty concrete table, set up like a cafe where they might have had saffron buns in The Time Before, seated across from one another on the two benches. They slid down onto the cushions, Lysander on one side and Magdelena and

Linnaea on the other. Linnaea leaned back against the wall and Lysander opened up the top of his tea mug. The steam hit his face abruptly while the glaring honeycomb lights crackled and popped above them in the booth.

"Yeah. I went to talk to her about getting myself some self-defense lessons and she told me it'll have to wait." He leaned back against the cushions as he signed.

"So the new mission starts immediately, then?" Magdelena signed, then lifted her eyebrows above the rim of her mug as she took a sip of her tea.

"That's what it sounds like."

"What about her leg?" Linnaea questioned. "I thought I might be able to learn something about what that Celtic doctor did to her and Lasse if I got to do work in The Infirmary like Petra said."

"Oh, I meant to ask, did they give you any more information about that yesterday in the school?" Magdelena asked and Linnaea shook her head.

"I think they are waiting until we get our bands to make it official," she signed in response, then lifted her spoon and took a half-hearted bite of porridge.

"So, how did you like the school, Sprout?" Lysander signed, then he put one of the three fresh orange slices on his tray into his mouth. It was juicy, unlike anything he had tasted in a long time. The cook had reminded them to separate out their orange skins after the meal, so the oils could be pressed and made into cleaning solution.

"It was fine," Linnaea replied without explaining further, so Lysander promoted her further.

"Just fine?" It was the first time she'd ever been to anything resembling a traditional school, so she must have found something interesting about it.

"Yeah, there were a couple of girls who showed me around and explained how it worked. They were kind of nice, they wanted to learn how to sign. They knew a bit already from a friend they used to have. The teacher knew sign language, too." Linnaea's face still displayed - not sadness, per se - but a disinterest he couldn't understand. "They showed me the tablets to read from or solve math problems on. They showed me some game called c-o-d-i-n-g?" She spelled out the word and Lysander couldn't help but smile.

"What?" Linnaea asked him.

"Coding is what I know how to do from school," he explained, "but I haven't had to do it in a long time. Maybe I should come join you in school for a little while!" He teased, but she wasn't as amused as he'd expected.

"They also have a hydroponic garden, but all they're growing is radishes and lettuce. It's not nearly as impressive as the plants we saw Above Ground," Linnaea continued, still generally unimpressed by her experience in the Mimameid school.

"Each plant serves a purpose, you know, Sprout," Magdelena signed, gently. "Even if that purpose is only to spark an interest in a young mind."

"I guess." Linnaea shrugged. "Then the teacher gave a history lesson, but it was really old, weird history." She finished and moved her porridge around in the bowl. She was definitely behaving more sullen than he'd ever known her to be, but perhaps they had come to the point she was most uncomfortable with.

"What was the lesson about?" he asked. She was clearly feeling more uncomfortable about school than excited, and he wanted to help if he could. "I had a teacher who used to tell me about really old history too and I always thought it was super boring. I wanted to do something with my hands instead of listening to stories about a bunch of famous dead people." He decided to leave out the part about how the history stories turned out to be self-fulfilling prophecies of how humanity would repeat the same mistakes over again and this time, the world would collapse in ecological disaster.

He should have paid better attention. A lot of people should have paid better attention. But the quick anecdote seemed to have struck a chord with Linnaea.

"Exactly," she agreed. " I could have been learning something useful in The Infirmary - how to cauterize wounds or tie off sutures - instead of learning about mistakes famous dead people made and how to grow plants that can't survive Above Ground, anyways." Lysander wanted to laugh, but he didn't want to crush her ambitious spirit. What students in his day would have given to be able to just reminisce about the mistakes of the good old days and grow plants instead of having to problem solve to keep the world from crumbling around them - unsuccessfully.

But, on the other hand, he could understand why she felt that way. Linnaea had grown up in a time and place where it wasn't about what you had studied, but about what skills you had. That's what Above Ground had been reduced to since the world collapsed. A part of him felt sad for her, that she had never known a life of peace, but another part of him was proud of who she was becoming, forged in the fires of 'Ragnarök'. He pivoted; it was only her first day of school, after all.

"What did you guys think about our conversation with Sigrid?" he signed, looking around to check if anyone was watching.

"About Ragnarök?" Magdelena confirmed, spelling out the word slowly. Lysander nodded. Linnaea stopped eating and put down her spoon.

"Yeah that's what was weird about the history lesson," she signed, "They were talking about that big snake and the god Thor and treating it like it was all true stories. Did all that stuff really happen? I thought they were just myths. You know? Bedtime stories." Lysander and Magdelena exchanged a look of unsurprised skepticism that only two scientists could share.

"I think -" There was a clattering as a tray across the room went tumbling from the table. A girl, maybe sixteen years old, with unruly brown curls, stood up abruptly, her face red with frustration. The room turned its sharp gaze on the girl and the uproar she was causing. Linnaea followed her mother's gaze over Lysander's shoulder and they watched.

"That's the problem. You guys don't care and you don't want to care. You can't shut your eyes to everything, you know!" She picked up the tray and threw it across the room and the girl's father stood up from the table, raising his hand in apology at the people she had narrowly missed hitting. Lysander interpreted quickly and discreetly at Linnaea's startled expression.

"Look, we made sacrifices too, to get you both here." The father gestured to the girl's younger brother, seated at the table, his legs dangling from the seat. The whole of B was looking down their noses at the display. The canteen stank of judgment.

"You have no idea what sacrifice means!" the girl screamed. "Maybe if you went down to D from time to time you might learn."

"If you want to be in D, then there's nothing stopping you," her father replied cooly.

"You're right, even the people who don't have enough water for themselves would take me in. Because that's the kind of people they are down there."

"Ingrid, this is something we can discuss privately. There's no reason for such a show."

"It would suit you just fine, wouldn't it? For me to be gone!" Ingrid's hair flew around her puffed-up cheeks. "Get rid of your problem child! Send her somewhere where she can't tarnish your precious reputation anymore." She threw her arms up, backing away from the family as the rest of B looked on, sternly. "Consider it done. I'll find a black market hacker who can help me with my band. You won't ever have to see me again, because I'll be down in D helping people actually get medicine!" The girl stormed out of the canteen, the doors sealed behind her ominously.

There was a split second of silence before the low chatter of lilting languages picked up again, as even-toned and pleasant as it had been before. As if nothing had happened. Resigning back to his seat, Ingrid's father hung his head and shook it back and forth, rubbing his face in frustration. When he stopped, he looked up at the young boy across from him and smiled.

It was unsettling, as if he had just wiped the entire altercation with his daughter from his face.

Lysander turned back to his food, porridge now cold, but his tea still sending swirls of steam up into the air. It felt decadent, he realized. To have a meal in front of him and sit leisurely in the canteen. There was something disingenuous about it. Like it was too good to be true.

What had the girl meant about having enough water and medicine down in D? He had wanted to feel good about their new situation, but guilt was creeping up as he looked into his cup of tea.

Linnaea was the first to say something again.

"They can come up to The Observation Deck from D too, right?" she signed, hesitantly.

"Of course they can, Sprout," Magdelena assured her and Lysander nodded in agreement.

"Yeah, your mom was down there yesterday and talked to the Icelanders, remember?"

"Honestly, they seemed to like it a lot. Prefer it, actually," Magdelena promised her daughter. Linnaea nodded slowly and put an orange slice in her mouth. In an instant, her eyes popped open, wide and warm in the bright lights. A little bit of juice leaked out the side of her mouth and she sucked on the fruit.

"*This* is what orange is supposed to taste like?" She gasped and her fingers moved rapid fire. Lysander recalled that the supply chains hadn't been able to deliver citrus to the north anymore, by the time she was born. She'd had the odd orange-flavored candy if they'd found some while scavenging houses, or as a welcome treat at one of the refugee camps, but never the real thing. For all the questions they had about Mimameid - its ideology, its hierarchy - there was something to be said for being able to have fresh fruit on your morning breakfast - the first taste of a real orange. He couldn't help but exchange a smile with Magdelena at the girl's reaction. Maybe it was all worth it if Linnaea could have a good life, and was provided for.

"Wow." Was all Linnaea could sign in response to their smiles.

"What do you guys have on your schedule today?" Lysander asked, steering the subject away from the girl named Ingrid.

"I've been given a place in The Gardens for a couple hours and Linnaea is headed back down to the school." Magdelena looked sideways at her daughter.

"Yay," Linnaea signed sarcastically, then she put her last orange slice into her mouth, carefully peeling the fruit off the rind.

"At least the nice girls will be there, again." Magdelena rubbed her daughters back, reassuringly. "What about you, L?"

When he returned to his room from breakfast a message beeped through on the panel by the door, reminding him in Yvonne's chipper voice of his next appointment.

He clicked on it, the screen lighting up with his schedule and his next appointment illuminated in red. The meeting was tagged with Sigrid's name, as well as a few others he didn't recognize, in the place called The Engine Room. A promising name.

"According to our calculations, you will arrive past the appointed time. Please leave promptly to ensure on-time arrival to The Engine Room," Yvonne's automated voice instructed him. He swiped the irritating message away and scrolled further down his schedule for the day.

After lunch, he had an appointment in Sigrid's office with Linnaea and Magdelena's names included. He was glad that he would have another opportunity to see them but wondered what another appointment for the three of them could mean. Their time was running out to decide about staying permanently, and he hadn't had a chance to talk to Magdelena about their decision after the disruption this morning at breakfast.

The thought slipped from his mind as the screen beeped and the blueprint plans of the engineering sector of Mimameid popped up. He was eager to see the older, repurposed parts of Mimameid where the core engineering was located. The part that had caught his attention yesterday, from the outside. He skimmed the documents, zeroing in on the Mimameid's reactor, just as the alert message about being late popped up again and started flashing.

It irritated him that he felt like he needed to head down there and he found himself wishing he had some sort of device that he could read through the plans on while he walked over to the meeting location. Something like - he grimaced even as he thought it - a band.

He took another minute to absorb as much of the information as possible and then took off, his door sealing with the now familiar gush of the airlock behind him.

Still not particularly trusting of the rusty, old elevator, he opted to descend via the concrete stairwell, taking in the bunker. For the first time, he felt, not like an outsider, but like a part of Mimameid.

The stairs were bustling with people, their jumpsuits emblazoned with the World Tree like his. He passed the hallway where they had gotten off to go to The Infirmary, hesitating as he considered visiting Lasse, but sighed and continued on. He was already too late for his meeting. Still, it felt good to have a sense of orientation, to know where he was, and recognize something.

Further down, he saw the turn-off to C level and he furrowed his brow, wondering again why Petra was being sent back out on another mission so soon. Lysander felt himself melting into the crowd as he sat deeper into Mimameid, but his eyes wandered up to the glass window at the top of the bunker, in the middle of that entrance hall floor. The foggy, green light of the fjord cast an eerie glow down into the cool concrete core of the bunker, throwing sunlight and shadows against the walls of their underwater home.

Lysander looked back around at all the people surrounding him and asked himself if they really knew what a truly miraculous feat of engineering it was, what an impossible place they were living in, this bunker hovering between rock and steel and glass, one tap away from depressurizing and killing them all.

He continued down into the belly of the bunker, past The Gardens, where he paused briefly, considering if Magdelena might already be inside. He passed under a flickering sign above the entrance to the next level that read "D" and followed a hallway with an illuminated arrow in the floor pointing him down to The Engine Room. It took him to a tight, spiral staircase, which he reluctantly climbed into. The smell of grizzly electricity and sweat greeted him before he made it to the bottom of the stairs and reminded him of the refugee camps he had worked at.

The bunker down here was small and cramped, made of a heavy, green-tinted metal. The lights here weren't hexagonal like the upper levels, but mounted on the walls behind metal cages, buzzing loudly in the salty air. The doors he passed had mounted wheel locks on them like an old submarine and he felt his heart flip with excitement at being in a piece of history from The Time Before.

He stepped into a hallway marked with the room number he was meant to find and followed it to a door. Raising his fist, he knocked on the metal, barely touching it before it opened with a hiss of air.

Inside, was a small group gathered around a table, some seated, some leaning against the walls. A man with a long, scraggly beard crossed his arms as Lysander came in. Two others, who looked like they could be twins, wore work belts around their waists and exchanged a salty look. The only man in the room who was moving, pacing actually, stopped and looked up when Lysander entered.

"In the boughs of Mimir's tree." There was an echo around the room of the words. Lysander gave a lackluster nod of his head, hand to his brow.

"Well, he's a bit young, isn't he?" He heard one of them say, though he wasn't sure who had spoken. The man who had been pacing, however, looked pleased. His face broke out into a smile.

"Odin's beard," the man said joyfully.

He was thin, perhaps a little jittery, and he moved like he was younger than the lines on his face and the glasses pushed into his long, grey-blonde hair suggested. He stuck his hand out to greet Lysander, eyes glimmering like the smoky waters of the fjord above.

Lysander took the sweaty palm offered to him and shook it, purposefully. The man squinted as he looked him in the eye and much to Lysander's surprise pulled him into a quick, powerful hug.

"Very pleased to meet you. We heard there was another engineer on board and we have just been dying to meet you ever since." Lysander looked around at the others in the room, the other men either averting their gaze or staring at him coolly. Maybe this one man had been dying to meet him, but only him.

"I'm Bjørn. It's truly a pleasure to have you here. I'm the lead engineer for Mimameid," he paused. "I hope the tools we sent up were in order for you."

"Lysander. Nice to meet you, too. And yeah, thank you. They were very helpful." He didn't want to put the man off already by insulting the toolkit, however rudimentary. He went around the table, shaking everyone else's hand before he came back around to Bjørn, who had pulled out a beaten-up, metal stool for him to sit on. Lysander nodded his thanks and dragged the stool up to the table, the legs scraping across the floor with a teeth-rattling sound. There was a small pause and the scraggly-bearded man uncrossed his arms and leaned against the wall, unimpressed.

"So, Lysander. What do you think of our little operation here?" Bjørn asked him, examining a hangnail and trying to appear casual from across the table, as though the entire room wasn't already full of his energy.

"I looked through the blueprints, but I'm curious to see it all with my own eyes." Bjørn pounded his hands into the table as he stood, enthusiastically.

"A tour!" he exclaimed keenly. "Yes. Let me show you around." Lysander thought he saw a few eye rolls at the table as they all stood, but Bjørn's own positivity was infectious enough to keep his interest piqued. He had a feeling Bjørn was just as much the engineer as he was. The man strutted to a door left of the table, pulling a lever which released the airlock with a hiss Lysander found himself growing accustomed to, and perhaps even fond of, down here in the deepest part of the bunker.

He followed Bjørn through the door into a room that looked like it could have served as a decontamination chamber at some point in the past and the rest of the men filed in behind him. When the door on the other end of the chamber whooshed open, the noises of engines moving, turning, clanking, and whirring assaulted Lysander's ears. The smile that spread onto his face was immediate.

It was the sound of a world that hadn't died, after all. It was the sounds of life and innovation. This was The Time Before as Lysander had known it.

He stepped over the threshold and into the beating heart of Mimameid.

He was standing on a catwalk suspended in a massive room, the ceiling high, like a vaulted, Gothic cathedral. Piping lined the walls, sprawling out around the room like a roadmap of a subway system across the walls. Some of the pipes were spitting out steam, some had cold, little droplets of water condensing on the outside of them and dripping to the floor below with slow and steady plops. Other pipes rattled and shuddered, echoing throughout the chamber.

In the center of the main floor below was what he thought must be the main reactor. It whirred rhythmically, humming in the center of the chaos, like a steady, guiding star. He felt himself being drawn to it. It wasn't like anything he had seen before.

As questions started bubbling up inside him, his gaze finally landed on Bjørn, who was watching his expression with delight. They grinned at each other, as young boys, kindred souls in a giant mechanical playground.

"It's made of carbonium," Bjørn explained to him, "that's why we can be in here without it doing any radiation damage. As far as I can tell, it was a hell of a thing to make. The engineer who was here before told me the military paid a lot of money for it. Old Norway had drained their own titanium supplies dry so they had to import Cornish titanium in order to make the carbonium for the reactor and Old Cornwall didn't want to honor the contract or something...I'm not exactly sure. It was around the time they joined the Celts, so it was all political nonsense."

Lysander nodded, but he hadn't really been paying attention to what Bjørn was saying as he'd followed him down the grated steps. He was far too distracted by the room around him. Set to the soundtrack of the whirring reactor, Lysander took in the pumps, valves, cables, and wires, all twisting and turning through the space in an elegance that only an engineer could appreciate. He ran his fingers through his hair, the energy in his fingertips itching to get started working.

"Anyways, we supplement energy with a wave generator to curb the need for more carbonium, but this is essentially it."

Bjørn led him down to the bottom of The Engine Room and around the corner, turning underneath the grated stair they had just crossed over. Along the back wall was a row of turbine fans working to dissipate the steam and heat from the engines and the pipes. Tanks lined the far end, with access points from above on the suspension bridge as well as at their bases.

Lysander followed Bjørn across the room as he led him past the towering tanks, to the wall on the other side. There were a dozen or so valves locked into place along various spots, but Bjørn stood beside one in particular, sort of covering it up with his body. He leaned casually against the wall, watching Lysander's face.

"Pretty beautiful, isn't it?" He grinned at Lysander and they looked together for a moment, standing next to one another in silence. Lysander closed his eyes and leaned his head back, letting the noises wash over him, envelope him. "It's a bit of a misnomer, to call it The Engine Room, of course." Bjørn gnawed on a hangnail as he spoke and Lysander opened his eyes again, looking curiously at Bjørn.

"Oh?"

"Well, it's not exactly a moving ship is it, so it doesn't have an engine," Bjørn said and Lysander shrugged.

"That's true," he agreed, feeling like Bjørn wanted to say more, so he let the silence hang in the filtered air, humoring him.

"But, I think the name is a call back to when it was still a submarine. This is the oldest part of Mimameid, made from the old engines of the submarines they pieced together. Well, this and level D. But I guess you noticed that on the way down." Bjørn ripped the hangnail out and spit it over to his right. Lysander reached up for his Iogr charm.

"Thanks for this," he sighed and Bjørn shrugged in reply.

"Well, I didn't make her, I'm just trying to keep her from falling apart, is all." The man brushed the compliment off.

"She's still going, so you must be treating her right." Bjørn ran his hand through his long, grey-blonde hair.

"Doing my best. I'm no electrical engineer, but I do my best."

"Oh?" Lysander queried.

"I trained civil. Specialized in building materials. I know a hell of a lot about concrete. But they heard the word 'engineer' and sent me down here. I'm not complaining, don't misunderstand, I've got a great team, but in terms of engineers - it's just you and me."

"And everyone else?" Lysander asked, looking at the rest of the team working around them.

"Electricians, plumbers, car mechanics, Selby installed heating units."

"You could do worse," Lysander responded.

"Oh, absolutely. And I know they don't always like that I'm in charge, but they get it done, no question. They take the work seriously. I can't ask for more than that." Bjørn's face had darkened as he spoke. It had gone from the delighted scientist in an engineering playground to a manager that dances with the line between the extinction of a whole human population daily. Lysander wasn't quite ready to think like that again.

"So, structural engineer?" he said, whipping Bjørn out of his head. "You must be thrilled to be working on such a...unique place, yeah?" Bjørn's face lifted slightly at Lysander's curiosity.

"You forget after a while. The novelty of it wears off, as it just becomes your day-to-day. But, yeah, when you put it like that. I guess I am." The sparkle returned to his blue eyes. "I mean how incredible is that -"

"The glass ceiling?" Lysander finished his sentence and Bjørn let out a hearty laugh that caused a couple of the nearby men to jump.

"Right?" He threw his head back in disbelief. "And have you seen The Observation Deck yet?" he asked, "With the -"

"Piezo crystal floor?" Lysander did it again. "I know, it's unbelievable. I've never seen anything like it." Now he could feel his own face starting to glow in awe.

"I've tried and tried to figure out who the team was that built this place - the engineers and the architects - but it's all classified. No one will give me any information. As if information like that being classified matters, anymore."

Bjørn rolled his eyes in frustration, but he was clearly too content with their camaraderie, to let it get him down right now.

"Listen, I have a job for you. If you're up for it. We haven't been able to come up with a solve so far. At least not one that holds."

He turned a crank that opened a door to another room under the suspension bridge. It was hot. Steam escaped out into The Engine Room after them as they entered. Along the walls were two of what looked to be identical systems installed side by side.

Lysander was drawn forward, raising his fingers to the old-fashioned knobs and dials. It looked like the control room in an old space craft from The Time Before. Back when they had thought that outer space might have been a way to escape their dying planet. But solar flares had destroyed their efforts to terraform Mars, and even if they had succeeded in the terraforming project, they never would have been able to evacuate enough people to start a varied and viable Martian community. He felt a flicker of gratitude that Mimameid had had a backup plan.

He shook his head at the control board, astounded that something so antiquated could still be operational.

"What is it?" he asked Bjørn. The lights on one of the systems were blinking rhythmically while the lights from the other weren't illuminated at all.

"Our air filtration system. The auxiliary system has been down for months, which is workable, as long as the primary stays up and running. But it's playing with fire, not to have a backup system in place with so many lives depending on clean air." Lysander looked from the dark console back to Bjørn, a twinkle in his eye. At last, a problem he could fix.

"Do you have a screwdriver I could borrow?" He grinned.

Still buzzed on the high of The Engine Room, Lysander climbed the stairs back up to the top of the bunker. All the way back up to Sigrid, in her high tower, just below that fragile glass ceiling, where he was meeting up with Magdelena and Linnaea. He didn't push himself but steadily climbed, his heartbeat pounding against his chest.

He couldn't tell if it was the pressure change, the exercise, or The Engine Room that had his blood pumping, but his fingers itched to turn back around and keep working with Bjørn on the auxiliary air filtration system they had left below. It wasn't like him to leave a project unfinished, but they had worked through lunch and now he was late for his appointment upstairs. Yvonne had even called down to The Engine Room to ask if he was on his way.

By all logic, this was another rule he had broken - not adhering to his assigned schedule - and would probably result in some lost privilege or punishment, but he couldn't worry about that now. This appointment, even though its purpose had not been disclosed, was likely to inject their implants and get their armbands.

Although he hadn't been initially thrilled at the idea of the bands, after seeing the work to do down in The Engine Room, he found himself looking forward to studying the blueprints in detail and seeing what the guts of the bunker really looked like, during meals and from the comfort of his bunk. As he huffed to the top of the concrete steps, he started to understand why people took the risky elevator from time to time instead of hiking up and down the entire length of the bunker every day.

He could hear Magdelena's voice ringing down the hallway from Sigrid's office. He nodded to Yvonne, tapping away at her desk as he passed her, she gave him a vacant smile in return and pushed gently on the door to Sigrid's office. It was already open.

Sigrid rose as he entered, her silhouette eerily contrasted against the fish and mollusks out in the fjord, and gestured for him to take a seat beside Linnaea in her familiar cordial manner.

"And now, you're all here." Her voice was the same pacifying tone it had been in their last meeting, something almost hypnotic about it. "I hope you all are finding your quarters and work assignments to your liking. We would, of course, like to offer you three permanent positions here in Mimameid, assuming you are prepared to adhere to the rules and regulations of our little haven." Her smile was fixed to her face, her grey eyes looking down at them over the bridge of her slender nose.

He ran his hands through his hair. He could tell that this was all a bit of a show put on for them. Their interactions with the soldiers in the canteen had told him that most people were processed before they were shown the inner workings of Mimameid, as a matter of security. They had taken a risk by allowing them a trial period and he respected them for it. But, the ceremoniousness of it all and the way Sigrid looked so thrilled to be rolling out the red carpet for them was more forced than he was comfortable with. Still, Magdelena seemed to have found something she was missing here and he felt that he could bear the falseness of it, if only for her sake.

"Thank you. After seeing the work that needs to be done down in The Engine Room, I am happy to accept," Lysander signed, then took Magdelena and Linnaea's hands in each of his own.

"I am as well, thank you." Magdelena's voice was soft as she inclined her head. Linnaea nodded beside Lysander as she raised her free hand to sign,

"Me too."

"Excellent," Sigrid replied, her voice rang clear, but her lips remained pursed as she raised her hands in cool celebration. She came around the desk, taking them in arm as they rose and walked together towards the door. "Now, Yvonne will escort you where you need to go." She used a tone that was sticky sweet, as if they had not already been down to the sterile Infirmary once before. Lysander felt himself recoil at it. When they reached the door, Sigrid squeezed their shoulders, her fingers digging into his collarbone before turning back to her desk.

"Welcome to the family!" she called out with her back turned as the door hissed shut.

The three of them spun around to see Yvonne. The girl hugged her tablet to her chest, her energy still as electric as a wired lightbulb as she had been when they had last been given the tour.

"Follow me, then." Tossing her long hair over her shoulder, she led the way back down the hall and they piled into the rusty elevator. Lysander shoved his hands into his pocket nervously where he felt the small bio-implant rolling around after he'd safely reassembled it.

A different nurse than before, a little older, with wisps of grey in her hair and warm, dark eyes, was on duty in The Infirmary. She greeted them as she led the way to the processing room and explained she'd already been briefed on who they were and what their appointment entailed.

"It's been such a long time since we've had *Opps*," the woman chattered excitedly as she prepared the implants.

The room was colder than he remembered. The lights were jarringly bright compared to the soft blue of the fjord-lit hallways. Yvonne stepped to one side and the nurse indicated an examination table where they would sit while they received their bio-implants. He felt Linnaea's hand reach up to his and he looked down at her, giving her a reassuring squeeze. She would have little memory of a doctor's office. In fact, she probably had never even seen a room like this save for the last time they were here.

"It's okay," he signed, "there's nothing to be afraid of." Stepping forward, he hopped up onto the examination table and rolled up the sleeves of his jumpsuit.

"Your non-dominant hand, if you please." The nurse briskly tapped a syringe as he stuck out his left hand. The nurse flipped his hand over, cleaning the injection site just above his wrist with iodine. There was a sharp pinch as she pushed the needle into his arm. He thought he could feel the bio-implant enter his body, as though with each pulse that followed, his blood was becoming aware of the foreign presence just beneath the surface of his skin. Not wanting to put Linnaea off, he held his face steady, ignoring the sudden drop in his stomach as the needle pulled out.

The nurse handed him gauze and told him to press it against the injection site for a minute. The words echoed in his ears as muffled, hazy directions. She turned away from him, messing with something over on the counter. Magdelena looked him in the eyes and he could see her asking, "Are you okay?", her lips moving but no sound except a sharp ringing. His hearing snapped back into clear focus at the sound of something tearing open.

When the nurse turned back around she held his band in her hand. It looked just like Petra's. The same sleek grey of their uniforms, with a glossy black screen. It was coated with an outer silicone layer and the two ends of the band wrapped around the wrist, clicking together magnetically to hold the band in place.

She took him briefly through the process of syncing it to the bio-implant and calibrating it.

"It will automatically activate when it senses the bio-implant, which triggers it to turn on. You'll just drag your finger down the middle of the screen to sync it up." He was listening, despite having already figured out the controls worked from observing Petra with her own band.

"We will calibrate it here before you leave and to recalibrate, which you need to do once a week or so and the band will alert you when it's time, you go to any home port and tap into the system. Most people tap into a home port more than once a week anyways, so if you do that regularly, then the band will automatically recalibrate, and you have nothing to worry about."

She checked to see if the injection site was still bleeding. The gauze had only a singular drop of blood on it, which had already begun to dry to a rusty, brown color.

He snapped it into place on his wrist. The screen sensed the bio-implant and as promised, immediately turned on and began synchronizing.

Lysander found himself embarrassingly fascinated by the level of technology that they had managed to preserve here in Mimameid. His fingers lingered on the band for a moment before the nurse patted the examination table.

"So, who's next?" Magdelena sat down on the table and Linnaea clamored up next to her, rolling up her sleeve.

8
PETRA

When she broke the surface of the water, the sky was already dark. The water around her was impenetrable, like ink.

Even though it had only been a few days since she'd seen the sky, she felt like there were even more stars up there in that vast darkness. She hovered in the water for a brief moment, letting the icy spray sprinkle her face.

Just to her left, Maike's head surfaced.

"All clear, Lieutenant?" Maike took off her helmet and sucked in a deep breath of air, her expression a little green. The Captain didn't like diving. Petra nodded, wordlessly, in response. "Good. Off we go then." Maike pulled her helmet back on and swam ahead of her towards the shadowed shoreline. Onni and Anja's heads bobbed up behind Benjáme's and together they fell into line behind their commander. With another glance at the stars, Petra swam after them.

They had intentionally come up on a beach far outside of the town. Their mission was classified, so much so that their absence from Mimameid couldn't be noticed, which meant they weren't supposed to be seen by the townspeople. Only a handful had been trusted with the knowledge of Mimameid's vulnerability and most of them were on the mission.

Petra gasped for air as the tide washed her up onto the sand. She pulled off her helmet and fins, crawling through the wet sand toward higher ground. She felt her hands sinking and looked down. Even in the night, she could make out that the sand was an unusual color. She reached one hand up to her headlamp and clicked it on. The light streaked across the beach and the sand glowed a wild reddish-purple in the beam. She'd never seen anything like it.

Another wave smacked her in the back, knocking the breath out of her. She pitched forward, forcing herself to stand as she pulled herself out of the surf and onto the red sand beach. Her booted feet sank as she trudged until she joined the others at the edge of the beach.

The nighttime temperatures had dropped well below freezing and they were soaking wet, but Fiske had stashed their equipment for the mission at the edge of the beach, and Petra could see Benjáme had already located them among the rocks. She collapsed on a large boulder next to him and peeled the camouflage off the stashed pack, just as the others were doing, pulling out the trekking clothes that had been vacuum-packed into the Mimameid-standard biodegradable algae-plastic prior to their departure.

They were no longer in the bunker, so gone were the insignia-emblazoned jumpsuits. Here, they needed to stay warm and blend into the landscape. Thick wool socks were shoved into lightweight, strapped boots. She slipped her legs into sleek, wind-resistant pants lined with a warm fleece, and pulled a thin thermal wool layer over her head. She buttoned up a black Lusekofte sweater and an insulated, waterproof outer shell. Judging by the smell, the second-hand sweater had been pulled out of The Closet, whereas the other clothes felt like they had been pieced together from reclaimed materials specifically for this mission.

As they dressed in the whipping, coastal wind, she cupped her hands and blew on her fingers, to get the blood moving again. She could feel herself warming up under the layers of clothing as she rubbed her long, copper curls dry, shoving a dark, woolen hat onto her head.

She stuck her hands into her jacket pocket and felt the pieces of red twine she'd placed there between her frozen fingers. She bit her lip as she thought about how she hadn't been able to keep it a secret. During the debrief, the Celtic love knot had come up, of course. Sigrid had then suggested Petra bring it along on the mission, to potentially help elicit more information from Arthur, although Petra was fighting against her better judgment on whether or not to follow through with that particular part of the directive. Her hand closed around a pair of gloves placed beside the knot in her pocket. She pulled them out and put them on, leaving the knot alone for the moment.

Rummaging around in the pack, she checked that all their required equipment was accounted for. Their bands stored their mission parameters as well as mapping and navigation, but she saw a sleeping bag and mat, binoculars, ammunition, a lock pick, a knife, basic first aid, water bottles, a small, single-person camp stove, and a week's worth of trekking food. She tried to hide a wince as she felt a twinge in her leg from the cold.

Benjáme stood up, having stowed his diving gear, and offered his hand to Petra. Feeling Maike's eyes on them, she nodded to him and took it. He pulled her up to standing. She turned to face the rock in silence, then shoved everything back into her pack and she maneuvered it onto her back. It felt heavy, although she had noticed there wasn't a tarp, tent, or weapons for the ammunition.

"I've got the tarp," Onni confirmed, clicking her headlamp on.

"And you two have the tent, correct?" Maike asked, looking at Anja and Benjáme, who both nodded. The weapons must have been divided up among the rest of them as well. It seemed they had divided up the heavier stuff in their own packs without telling Petra. Normally, it was protocol to have the weight of the packs calculated out and matched accordingly to the prospective soldiers' capabilities. But perhaps her injury had changed her algorithm. Benjáme seemed to understand the evaluation Petra was making. He tried to shrug his shoulders discreetly, but Petra felt the pity coming from him and her stomach roiled at it. He reached into his pack and handed her an empty handgun.

The rest of the group clicked their headlamps on and they set off up the hillside away from the beach, keeping the coastline just at the edge of their line of sight.

Mimameid scouts had last sent reports of the Celts heading into the North Country, so once they left the valley of the red-sand beach, they hiked along a path glittering with boulders of granite that would eventually lead them toward the Arctic Circle.

By the time daylight broke over the mountain peaks, Petra's legs were aching, but Maike, Anja, and Onni showed no signs of slowing down. Forcing herself onwards, she was grateful that Benjáme, at least, hung back with her. The cut above his eye from the Celtic girl gleamed. The pink skin would soon fade to white and match Benjáme's other Celtic scar across his scalp. She sighed and tried to think of how Sigrid and the people of Mimameid - Lasse, Milla, and Lysander among them - were counting on them. She felt her hand find the twine in her pocket once again.

But Mimameid was so far away up here, and as they trudged across the rugged landscape, guided by hazy sunlight glowing faintly overhead, something awoke in her. It was the same stirring she had felt their last time Above Ground, when that whisper of green and purple had shot across the night sky and now, in the open air again, she felt herself coming alive. The faint red of the morning sun bathed her like a bird in the surf, hit by a wave. The frigid wind cut against her cheeks and her long curls danced in the air, and as she leaned into the feeling, the pain in her legs melting away.

Deeper into the North Country, the path became dusted with ashen snow. The mountain peaks around them were white-tipped and shining. It was a part of Old Norway Petra hadn't seen since she'd joined Mimameid. The trek down from where Sigrid had found her in the northern woods of Old Sweden was a blur in her memory. She had been in and out of consciousness and the world around them had still been burning. She recalled flashes of charred villages and ancient pines ablaze, the feeling of hands gripped tight around her, though she now knew the restraining hands were because she had been bound to a sleigh. Even so, the grip had reminded her of the men who had found her, and she had gone limp at the touch, utterly drained of the will to fight. Sigrid's honey voice had seeped into her unconscious mind, forbidding her from giving up and giving in.

Now, as they continued onwards, Maike instructed them to use the time to work on their Gaelic. They had a long walk ahead of them, therefore plenty of time to practice and the language wasn't the easiest one.

Anja explained to them that as an act of good faith, the Irish allowed their allies to continue speaking their native Gaelic and accompanying dialects after being absorbed into the Celtic tribe. The result was a lot of variation in accent and vocabulary, which would work in their favor.

"It'll be easier for you guys to blend in and pass off your unpolished Gaelic as a difference in dialect," she told them, the snow crunching lightly under their boots while they walked. Benjáme opened his mouth to speak and she raised an eyebrow. "It's not an excuse to not practice," she continued, sternly. "Simply a comfort to fall back on, if you're feeling nervous."

Ever the instigator, Benjáme pressed on, "I heard the Celts forced the Cornish and Welsh to learn Gaelic and that they aren't allowed to speak their languages anymore. If they get caught speaking their native language, then they brand them as a traitor to the clan." Looking smugly at her he continued, "They aren't as progressive as they'd like you to think," he insisted. It was true, Anja's attitude towards the Celts wasn't as hostile as other Norse Petra had encountered and she wondered why exactly that was. But even Petra wanted to roll her eyes at Benjáme's insolence, talking back to a specialist. She would have chided him, except she had heard the same rhetoric from Sigrid. It seemed uncharacteristically compromising of the Celts to allow people to continue speaking their native languages. But Anja didn't look phased and continued walking.

"That's a common misconception in Mimameid." Her face remained steady and academic as she contradicted him. "Cornish and Welsh are still tolerated and spoken within private homes, but any time you step outside your dwelling, you must speak Gaelic." She didn't look at them as she answered, simply continuing in her matter-of-fact way. Childish as it was, Benjáme stuck his tongue out at her behind her back. Petra stifled a small laugh at the nonsense, but the fact remained that Anja had effectively ended the conversation. She was the expert, after all.

Anja turned back around at the noise, giving the two of them a glare that wasn't so much angry as confused by their antics. She narrowed her eyes and continued walking.

Petra patted her defeated colleague on the back and overtook him on the path with a shrug of her shoulders, using the lighthearted moment to mask her uncertainty with nonchalance. Really, she was wondering why Sigrid wouldn't have told her the truth about the Celts. Did she not know? Maybe Sigrid had misunderstood, or had Anja intentionally not shared all of her information with her superiors, like Petra hadn't?

She looked at the quiet woman walking ahead of her, her stringy, blonde hair sticking out of the bottom of her own woolen cap, and had a hard time reckoning with the fact that she would withhold information that might jeopardize Mimameid. That she was somehow a rebel. But, then the only logical answer remaining was that Sigrid wasn't being honest with Petra about the Celts.

"Another thing to remember about Gaelic is that it's an incredibly descriptive language, very bonded to the natural world," Anja continued, smoothing her hat on her head and looking over at Maike as she spoke. "Their word for wolf literally means 'son of the land' and they describe a choppy sea by saying that "the fishermen's field is under white flowers'."

"Don't they have a funny name for whiskey, too?" Onni's voice was light, familiar with Anja.

"Oh, yeah. They call it the 'water of life'," Anja said and Onni's laugh lifted into the thin, cold air like bells.

"Water of life," she sighed, amused. "What a way to live."

"I think it's deceptive of them, not to say what they really mean," Benjáme countered, and Petra saw that although Maike didn't say anything, her eyebrow arched. She flipped her long braids over her shoulder and cleared her throat as she gave Anja an anticipatory look, wondering how she might respond.

"Well, their language formed, as I said, around a connection to the land. I'd call it more poetic than anything else..." Anja offered in reply, trailing off.

"It says a lot about them as a culture, that they don't speak clearly," Benjáme responded, cutting her short. Petra knew he had a personal grudge against the Celts for what had happened with Taavi, but she wasn't sure she agreed with him. What she found more interesting though, was how Maike was very intentionally remaining uninvolved.

When they had mastered a few simple phrases like '*Dia duit is ainm dom*' and '*Cá bhfuil an leithreas?*, they took a short break from language lessons.

Petra stopped in what could have been the midday sun, atop a ridge of marbled granite looking around at the wild northern countryside, and pulled her dancing hair back into a knot at the base of her neck as she looked around. Ahead of them was a vast, deep blue lake, suspended against the ridge line, bottle-necking into a waterfall that rushed straight over a cliff face of solid rock. It fed into the valley below, plunging into a sweeping river that pushed out into the sea.

Benjáme tapped her on her shoulder.

"Have you ever seen anything like it, Lieutenant?" he huffed, wiping sweat from his forehead, careful around the cut as he did.

"It's so..." she searched the crisp air for the right word, "untouched."

"It doesn't look like the Celts ever came this way," Benjáme agreed.

"They would have stuck to the roads." Onni put a hand on Benjáme's shoulder as she passed them, pausing. "They like to be seen as the dominant force when they are entering a new area, known as a threat. And then once they are settled, that's when they deploy their guerrilla teams to enforce their rule of law." She started the descent towards the lake and Petra felt a chill down her spine at how impersonal Onni's analysis had been. She was starting to feel like she was the only Norse on the mission who really knew a Celt, like really *knew* a Celt. Benjáme, fell into line behind Onni, beckoning Petra onwards.

They followed the others down the rocks towards the waterfall where, as they got closer, Petra could see the remains of a bridge hanging over its rushing waters.

Maike turned to them, adjusting her pack on her back and then leading the way, dexterously advancing across the broken beams and metal foundation, drilled into the bedrock. She hopped gracefully from one foot to the other, sussing out a stable path for them to mimic. Onni pushed ahead of Anja, stepping lithely onto the bridge, a mischievous smirk on her merry cheeks. Anja was more timid as she followed behind them, taking each calculated step with caution. One simple misstep and they would be carried over the rocky edge. It was a fall no one could survive.

Petra stepped up onto the first of the broken beams hesitantly, aware that her uneasiness could jeopardize her crossing. She tried to steady her breath as she took the first step onto the metal frame. She found it easier than she'd expected, to balance, cat-like on the remains of the broken-down crossing.

When she was nearly across, she turned around to invite Benjáme on up, but he had already begun his crossing. Turning back, Petra leaped from the final foothold onto the granite bank, feeling the rock she'd leaped from shift under the pressure of her foot. She unclipped her pack and shimmied it off onto the bank so as to reach back and help Benjáme with the now-treacherous last step.

Just as she felt his hand in hers, the rock slipped out from under Benjáme's boot and the water caught him in its current. Petra held firm, her eyes locked on his deep-set, brown ones, panic darkening them like a puff of smoke.

"Help!" she called out hoarsely. Her feet began to slide on the smooth surface of the rock. Before the word had fully left her mouth, she felt two strong arms wrap around her waist, locking together. Blood pumped in her ears as she steadied her feet and reached for Benjáme with her other hand, heaving him up.

A blonde head of hair burst over Petra's right shoulder, grabbing onto Benjáme's other hand and heaving until the two of them could reach around Benjáme's waist and drag him up to safety.

They collapsed on top of one another, gasping for air. Benjáme was soaked and pale, the blood drained from his cheeks. Petra looked up to see the blonde head had been Anja, her pale blue eyes shining beneath her damped brow. She tucked the wet strands of hair behind her ears and squashed her hat down - which had fallen off as she'd leaped towards them - back onto her head. Petra nodded a breathless thanks and pushed herself up to sitting. Behind her, Maike's voice rang out, and Petra realized it had been the Captain who had held her steady.

"Everyone alright?" Nodding as she stood up, Petra observed the way Maike moved. Even if she had only rescued them because she needed them to get into the Celtic camp, the act cast doubt on Benjáme's theory that they had only been sent on the mission as cannon fodder. To make their deaths look like an accident. Hadn't that been the perfect opportunity to get rid of them both? Maike certainly looked like a soldier who would follow orders without question, so why had she saved them? Her face was angular and severe, but there was a flicker of vulnerability in her bright eyes that hadn't been there before. Maike tossed her Valkyrie-braids over her shoulder and offered a hand to Benjáme, who was still on his hands and knees, trying to catch his breath.

"Thank you, Captain," Benjáme panted as she helped him up. Perhaps there was more to Maike than Petra had thought.

"No one is going over the edge on my watch," the Captain replied, and Petra could see something soften in her expression as she said it.

Onni, who had been scrambling around, picking up people's packs, helped Petra get back into hers.

She smiled warmly at her before turning to help Benjáme with his pack.

"That's a nice knife." She heard the small woman say, pointing down at the reindeer antler knife. The one she knew Benjáme had gotten from his husband.

"Thanks," Benjáme replied and Petra heard the conflict in his voice, warming to Onni, even though he didn't trust the mission. But, here was someone from home.

Petra herself hadn't grown up among the Sámi people. She had learned the language and traditions from her father, but she hadn't known many others like herself. Certainly no other murky, mixed-bloods like her. When Benjáme had discovered that she was also Sámi, he'd been overjoyed.

There were a few Sámi living in Mimameid, but none in such a high-ranking position as Petra. None with such influence and certainly none with such a personal relationship with Sigrid. He had been sure that she could somehow use that position to help make things better for the Sámi peoples in Mimameid, who were so often looked down upon by the others and taken advantage of, even more so than the refugee Danes and the outcast Finns.

But, Benjáme had been wrong about her. After all, here was another Sámi, hidden in plain sight among the upper ranks.

After they were well past the cliffside waterfall, Maike opened up the conversation to some strategy planning. Petra found herself grateful to be back on a topic she was more familiar with.

"The Celts have become masters of guerrilla tactics," Maike told them. "Now, we know they deployed and developed these tactics against each other for generations. They became particularly notorious for their use of car bombs. Particularly driving them into crowds and letting the casualties cause chaos for cover. But, because they use them so frequently, they also know how to protect against them. Even when they are traveling to a new campsite location, they split up into units and travel undetected through the villages, using hit-and-run to gather any supplies they need to restock on."

Somewhere in the distance, Petra could hear the waves crashing against the coastline. They were closer to the water than she'd realized and she hoped the sound would conceal them. Instinctively, she looked around, checking to see if they were being followed, while Maike continued,

"Car bombs aren't the only thing they were infamous for. They are also masters of infiltration." She seemed to be in her element as she walked and talked - hands gesticulating to illustrate her words with animated fervor, "Beyond the standard scorched earth method of destroying any viable resources left behind, they will often use an infiltrated member posing as a stray Norseman to go in and plant bombs in an otherwise peaceful Norse village so as to strip them of any valuable supplies. I'd like to use this tactic against them and get into their camp by imitating -"

She stopped mid-sentence and Petra lifted her eyes from the pebbled path to see Maike had come to a complete stop up ahead. She hurried up to join her, and when they were shoulder to shoulder she followed Maike's gaze to the horizon.

Lying before them, across a flat, rocky beach freshly carved out by the receding ice, was a metal submarine. And though it looked rusted enough to be from The Time Before, when Petra squinted, she could make out the faded World Tree of Mimameid painted on the hull.

She had heard of these ships.

Mimameid had used them even before Ragnarök. They had taken anyone willing into the bunker, transporting people by the hundreds on submarines that departed from all major Scandinavian ports and delivered them right to Mimameid's Back Door. The service entrance, Sigrid had told her.

Petra herself had never seen one of the ships, only the four six-seater pods they used to ferry supplies down, like what Lasse had been brought home in.

No, she was found by Mimameid after the time of these massive subs, but, a few years back, Sigrid had wanted them to recover the subs as part of an emergency evacuation plan. That's when Petra had learned of their existence and that they'd been washed away by the tremors and eruptions of Ragnarök. Whether or not they were even still intact had been a controversial question during the recovery project, Petra recalled. A lot of time and resources had been dumped into it before the project was determined no longer a priority.

And yet, here one was, on a beach that hadn't even existed five years ago.

Maike caught her breath again, squeezing Petra's shoulder excitedly before leading the way down the hillside toward the beach. They followed after her, scrambling over boulders and skidding on the smaller pebbles as they descended. The waves bellowed against the rocky shore and sent brackish spray up into the air.

Petra pulled her glove from her hand and gently raised a hand to the rusted iron, her fingers running along the flaky, salted surface. It looked to her like a beached whale, long-dead and grey skin curling back against the white bones, sticking out starkly from the dark shores of the rocky beach. The ship creaked in the powerful winds that howled across the expansive beach, wild and unopposed.

"Is this what I think it is?" Benjáme asked the question that Petra could see was on everyone's mind. "I thought, I mean - I came in on one of these. How did it end up out here?" he continued, confused. Maike scanned the wreck, shaking her head, at a loss. Her hand stopped, hovering above where the faded World Tree was painted on the side of the ship.

"I have no idea," she confessed. This wasn't actually her area of expertise, Petra realized. Maike was an expert on Celts, but not on Mimameid.

"It's one of what were three ships." Petra stepped in, her palms pressed against the metal, reverently. "The three roots of our World Tree." She barely breathed as she remember how Sigrid had explained it to her. "They brought life to Mimameid: the things they needed to build her, the plants they needed to sustain her, and then the people. They named the ships for the roots because they connect the worlds to the Tree, just as the ships connected The Time Before to Mimameid."

"There's a name on the side!" Benjáme shouted out to her from further down the bow of the ship. Petra walked towards him. "It starts with an N, but I can't read the end of it."

"*Niflheim*," Petra said, offering her hand to help him up. "The smallest of the ships that were built, but also the most advanced." She looked up at the wreckage sadly, thinking of the technology inside they could have reclaimed, probably now beyond repair from exposure to the salt and wind. What a waste.

"There's something else over here!" Onni waved for them to join her. Petra picked her way across the rocks, running her fingertips along the edge of the ship until she reach Onni.

She clambered up the side and looked over at the other side, where Onni was pointing. The great, round belly of the ship was white with salt, but at the base, where it would have sat in the water, was a scorched, black spot. Petra leaned forward, squinting at the large pile of charred wood. Something jumped inside of her, was it more survivors - or more Celts?

Warily, she made her way over to the remains of the fire. Up close, it was enormous - it looked like it had been a bonfire of some sort. *Maybe a ritual*, Petra thought. But the charcoal had a fine layer of snow over it that looked like had melted and refroze a couple of times. Whomever it was that had been here, was long gone.

"Celts?" Onni shouted down at her. Petra bent and picked up a piece of the charcoal, turning it over in her hands. She looked up at the others and nodded.

"Looks like it. But it's old, they haven't been here recently." She turned to toss the charcoal back in the pile when a drawing on a panel of the ship caught her eye, etched across the grey wall in thick strokes of charcoal. It was on the far side, so the team couldn't see it from their vantage point, but the twists and twirls of the love knot were familiar to Petra. Instead of throwing the piece of burnt wood back into the pile, she slipped it into her pocket and returned to the others in silence.

They continued along the length of the beach, littered with more piles of black and burnt wood scattered among the rocks. The Celts were not small in number, that much they knew, but Petra was still surprised at how many fire pits were there.

She watched Benjáme talking with Onni as they made their way through the maze of Celtic fire pits. She couldn't hear what they were saying, but he moved differently with her than the others, as though she was a family member. It set off a small twang in her chest. Maybe Benjáme wasn't comfortable with her like that because she wasn't Sámi enough. Maybe because she was his direct superior officer. Either way, seeing them chattering together like old friends ushered in a coldness in her that she hadn't expected.

After walking the length of the beach, they found a cave to tuck into for the night. It was protected from the biting northern cold and Petra slipped wordlessly asleep after such an exhausting day.

In the morning, her leg still ached, but she found it easier to ignore the pain. Whether because she was getting used to it or because it was healing, she couldn't say.

Following the trail they had picked up from the Celts on the rocky beach, they continued north along the coast, using the cracked and broken road for vague orientation.

A burnt, orange sun worked hard to break through the ashen sky over the mountaintops, punching a spotty, golden light back across the wilderness.

In the distance, they could see ice-kissed buildings being illuminated by the sunlight. Their shingled rooftops still visible under a gleaming layer of snow. It wasn't an unusual sight, an abandoned village, but Petra still found it sobering all the same.

As they approached it, it became apparent, just how dilapidated the buildings really were. Red paint peeled from the wooden frames of the houses. Broken windows whistled and doors hanging by a single hinge creaked in the wind. Those were certainly the signs of a house that had been raided, stripped for parts. But it looked like the buildings had been cleaned out long before the Celts were here. The village, after all, hadn't been burned. The shabby wooden frames looked so forgotten and run down, even the Celts didn't see any use for them. Not even firewood.

Onni walked up to one of the houses and put out a hand to the paint, which crumbled to dust the moment her fingers touched it.

"It never gets easier, does it? Seeing these places from our old world," she said, wistfully.

"It's good that Mimameid doesn't allow too many people Above Ground," Maike replied, her voice bitter with sadness from some festering loss. "Better for morale if people can be allowed to forget and move on."

"But *we* can't," Benjáme muttered under his breath, anger laced in it.

"That is the cross that every Mimameid soldier must bear," Maike said coarsely. The sadness was masked now by the resounding authority her position demanded.

The cracking of the icy road under their feet was all they could hear as they walked on in silence, passing a long-empty grocery store where the sign swung crooked, back and forth in the wind. An old motel sign had been smashed in and robbed of its lightbulbs.

More flat, white hills against a grey sky awaited them on the other end of the small village. The further north they went, the more Petra felt an aching in her heart. A tug like the first drop of water from an icicle in the sunlight. At first, she had thought maybe it had something to do with seeing Arthur, but the more they walked, the more she realized, it had nothing at all to do with him.

What she felt was the pull of home.

And it felt so raw, like the landscape of the North Country being pulled free from the receding ice. The frozen layers that protected her heart were melting away. The wild North was calling to her.

The pine trees that scattered the hills here were older, they hadn't been destroyed by the initial darkness of Ragnarök. The snow glistened atop their needles, even in the dim light. Petra inhaled, trying to imagine that sweet scent of pine atop a roaring fire.

As the dark sunlight began to wane, Petra spotted something rising over a ridge dappled with ribbons of snow before them. It had been impossible to see against the grey backdrop of clouds during the day, but the smoky plume grew paler as the sky darkened, the sparks from some great, distant fire dancing up ahead. She raised her hand.

"Onni," She tapped her on the shoulder and pointed, "is that what I think it is?" One look at the woman's dark face told her all she needed to know.

They had found the Celts.

It took several more hours for them to summit the ridge, but when they had, Maike gave them the all-clear, and she and Benjáme tossed their packs aside. They bent low to the ground and moved across the ridge like shadows towards the camp.

The two of them crept along to an outcropping of rock above the valley where the Celts had made their temporary home. Snow glazed a steep cliffside that curved gracefully down the wooded mountainside. Equal parts protective for the Celts and treacherous to any invaders, Petra could understand the appeal of this particular valley to them.

From the distance, Petra could make out the dark outlines of transport trucks, circled around their campsite-village, forming a protective wall around the great bonfire in the middle. Other, smaller vehicles were parked like the rings of a tree within the confines of the makeshift camp. The innermost circles of the bonfire were rows of tents, sagging under the weight of the snow.

Eyes scanning the flickering flow of movement among the people, Petra gauged any possible access points. There were guards posted at every break between the transports, torches of Celtic fire jammed into the snow illuminating the perimeter. If they could stay in the shadows, they might be able to enter by crawling under one of the trucks. She had a pretty good idea who would be sent in first.

Her eyes were drawn back to the blazing fire in the middle of the camp. People were gathered around it, even with the temperature plummeting into night. A light melody floated up into the air with the smoke. Petra had to concentrate to hear it, but the faint whistle of a song was there. Softer and more tender than she had expected, there was something sorrowful about it. Certainly not a cry to battle.

Her heart skipped a beat as a blonde head bobbed out of one of the bigger tents near the bonfire. She squinted in the darkness, trying to make out the face. It seemed familiar enough to be Arthur's, but she wasn't convinced. The movements were too stiff.

As though the gods knew she was watching, a second blonde head exited the tent, donned in a surgical bib smeared bright with blood. He had a bag hung over his shoulder that she would know anywhere. In an instant, her heartbeat rose into her ears. She grew hot and quickly tore her gaze away from him. Benjáme reached out to her at the sudden movement.

"You okay?" he whispered and she nodded, voice caught in her throat. "How many do you think are down there?" He jerked his head down to the camp. Petra quickly numbered up the vehicles, calculating in her head. It was strange.

"A thousand, maybe?" She watched Benjáme count silently, too. "Enough for one of us to blend in maybe, but not nearly what I was expecting," she continued while Benjáme lifted his hand, pointing beyond the valley at something. Petra followed his finger across the next ridge of mountains to where four more pillars of smoke were lifting into the sky.

"What about those?"

9
LYSANDER

"I'M SORRY THAT I didn't say something sooner." Magdelena's green eyes clouded as she spoke. He nodded at her, a sad smile on his face, in the warm light of his bunk.

"I wish you had, Mag. If only to avoid the trouble of getting," he gestured down to his band, "these things. But I understand." His voice was gentle and sincere. "Listen, I made a promise -"

She raised her hand and cut him off.

"You have more than fulfilled your promise, Lysander." Her voice was heavy and tender as she spoke his full name.

"I'll never be able to pay back what you did for me in Lillehammer," he told her, dejected. "Seeing Judit's face-" He stopped himself before he conjured up the image of her cold body in the morgue tent.

"Look at me, L," she said, "You can actually make a difference here." He sniffed and nodded and she continued. "You know I'm right." She took his chin in her hand and lifted it to look into his eyes, sternly. "You have taken good care of us. You have fulfilled your promise."

His stomach twisted, aching at losing them. Understanding why they needed to go, yet still wishing Magdelena was wrong.

It felt like losing his parents and sister all over again. "You have to stay, L. You have to help these people."

Resigned, he nodded, lowering his head again as he did. Magdelena pulled him into an embrace and he clung to her.

"When will you all leave?"

"Early in the morning."

"And Linnaea?"

"It's what she wants. To keep looking for her father."

"Good. Then you're doing the right thing," he replied while Magdelena nodded solemnly. Lysander's band beeped gently, interrupting the moment. He glanced down at the feed and saw a massive, broad figure nervously bouncing in front of the door. Curiously, He opened it with a touch of his band, and the airlock released.

Looking sweaty and disoriented in a hospital gown, Lasse stumbled over the threshold into Lysander's bunk. His feet were bare and his cheeks were flushed. His topknot sagged to one side and his beard was matted and unkempt. Magdelena jumped to her feet, alarmed at his haggard appearance.

"I heard you were leaving," Lasse panted at the two of them, looking back and forth between as he caught his breath. Magdelena nodded, attempting to guide him to her chair. He tried to lumber over, but his huge limbs wouldn't obey and instead, he sank to the floor, clutching at his side where he had been wounded.

"Are you okay? Let me have a look at you," Magdelena insisted, but Lasse shook his head and swatted her hand away from him, startling them both.

"No time for that. Listen, I came to warn you." He reached up with a large hand and wiped the sweat from his disheveled hair.

"Warn us? What for?" Magdelena crouched beside him, trying to look into his eyes. Lasse tapped his band, but no words came out as he tried to breathe deeply.

"The bands?" Lysander asked and Lasse nodded, coughing, ferociously. "What about them?" Lasse just tapped his wrist again insistently and Lysander looked at Magdelena for help. She shrugged as Lasse dissolved into a coughing fit. Magdelena held onto him, rubbing his back to help warm the bronchial muscles until he got his breathing under control. Still wheezing, he managed a couple of steadying breaths.

"Whatever you do, don't take off the bands." Lysander and Magdelena exchanged a startled look. "No matter how far away you are, no matter how safe you think you might be. Don't take them off!"

"What?" Magdelena was confused, but Lysander had a sinking feeling he might know what Lasse was talking about. He gulped.

"They're coming for me-" Lasse gasped and almost immediately, Lysander's door gushed back open, unprompted. Two nurses - one male and one female - entered the room along with a rather sanitized-looking doctor. They raised their hands politely to their brows and murmured, "In the boughs of Mimir's tree," respectfully before encircling Lasse, who Lysander now realized by the gown, must have escaped from The Infirmary to get to them. When they wrapped their arms around the viking-warrior, he protested, thrashing dangerously in the tight room.

"No! No!" Lasse shouted.

"It's alright, we are going to get you back to the ward now." It was the dark-eyed female nurse from when they got their bands that spoke to him, her voice ringing with a practiced patience as she injected a clear liquid into his shoulder. "Just relax." The medicine did its work and he went limp, eyes rolling back and his legs buckling. The burly male nurse and the doctor caught him as he fell, hoisting his arms over their shoulders and supporting his massive weight as they dragged him out into the hallway. The dark-eyed nurse turned to them and spoke with the same levelness in her voice as she had used on Lasse while her colleagues loaded him onto a gurney.

"I'm so sorry about that," she said apologetically, reaching a friendly hand out to Lysander's arm. His concern for Lasse overwhelmed any calm she was trying to exude and he tried to brush her away. But the woman was stronger than she appeared and remained rooted to the spot. "Lasse slipped out when we weren't there, poor man. He's been feverish and delirious since he was admitted and something must have just come over him today." The burley nurse pulled a strap tight over Lasse's unconscious body. "But, don't you worry. He'll be right as rain in no time." She turned on her heel.

Unable to ignore the laughable metaphor, since it never rained down here in Mimameid, Lysander and Magdelena exchanged a look. Magdelena's eyes were wary, warning him not to attempt anything. The others had already begun wheeling him away as the dark-eyed nurse fell into step behind the squeaky gurney.

When the medical team had turned the corner, they retreated into Lysander's room and the door hissed closed. Magdelena sank back down into her chair, but Lysander stood in silence, trying to work out what exactly had just happened. Hadn't they seen Lasse only two days ago in The Infirmary and he'd been completely fine? He felt his brow furrow and his hands running through his hair, furiously.

"One last dinner together tonight?" Magdelena stood up again, rearranging her elfin features so it looked as if nothing out of the ordinary had happened. It was unsettling and he stopped running his hands through his hair to recoil from her. It was intentional and practiced, as the nurse had been. He didn't understand. Magdelena used her band to open his door and step out into the hallway.

"Why would he risk coming here if it wasn't important?" Lysander urged, stepping forward to follow her into the hallway.

"Shh," she hushed him, her mossy eyes flashed while the rest of her face remained placid. Lysander tightened his lips. "Later," she promised, jerking her head up to the camera above his door frame, pointed down at where they were standing. It was angled to see Magdelena's face. Was someone watching them? He looked across the hall to see if there was one angled towards him and sure enough, there was one camera in each direction, both equidistant from his door and diagonally positioned so they could face either him or his coinciding neighbor. He hadn't noticed them before, but now it made his throat tighten.

"Dinner, 1800h?" he asked and she smiled sweetly, both of them aware that the time itself was essentially a construct down here, beneath the water. Nonetheless, it felt normal to say it like that, so they carried on pretending.

"We'll see you then, L."

He slunk down to The Engine Room once Magdelena was gone in hopes of appearing normal to those who were monitoring the other end of that camera. He was certain his armband data, his increased heart rate at the very least, would have given them away anyhow. Hastily, to throw them off the scent, he had messaged Bjørn with a new idea on how to fix the auxiliary air filtration system and asked if he wanted to try it out. He figured it was also a good way to pass the time before he and Magdelena would be able to talk again at dinner. He'd been meaning to bring the cable rippers he'd snagged Above Ground down to The Engine Room anyways to add to their supplies.

As he descended into the hissing and cranking of The Engine Room, his worries evaporated into the air with the exhaust. Bjørn was already in the filtration room; his quarters were in D with his family, so he had a much quicker commute down than Lysander up in B.

"How's it going so far?" Lysander asked through a cloud of steam, the door to the room closing behind him.

"Oh, hey there!" he called out, enthusiastically. "I just thought I'd get a head start on exposing the switchboard for you." Bjørn's face was bright with sweat and his thick-rimmed glasses were balanced on the bridge of his nose. He scooted over to make room for Lysander, the screws balanced between his teeth.

When Lysander looked in, he could see from the frayed wiring that they had tried to repair it themselves more than once. He was glad he'd brought the cable rippers.

It took Lysander more than a few minutes to find the problem as the sensor that measured the quality of the air had been compromised. Therefore,

Lysander needed to completely reprogram the system to bypass the sensor and operate it manually instead.

Bjørn retrieved a dusty, old computer for him and Lysander began the long process of reprogramming while Bjørn talked through the different steps of what he was doing, just in case he ever needed to do it again in the future and without Lysander.

They worked together for a couple of hours, moving their way gradually through the problem. Bjørn carried on about all the different problems they had encountered since his arrival at Mimameid four years prior.

There had been another engineer there at that time, the guy who had shown Bjørn the ropes around The Engine Room, but he had gone missing shortly after Bjørn and his family arrived, leaving him on his own to discover the quirks and problems of The Engine Room and her reactor.

With an air of ease and merriment, Bjørn flowed right from one story to another. Before he knew it Bjørn was telling Lysander about his family.

Bjørn and his wife, Runa, were childhood sweethearts who had grown up on adjacent farms in northern Scandinavia. They moved south to the city when he wanted to study engineering. But after a few years of constant flooding, evacuations, food shortages, and noise, they missed the wilderness they had grown up in, so when Runa got pregnant they decided to return to the north.

"We built the Fylke - our homestead - with our own hands. Runa about as round as you can get and me working as fast as I could to get the place up before winter set in. Our baby girl was born on the living room floor the morning of the first snowfall." He took off his glasses and tried to clean a smudge with the edge of his jumpsuit. "We had chickens and goats and sheep, and in the springs and summers, Runa would strap her on her back and go foraging in the forest." He put his glasses on and reached back into the switchboard to expose the wires they would be re-enforcing next.

"Runa has this way with people - she always has. She's like the All-Mother incarnate. You never met someone who cares so much about every living creature - plant or animal," Bjørn explained. "It's one of the things that set her apart from the others, even when we were kids. You know, new species were dying every year, and for most of us that was just expected. But for Runa, it was a calling. She'd be out there literally bringing goat milk to orphaned baby bunnies or building shelter for injured bugs from twigs and leaves. In the end, her family was hiding people who were being deported. People born here for generations, but they had the wrong skin color or the wrong religion." The older man sighed, heavily. "Anyway." He kept working as he spoke, but his jaw tightened. "That's what made it so much harder on Runa when our girl died." Lysander stopped what he was doing.

"She would have been three." Bjørn was still for a second, but his hands were still deep inside the machine they were fixing. "She fell from a ladder in the barn," he said, picking back up with the wires, "and after that, Runa changed. She wasn't this carefree, hopeful person she had been. She-" he tried to explain as he yanked on a stubborn cable, "she- it was like she got lost inside herself." His shoulders slumped. "Those were the hardest years." He conceded and leaned back against the wall.

"How did you get through it?" Lysander barely knew how to ask the question. He knew loss, but not like that. Bjørn pushed the hair that had shaken loose behind his ears.

"Well, a few years later, Runa said she wanted to expand the Fylke," he continued, resting his arms on his knees. "See, she had grown up on a dairy farm, watching her mother call the cows in from the field and she wanted to have cows again. After that, Runa came back to life. She knew all the cows by name and she would sing them back home every night."

Her voice is like-" he thought about it for a second, "she has a voice like water droplets on glass, like the sound of fresh dew on leaves in the morning." Lysander tried to imagine what dew sounded like, but it honestly made no sense to him.

"There are many things about Mimameid that are good, the one thing that makes me sad is that there is no wilderness for Runa to sing in." Bjørn's voice, usually so cheerful, bore a hint of melancholy. But it was only temporary.

"Shortly after we got the cows, Runa bore another daughter, and then another." The older man smiled and he told Lysander about them. His two daughters, Åsa and Tuva, were now near Linnaea's age. What would have been Judit's age.

"Åsa has her mother's voice and the two of them singing together, it's like the magic of the old sagas. I half expect fairies to come springing out of these old metal walls. But Tuva, she takes after me. She's interested in how things are put together, a little engineer in the making. She'll be here in The Engine Room getting her elbows dirty in no time." His eyes shone a blue as clear as a fjord in spring as he spoke about his family. Lysander could feel the pang of longing for that feeling of family.

"You should come and meet them!" Bjørn exclaimed, suddenly hit with the idea. "Perhaps we can all get dinner tonight? I could send in a request so you can eat with us in D? They will love to hear from someone from Above Ground. You know, to hear what it is like up there now." Lysander almost accepted when the words died on his tongue. He felt his heart sink. He wanted so badly to accept Bjørn's offer, to be a part of the family Bjørn had described, but he had unfinished business that needed attending to.

"There's something I have to do tonight. But, another time, I would love nothing more." Bjørn's eyes still glistened, not even momentarily put off by Lysander's rejection.

"Another time, then. I look forward to it." Bjørn smiled, looking back at the computer screen in front of Lysander. The code Lysander had written was doing its job and a window popped up indicating that the sensor had been successfully bypassed. Lysander handed Bjørn the laptop.

"Want to reboot the system to see if it worked?" he asked.

"It's your work, you go for it," Bjørn replied graciously. Lysander hit the button, rebooting the system. All the lights shut off and the fans stopped whirring for a split second. Lysander felt his stomach jump to his throat, thinking maybe he had broken both air systems now, but then the lights kicked back on and the fans began to speed back up.

Bjørn threw his head back and let out a deep roar of success. Lysander sighed, putting his hand on the air filter. *Good girl*, he thought and he felt the warmth in his chest at being able to fix something again.

※※※※※

Almost as soon as the doors opened to B, Linnaea's body slammed into his. She wrapped her arms around his middle and Lysander melted down to squeeze her tight. He stood back up and she put her arm around the small of his back as they walked to the concrete table where Magdelena was sitting. She rose as they arrived and reached around into a hug that Lysander sighed into. She was the person in all the world who knew him the best; she had gotten to know the him that remained after the world had fallen. Now he was losing her. He sniffed back his sadness, trying to keep the mood light for their dinner. Magdelena pulled back from the hug.

"Shall we get something to eat, then, Sprout?" They retrieved their dinner packs together from the automats using their bands. Lysander already felt himself growing accustomed to the regularity of meals. The food was warm and filling and it was easy to feel at home with a full belly.

As he bit into a steaming piece of honey-glazed salmon, Magdelena asked him casually about the rest of his day. Happy for the distraction from the fact that they were leaving, he detailed the day he'd spent fixing the air filtration system, but the longer he went on about it, the harder it was to stay enthusiastic and light-hearted when really, he was anxious to talk about what Lasse had meant earlier.

"Runa? Well, we met Runa." Magdelena spelled out the name when he started talking about Bjørn and his family.

"Yeah?"

"Yeah, remember? She works in The Gardens. I talked to her a little when I was doing my work assignment there, too." She lowered her hands slightly and looked around as if she was trying to avoid a hidden camera. "She was quiet, but patient with me learning the new systems," Magdelena paused, fidgeting with her fork for a moment, uneasily, as if she was trying to decide how much information to give him, before continuing, "Oh, and her daughters were friendly with Linnaea in the school, especially the younger one."

Lysander was curious what she had chosen not to say. It wasn't like her to be secretive, but maybe this was one of the ways she was pulling herself away, making it easier for her to leave.

"Yeah, they were the ones who practiced their sign language with me," Linnaea told Lysander, pulling him away from his suspicions. Magdelena took a sip of her ginger-green tea and Lysander watched her, graceful, but cautious. He had opted to try the Mimameid beer tonight, one of the three he was allotted per week. and he mirrored her, taking a sip of the dark, creamy liquid. They both set down their glasses and Magdelena continued, "Anyway, Runa's worth getting to know, L." She paused again and this time her eyes twinkled, knowingly. "She seems like the kind of person who sees things others don't."

"Huh. Good to know. I guess Bjørn's a useful person to know in more than one way." Lysander scooted forwards in his chair, the dull roar of people chattering growing louder around them. "But, enough of that." He couldn't wait any longer and he hoped the commotion would distract whomever Magdelena thought was watching them. "Should we be worried about Lasse?" His fingers were tense, and he didn't want to alarm Linnaea. She hadn't been there, she hadn't seen what they had seen.

Magdelena's eye twitched as she saw something over his shoulders. She wrapped the table with her knuckles while she considered something. Angling her body to obstruct anyone else's view, including the camera's, from seeing her hands in full, she covertly signed to him and Linnaea.

"He seemed completely fine when we saw him in The Infirmary a few days ago, right?"

"Right? I thought so," Lysander signed back.

"Definitely not feverish or delirious." Magdelena's eyes were shifting around as she signed, watching the people of B suspiciously.

"Why would Lasse risk coming to find us if what he was saying was just the ravings of a fever dream anyways?" Lysander also looked around as he signed his response.

It was the peak of dinner time, so most of the people who bunked around them in B were there. It was clearly a different class of people than down in C; maybe more educated, and definitely had more money in The Time Before.

Linnaea picked up her fork, moving a potato around in some mushroom sauce before shoveling it into her cheek. Magdelena smiled and took a bite of her food as well. Lysander let his eyes wander while his question hung in the air, unanswered. The only thing they knew for sure was what Lasse had been willing to risk for them Above Ground.

There seemed to be more food automats up here - or maybe fewer people, he couldn't decide - because the lines moved quickly and were shorter than in C. There wasn't any fighting in lines, or people slamming other people's faces into tables. There were also no whispers of Sámi or Danish or Icelandic floating among the people, fewer tattoos, and no warrior-braids. The languages lilting through the air were mostly Swedish and Norwegian, and they all seemed somehow softer, their movements and words deliberate and precise.

"Look," Magdelena signed, her face grave as she put down her fork to continue. "You have to be careful. They need you here, but they need you *alive*. And that's your advantage. No one wants to see you become a martyr, L." She tilted her head again to where, out of the corner of his eyes, Lysander saw decorative hanging plants. If he looked close enough, he could see the dark lens Magdelena was referring to, hidden between the foliage. Linnaea raised her hands.

"And I want to see you again when I get back here with my father!" she interjected and Lysander nodded, reaching his pinky across the table to pinky swear with hers. She lifted the hand that was wearing the band on for the swear, closing her pinky finger around his.

"How did you know about the cameras?" Lysander signed and Magdelena's face lifted a little.

"You want to tell him, Sprout?" she signed to Linnaea. The girl smiled.

"I could feel the intermittent vibrations in the walls every time they moved. I couldn't figure out where it was coming from at first, but once we knew, we realized how many of them there actually are everywhere. How much they are actually watching us."

"But why? To what end?" Lysander leaned in as he signed and both of the girls shrugged.

"No idea," Magdelena signed.

"What are you going to do about the bands?" Lysander asked them, and Magdelena looked across at Linnaea, reluctantly.

"You inspected the implant, right? Is there any reason we should be concerned?" As the words left her lips, Lysander thought about the capsules he hadn't been able to identify on the implant, with the small valve between them. But he didn't want to worry her. "I don't think so, but there are these capsules inside…" His voice trailed off. "I'm so sorry I didn't ask more questions, didn't think about it sooner." He pinched the bridge of his nose, frustrated.

"We won't take them off then, that simple," Linnaea signed and Magdelena nodded. "We don't know what will happen if we do, so we just won't take the risk. Besides, they can't track us once we get far enough away from the bunker anyways. All they'll know is we're going north."

"And that way, when we come back, you'll be able to see us coming." She smiled as she tapped her band. Lysander reached out across the table, wanting to hug her again for her optimism, despite everything that had happened to her in her short life.

"I'll come pick you up myself," he promised her with a wink.

"You'll hold down the fort for us here?" Magdelena asked him, "Learn as much as you can about this place?" Lysander nodded, still wishing they weren't leaving.

"I'll wait for you all here."

They bussed their dishes from dinner and Lysander walked them back to their bunk quietly. The halls were illuminated in a fainter, evening glow. Although he imagined it was supposed to be soothing, to him it just felt darker, more like a cave. At the door, Magdelena turned back to him.

"If you need help, go to Ned. He's an old drunk, but you can trust him," she signed earnestly. Again, Lysander nodded, choking on the goodbye that was stuck in his throat. Lysander felt a small bout of jealousy flare up inside him.

"Are you seeing him too before you leave?"

"No, no. He'd never say it, but I remind him too much of The Time Before." Her face fell a little and Lysander suddenly felt guilty for the bout of jealousy. He knew she was only searching for some feeling of familiarity, the same as he was.

Linnaea reached out and hugged him.

"I'll miss you, L," she signed when they had pulled back.

"I'll miss you, too, Mag," he signed in response, looking at how her eyes mirrored his own reluctance to let them go. "Take care of your mom, Sprout." Linnaea nodded and they looked together at Magdelena, her mossy eyes had darkened. "Oh! And," he reached around his neck and pulled off Judit's lögr charm, "for safe travels on the sea," he signed and Linnaea reached out to hug him one more time, this time tighter than before. He held her tight, trying not to think of the last time he said goodbye to his sister. When they released, he looked back to Magdelena.

"You have helped us more than you know," she signed to him before pressing her forehead gently to his. He closed his eyes. He could feel her wanting to stay with him too, to stay with what felt secure and safe.

"He's out there, waiting for you both," Lysander whispered to her, giving her the push she needed. "You have to find him." He felt her nodding. And though a silent tear had slipped down her cheek, when he opened his eyes again, she was smiling at him.

10
PETRA

Petra sat down on an outcropping of granite rock and let Benjáme brief them while she hung back in silence. Onni's face fell at Benjáme's explanation.

The image of Arthur's blonde head down in the camp was seared in her mind. Like the way his fingertips had burned white-hot on her cheek in the hut. Like the feeling of the knot in the palm of her hand. It was like a warmth rising in her from a singular pointed brand. When Benjáme had finished, Maike turned to Petra.

"And you can confirm all this?" She was direct. Despite the abruptness of the situation now, Petra felt surprisingly calm. She nodded once in response. All their intel, all they had discussed, and yet they hadn't been prepared for this, for separate camps. She could see it in Maike's searching eyes as they followed the ribbons of snow over the ridge and down, deep into the valley below.

"We should send someone in under the cover of darkness. We don't have any time to waste," Benjáme interjected.

"If there are several camps, maybe we should consider sending someone into each of the camps to get more complete information?" Anja suggested, crouched and dragging the end of a stick absentmindedly through the snow as she spoke. Maike held up her hand, her eyes tracing the footprints in the snow back to Petra, still perched on the rock.

"We must assume that the camps communicate with one another and we can give them no cause for suspicion. We send one person to one camp. It will be enough to get our footing and even if it delays the mission, we have a greater chance of success." Her brow furrowed and she set her jaw, "Benjáme and Onni, you two head over the next ridge and scout out the other camps so we can assess which is the most viable. Anja, go keep watch on this camp, for now. I will come to relieve you in a bit." Although it looked like Benjáme wanted to continue discussing, Onni tapped him on the shoulder and he nodded reluctantly. They turned and headed out into the falling darkness. Anja stood, smoothed her cap down on her head, and inclined her head to the Captain.

Maike straightened herself up as her men left for their posts - to her full, towering height - as tall as the mythical warrior-maiden Lagertha. Within three long strides, she was beside Petra.

"Lieutenant, are you ready?" Petra felt herself instinctively sitting up straighter, mirroring Maike's confidence. It felt odd. She seemed to have spent their entire journey orbiting the Captain, but had never stood side by side with her. It made her feel small somehow and insufficient at first, but when she made eye contact with the woman's determined face, she swelled with courage.

"I am, sir."

"Your Celt. He is down there, yes?" Petra felt her face flush, caught off guard by her directness.

"I believe so, yes, sir."

"Believe so, or know so?" she asked her, pouring over Petra's expression. She looked off into the valley, the direction of the flickering lights. Her stomach twisted.

"I know so."

"Good," Maike replied. They were silent for a minute, the only sounds were the whipping wind and the crackling of the old trees in the cold. Maike walked back towards the camp and sat down. Obediently, Petra followed her. She dragged her pack behind her and started rifling through it, sorting out what she'd need down below and what would stay with her team. She hoped the task would distract her from the conflicting feelings rising up in her. "We will wait to see what the others say when they return as to which camp seems to be the headquarters, but I think I already see the answer in your eyes," Maike continued, her eyes shifting as she tried to read Petra's face.

Her gun and ammunition went into the pile that would stay here, while her knife she could hide on her person more discreetly. The Captain continued, "We will only have one shot at this. We need to know what they know. We need to know what their next move will be." Petra bit her lip but continued sorting. The lock pick set and binoculars came with her, but the first aid kit stayed - that's what Arthur was for. Petra's heart skipped as she felt her hand move involuntarily to the brand on her leg. "There is no room for hesitation," Maike said.

Embarrassed that her body had betrayed her thoughts, Petra dropped her head and kept sorting; extra socks and base layers got rolled up small, but her mat and sleeping bag stayed behind. Her camping stove stayed, but some old protein bars, seaweed, and dried fish came with her, tucked into her inner jacket pockets. "Do not let your feelings get the better of you." Maike's voice was suddenly soft, which made Petra look up, curiously. Maike unclasped her pack and rooted around in it for something.

When she raised her head again, the Captain's brown eyes were full of understanding, as if she knew the struggle Petra was faced with, as if she herself had been in this position. "You are a good soldier and you must hold to that when you are with him." The woman's voice was heavy. "You must think of Mimameid and the people depending on you."

Petra cocked her head to the side as she listened, wondering what kind of life the Captain had lived, and where the words were coming from inside her. But she felt the connection that Maike felt too, like they had some shared experience, and she wanted to make her Captain proud of her. She felt like a little girl again, Maike's faith in her filling a space that yearned to be recognized.

Maike produced a dented and rusting flask from her pack, popping open the lid. Though she arranged her face to hide it, Petra was surprised that Maike, who she saw as a straight-laced, shining example of a Mimameid officer, would be one to partake in the illegal booze trade. *Everyone has their vices,* she thought with a shrug. Maike stuck out her hand, offering the flask to her. She sat down on a rock an arm's length away and swung her long braid over her shoulder, while Petra tentatively took a swig. It warmed her insides as the sweet, herbal schnapps tickled her tongue, slipping down her throat and into her belly. It was far more pleasant than she had been expecting, completely unlike the flavorless homebrew Milla traded with. No, this was expensive. This was something personal, something Maike held onto from The Time Before.

"Thanks." She coughed a little as she passed the flask back. She wasn't used to drinking any alcohol, having never wanted to dull her senses with it, but it tickled pleasantly on the way down. Even the sweet smell of it made her head start to spin.

"You'll need it down there. The Celts, well, they aren't for the faint of heart." Maike took her flask back from Petra's outstretched hand and tucked it into the pocket of her jacket without explaining what she meant by that.

"I'm going to relieve Anja." Maike cleared her throat and stood up, tossing Petra a pair of flint stones. Whatever moment she had been having, it had passed. "You should work on your Gaelic a little more in the time you have left. We'll send you in just after dark." Petra nodded, handing Maike a magazine of ammunition from her pack. The Captain strapped a gun to one leg and sheathed a hunting knife into her boot.

"One more thing, Lieutenant." Maike stopped and turned back around to face her. "Never let anyone else tell you who you are. Only you can do that." She ducked off into the snow. Petra tied back her long hair and made herself busy with the flint stones.

By the time Anja returned, the fire was in full blaze and she welcomed the warmth, stripping off her gloves and hovering as close to the flames as she could safely get. They worked on Petra's word order, Anja telling her that because of her red hair, they wouldn't scrutinize her as thoroughly if her pronunciation sounded odd, but the wrong syntax would be a dead giveaway that she didn't belong. She used the light to fish out a few other odds and ends she'd need to take with her into camp - her headlamp, the flintstones Maike had tossed her, and an emergency thermal blanket.

When Onni and Benjáme returned, Petra used her band to signal to Maike and Anja left to replace her as the lookout, having sufficiently warmed by the fire and eaten a small dinner.

According to Benjáme, the other camps looked similar in size to the first one, so it was difficult to tell if one site was more important than the others.

"But I don't believe the Celts would separate their leaders into different camps," Onni reassured them. "It makes them less vulnerable, but also less efficient. For them to operate as effectively as they do, the leaders must be able to make decisions fast, decisively, and adaptively."

"And you think they may be in the first camp together?" Maike asked her specialist.

"I have no way of knowing what camp they are in. They operate off of misinformation and illusion, so even if there was a way to tell, it would be unreliable. But I also wouldn't necessarily see it as an advantage to be in the camp where the leaders are. It's much riskier to have our asset so close to being caught," Onni pointed out.

"But also means we get information faster," Benjáme interjected.

"True. But that doesn't help us if Petra is caught, thus our source of information is removed from the equation entirely," Onni countered. Petra tried not to think about what "being removed from the equation" was code for. Maike was quiet as she thought through all Onni said. She stood up, walking a few paces back and forth, her eyes calculating some intangible risk analysis in the flickering firelight. Benjáme's eyes narrowed.

"So, you would rather waste precious time than take a little risk?" He was as provocative as ever. Petra wondered if he was letting his personal grudge against the Celts cloud his thinking. It certainly wasn't the first time his hotheadedness had almost gotten them caught. The very day they had found Lysander, it had been his idea to pick off the dead before the Celts could. She shifted her smaller pack around, unsure whether to interject or not.

"It's not exactly our risk to take, it's Petra's," Onni responded. But Benjáme wasn't convinced.

"If we are concerned about which camp to infiltrate, we should send multiple people in." He really wanted the chance to face the Celts head-on.

"No." Maike's voice was sharp. "We cannot compromise our only opportunity to slip in undetected by raising unwanted suspicion. We have an 'in' with the Lieutenant and I, for one, am comfortable trusting her." Maike's trust in her was everything. Petra raised her hand to the back of her neck and rubbed it uncomfortably, unsure if she wanted this vote of confidence from Maike, this added pressure that went directly against what her instincts were telling her. "Anyone else have something to add?" Maike asked and Benjáme's eyes flashed deviously, but he held his tongue. The Captain turned her gaze back to Onni.

"The stakes are high, Captain. That's all I'm saying," the petite woman ventured.

"We all have family in Mimameid, Private. We all have someone to lose," Maike answered, her voice hard, but as true as the North they followed. "So, no matter what we do, we are essentially sending Petra in at a disadvantage, yes?"

Onni nodded hesitantly, unsure of whether or not she was going to be told off for incompetence. This was her job, after all, to be able to predict the Celts' next move. But, it wasn't her fault that Mimameid had secluded itself for so long that their information was outdated. Onni alone wasn't responsible for Petra's safety, or the success of the mission. Although Maike's face was stern, Petra was sure the Captain knew it, too. She turned instead to Petra.

"Lieutenant, are you clear on how to pass information back to us?" Maike asked.

"Yes, sir."

"Are you certain? This mission cannot be in vain." Again her words dropped like rocks sinking to the bottom of a lake. Petra nodded.

"Use the charcoal from the *Nilfheim* to inscribe the corresponding rune on the outside of the truck I use to get in with when I have something we need to meet about." She patted her outer jacket pocket where she had stashed the burnt wood. Maike turned around to face the fire and crouched low, putting her hands out to warm them from the flames. The heat danced on her lined face.

"Okay, then," she spoke into the fire, "we don't waste time. You'll slip in under cover of darkness." Maike picked up a stay twig and fiddled with it for a moment then she used the twig to point to Petra. "Objective being to locate your Celt and extract him for information." Petra felt her eyes dart to Benjáme quickly as Maike said *your Celt*. His jaw tightened and he sniffed, irritated. She lowered her eyes to the ground apologetically, then let a breath out and looked back up at her team, scanning them until she landed on the Captain. Maike's face was compassionate again, "First contact should be after you have located your mark."

"And if he's in another camp?" Petra stood up and pulled her pack onto her back, zipping her jacket tight around her neck.

"Don't risk making contact over that. We will be watching," Maike told her, still fiddling with the twig in her hands. "If you leave for another camp, we will know." Petra looked around at the team, feeling conflicted, but not wanting to disappoint them. Benjamé was her friend and Onni was kind and caring. Even cool, distant Anja bore a compassion she didn't know soldiers in Mimameid still had for outsiders.

But, today it was Maike she couldn't bear to disappoint. She saw in the Captain who she could become for Mimameid, should she put her whole heart into the mission. Someone who knew how to put others' needs above their own. Someone who could make the hard calls, but do so with a gentle, firm hand. The kind of woman she had always aspired to be, but for that pull at her heartstrings leading her North. That sound like a familiar song that lilted in the thin air. She tried to put it from her mind.

Petra shoved her hands into her pockets and they balled up into fists, one hand wrapped around the love knot, the other the piece of charcoal. "Time to get in position," the Captain said as she tossed the twig into the fire.

She turned back for one last look at Benjáme. He was a dot, climbing back up towards camp through the arctic brush and snow, growing more distant.

He was angry, she knew, that she was being sent into the camp and he wasn't. But she understood the decision their commander had made. He was so full of rage towards the Celts, too unstable to be left to his own devices among them. Like a loose bullet waiting to be loaded into the right weapon.

But then, here she was. A different kind of risk to send into the camp, a different bullet. But, one that could potentially pay off, although she'd also be just as likely to backfire. Their trust in her was overwhelming and she also felt her stomach knot up when she pictured Arthur's midnight blue eyes. After what he'd done for her and her men, how could she betray him? Maike's trust was explicit - something she appreciated - but what struck her about their plan was the gravity of Sigrid's trust in her. This was no simple job promotion. Mimameid had been the guiding light that brought her back after she'd lost her family. And this mission was the most responsibility she'd ever assigned, so she savored the feeling of Sigrid being so sure of her. Arthur or no, Sigrid knew what it meant to her.

Petra raised her hand to Benjáme and he returned the gesture, before placing his hands over his heart. For all his rage at the Celts, he had always been a fierce friend to her.

"Give them hell," he'd said as he accompanied her down the cliffside into the valley. They had hidden in the shadows of the fallen trees and boulders until the guards changed.

The new guard, now fresh at his post, not yet fully awake for his night shift, would provide the perfect chance for Petra to scurry off into the darkness. With a last glimpse up at Benjáme - a last glimpse of Mimameid and who it stood for - she ducked silently under one of the trailer trucks.

It stank of oil and smoke as she crawled on her belly like a snake through the muddy sludge that carpeted the ground beneath the truck.

Shadows moved beside the back tires and she sucked in her breath. She heard the soft lisp of Gaelic and her heart pounded, listening. Their boots crunched in the snow as they walked away and the conversation faded.

She slid silently towards the other end of the transport, curling herself up around the front tires and peering out to see her first glimpse of the Celtic camp up close.

Despite it being dark, people wrapped in furs and tartans walked shoulder to shoulder along the makeshift streets formed by the vehicles. Small torches blazed every couple of paces, lighting the narrow streets as people passed each other by. Smoke rose like ashy ribbons into the night sky from both the street torches and the giant bonfire in the center of the camp, still aflame.

Thinking quickly, she eyed a cluster of young people chattering as they drew closer to the truck. She scrambled, brushing the dirt and snow from her jacket as the group began to pass and slipped out from under the truck. She fell into step behind them as if she was the tail end of the group. She trailed them around the curve of the street, clocking how far it was to the next guard post. The people around her were unsuspecting and relaxed, laughing with one another and engaged in deep conversation, the Gaelic flying out of their mouths tumultuous and melodic. The camp had an air of safety and security about it. There was nothing to suggest that they were on alert or a militant people. In fact, the camp felt almost festive. She looked around at the varying, bright patterns of tartan - cherry reds, luminous yellows, brilliant blues, and emerald greens - catching in the firelight and could see that rather than her all-black attire allowing her to blend in it was actually making her stand out. The women all had long tartans wrapped over their heads and shoulders like shawls. The style seemed to be wearing it long - for the young women, loose locks fell from their tartans, and for the older women, plaited braids wound around their heads in intricate patterns. Their lengths of cheerful tartans covered patched elbows and threadbare kneecaps, whatever was left of their tattered, old-world clothing. The men too, had tartans of all various clans draped across their chests as sashes, hiding the wear and tear of their normal clothes behind the ribbons and folds of color.

When the group she was following took a left at the next intersection, heading deeper into the circle towards the bonfire, she sidestepped to a larger van, put her hands up on the cold metal exterior, and peered into the window. The vehicle was dark and empty and the doors were locked. As nonchalantly as she could, she pulled her lock-picking kit from her pants pocket and slipped it into the handle, fiddling with the barrels until the lock shifted with a gentle click.

She popped the door open and climbed onto the worn leather driver's seat, slamming the door shut behind her. The seat was ripped in several places, the stuffing poking out from beneath the leather, but it was warm to her touch. There must be some sort of heating unit inside the vehicle. Pocketing her lock tools, she scaled the front seats and tumbled into the back of the van. She clicked on her light.

It was outfitted like an old camper van with a bed, some sleeping bags and thick blankets, a gas stove, and a few drawers for storage. She yanked them out one by one, digging through for anything that looked vaguely like a tartan she could use to look more Celtic. A flash of green caught her eye in the bottom of one of the drawers and she dug down, producing a pine-colored, woolen shawl with triumph.

She ripped off her knit cap and shoved it haphazardly into her jacket pocket. Delicately, trying to imitate the precise folds she had seen on the other women, she wrapped the tartan around her head and draped it over her shoulders. Climbing back over the driver's seat, she jerked the car door open and slipped into the flock of people headed towards the center of camp.

Drumbeats that seemed to pound against her ribcage pulsed faster as she found herself being swept through the crowd further toward the edge of the bonfire that was positioned right at the center of the Celtic camp. She adjusted the shawl around her face, pulling it further forward to mask her features, but intentionally pulled a few strands of red curls out as camouflage. There were - as she had been promised - many various shades of ginger bobbing in the crowded gathering of Celts. Here, finally, her flaming hair was a sign that she belonged. She let the prattle and song in the camp's rising, melodic voices intoxicate her, as they swirled like bonfire smoke up into the air with a haunting song.

She could no longer feel the cold of the North Country here, surrounded by the Celts, in a river of tartan flowing towards the center circle. Someone shoved her in the dark and she tripped forward into the innermost perimeter of the crowd, almost losing her balance. She steadied herself and looked up.

The fire rose, lighting the faces of the Celts that danced around her with a copper glow. They moved in a way that seemed feral to her, savage even, but she couldn't tear her eyes from them. The beat of the drums commanded the onlookers the same way as the musicians, pulsing together as one heartbeat. Petra noticed that the people gathered had small crosses formed from dried reeds pressed in the palms of their hands. Ash landed in her loose strands of hair and she let the sounds of their song wash over her, the wildness of the language, the grief that she could feel within the music. Although she couldn't make out the words they were singing, it overwhelmed her.

Suddenly, like a flush in her cheeks, she felt very unsure, exposed, and foreign on the edge of the Celtic circle. She shrank back, easily absorbed back into the crowd, allowing the people to swallow her up until the heat of the festival was beyond her. The glow of the fire dimmed by the festival-goers. Their song receded from her body, back into the soil beneath her feet.

She felt the cold of the North Country sweep up against her back and a wash of fresh air filled her lungs. She sighed with relief.

"*Go raibh maith agat,*" Petra thanked an old woman with a cringe, annoyed at her own rough accent. Lush, grey locks of hair cascaded from the woman's tartan as she inclined her head and wordlessly left a bowl of warm, golden liquid in Petra's hands. With a gummy, toothless smile and dark eyes full of mischief, she turned and melted back into the crowd.

Raising the bowl to her face, Petra inhaled the steam coming off the liquid. With a sip, she knew it to be some sort of homemade ale. The strong, yeasty taste made her stomach lurch at first, but Petra found that when the drink hit her belly, it was soothing, the warmth placating any worries she still had about being caught. It was different from the oat beer in Mimameid, different from the cheap spirits her father had slipped her a sip of from time to time, different even from the herbal liquor she'd shared with Maike. She felt her body physically relax into the warmth, and though it wasn't something she'd ever done before, she imagined this was what it felt like to be snuggled in a blanket on a cold, snowy day.

She retreated towards a dimly lit torch that was struggling a bit in the wind, somewhat removed from the congregation, and watched the old woman curiously as she continued handing out bowls of ale to the stragglers hovering around the edges of the festival. The torch Petra had chosen was positioned beneath the branches of a dry, old birch tree with branches that hung low. Petra felt protected here, observing instead of being observed. She sipped her ale in the shadows, reigning her curiosity back in as the drums and the dances carried on before her. She tried to focus, instead, on finding something useful for the mission.

People were laughing, tossing their heads far back into the night in drunken revelry and cheer. They lit candles from the torches, passing the light from candle to candle, wishing each other good fortune as they did. Soon, the entire crowd twinkled with the little, flickering lights.

Just inside the tent nearest to her was a group of small children bent over a low table, carving into small pieces of wood. She watched them string a cord through each talisman, then line them up on their arms. When their arms were dripping with the little charms, they dispersed, donning each person at the festival with a little wooden necklace.

As Petra watched, a small girl, barely old enough to be walking, with an ash-smeared face and a luminescent grin tapped her leg. Petra looked down. The girl lifted her chubby little fingers to present a wooden charm on a necklace. Petra tilted her head, her curiosity captured. She took the necklace in her hand, cradling the charm delicately. The little girl tottled off, wishing Petra, '*Beannaithe Imbolc!*' in a small, shy voice.

The word made her pause: *Imbolc*. Hadn't Anja mentioned something about that when she was talking about the Celtic calendar? She had thought it was so ridiculous at the time, that the Celts didn't just adhere to the same passage of time as the rest of the known world. But now she racked her brain, trying to recall the details of the conversation. Wasn't it the season of transformation? Or was there a better translation? Anja had been prattling on for so long during their lessons about how interconnected language and culture were that she'd found it difficult to concentrate. But then the word came to her, that Anja had used to describe it - *rebirth*.

Her gaze followed the little girl back to the crowd of Celts with their carefully kept family colors now draped over their shoulders with pride, the way they embraced one another no matter the colors. Their bright songs and laughter roared as they shared all the food and drink with one another around a blazing fire, even as they were surrounded by enemies in a cold, dead world.

There was nothing about this that was meant for survival. This was, by all assessments, a total waste of their finite resources. And yet, here they were, celebrating. Feasting. Dancing. There was something here in their camp, a community - no, a culture - that had endured through all their tragedies.

Petra looked back down at the charm in her hand and found she recognized the symbol carved into its bark. It was a jagged 'p' shape that was meant - at least to the Norse - to bring kinship and joy to her. She slid the string over her head, letting the tartan fall from her face as she did. The air rushed under her curls and around the nape of her neck like a breath of life from the wild.

Sighing, she leaned back against the tree trunk, looking up through the barren branches at the smoke rising from the fire and how it spiraled into the starless, night sky.

"It cannot be."

His words were barely more than a whisper, but Petra had heard them slip out. She almost dropped her bowl of ale, hissing as the hot liquid spilled over, searing her gloved hands. "Oh *cac*, sorry!" He appeared from around the other side of the tree, hands snatching at the hot bowl and setting it down, carefully, in the snow beside them. He rose slowly and adjusted the golden tartan pinned across his chest. She was immobile, startled like a deer in the woods, but he was no hunter. He reached out to her, gently pulling her wet gloves from her hands one finger at a time, and stuffing them into his pocket. She saw his eyes light up a magnificent, midnight blue when her fingertips met his own and her heart jumped. Like the feeling of the first rush of air each time she surfaced from Mimameid.

"Arthur." It was the first time she had actually said his name out loud; it felt so foreign, so clumsy on her lips. But it made her smile, to feel it playing on her tongue. "Hi," she said, watching the way his jaw caught the light of the fire, as his face broke out into a warm smile, too.

"Petra," he sighed like he was shedding a layer of clothing, "hi." he gave a light-hearted laugh and rubbed his chin in disbelief, his eyes still shining. Her name coming out of his mouth warm and rich, like the ale in her belly.

"You're here," she said as she followed the line of his jaw down to his freckled neck, and then to the goldenrod-and-smoke tartan draped over his shoulder, speckles of robin's-egg blue and soft red from the pattern catching in the light from the torch. His feet were shoved into worn, fur-lined boots, his legs wrapped in high, woolen stockings and a long tartan kilt. He had on a thick knit sweater with visible moth holes around the collar and a parka that was halfway unzipped. A wool hat now concealed his golden hair, a vibrant sash hung over his shoulder and trailed beyond his fingertips, a sash pin glimmering softly in the torchlight. She saw his hands were balled up into fists and his arms flexed tensely. She clenched her jaw for a moment, feeling the urge to take a step back. But his face still displayed relative calm, and his twinkling eyes told her to trust him. She wasn't sure what to make of the mixed body signals, but with a nervous twitch of her eyebrow, she decided to roll with whatever game he was playing.

"Somewhat less surprising than the fact that you're here, but yes. I am," he chuckled, taking her hands in his and squeezing them gently, as he did.

"No, I just meant -" She felt her mind fogging up, a blend of elation mixing with Maike's words to her. *Think of the people depending on you.* She took a steadying exhale. Arthur cocked his head to the side, one eyebrow raised, curiously, or maybe concerned?

"Is everything okay?" he asked and she nodded, lowering her eyes, finding herself following the curve of his calf muscle. She hadn't been able to remember him in such detail.

"Yeah. Yeah, it actually is." She lifted her face again to his and shook her hair from her face. A stubborn lock of red fell back down to her cheek and she felt Arthur's hand reach up, tucking it behind her ear, slowly, intentionally.

"Do you want to go somewhere, maybe more private?" he asked her, searching her face. Petra nodded and tried to bite back a smile. He took her by the arm, so confidently that she was surprised. His cool fingertips sent the same breath of air up through her arm as he led her away from the gathering. She pulled her own tartan tighter around her shoulders, looking around nervously.

They wove through the rows of tents and vehicles, flitting in and out of the shadows thrown by the torches. The streets were now all but abandoned, nearly everyone having been drawn to the bonfire.

"Was that *Imbolc*?" she asked, her voice quiet in the cold air. Her tongue had a hard time with the pronunciation, and the word came out harsher than when the little girl had said it to her.

"Yeah," Arthur shoved his hands into his pockets, looking impressed, "it was. How'd you know that? I thought the Norse forbade the study of anything other than Nordic lore."

"What do you mean?" She was shocked that he knew anything about life in Mimameid, it was supposed to be such a well-kept Nordic secret.

In The Time Before, the Norse had tried to share their way of life with the outside world, but as the world descended into chaos and people became more desperate, radical factions crawled out of hiding. Mimameid had been such a faction, at first only accepting people who could prove they came from the purest Nordic bloodlines. But that was before Ragnarök actually happened and Sigrid assumed leadership. She'd opened their doors to all who were looking for safety, all who were willing to sacrifice for the greater good of others. But, Petra didn't know how Arthur could know about any of that.

"The Celts have their own ways of getting information about you guys," he explained, looking at the ground and kicking at some snow as he walked. She would have to circle back to that another time. She had noticed he had said 'the Celts' instead of 'we'.

"You don't consider yourself a Celt?" He yanked his hands out of his pockets and gestured to the brightly colored tartan sash hanging from his shoulder.

"Cornish," he said as if it explained. The Cornish were still English and the English were still Celts, last she had heard. "Born and raised by good, Cornish miners. Everyone has to wear the tartan issued to them by the Celts at festivals, and this one's the Cornish one. Women wear them more regularly though, as a way to keep track of bloodlines and marriages." Petra nodded slowly, intrigued by the insight.

"I see." So, this was the Celtic way of making sure they knew where everyone was on the hierarchical food chain. No one could hide who they were. It also explained why they let everyone keep speaking their own languages. "So, they force you?" she asked.

"Well, it's mandatory, yes. But, I'm proud to wear the colors of my forefathers," Arthur replied, nonchalantly.

"It's never created any problems for you?" From his querying expression, he could tell she was prying. He stopped walking and glanced around to make sure they were alone before answering.

"I don't always agree with the decisions the Celts make, but no, I've never regretted wearing my tartan. Or standing up for my people." He bit his lip nervously as if he'd just committed heresy, before turning and continuing on.

When they had walked what Petra determined to be as far away as possible from the bonfire, Arthur took out a ring of keys and fiddled with them in front of a battered, white van. He slipped on into the lock and turned around to look at her, his eyes uncharacteristically sheepish.

"I'm sorry it's not cleaner." He slid the door open, exposing the back of his own little, outfitted camper van. "I'm at work a lot -" He started to say as Petra climbed in, the sentence falling flat.

She glanced around, trying not to pass judgment. The bed, which took up most of the back of the van, was wrapped in wrinkled, old flannel sheets and a sleeping bag tossed together with a pile of dirty laundry, some of it speckled with red flecks that looked like they could be blood. She let her hand run across the threadbare flannel. There was a roughly patched-in kitchenette top to her left with a camp stove and a privacy curtain hung between them and the front seats, where a pair of dirty socks were airing out. She turned to sit down on the bed and Arthur slammed the van door shut behind them.

She exhaled shakily. This was the moment Maike had tried to prepare her for. He pulled off his tartan sash, sat down on the other end of the bed, and kicked off his boots with a heavy thud. He put his feet up on the bed and she felt her own feet glued to the floor. Try as she might have, Maike could not have prepared her for *this*.

"It's nice." Petra attempted awkwardly, gesturing around to the bed piled with dirty clothes, camping stove crusty with old food, and floor wet with sludgy, melted snow. Arthur let out a warm laugh and the sound made her lips slip into a smile. "What?" she asked, innocently.

"It's an absolute pigsty in here," he replied pointedly, still laughing. She shrugged, feeling herself relax a little. This was the Arthur she had met out there in the wild.

"Well, yes." A chuckle escaped her.

"I appreciate your honesty, at least," he sighed, leaning back against the passenger seat headrest, content. "Normally these vehicles are reserved for families, and I'd be in one of the big bunk vans with the rest of the people who aren't coupled." He raised one hand to the side of the van and touched it. "But, doctors' hours are unpredictable, so I'm one of the lucky few who gets one of these. I do have to handle all the maintenance on her myself though, which," he paused, "it's fair to say that was a bit of a learning curve." He pasted a goofy smile on his face and lifted his arms comically as he shrugged his shoulders.

"So, there is something you aren't good at?" Petra watched the way his chest moved up and down, how at ease he was in here, no trace of the nervousness he'd had as he'd talked about the Celts outside.

"You mean, besides cleaning?" Arthur joked with a tense smile on his face as he ran his hands over his hair and Petra cocked her head to the side, the tartan falling to her shoulders, "I'm just always at work, hence the mess," he repeated, abashed.

"You don't know what my bunk looks like. I could be just as much of a pig," she offered.

"Military girl like you?" He raised an eyebrow. "I'm skeptical." She flushed. *Was she so predictable?* She thought, hiding her face as the color rose to her cheeks. "Nice tartan by the way." He tugged on the edge of the shawl that trailed across her lower leg.

"Huh? Oh, thanks." Grinning a little mischievously, she said, "I probably shouldn't tell you this, but I broke into someone's van for it." She adjusted the tartan, pulling it tighter. Arthur's van wasn't as warm as the other one had been.

"They will just get another one," he reassured her, "And anyways," he reached out to run his hand over the dark green fabric, "the color suits you."

His eyes sobered, as he spoke. "Petra," he continued, her name tumbled from his lips again and she felt her chest warm at the sound.

"Yes?" She caught his gaze for a second. Then, her eyes flitting around, studying the lines on his face - the edges of his playful mouth, the deep, dimpled cheeks, and up to the corners of those eyes - as blue as a summer evening. She could see from his furrowed brow what he was thinking, trying to figure out why she was here, in the camp. Did he think she had come for him?

"I'm sorry about outside, earlier," he said quietly and she tried to arrange her face like it hadn't bothered her, but she was evidently unsuccessful because he continued, "I have to be so careful out there. I never know who is watching." It was a cryptic answer, but one Petra identified with. She sighed.

"It's okay, I know the feeling." She tucked a lock of hair behind her ear. In one sudden motion, Arthur lurched forward and she felt his hand on her upper thigh. Her heart pounded, she closed her eyes and tried to think of something else, anything else.

But his hand stayed put, poised just below the scar from the knife blade.

"How is your leg? Did it heal up okay?" She opened her eyes and saw his watching her. Her fingers found the love knot in her pocket and twisted around it.

"Yeah, it's good. You saved it." Her reply was breathless and she could feel the outline of the "T" scar from the knife blade burn on her leg. She could feel the weight of his hand.

"I'm sorry if it scarred or..." His voice trailed off and Petra felt herself running her fingers over the edge of the love knot in the silence. "I didn't have all my equipment with me, you know." He paused again. "If I'd had a proper needle..." His quizzical gaze was fixed on her, but he couldn't bring himself to say the words. She knew what he wanted to ask.

"I'm here because I need your help," she said, finally and his eyes softened, like a wave that crashed and melted against the shoreline.

"You do?" he prompted. She wet her lips, raising her chin to him and tucking her hair behind her ears. How to phrase it? How to tell him she was there to gather information for Mimameid, but that she wasn't sure she could trust Sigrid anymore?

"Something is happening. Something is wrong. At the Norse camp." She felt the truth behind the words, even as she said them. He lifted his head.

"What do you mean?"

11

LYSANDER

The alarm filled the room and he tumbled off the bed, rubbing sleep from his eyes. He stood up and stretched, his neck cracking in several places as he looked out the small, portico window with his view into the fjord. He kicked the pull-out bed back into the wall, blankets balled up and pillow still full of lumps, but it bounced back and it hit him in the back of the knees. He groaned from both the pain and frustration at the mechanics of the bed. With an annoyed exhale, he turned around and haphazardly attempted to flatten out the covers, before rolling it in gently until he heard the lock click into place. He turned back around with a sigh. Although the night had been an improvement on his first few nights there, he'd still not been able to manage to get much sleep without the sound of Linnaea's soft snores nearby.

It had been a little more than a week since Magdelena and Linnaea had left and each day he'd woken up with an ache for their absence. Having lived for the better part of four years together, he felt like a piece of himself was missing without them. His fingers popped as he finished stretching and rolled his shoulders up and down, as his band started lighting up. He strolled over to the sink to splash water on his face, grinning when he saw the messages rolling in were from Bjørn.

He wiped the water from his stubble and let curiosity get the better of him, opening up the messages. The enthusiastic man was an early bird, likely a habit from his farming days, as he was always in The Engine Room at least an hour earlier than anyone else.

Lysander put a tooth-tab in his mouth and bit down. The powdery tab split open, coating his mouth, chalky and flavorless. It wasn't the most delicious thing he'd ever put in his mouth, but he definitely liked the feeling of having clean teeth. Above Ground, you had to choose between scavenging dodgy toothpaste tubes that had long since crusted and smelled, or risk contracting serious dental complications, a horror he and Magdelena had seen take people's lives in the camps with the worst conditions. Festering cavities, rotting gums, and rancid infections were commonplace. Even before Ragnarök, nutrition had just been disgracefully poor, and knowledgeable people to help were scarce, to say the least.

So now, the chalky powder was a blessed luxury and in the light of his room, rising slowly, like a fresh dawn, he breathed his new reality in. Whatever future that might bring.

When he finished with his teeth, he spat into the sink, washing the waste away with a bit of water from the faucet, another detail that hadn't escaped his notice. He loved having running water at his fingertips again. He let the water run for a few seconds longer until it ran warm over his fingertips. It felt *so* good to have warm water.

Before too much was wasted, he shut it off, not wanting to overindulge. He glanced up into the tarnished mirror at his disheveled, chestnut-brown hair, hair that Magdelena would have trimmed back by now. His fingers combed through it, catching on a tangle on the bottom behind his ear. It left a knot in his stomach.

This was the same feeling when he had been sent away for school and couldn't see his little sister anymore. He learned to live with the dull pain of not watching her grow up, being absent from her formative joys and pains every day. And though it had been many years since the sound of her piano keys had faded forever and he learned a new lesson in how to live with that deafening silence, the wound left by Magdelena and Linnaea's absence was fresh. He knew their smell, their laughs, their dreams for when this was all over and he felt the loss heaviest when the lights in his room went out and the silence of the water outside engulfed him.

Instead of doing anything about his unkempt appearance, however, he turned away from the mirror and grabbed the inhaler he'd been prescribed by The Infirmary doctors off the shelf. Reluctantly, he put his lips to it. They'd determined that his lung capacity was suboptimal after being exposed to so much smoke in the air for all those years he'd been Above Ground. The inhaler was temporary, but it was still weird, after all this time, to have a doctor prescribe him medicine. He was sure such things had died out with The Time Before.

He'd grown up relying on home remedies his parents bartered with neighbors for, and it had been no different with Magdelena finding wild mint to ease lung strain or caraway seeds for digestion. But most people had just accepted that working in those modern conditions, like around exhaust fumes or mines, was just a part of survival, even if it wasn't your own survival. There was no thought about individual longevity, only about managing the problem right in front of you.

After replacing the inhaler, he approached the wardrobe, pulling from the scant selection the long-sleeved, waffle-knit tee from The Closet. The cuffs were frayed and the collar was a little worn, but it was fluffy, clean, and surprisingly warm. He pulled up some thermal pants and zipped up his Mimameid jumpsuit. He wiggled his toes into his new socks, feeling out where his other socks had holes in them and then stepped into his boots. With an alarming 'ding,' a second wave of messages began to cascade in from Bjørn.

Without fully tying his laces, he made for the door and down the hall, clomping along to Canteen B. He grabbed his breakfast from the automat and shoved the orange into the pocket of his jumpsuit before scarfing back porridge on his way back out the door. He had no interest in sitting alone in the canteen and watching the people who all had family with them. A lock of messy hair fell into his eyes and he shoved back the reminder of

Magdelena and Linnaea with a determined hand. No, he wanted to be in The Engine Room, surrounded by the drumming and whirring of machines, problem-solving with Bjørn.

Most people were still on their way to breakfast or coming back from the night shift as Lysander hurried down the staircase to The Engine Room, his lanky legs already ahead of him. He paused briefly, just as he had every day that week, to briefly look up at the skylight out into the fjord above him. The murky blue-green shone a little extra today as rays of determined sunlight pierced the surface of the water, far above them. He took a deep breath and continued down.

When he arrived, Bjørn was downstairs near the reactor, glasses pushed onto his head with sweat beading his forehead. He waved to Lysander as he entered, signaling to come join him on the floor.

"Are you finally going to come to dinner tonight?" he asked when Lysander was beside him, pausing to look up from the tank he was bent over.

Lysander didn't know exactly why, but he had been avoiding the topic with Bjørn, maybe out of fear of replacing Magdelena and Linnaea somehow. He wasn't ready to connect with anyone new, he just wanted his own family back. But apparently, this hadn't put Bjørn off. He wiped the sweat from his brow and looked at Lysander with his intent blue eyes. His gaze didn't waver and a smile played in the corners of his mouth.

"Yes," Lysander conceded, "yes, let's do it." The older man's face broke out into a bright smile that reached all the way up to his hairline, wrinkling his forehead with joy and causing his glasses to shift and fall down onto the bridge of his nose.

"Excellent." He grinned and pushed his glasses up against his face. "I'll go send Runa a message right now so she can put in a request for food in D." He jumped up, all thought of the project in front of him temporarily forgotten and ran up the stairs into the office.

Lysander stood up and pulled out the orange from his pocket, peeling it and popping the sweet, plump slices into his mouth. He stopped mid-chew when he spotted the broken valve that he'd seen on his tour that first day.

He hadn't forgotten about it, but it had been pushed to the back of his mind, distracted by the auxiliary air filtration system and then everything that had happened with Magdelena. Not to mention that there had been no word on Petra's Above Ground mission. He'd hoped that Lasse or Milla might have had some news for him, maybe even Sigrid, but it was as if she had disappeared without a trace.

But here it was, this strange replacement piece on the valve, tinkered together from whatever spare parts they had had lying around and somehow it was still kicking, still pumping out the unfiltered water. He reached his hand out to it just as Bjørn popped his head back through the door at the top of the stairs.

"Alright, it's all taken care of. We can leave right from here after work." He pounded back down the metal steps to the tank he'd been working on. "Will you give me a hand over here? The other guys won't be rolling in here for at least another half hour and I'd like to have this ol' gal up and running by the time we break for lunch." One eye still on the valve, Lysander wistfully wiped his citrus-coated hands on the front of his jumpsuit and went to help. It didn't take long before he was wrapped up again in the stories Bjørn told about his girls.

"Tuva, the fifteen-year-old," Bjørn explained, "keeps getting in trouble in school. She's started taking things apart during her free time and putting them back together. She told them she's trying to look for patterns in the machinery, but I guess that was considered a cheeky answer. The teacher didn't like it too much." Bjørn shrugged.

"I don't understand what the big deal is, as long as she puts it back together when she's done." Lysander soon found himself engrossed in the story of Tuva opening up one of the cameras mounted in the back of the classroom and Bjørn laughed.

"That's what I told the teacher!" He raised an eyebrow. "But, no apparently that's not considered 'proper' behavior for a woman. Not when she has to learn how to be a good mother for the next generation. How insane is that? I thought Ragnarök happened, not a time warp back to the ridiculous notions of gender-role stereotypes. Anyways, since she turned fifteen she'll be up for a job assignment in Mimameid any day now. Anyhow, she won't have to put up with that ridiculous teacher anymore."

"I thought most people didn't get their job assignments until they were seventeen?" Lysander asked. He'd overheard someone talking about it B last night at dinner. Perhaps Tuva's intelligence had accelerated her somehow, as he had been?

"That might be how it works in the upper levels," Bjørn laughed a little, lighthearted, but with an edge of bitterness, "but down in D we have to pull our own weight a little earlier than that. Mimameid doesn't work any other way." While they'd been talking, the other men and women who worked in The Engine Room had come in one by one and started peeling off to their prospective work stations after a customary Mimir greeting. Toolboxes in hands and grumbles about what had been in the canteen for breakfast began to swirl in the air. The twins, Arne and Bo, who Bjørn had said worked as appliance manufacturers in The Time Before, were eyeing Lysander with particularly critical gazes.

Paying no mind to them, Bjørn and Lysander worked right up until lunch, at which point Lysander's band told him he needed to get his heart rate up to meet his health requirements for the day as if he's been sitting idly all day. So, at Bjørn's recommendation, he took the opportunity to climb the stairs up to The Observation Deck.

Although he wasn't the only member of Mimameid that had decided to take a small break there, it was still relatively quiet. Although everyone wore their jumpsuits, he could see some stained with soot, some with grease, some smelled like fish, some like chemicals. It looked like all the skilled laborers in Mimameid took advantage of the peace that the room afforded. He even saw one teacher who had brought her class of small children there for a lunchtime field trip. There was something about the glass and the water outside and the glowing piezo crystals that made everyone hush. It was a different kind of quiet than the room at the top of the bunker, where the people from A had lounged, looking for something to do to pass the time, just something to entertain themselves. This room down here was filled with a kind of mystical reverence that everyone who came here was seeking, yearning for.

Lysander watched a corner of the seaweed farms swaying in the current. By the looks of it, this particular section still had a little ways to go before it would be harvested, but it was grown enough to offer a soothing sway.

He sat down in a darker corner, enraptured by the crystals reacting to the pressure from his hands. He tried to remember the motions of playing the piano, like he had when he was a child, tapping out the notes against the glass floor, imagining that it sounded like when Judit had played. He felt his hand move longingly to where her charm had hung around his neck, now bare. She had always been better at music than he was, even though she'd been so much younger.

Lysander's band beeped at him and Yvonne's voice told him that he was needed back in The Engine Room. His cheeks burned as the other people in the room glared at him for forgetting to put his band on mute. He stood up, crossed the room hastily, bumping into a couple entering hand in hand, and scurried out to descend the stairs.

When he entered The Engine Room, one of the twins and Selby, the man with the long, scraggly beard, were in the midst of a row in the middle of the floor. It looked like a piece of equipment usually mounted on the wall had been tossed - at who he couldn't say. Parties were forming on each side of the fight, egging them on and jeering.

He reached the bottom of the stairs just in time to see Bjørn throw a punch straight into Selby's nose, only to notice that the twin already had blood on his face. Both men spit blood out onto the floor angrily, but moved away from each other, back to their perspective work stations. The small crowd scattered and Lysander approached Bjørn, who was nursing his right hook.

"Let's head up to the office," he muttered and they climbed back up the staircase together.

"What was that about?" Lysander asked as the door closed behind them and the roar of the engines faded.

"That? Oh, nothing, just a little disagreement. I think we've all been down here just a little too long, that's all," he said dismissively, still shaking out his hand. Lysander wanted to press him further, but the knuckles were starting to swell and Lysander could tell Bjørn needed to head to The Infirmary. There would be time later.

"You should probably get some ice on that," Lysander told him.

"Odin's beard, Runa will kill me if I can't make it to dinner because I got in a fight. The last time I missed dinner for a scuffle, my brothers were still alive." His laugh was bittersweet. "You'll cover for me, downstairs, yeah? I opened up another switchboard in the back room I want you to patch up." Lysander nodded, grateful there was already more work set up for him below. "I'll see you for dinner," Bjørn confirmed, pointing at him with the hand that wasn't swelling.

When Bjørn had left for The Infirmary, he disappeared into the back room and lost himself in the switchboard until his band beeped with the address for Bjørn's family bunker, the phantom sound of Judit's melody in his ears.

Besides what he saw of it walking down to The Engine Room - the winding, narrow passages and strange smells wafting past tiny, portico windows - D was a section of the bunker he was wholly unfamiliar with.

He followed the directions that the band had given him, curiously dodging lines of laundry strung up across the narrow hallways, although he didn't know why they needed to when they had a laundry service. Down another twist in the hallway sat a gaggle of old men with chairs propped up in the doorways, shouting back and forth at one another in a mix of Sámi, Finnish, and Danish. In an attempt to duck past them, he bumped one of the men and something spilled over across shoulders that reeked of pungent alcohol. He jumped back in surprise, knocking another man from his seat, and then, in embarrassment, tried to help the man back up. When his attempt left the man even more entangled than before, Lysander hastened away while furious, barely-discernible shouts chased after him.

When he arrived at Bjørn's door, he found he didn't even need to knock. A fuming, teenage girl with dirty-blonde hair and eyes that flashed as brilliantly as Bjørn's came stomping out and down the hall past Lysander, her arms folded across her chest. Given the circumstances, he was left assuming this was Tuva. Lysander was still watching her storm away until Bjørn hurried out after her, his face very much that of a crestfallen father. But, upon seeing Lysander, his expression lifted immediately into a warm smile.

"Hey!" Bjørn welcomed him in with a bear hug, clapping him on the back as if he were his own son, come home after a long trip. He was grateful they weren't greeting him with the typical, stiff 'Mimir's tree' mantra of Mimameid. "Welcome, welcome to D. Come on in! Sorry about that, apparently I am just having one of those days today." His hand was wrapped in a makeshift cast, the edges of a splint poking out from the side as he guided Lysander into their family bunk. It was bigger than Lysander's own bunk, but not by as much as he was expecting. Runa and Åsa were pushing in the set of double bunk beds when they entered. Lysander had a vague recollection of Runa from The Gardens, but seeing her next to her daughter was like seeing double. Although her hair was dirty-blonde to Åsa's ash blonde, they shared long, willowy locks, smoky eyes, and the rosy, laughing cheeks, dappled with freckles.

"Welcome!" Runa greeted him with open arms and two kisses, one on each side of his face, recognizing him at once. Åsa helped her dad pull out the table and unfold some chairs, setting them onto a well-loved, fur rug, in the same spot where his room had a sealskin rug. He reached down and let the thick, coarse fur run through his fingers.

"What kind of animal is this? It's different from the one I have in my room," he asked.

"It's reindeer. Our old neighbor gifted that to us before she passed away," Runa explained. "She was an old Sámi lady and it was all she brought with her from The Time Before."

"You'll have a sealskin rug being in B, right?" Bjørn asked him, pulling Åsa onto his lap as he sat down.

"Yeah, how did you know?" He was surprised.

"Standard issue Mimameid for A and B. Nothing but the best for the top floors," Bjørn spoke in a tone Lysander didn't recognize, Runa throwing him a warning look.

"Thank you for inviting me to dinner," Lysander said quickly in an embarrassed effort to change the subject; Runa squeezed his shoulder with a soft smile.

"Of course. The pleasure is all ours. Bjørn hasn't been able to stop talking about his new colleague, so it was time for us to finally meet you. Something to drink?" She walked over to the sink and started pouring several glasses of water.

"Yes, thank you. I thought we were going to eat in the canteen, though?" he asked, a little confused and Bjørn laughed lightly.

"Oh, we are. I think we just have to wait a few minutes for uh, Tuva to cool off." He jerked his head, indicating the hallway outside the open door. Åsa shifted in her father's lap and rolled her eyes.

"She can be *so* theatrical sometimes," the younger girl moaned, and Lysander couldn't help but laugh. The words sounded like something she had heard from the mouth of her parents.

"Now, be nice," Runa said gently, tucking a stray lock of hair behind her ear as she set the glasses of water down on the table and gave Lysander an apologetic look for her daughter's audaciousness.

"I am being nice!" Åsa replied to her mother, absentmindedly tucking a lock of her own hair behind her ear, exactly like Runa had just done. It was uncanny. Lysander exchanged a glance with Bjørn, who raised his eyebrows at Lysander knowingly. Åsa really was her mother's daughter.

"What happened?" Lysander asked Åsa, and the girl looked at her dad, who nodded his head in resigning permission.

"*Pappa* won't let her meet up with a boy instead of eating with us tonight." She crossed her arms matter-of-factly and Runa looked at her, rolling her eyes lightheartedly.

"Not because of me, I hope?" he asked.

"No, no," Bjørn told him. "Well, it was a good excuse, let's say. But the boy in question is also a *tjockskalle*. So, there's that." Runa slapped Bjørn playfully with a towel for his language and Bjørn shrugged in response, "What? He is!" he defended himself against Runa's scorn, which made them all erupt into laughter. Lysander sighed, he couldn't believe how quickly being with Bjørn and his family had turned his mood.

A few minutes later, Tuva returned to the bunk, sullen, but muttering an apology for storming out on them. As Bjørn hugged his daughter Lysander could see that as Åsa was Runa's daughter, so Tuva was Bjørn's, down to the dimples and adamant blue eyes. He promised her they could talk later about the boy in question. Lysander exchanged a weary look with Åsa, who clearly wasn't amused with her sister becoming such a moody teenager. They all headed out to the canteen, Runa herding the girls through the door, with Bjørn and Lysander bringing up the rear.

As they walked back down the hall, again dodging the laundry lines and drunk old men Lysander turned to Bjørn.

"D isn't really what I pictured," he started to say, but Bjørn turned his head, talking loudly over the arguing neighbors. Between the laundry lines and the old men, he wasn't sure what he had expected, but it wasn't that.

"D is kind of made up of everybody's leftovers. All the city people that evacuated Copenhagen, Oslo, and Stockholm, they all ended up in A and B where the rooms are bigger and there are fewer people because so many of them got here first and well - no one says it outright - but because they all donated more money than the rest of us could. I think a lot of A is even reserved for the original people that funded the bunker in the first place - so yeah - money." He shrugged. "Then, C is military personnel. Originally, it was a private military, but they merged with what was left of the state once the government took on the project. The military is who built Mimameid though, so they lived all over before finally settling into C because they needed to house more people as the survivors started flooding the bunker." From a bunk somewhere behind them, Lysander heard a nasty coughing fit erupt. He hoped it wasn't one of the old men from earlier. Unperturbed, Bjørn raised his voice over the coughing.

"And then there's the rest of us. The stragglers, like the Sámi when their herds died out Above Ground, any Finns who made it to safety from the Rus invasions, Dane refugees who couldn't buy or barter their way to the top once their cities flooded, the countryside Swedes and Nordmenn like us who don't have enough manners or education to socialize with the uppers. Oh and, of course, the old, who are no longer able to contribute to rebuilding the Norse population - because that's at the top of our leader's agenda. It's all about how we can contribute to her political goal, you know?" Bjørn said, sarcastically. "If you're a family - like us - you're safe from being too much involved. But, you better be careful," Bjørn joked, "genes like yours - she's going to send you straight to the breeding tanks!" Lysander didn't know whether to take him seriously or not at this point. "But, anyways, that's why the Icelanders hide out down here, too, just to stay away from all the politics," Bjørn finished, this time more earnestly.

"That doesn't really seem like..." Lysander started to say, but he didn't know exactly how to finish. What did he really know about Mimameid?

"Like the spirit of Mimameid?" Bjørn took the liberty of finishing his sentence for him and chuckled as he said it. Lysander nodded. "Unfortunately, that's exactly the spirit of Mimameid." His tone sobered for a moment. "But it doesn't bother us so much." He continued as the doors to the canteen opened before them and roaring, fiddle music spilled out into the dank hallway. "We have more fun down here anyways." Bjørn winked, taking Lysander by the arm and leading him through the crowd gathered around the musicians, towards the automats.

D was bursting with color and music. The people were sporting their traditional sweaters and dresses, the polished, metal clasps and buttons catching in the flickering overhead lights. Somewhere, a circuit needed to be fixed. True blues, reds, yellows, and greens were painted across the dull concrete in patterns and symbols Lysander didn't recognize.

The tables and chairs were haphazardly made, similar to the ones he's seen in C, from scraps of old submarine and recycled trash. But unlike the ones in the military canteen, these had been put together like little pieces of art, using whatever tools and materials they could find to weld them, paint them, tack them together into hodgepodge channels of creativity. He saw plants dripping from every available shelf and nook and looked up to see the long tendrils of a plant he couldn't name touching his shoulder as he stepped into line to get his food from the automat.

"What's with all the plants?" Lysander leaned over to ask Bjørn, his eyes still wide at all the excitement.

"Oh, Runa and the other gardeners have been making clippings of them for years and sneaking them out. They ease the strain on the older air filters since the air quality is worse down here than anywhere else in Mimameid." Lysander tried to match Bjørn's smile, but he was horrified they even had to think like that when A and B wanted for nothing. Literally using VR to pass the time they were so bored. But, Bjørn was so proud of Runa. "She's even made sure everyone in D has a plant or two in their bunk as well." Lysander sighed. There was nothing that could stop their optimism.

When they had gotten their dinner, Bjørn and Runa squeezed into a spot at a wobbly table facing the *Hardanger* fiddlers, who had been joined by a dulcimer and an accordion player. The music was lively and the portions of food were a good size, with generous portions of seaweed and potatoes, although Lysander did notice that the fish was a fattier one than he'd ever gotten in B. He couldn't say exactly what kind of fish it was, but certainly lower quality than what he was used to in B.

The girls squirreled down their food faster than even Linnaea had that first day in Mimameid and jumped up to join the dancing around the musicians before Lysander's piece of fish had stopped steaming. Runa laughed and clapped as the girls danced, spinning and bouncing to the fiddle's melody. Bjørn leaned over towards Lysander.

"The girls started learning to dance from the family down the hall about a year ago," he explained. "Runa's always been the musician in the family of course, but she never was the dancer and she's so glad someone can teach them our traditional dances." He was glowing as he watched them. "You can tell Tuva's my girl," he laughed heartily and pointed to her. "The poor thing. Next to her sister, she's got no sense of rhythm at all. But she *loves* it," Bjørn grinned. Lysander found he couldn't help but laugh and clap along with everyone else.

The atmosphere in the canteen was infectious and he started to wonder if there wasn't a way for him to transfer down here to D somehow. They definitely did have more fun.

After they had finished their food, a flask of dangerous-smelling liquid that was being passed around the canteen made its way to their end of the table. Lysander accepted the flask from Bjørn's outstretched hand and knocked back a swig of the spirits. It burned like gasoline down the back of his throat and sent a tickle straight to his head.

When he handed the flask to Runa, Bjørn winked at Lysander. "Watch this." He motioned as she took a swig of the homebrew, shaking her head at its awful taste. Bjørn stood up and started clapping and chanting her name, slow at first but growing faster and faster as more people joined in.

Runa shot Bjørn a look that could have knocked him dead, but the corners of her lips twitched with a smile. The musicians quieted, joining in with Bjørn until even Lysander himself had joined the call.

"Ru-na, Ru-na, Ru-na!" She threw her hands up in concession and the room erupted in cheers as she walked toward the center of the dance floor. She draped her arm over Åsa's shoulder, who grabbed a hold of her mother's hand, then winked over at Tuva, who was sitting on a table, her arms wrapped around a dark-haired young man below her on the chair. Everyone was still in anticipation, and when Runa opened her mouth, Lysander understood why.

She let out a call like nothing he'd ever heard. Something otherworldly, as though she had reached straight into the Eddic lore. Clear and cutting, it echoed like glass upon the walls of the canteen, carrying Lysander far from Mimameid and high into the hills of Old Sweden.

Her voice was like a soft touch of light breaking through a cloud, but the song was interlaced with melancholy. A longing for something that was no longer attainable, Lysander thought. It held her audience captive, the breathy tones rising to a climax as Runa clung tightly to her daughter. She let out a wild call that wove its way between Lysander's ribs and into his chest, the last note still reverberating in him even after she had closed her mouth. There was an aching silence and then her voice cut through the air, repeating the first part had been again, this time softer, sweeter, and sadder.

The song ended and Lysander had tears on his cheeks, though he couldn't remember when he started crying. Blinking, he looked around and saw that he wasn't the only one. Bjørn was wiping his eyes dry as Runa took a small flustered bow and returned to her seat beside him.

The musicians gradually began to strike their instruments back up and the chatter and dancing resumed. Bjørn put his arm around his wife and kissed her full on the mouth as she sat back down.

"That was beautiful, *sötnos*," he told her and then he looked over at Lysander. "Now, why don't you tell him what you were singing about?" Runa, looking embarrassed, obliged her doting husband.

"I wrote that song when we had to leave. It's the song of home."

The night eventually died down to a low rumble, the accordion pumping out a romantic little folk melody from the corner of the canteen, followed by the occasional roar of approval from a group of drunk men.

Bjørn and Runa were settled back into their chairs watching Åsa play with some of her friends and trying not to watch Tuva too closely since she had been allowed to go and sit with the boy from her class after all.

"You're so good with the girl. Do you have sisters?" Bjørn asked Lysander, his arm draped over Runa, fingers running through her long, willowy hair, lazily. The question surprised him.

"One, but she died."

"Oh, I'm sorry to hear that," Runa said, reaching out to him and he could see the sincerity on her face.

"I hadn't seen her in a long time, but thank you. She was sweet, quiet. She liked to play the piano," he said. "Since Ragnarök, the closest thing I had to a sibling was Linnaea, the girl I came to Mimameid with," Lysander told him, though the words felt heavy on his tongue.

"Ah, yeah. You were telling me about them. Linnaea and what's her mother's name?" Bjørn asked.

"Magdelena." He felt a breath of air release from his lungs, relief to be able to say their names, mixed with a bittersweetness.

"Right. The biologist, right?" Lysander nodded.

"Yeah, botanist. Married to the Icelandic scientist."

"The one on the island in the north." Lysander was surprised by how much of his story he had actually listened to down in The Engine Room while they worked, forgetting for a moment that Runa had met Magdelena, too. Runa leaned forward and pointed to the group of drunk, old men at the other end of the canteen, the group that kept making noise.

"You see the one there, with the long, red beard?" she asked Lysander and he followed her gaze. The man was standing, telling an animated story to the group, the drink in his hand spilling over as he raised and lowered his arms, the smile on his lined face was wide enough that Lysander could see his chipped teeth from across the room.

"Yeah?" He looked back at Runa.

"That's the Celt, Ned Wallace. The one that Magdelena talked to while she was here." Lysander snapped his face back towards the man, his interest piqued.

"Do you think he'd talk to me?" he asked Runa, and she shrugged. It was Bjørn who answered.

"You get Ned drunk enough and he'll talk to anyone. Not exactly the tightest lips around here," he laughed and Lysander smiled back but wondered. Magdelena had told him exactly the opposite about Ned. That he was in fact, her secret keeper. Runa looked at her Bjørn with a skeptical eyebrow raised.

"Are you sure you aren't talking about yourself, *sötnos*?" she scolded him playfully and he laughed even more warmly.

Lysander reclined in his seat and surveyed D. Bjørn leaned over, pointing to an old woman with thick, silver curls who was hunched low in her seat before a captive audience of young children, animated as she depicted a retelling of Egil's Saga.

"And don't listen too closely to old Liddie, yeah?" he said pointedly.

"Liddie?" Lysander repeated, zeroing in on the old woman.

"Yeah. She's our Seer. She's been around a long time, seen a lot of things - even has a family name - but don't take her too seriously, yeah? And don't tell Runa I said so. She'll have my hide. Liddie's a friend." Lysander nodded, but his eyes were wide with curiosity. He was watching her when she looked up and marked him from across the room. Striking, cornflower blue eyes met his with a jolt and he felt them pierce something deep inside of him before he ripped his gaze away.

Åsa and her playmates, fraternal twins with oversized ears sticking out the side of their heads, had produced some chalk and were decorating the cement floor with runic seals, copying something they had learned about in school. The walls around them reverberated with the sounds of their ancient, folk music. The mix of languages roared so harmoniously, they didn't need a fire to keep them warm, like the upper levels. Their energy, their music, and their dancing did that. If the Norse peoples and the essence of all they were was being preserved anywhere in Mimameid, it was down here in D.

Across the room, Ned belched, announcing loudly that he was getting another drink, and stood up to head over to the automat. Lysander seized his chance and jumped up to intercept the old Celt. He fell into step beside him and after a few paces, Ned stopped and looked at him.

"Can I-" he burped again, "help you?" he asked, his breath rank, his voice gravelly and with a hint of an accent he thought must be Scottish, but he couldn't be sure.

"Hi uh, Ned Wallace, right?" Lysander began. Ned rolled his dark eyes, running a gnarled hand through his long scraggly beard.

"Yes, I'm the Celt. No, I'm not a spy. I don't know how you got in here, but if you don't mind, I'm just trying to have a quiet drink. Please leave me alone." He pushed Lysander aside and continued toward the automat. Lysander sidestepped him and grabbed a hold of his arm. Ned, stronger than he looked, easily escaped Lysander's grip, taking a hold of his wrist forcefully. Lysander winced as Ned's grasp tightened.

"Sorry. I'm Lysander, I'm a friend of Magdelena's." He spoke quickly and Ned's eyes shifted, his grip relaxing ever so slightly.

"Walk with me," he instructed him, his tone suddenly sober. "Sorry about that, laddie. I can't be too careful, especially with people who look like you." He raised a wiry eyebrow as he scanned Lysander up and down.

"What do you mean?" he asked, feeling scrutinized.

"People from the upper levels," Ned explained, as though it were obvious. "Not always welcome here, am I? Being who I am." They were at the automats. "What took you so long to get down here?" he asked, surprising Lysander.

"Huh?"

"Magdelena said I should be expecting you," he answered nonchalantly.

"She did?"

"Ha. I guess I shouldn't be surprised she knows you better than you know yourself." He let out a light chuckle. "That woman never ceases to amaze me. How Helgi earned her, I'll never understand." The last bit was more for himself than for Lysander.

"You know him, right? Her husband? From Svalbard?"

"Knew. I'm not sure I believe anyone who was there is still alive."

"But you told Magdelena -" he began, quick to feel indignant that Ned might have fed Magdelena false hope.

"She would have left regardless of what I had said to her, lad. If only to say goodbye." Ned spoke with finality and Lysander knew he was right. "She's been through enough. She didn't need more pain from a friend."

Ned stuck out his band up to the automat and Lysander watched it dispense the Mimameid specialty oatmeal beer. "You want one?" Ned asked him.

"A beer?" Lysander was confused. "Aren't we only allotted one every three days?" Ned smirked at him.

"No one's shown you the trick yet?" he asked and pulled out his wristband. "You slide down to reset and while it's resetting, order your beer." Ned showed him as he explained and sure enough, the dark liquid came pouring out of the dispenser into a mug below. Eyes wide, he looked at Ned.

"And what happens when the implant reads your blood alcohol levels?" he challenged him, curious. Surely, they must be monitoring this somehow.

"Don't let them get too high." Ned winked, pulling out a flask and tipping what smelled like whiskey into his beer.

Lysander picked up his beer and tipped it back, taking a small sip. He grimaced, unaccustomed to the malty flavor.

"So what is it you want from me, exactly?" Ned asked him again, as they started back across the room. Lysander paused.

"Just to talk," he said vaguely, but looking Ned directly in his cloudy, sea-green eyes. The man nodded.

"We can talk, laddie. But not here. Come by my bunk after work tomorrow." He didn't wait for Lysander to answer, instead returning to his cheering group of drinking buddies, the accordion player striking back up a lively, if slightly out of tune at this point, melody at his reappearance.

Lysander took his seat across from Runa and Bjørn, who looked at him expectantly, clearly wanting to know what had happened with Ned.

"And?" Bjørn said, after Lysander was quiet.

"I like it down here in D," Lysander replied, taking another sip of his beer. This one was better, a bit smoother as it went down. Bjørn grinned at him.

"I thought you might."

12
PETRA

"...AND YOU WOULDN'T BELIEVE what the mountains are hiding up there. I found more of that - what was it - that peculiar moss we used on Lasse up there." Petra grinned sheepishly as he carried on. She was grateful to see Benjáme again, any remaining bitterness between them having floated away with the winds of the mountains.

Above Ground life suited him. His eyes sparkled like an agate stone in the sun as he told her about camp life on the ridge. They had built semi-permanent sleeping quarters so they could stay on as support without the weather affecting their ability to observe her. Anja and Onni were happy as could be to study the Celts firsthand. Meanwhile, Maike was keeping them all on task, making sure they had enough food and water to sustain them as long as the mission continued, as well as running point on communications with Mimameid. Benjáme, in addition to being Petra's primary contact, had taken it upon himself to map the rugged landscape and was enjoying the long days of solitude that his expeditions were affording him.

Although he told Maike it was for Mimameid, he confided in Petra that secretly he was using it to orientate himself so that when the opportunity presented itself, he would go find Taavi. It had been a long time since Petra had heard him talk about his husband and she was glad to see Benjáme with a sense of purpose other than revenge.

Though with discipline and training he had learned to channel his rage, he carried his hatred with him always. It informed his every decision over the years, including whether to buck the alcohol limit or pick a fight with someone to get himself a disciplinary hearing, just so he could jump the queue for an audience to argue with Sigrid. Blind, reckless, and consuming.

Before this mission, she might not have considered it, but this hotheadedness made him an easy person to pin mistakes on, especially if he wasn't there to defend himself. Now to see that fire being channeled into something productive - to see that light in his eyes burn for justice, instead of revenge - made her glad, but cautious. That light as he spoke reminded her of Arthur. She hoped that while she was on-mission and unable to help him, it wouldn't be snuffed out.

She let Benjáme carry on for several more minutes before interrupting to refocus the topic. She cleared her throat.

"I'm going to have to get back soon, before they start to notice that I'm gone." Her smile was a little impatient but he luckily didn't notice.

She had left Arthur at the exit of the dining truck, promising to bring ale back with her when she met him later at his camper van. She had told him about the need to meet with her people, but for his own safety, he didn't know when or where she met them. He would certainly start to get suspicious if she took too long now, getting that ale.

"Oh, right. Of course. Also, Maike really needs to know about any more upcoming festival bonfires. When they might have their guard lowered, you know? I can tell it's starting to get to her, the stress coming from the Mimameid end of things, so even if you don't have much, it would be helpful for next time." Benjáme's eyes were reluctant to have to bring it up. He had also been enjoying simply being about to catch up with her.

"I'll do my best," she promised and she meant it. She felt for Maike. The pressure from Sigrid could be relentless. She was grateful that pressure didn't fall so immediately on her shoulders this mission.

"And Petra?" Benjáme ran his hand over his scar, hesitantly. "You will ask around about Taavi? See if they have any Norse prisoners?" He fingered his reindeer bone knife as he asked and Petra nodded, trying to arrange something like confidence onto her face for him.

She was skeptical of there being any Norse prisoners in the Celtic camp, but maybe that had been what Arthur had meant about how they got their information on the Norse. She still hadn't visited any of the other camps either, so just because she hadn't seen them didn't mean they weren't there. Regardless, she wanted to help her friend. "I will, I promise."

He reached out and hugged her. The gesture came as a surprise, her stomach lurching before she relaxed and hugged him back.

"Take care of yourself," Benjáme told her as they released one another. She nodded, half a smile creeping into the corner of her mouth.

"You too."

She turned, heading back through the small grove that led to camp. The trees were tucked in here, sheltered in the valley by the mountainside, growing taller and thicker than any other trees she had seen since Ragnarök. Smoke from the evening bonfire was just beginning to swirl up into the air, even though night hadn't completely fallen yet. The sky still clung to a misty grey of dusk, twinkling half-heartedly.

Petra's heart suddenly stopped when she saw the guard posted at the entrance. *Perkele,* she thought. She'd let Benjáme carry on for too long and now it wasn't who she was expecting. The young, impressionable boy she'd been timing her meetings with was gone.

Standing in his place was a burly man with orange hair streaked with grey atop his head and a rugged brow, furrowed with discontent. Still partially obscured from view by the trees, she adjusted her tartan nervously around her hair, pulled a few copper locks out, and took a step forwards, leaves crunching under her boots in the snow. He was immediately alert, unsheathing a jagged hunting knife from a leather strap. She stepped out of the shadows of the tree line and put her hands up.

"Hi, sorry." She stumbled over her Gaelic and the man lowered his weapon. "Sorry, I just got a little turned around-" He sheathed the knife, rolling his eyes and grabbing her by the shirt, her tartan shawl dropping into the snow. As he dragged her across the frozen ground into the encampment's borders, she scrambled for any plausible reason to be beyond the bounds of camp. Her thoughts racing, the guard grunted as he slammed her up against the side of a transport truck.

"Just a little turned around, eh?"

"Petra!" The usually-laughing voice rang desperate in the cold evening air and she let out an audible sigh of relief. "Petra. What took you so long?" Arthur's words fell indignantly into the snow around them. The guard lowered her to the ground, still gripping tight, and Petra hung her head, feeling Arthur's disappointment.

"I was just -" she started to say, but then she saw Arthur's wink and realized he was putting on a show. He turned to the guard, clapping him on his enormous bicep.

"Angus, you ever try to take a girl to the clootie well and it just *does not* go like you planned?" Arthur asked. Angus - who was easily a head taller than him and had shoulders twice as wide - grunted back, confused by what was happening. "Well, this girl just takes off, just starts running!" Arthur continued.

Angus nodded slowly, having understood some part of the nonsense Arthur was saying - even though Petra didn't - because his grip on her eased up. "Gotta show her what we do to women who don't respect us, you know what I mean?" Arthur tried to puff out his chest to look tough but instead looked so ridiculous, Petra had to swallow to keep from chortling.

Angus nodded again and dropped his hold on her. She glared at the large man, annoyed, and straightened her jacket.

"You just can't be too careful, you know. We just had a rotation in from one of the other camps and I swear, I've never seen any of those people before," Angus told Arthur.

"How is it we've been on this rock for six years and you've never seen them?" Arthur asked incredulously, grabbing Petra's fallen tartan from the ground.

"That's what I was asking myself." The guard shrugged his shoulders.

"Well, say hi to the missus for me, yeah?" Arthur told Angus, stepping in front of Petra to hide her from the small crowd that was starting to gather at the commotion and she threw her tartan back over her head. Hand in hand, they hurried away. "Well, that was fun," Arthur finally said when they were clear of the other people. His voice was low, but his eyes still sparkling, playfully. "Shall we get that drink and you can tell me what that was all about?"

"So you're saying you believe this woman is trying to have you killed?" he asked, eyes narrowed as he riddled it out.

"Sigrid. And I'm not sure. It's just a theory." Petra looked down into her empty mug.

"Right, Sigrid. Even though she's been your mentor for years. You know that sounds a little..." he raised his hands to his head as he searched for the word, "*dúsachtach*." He found it in Gaelic faster.

"I know, I know I sound crazy. But think about it, would you have sent me out on a such dangerous mission with a still-healing leg wound?"

"I mean, I'm a little biased," he teased and she felt her cheeks burning. She was still getting used to this part of him. He was so brash sometimes, so unembarrassed by his feelings, so unafraid of them. Was it the Celtic way, to be so...forward?

"Would any responsible leader, then? Without an ulterior motive?" she asked him with a raised eyebrow.

"No, no you make a good point." He glanced down at his old-timer watch, blowing on the scratched glass and rubbing it. "Oh *cac*. I told Iain and Gwenna we'd be there for dinner." He jumped up from his seat and grabbed Petra's tartan off the table.

She stood up quickly, almost knocking her mug of ale over on the table. Arthur had arranged for her to stay with his brother, Iain and his wife Gwenna, in their family trailer, but there hadn't been an evening yet where Arthur hadn't been working in the clinic. This would be the first time they were all together. She took her shawl from his outstretched hand, wrapped herself up tightly, and followed him away from the pub, into the dark.

"So what are you going to do? If you aren't sure if you can trust your people?" he asked.

"I mean, I can trust Benjáme. And I don't think Onni or the others would do anything to intentionally harm me. It's just..."

"They will do what it takes to protect what they love." Arthur's voice was surprisingly grave as he finished her sentence.

"Yeah."

The wind was whipping as they made their way across the camp, stirring up the ashes and causing Petra to pull her woolen tartan tighter around her face. Usually, the valley was relatively protected from such bracing weather, but something must have swept in from the north.

"So, what are you going to do, then?" he pressed her again.

"I'm not sure. I think I need more information. From both sides."

"And how do you plan on getting information on the Norse from inside the Celtic camp?" he asked, hands shoved in his pockets, shoulders hunched in the wind.

"I'm still working that one out." She looked sideways at him, cheekily.

Arthur led the way through the maze of tents and trailers until they were back at the faded camping trailer that belonged to Iain's family. He raised a raw, red hand and rapped on the door in a playful rhythm.

The door opened, but no face appeared. Petra followed the open frame down to see Arthur's seven-year-old nephew, Aeron, standing there to greet them with his full head of auburn hair and glittering eyes.

"Uncle Art's here!" he called back into the trailer as they heard a clattering of dishes and the wails of the youngest member of the family, baby Domnall, coming from inside. Iain's head appeared around the edge of the door.

"Come in, come in! We didn't know if you were going to make it in time." Arthur gestured for her to go first and Petra climbed the steps only to be ambushed by Iain, wrapped in a warm hug. Something Petra was learning to appreciate about Iain was his seemingly boundless warmth, but it could at times, be overwhelming. He released her and moved on to Arthur as Petra made her way further into the trailer.

"Can I help with anything?" she asked Gwenna, who looked up from the table, having lulled Domnall back into a sort of calm.

"No, no everything is already done. We were about to start eating. Just wash up and take a seat." Petra pumped some sanitizer onto her hands from the bottle on the counter and slide into her seat, rubbing her hands together. She was starting to get used to the filmy feeling the sanitizer left behind. It was a luxury not everyone in the camp had, but because Arthur worked in the clinic, he could get his hands on some extra occasionally. Gwenna insisted it go to the family, aware that it was a small measure, but a helpful one when one disease or another swept through the camp.

"It smells good." Petra tried to match Iain's level of friendliness to show how grateful she was that they were taking care of her. Gwenna raised an eyebrow, suspiciously.

"We got pasta, canned tomatoes, and canned corned beef in rations today. I just balled them up and hoped it might taste something like bolognese. And lucky us, only the tomatoes are past their expiration date." Her voice was a little sour, but she arranged her face as though she was trying to hide it. She dished it out and handed a plate to Petra.

"Thank you." She accepted the plate as Aeron slid in beside her before Arthur could. He took the next plate from his mother's hands as Arthur and Iain joined the table.

"Are you staying with us, again?" Aeron asked Petra, his eyes hopeful. She glanced up at Gwenna, not wanting to overstay her welcome, but Gwenna gave her an approving nod. She was grateful to have someone to entertain Aeron when she was busy with the baby.

"I am, actually. Is that okay?" she asked Aeron and he nodded with his father's unbridled warmth. Kids weren't exactly her thing, but she found that Aeron was uncommonly quick-witted and she enjoyed her conversations with him.

"So I heard you gave the guards a little trouble earlier?" Iain said as he started shoveling the pasta into his mouth. Petra fiddled with a noodle she was twirling around her fork, looking sideways at Arthur.

"That's true, I did," she started, trying to decide where to steer the conversation.

Iain and Gwenna didn't know her true purpose in the camp. She was actually quite surprised how much Iain trusted his younger brother, to simply agree to welcome a perfect stranger with an odd accent into their home. She decided to redirect the conversation as casually as possible. "But of course, thankfully I had this knight in shining armor there to protect me," she replied sarcastically. Iain threw his head back and let out a howl of laughter that earned him a stern look from his wife. Baby Domnall babbled happily at the interaction between his parents.

"I like her," Iain chuffed generously at Arthur. "She's some lady. And Pa would have, too." The last comment hit Arthur a little harder, but he tried to brush it off.

"Weather-beaten old miner he was, he'd probably marry her himself," Arthur joked, though a little crestfallen.

"Oof. Baby brother, you're just as fallible as the rest of us," Iain replied, grabbing his brother's shoulder and shaking him. "This confidence he has, it's just a façade," Iain assured Petra with a wink that reminded her of Arthur. Maybe their Pa had had it, too. It was impossible not to see the similarities between the brothers. She couldn't understand how, after all they had been through - the massacre she remembered from the TV, whatever had happened to their parents - they had remained so light-hearted, so idealistic.

"That's Cornish men for you. All bark and no bite," Gwenna scowled playfully at her husband as she set down a plate of canned corned beef on the table, wobbling in its gelatinous, packaged form.

"All bark and no bite?" Petra asked, glancing between the two men, Arthur reaching over and helping himself to the bland beef.

"Ah, well," Gwenna sat down next to Iain, who put his arm around her as she picked up a spoon and started to feed baby Domnall something mashed, "see Cornish men, they like to put on that they are so sure of themselves. That they don't take life too seriously. But when it comes down to it, it's the women they marry that are *really* made of steel." Both Arthur and Iain raised their voices in protest. Even Aeron stood up on his chair in defiance. But the noise was warm and jolly.

"Oi! Those are fighting words, *fy nghariad*!" Iain said, the word unfamiliar to Petra.

"*Fy nghariad*?" she asked as Arthur leaned across the table to grab the pitcher of water for a refill. "That's a new one for me." She saw Gwenna squirm uncomfortably.

"That's because it's not Gaelic, it's Welsh," Arthur explained, without skipping a beat. "Gwenna here is one of the handful of Welsh we have left, so my brother here -" he reached over and punched Iain's shoulder, "went to the trouble of learning the language to impress her." Gwenna's comfort level didn't seem to change with the explanation and her eyes shifted around the table.

"Well it worked, didn't it?" Iain declared triumphantly, slapping the back of the chair beside him.

"No, what worked was you getting me pregnant," she reminded him, "and then pregnant again. With his little *cyw*." Gwenna leaned forward and tapped baby Domnall's pudgy nose sending him into a fit of giggles.

When the children were both in bed, bedtime stories of Annwfn having been read aloud from a threadbare old book, and then read aloud again, Iain pulled out a few bottles of ale he'd traded for at his work down at the water reclamation truck while Petra helped Gwenna with the washing.

"So, how are things going back at the clinic, then?" Iain asked as he reclined on the sofa, now that the dinner table had been stowed.

"Oh, fine. Nothing exciting really. A couple of cases of vitamin D deficiency, and we think there might be upcoming problems with vitamin A... but beyond the expected illnesses in the elderly, nothing to report." Petra was surprised at his response. She hadn't spent much time in The Infirmary of Mimameid, but it sounded like the Celts had far more day-to-day problems to deal with here Above Ground than the Norse, with their perfectly curated meals and exercise routines. Not to mention safety and security that granted them peace of mind. Even the people in the lower levels had access to those things.

She finished drying the last of the plates and put them away in the cabinet above the sink before accepting a drink from Iain and sitting down on the couch opposite them.

"So, where do you get those vitamins from?" Petra asked, taking a sip of her ale.

"Ideally, we'd be able to solve a lot of our nutrition problems if we were able to fish," Arthur said, watching her.

"But then, why not fish?" she urged him to continue, "We -" she stopped herself, realizing that Iain and Gwenna were still there.

"Well, the fjords are contaminated because of the ash in the atmosphere. The fish populations are so decimated by it, we couldn't possibly find a sustainable way to fish them while also screening them for healthy levels of toxins. We'd destroy the fish and then we'd be right back where we started," Arthur explained. Petra was starting to understand the true level of desperation in the Celts.

Mimameid maintained a small level of saltwater fish from the fjord, but also relied heavily on their own freshwater fish, grown and harvested safely within the confines of the bunker. The Celts didn't have such a luxury. There was a clock ticking on how long they could continue to exist like this.

"Can't you test the waters to find out when the water levels have become safe again for the fish?" Petra asked, wanting to find a solution. "What kind of equipment does the water reclamation truck have, anything that could be useful?" She directed her question this time to Iain. He was quiet for a moment before a smile crept onto his face.

"Arthur, I really like her."

The ale swam in her belly, warm and bubbly as she walked with Arthur back to his camper van. It hadn't really been the plan, but they were on such a high after talking about the possibility of a water testing project that they'd finished off Iain's ale and now they were clinging to the remaining buzz of the evening.

She still hadn't gotten used to drinking and her head hummed pleasantly. Arthur's arm wrapped around her waist, holding her steady.

"You ready to talk about why you got caught outside of camp now?" Arthur asked her as they leaned back against the trailer. She looked up at his eyes, striking against the dark sky.

"Did you just get me drunk so you could interrogate me?" She pointed a finger at him and squinted skeptically.

"Maybe," he answered with a lighthearted chuckle.

"You want to tell me why you haven't told anyone I'm Norse yet? Not even Iain?" she ventured and he raised an eyebrow at her question, a bemused expression playing on his face.

"Who says I haven't?" A twinkle danced in his eyes.

"Because that guard would have taken that whole thing a lot more seriously if he'd been told to keep an eye out for an infiltrator. And Iain wouldn't be so nice," Petra shot back, even though her brain felt a little like it was moving in slow motion.

"Okay, okay you're right. But Iain is nice to everyone." Arthur raised his hands in surrender and fumbled for his keys, unlocking the door and guiding her inside.

When they were sitting on the bed, Arthur poured them each a glass of water and together they leaned against the wall. Petra sipped quietly, tilting her head back and sighing.

"I had to make contact with my people," she confessed softly, throwing him a sideways glance as she spoke.

"Of course," Arthur replied, "I should have known enough to work that one out on my own."

"Hmmm," she just sighed, thinking about what he had said about being biased about her.

"Well, what did they say?" he responded and she chuffed.

"That I'm not giving them enough information."

"Do they think maybe you've been compromised? Turned?" He took a loud gulp of water and Petra shrugged.

"By whom?" she asked and he raised his eyebrows, looking at her. "By you?" Her voice was probing. "You don't even like the Celts." Arthur's eyes got wide, the part of his irises tinted with purple glowing precariously.

"How would you know that?" he said, suddenly very serious.

"Iain said," she started to say but stopped herself, seeing the regret creeping up onto his face. She hoped it wasn't because of her, but it made her sad.

"Iain, you idiot," Arthur murmured under his breath. Suddenly, she felt bad, a pit in her stomach. The alcohol had made her tongue loose and now he was upset with her.

"Look, I'm not going to tell anyone, Norse or otherwise," she said quickly.

"No, no it's not that. Sorry. It's just Iain, he can't keep his mouth shut. He and that busybody, Gwenna, were made for each other, I swear." His brow was furrowed, but he didn't elaborate further.

"So, is that why you haven't told anyone the truth about me?" she asked him, tentatively. "Because you don't like the Celts either?"

"It's not like that. It's just, they take care of us - me and my brother. I have a good job here, and they leave us be. But the price I had to pay..."

"Because you're English?" she asked, slowly. He nodded, silently. "Because of the massacre?" The word felt like poison on her tongue. He leaned back, running his hands through his messy hair, anxiously.

"How much do you know about it?"

"Only what I heard from the news. Not too much, I imagine." She shrugged and Arthur was quiet for a moment.

"They came in the night. Always raiding at night, town after town. Until we couldn't sleep anymore for fear of being burned alive." Petra nodded. She had heard about their raiding methods from other Norse, but the Celts never made it as far north as her little base in Old Finland.

"We lived on a mountain outside of Old Penzance. Our land didn't flood because we were too high up on the cliffs. We had a big family - our younger siblings and our parents. So we offered to join the ranks, Iain and I, as soldiers, if they let our family be. And we thought they'd agreed to that, of course, right up until they lit our house on fire and held us down to listen to the screams of our family burning inside." Petra was quiet. She didn't know what to say. How could anyone know what to say to that? It was worse, far worse than she had imagined.

"We didn't have any choice after that. We joined, and they found out I was a doctor after a little while, treating people in secret. So they traded out my gun, put me and my brother up in private quarters on the contingency that I stitch them up and..." His face fell into his hands. Petra reached out to him, placing her rough fingers gently on his back. He sucked in a breath and let it out again, haltingly. He raised his head and sighed. "Anyways, that's why I haven't told anyone about who you are."

"I understand," she breathed. And she really did. It had been subtle at first, but she had started to notice the way the English were treated here, as second-class citizens, as traitors to their own people. It reminded her of the way the Sámi, the Finns, and the Danes were sometimes treated in Mimameid. It was something she had tried to push from her mind because she was better off than most, but every so often a comment from Milla or Benjáme would catch her off guard.

Of course, Milla's family had died down in D during the quarantine. And Benjáme, well, he had spent more nights in The Infirmary than anyone else combined from being beaten up for his Sámi tattoos or refusing to back down after another provocation that turned into a fight. She didn't know Aksel as well, but he was always right there beside Benjáme in those fights. They were only a few of the people she felt were justified in their anger.

But even the most sympathetic Norse knew that Sigrid had no love of the Celts - English or other - and the story of the English plight wouldn't be enough to evoke mercy from her. They had done too much damage since coming to Scandinavia, whether they had been coerced into it or not, they had been a part of that. She was coming to understand that no matter what she or anyone else did, both sides were bracing for a confrontation, each thinking they had been wronged by the other. Petra was inclined to agree that there were good people, innocent people on both sides. But of course, only one of their leaders had condemned entire peoples to death. Even Arthur wouldn't deny that they had it coming.

"And what if the Norse come? What would happen if they attack?" Petra barely breathed out the words. Arthur's gaze was fixated on the hideous orange-purple-blue pattern he had strung up as curtains.

"I trust you." He broke his stare and looked over at her, taking her hand in his and running his thumb over the soft skin in little circles. "I don't know what it is about you, but I trust you." It wasn't really an answer, but it satisfied her and the air softened around them at his words. She felt the same way, after all, with no rational explanation for it. He continued making the little circles on her skin and she felt her heart getting faster.

"I'm glad I have some time to think about this," she said breathlessly. Arthur stopped what he was doing and she let out a sigh. She pushed her craving for his touch from her mind.

"What will you tell your men, the next time you meet them?" he asked her, and she considered the question carefully.

"Everything I know about the Celts that might help them. Nothing more, nothing less," she answered plainly. Arthur nodded, taking her hand back and kissing the top of it gently. "I do have some new things to tell them now, anyways," she reassured him.

"Thank you," he whispered and leaned his forehead against her own.

⨯⨯⨯⨯⨯

When she woke the next morning, she found herself alone in Arthur's camper van. A grey, morning light was shining through the curtains as the happenings of the night came flooding back.

They had agreed it would sell the story to the onlookers of last night's disturbance by the camp entrance better if she stayed in Arthur's camper van and he snuck out to bunk with Iain's family.

A heavy knock on the car door made her hand jump to her heart as she swung her legs over the edge of the dirty mattress. She leaned forward and rolled the door open, the misty morning light spilling in.

"Alright?" Iain chimed as he, long blonde hair rippling in the frigid wind, climbed into the van, Arthur slipping in behind him. "We brought you some coffee since I know my brother's amenities are...less than satisfactory." Iain scrutinized the place with a critical eye and grin as he sat down on the mattress. Petra scooted over, accepting the coffee. The powdery mix that they drank here in the Celtic camp wasn't real coffee like they'd had in The Time Before, and it certainly wasn't the green tea that she enjoyed back in Mimameid, but it was at least something to warm her fingers.

"Morning," Petra replied, groggily.

"Sleep well?" Arthur asked her, the carefree sparkle having returned to his eye after the intensity of last night. She nodded, a smile unwittingly creeping onto her face as she took him in. Dirty-blonde hair unkempt, and his stubble a few days old. His shoulders were slumped under a sheep-skin jacket, his boots stained with muddy, melting snow. Iain let out a cheerful laugh.

"You two," he said, rolling his eyes and standing up again. He climbed out of the van, bending into a goofy little bow at them. "Enjoy the day. And come by later!" Iain shouted, starting to walk away, but turning quickly to point at Petra and added, "You promised Aeron!", who couldn't help but laugh and nod.

"I'll be there!" she shouted back at him.

"That little boy is going to be very upset if you stand him up for his uncle again," Arthur chided playfully as he sat down next to her, sipping his own mug of coffee.

"Yes, Uncle Art," she smirked, "I won't stand him up - he's much better company, anyways." To which Arthur raised an eyebrow.

"Uh-huh," he smirked, setting his coffee mug down on the floor. "Listen, I had an idea this morning."

"Okay." She waited.

"I thought you could come assist me in the clinic. People generally feel pretty comfortable there and their tongues start wagging. I thought maybe you could, you know, keep your ears open. Maybe it'll help get Sigrid off your back, buy you some more time."

"Thanks. That could be really helpful, actually."

"Of course, my motives have a selfish angle," he admitted sheepishly. With a flush in her cheeks, she knocked her coffee back, feeling the electricity between them rising, then tied her long copper waves back into a loose braid. She picked up her tartan and stepped out of the van, wrapping the shawl around her as the morning air washed over her face.

As they wove through the maze of vehicles, Petra noticed the looks that seemingly every passerby gave them. Despite feeling more scrutinized than she preferred, she allowed Arthur to guide her down the camp's main road, his hand hovering in the small of her back protectively. It wasn't a gesture she was used to, nor one she felt particularly comfortable with, but she knew after last night why it was his first instinct. To protect, like her own instincts. She attempted to distract herself.

"Can I ask you something?" She looked sideways up at him.

"Sure," Arthur replied, clearly unmoved by being so observed.

"Do you ever have to treat..." she didn't want anyone overhearing them, so she lowered her voice for the last word, "prisoners?" Arthur turned his head, the slight hiccup in his step the only tell that he hadn't been prepared for the question. But she had promised.

"Interesting. Is there someone, in particular, you are looking for?" It wasn't a no.

"I'm asking for a friend," she replied coyly, not wanting to give him too much information before she had reason to. But his face was soft when he opened his mouth again.

"Well, officially," he sighed, "the Celts leave no survivors. Part of their scorched earth philosophy. But I patch up all kinds of people in my hospital," he replied, equally cryptically, "and the stories have to come from somewhere." They arrived at the edge of the bonfire perimeter and Arthur drew back the flap of the tent on the right as he spoke. "Step inside my office." He winked as she passed him and entered the Celtic clinic. She would get back to the prisoner question when they were somewhere more private.

It was somehow quieter inside the tent than she had imagined. And warmer. The lights hummed overhead, but the flap of the tent shut out everything that made the Celtic camp feel foreign to her. If it was a little bigger, she could easily imagine she was back in the Mimameid Infirmary. There were rows of cots lined up down the walls of the tent.

On the right-hand side was a small draw in the curtain leading to another room, presumably the surgery suite or storage. About half of the beds were occupied with patients, either sleeping or sitting up, propped against the thin mattresses and wrapped in foil blankets.

Arthur slipped past her, snapping on a pair of latex gloves and picking up a clipboard and pen. He read something on the papers, made a mark, and turned to the nurse at the other end of the tent - a woman with short, dark hair and kind, grey-blue eyes. She wore an old pair of scrubs over a layer of thermals with thick, fur-lined boots on her feet and latex gloves like Arthur on her hands.

"Did you already give Keeley her medication?" Arthur asked and the nurse nodded.

"Just ten minutes ago," she told him over her shoulder as she handed out the last of what looked to be breakfast on each of the patients' tables.

"And there's been no change since yesterday morning?" he confirmed with her. She nodded again and approached them with the empty tray.

"No change at all. But between you and me," she leaned in, "I don't think it was Duncan who gave her mono." Her eyes shifted and Arthur's top lip curled into an amused smile.

"Okay, thank you, Darcy. Let's keep her under observation for another twelve hours before we send her home. Maybe keeping her under lock and key will keep it from spreading faster than it needs to." The woman returned his smile and nodded in response. She then turned her gaze to Petra, welcoming, but Petra sensed she felt that her territory was being infringed upon by some stranger.

"Can we help you?" she asked, her voice cordial.

"Oh sorry!" Arthur laughed and quickly introduced her. " Darcy, Petra. Petra, Darcy." He gestured back and forth between the two of them. "Petra offered to help us out today. She has some field training in medicine and thought she'd see if she wants to make it a more permanent job position." Petra shook Darcy's hand, impressed, but also a little unnerved at how seamlessly the lie had slipped out of Arthur's mouth.

"Always glad to have an extra set of hands. I'll show you around then." Petra relaxed a little with the warm smile Darcy gave, following her down the tent to a cart of what she could see were various medical supplies.

Petra turned back to see Arthur wink at her one more time before he stepped towards his first patient - an ornery old man with bushy, white eyebrows.

Quietly and carefully she made herself busy and kept her head down, administering IV fluids and taking people's blood pressure without over-involving herself in any one particular person.

Darcy and Arthur chatted as they worked about all kinds of goings on in camp. Petra's ears rang with the echoes of the rising cases of pneumonia and their thinning supply of antibiotics. They talked about a baby that was born blind, a woman who died after a miscarriage a few days before, and how they were both likely to be yet another result of the growing vitamin A deficiency.

"Siobhan won't be pleased," Darcy told him, her voice a little chilled when she said the name. It seemed to mean something to Arthur though, who sighed and looked at Darcy, half-heartedly.

"Don't worry about Siobhan, I will talk to her. You have enough on your plate without getting involved in politics," Arthur reassured her. "On that subject, how are the kids getting on?" Arthur asked her and Darcy's face fell a little.

"Better, I suppose. I haven't been sleeping much since Ben passed, but Fergus is good with the little ones. He's taking good care of the baby." The more Petra listened, the more she learned and saw why Darcy was around to help Arthur.

Despite, what Petra gleaned, the death of her husband and having three young kids at home, Darcy had seemingly unending patience with the sick, and she always listened to whatever they wanted to talk to her about. If she hadn't been ten years his senior, Petra might have found herself feeling jealous of the bond between the two of them. But their rapport with one another was professional, aside from the tidbits of camp gossip that Darcy shared with him from time to time. It was easy to see how she knew so much about the goings-on. She was so full of compassion and empathy that it was natural for people to confide in her. Perhaps she had been the person Arthur had meant for her to speak with to gather information.

He, to Petra's surprise, was a completely different person than the younger brother figure she saw when he was with Iain. Here, he was in his element.

His movements as he inserted an IV or redressed a wound were organic, pure muscle memory. And his manner was that of calm authority and earnestness. All day long, he assured one after another patient that there was no problem he couldn't solve, no length he wouldn't go to help them. Petra found that she, like Darcy and his patients, was drawn to his charisma like a magnet. It was the same unflinching compassion he had shown them out in the wild and she saw here that it was in fact, inherent in him.

She was amazed that out here in this little makeshift clinic, in the bitter cold of the North Country, she felt so warm and at home. She was almost scared to say it, but even more at home than in Mimameid. Though being here wasn't familiar like the bunker was - where she knew every nook and cranny - the camp, the Celts, and Arthur - they awakened in her something deep, something she had been silencing inside of herself.

Lunch was delivered to them in the tent: cans of tinned fish, as well as one can of peas and carrots to be split among the patients. As she helped Darcy pass the food out, the nurse gave her background on the various patients they had.

"That's Leith, he got his girlfriend pregnant last year, but then she miscarried and that was one of the first cases that made us start looking into the vitamin A supply. And now she's pregnant again, so here's hoping things go well. You heard about Keeley, I guess. Duncan is her husband and he's a sweet old man, but they seem to be on different pages these days if you know what I mean," she smirked, "and then there's old Deirdre whose husband died ages ago and she's lived through so many wars, gods only knows, so she's known to say the odd racist thing or two. Gotta be careful around her. Oh, but with such lovely red hair like you have, she'll absolutely adore you." She chattered on happily, unfortunately not saying anything of much substance that Petra would be able to report back to Benjáme and the others. But she found that she didn't mind much, that there was something peaceful about just doing simple tasks and helping around the clinic.

Petra watched everyone eat together as if she was looking in from the outside, sitting on the edge of a glow that radiated from the others, but not able to bask in it. She wanted to feel sad for herself, but she found instead that she was only curious how the people of Mimameid could have such a false understanding of the Celts.

They didn't cannibalize people for their bonfire festivals as a ritual sacrifice to please their gods. They didn't even seem to be militarized, to be quite honest. The leaders had massacred the English all those years ago, it was true and no one could deny it, but not every Celt should answer for that.

Maybe she'd been wrong. Some of them were just as much the victims of their leader's greed as the Norse, like Arthur and Iain, and Gwenna.

These people, the people that made up the Celts, on the whole, were just people. Just trying to find enough food to feed their families. Just trying to survive in the post-Ragnarök world.

Yanking her from her thoughts, Petra looked up to see a panicked woman come in cradling a small boy in her arms who was wailing.

The boy's arm had been badly broken, the bone poking out, tendons ripped apart. Arthur jumped up, dexterously taking the boy from the woman's arms and disappearing into the other room of the tent, away from the other patients. The young mother dissolved into tears on Darcy's shoulder and Arthur called to them, the slightest trace of panic in his voice,

"I need an assist!"

Darcy, with the woman still sobbing into her shoulder, jerked her head towards Petra.

"Go on," she said softly, her voice full of encouragement. Petra found her feet moving toward the room before her brain had fully processed what was happening.

She ripped back the curtain, seeing the provisional operating suite set up beside cabinets half-filled with overflow medicines. They certainly weren't as well stocked as Mimameid. It was colder than the main room, and she thought fleetingly that it must have something to do with keeping the medicines cool. She tried to pull herself back to the situation at hand.

"Gloves," Arthur instructed and they both put on fresh pairs before beginning. "Masks." He handed her one off the cart. Once they had secured them in place, he held her gaze for a moment, the midnight blue steadying her. "Are you ready?" he asked and she let out a shaky breath, trying to nod. She had never had to do anything like this before.

"Yes." The word came out, but she wasn't sure she meant it. She was, however, as ready as she could be. He reached out over the boy on the table to squeeze her gloved hands reassuringly before picking up the scalpel. He pressed it to the boy's skin and they began.

He explained every step as he was doing it, just as he had when he worked on Lasse. Stop the bleeding. Clean the wound. Reset the bone. Put in the pins. Repair the tendons. His voice didn't falter as he asked her for various-sized clamps and needles. Petra found herself generally in awe at how intuitive the process was for him, even when he needed to pause to work through a different approach halfway through. Once the situation was, however under control, the atmosphere in the room relaxed again and Petra could lean into that awe as she watched Arthur work, a pair of forceps in one hand and bloody gauze she'd forgotten she was holding in the other.

"Is this how you pictured it? Your day in the clinic?" he asked with a teasing, if still a bit tense, light in his eyes. He guided the needle into the unconscious boy's arm and pulled the first suture tight.

"Very funny," Petra replied uneasily, but then continued. "Other than this poor kid though. It's kind of a nice place to be," she answered honestly, but she could see in his eyes that he was curious about exactly what she meant. "I like it better than The Infirmary in Mimameid," she said, the confession slipping out.

"Well, that means a lot. We really try to make it not such a scary place to be." His voice was modest. "But, what's Mimameid?" he asked her, without looking up from the stitching.

"It's," she thought quickly, eyes darting, "it's what we call the Norse camp." She didn't know why she didn't tell him that it was underwater and that it was a little bit more than a camp, but it somehow didn't feel safe, out here in the open. Exposed as they were in the cold, operating suite. She decided to ask him something, instead, since he was so at ease. And she was curious what he would say, as it seemed to be the one useful piece of information she had been able to extract from Darcy all day.

"Arthur?" she began.

"Hm?" he asked, still not looking up from his work.

"Who's Siobhan?" She saw him react to the name, just as he had earlier. He steadied his hands and continued working.

"Siobhan? Why do you want to know about Siobhan?" The question was abrupt, but Petra could see him trying to soften it by avoiding her gaze.

"Darcy mentioned a woman called Siobhan earlier." She shifted her weight. "It's just, she seemed *afraid* of her." She tried to sound innocent. Arthur stopped what he was doing. His eyes darted between hers - back and forth - searching. After a minute, he cast his face back down to the boy on the table and carried on with the sutures.

"Siobhan is our leader. She's the leader of the Celts." He spoke the answer down as if he was talking to the boy and pulled the thread high back up to look her in the eyes again. The question, it seemed, had been answered in its entirety. Arthur's face remained unchanged, steady. Pleasant, but not too revealing. It was like the first night at the bonfire, before they had made it to his van. Back then, he had been leaving some pieces of the story out and after spending so much time with him, she could tell he was now, too. She wasn't sure what he had omitted, but she assumed it had to do with his family. She opened her mouth to ask, but he changed the subject. "So, first surgery." He wiggled his blonde eyebrows in a goofy dance, "Do you want to cut the thread from the final stitch?" he asked her, proudly. She couldn't help but let out a little chuckle.

"Okay, yeah. Sure." She tried not to blush. It was a very bizarre thing to blush about, she knew, but she liked the feeling of him being proud of her. Arthur twisted the thread through the loop and pulled it tight. Even as she watched him though, a feeling of unease began to creep back up in her. Why hadn't she been briefed on Siobhan before the mission? Even if Maike and the others didn't know about her, or didn't want to say too much, Sigrid, at least, should have said something. They'd been alone, after all, in the briefing room.

That odd feeling of distrust of Sigrid was starting to slither back up into her spine with a prickle. She tried to shake the feeling off as she reached for the scissors. With a single cut, the surgery was complete.

"Nicely done," Arthur said when she had finished, ripping off his mask and throwing her a radiant look. He loved every bit about being a doctor. "Okay, now we just have to clean everything up and then we can get this brave guy back to his mom," Arthur said to her, pointing to something over her shoulder. "Can you hand me the iodine?" he asked.

Then everything went black.

13
LYSANDER

STILL FLOATING ON THE high of the music and cheer, and admittedly a bit from the beer, Lysander ascended back up to B with some difficulty. On a good day, the climb to the top of Mimameid took the wind out of him. On those days, he was grateful for the inhaler the doctors had given him, but tonight, he didn't think it would help. Tonight it wasn't the physical act of climbing that fatigued him, but quite simply that he wanted to stay down in D. It felt safe down there in the bellows of the bunker. Cocooned. It didn't help that the walls were spinning ever so slightly.

Rounding a corner that exited to C, he caught sight of several familiar, if stern, faces. Unsure of whether the beer was fogging up his brain, he squinted at them in the dim light, but the faces remained the same. Rosy-cheeked and arguing, but the same. They were in the middle of a heated debate.

"You are going and that's that!" The voice speaking was Petra's dark-haired cook friend from the Canteen in C, Milla. "I don't know what they did to you up there, but this isn't you." She was clearly upset.

"Thank you! Exactly. That's what I said." The second voice came from a slighter man beside her with dark, curly hair. Aksel was his name, the disgruntled one; Lysander remembered from the meal in C. They were both talking to the same person - a tall, well-built man with a blonde topknot and a cropped red-blonde beard. Milla, Lysander observed with a drunken wobble, was standing on her tiptoes as she held the tall man's face firmly in her hands. It was a face he knew right away, even if it was a little shinier than usual.

"Lasse." As his voice spilled out, he became aware of just how inebriated he actually was. He thought of the last time he had seen Lasse, being dragged off to The Infirmary unconscious after warning them about the armbands. It was a sobering memory, but not sobering enough.

He looked down at his armband with a grin of recognition and then back up at the viking-face. "Hey. Glad you're okay." He knew his words were coming out sloppy, but he couldn't stop, "We were worried after, well, you know." He tried not to laugh, but couldn't suppress a small snort.

"Woah, who got the straight-laced engineer plastered?" The third voice had a lilt to it that Lysander was positive he'd heard before. Sure enough, when he looked it was Anders, the Icelandic soldier who had picked them up at the coast, his scarred neck gleaming in the dimmed, 'evening' lighting from under a rebellious *lopi* sweater.

"Hey, guys!" Lysander's arms spread wide as he stepped back and nearly slipped on the step behind him. "Whoops." He hiccuped as Anders reached out to steady him and took them all in as a group. "Well, that would be the uh...Ned down in D," he put a finger to his lips. "but, shhhhh because I'm pretty sure he put a little of the uh, *you know*," he pointed down at nothing in particular and whispered behind his hand, "whiskey stuff in my oat-beer."

Anders let out a hearty laugh and Milla punched him in the arm.

"Shut up," she hissed. "We're going to get caught."

"Yeah, because this B-level can't hold his drink." He laughed again, quieter, while Lysander lifted his finger back up to his lips, trying to open his eyes wide.

"Shhhhhh!"

Milla rolled her eyes at Lysander, taking Lasse by the hand and leading him down the steps, around Lysander. Aksel followed behind her, but Anders held back.

"Look, someone has to get this *fíflingur* back to his room or we're all screwed. I'll take him and meet you guys there," he told them, his hand still steadying Lysander on the steps.

"It'll probably be better to arrive separately anyways," Aksel offered and Milla conceded.

"Fine. I'll tell one of the others to wait for you by the back to let you in," she instructed him and Anders nodded. "Twenty minutes," she confirmed.

"I'll see you then," Anders said, a confident grin on his face. As the others disappeared down the stairs, Anders took Lysander by the arm and guided him up the steps.

"You were lucky Milla was with Lasse tonight, mate," he told him as they climbed. "She can be in a real mood sometimes, but she didn't want him to get caught. You got off easy." Lysander was aware that he hadn't understood everything that had just happened, but it dawned on him that they were all, except for maybe Milla, a part of C and therefore had no reason to be headed down to D. Anders and Aksel had even specifically said they had moved up to C because they enlisted.

"Little Milla?" he asked and Anders snorted again, laughing at him and the way he had made his hands into a little box shape.

"Yes, *little Milla* can really mess you up if she wants to," Anders assured him.

"Wait, but where were you guys all going?" he asked, tripping on a step and letting out another 'whoops.' Anders caught his elbow, still grinning at him as he hoisted him up. "The party in D is over, you guys know that right?" His words were slurred he knew, but he didn't know how to fix it.

"Yeah, I figured, boy genius," Anders chuckled and rolled his eyes. "What were you doing down there getting pissed in D?" Lysander put his hands up in the air.

"I'm innocent. I just got invited to dinner by a friend." The words slipped off his tongue a little jumbled up.

"A friend, huh?" Anders replied, distracted as they passed a group of people who, by the look of them, had never been further below than B. They looked at Anders' sweater, disgust evident on their faces, at a rule being broken. "So, where's your bunk?" he asked, unaffected by their stares.

Lysander pointed up, snickering at the expression on Anders' face when he did. Anders rolled his eyes again and continued up the stairs until they got to the entrance to B. "You're a real smart-ass, you know that? Next time I'm going to leave you with Milla," the blonde man told him. "And now?" Anders helped him off the stairs and onto the even floor, but Lysander felt the bunker start to spin, uncomfortably. He pointed down the right hallway.

"Oh no." He swallowed back something hot before bending over towards the spinning cement floor, the alcohol rising in the back up.

"Not yet, mate." Anders hoisted him up, dragging him down the hall until they got to his room.

"That's the one," he told Anders and held up his band, praying he was right. The numbers on the doors were moving a little too fast for him to be completely sure. Luckily, the light turned green and the door opened with a gush. Anders helped him over the threshold and pulled out his bed from the wall with the toes of his boot.

"Nice place," he said, reaching down and feeling the sealskin rug. Lysander kicked off his boots and fell back onto the bed.

"Thanks, man," he said, shielding his eyes from the lights that were slowly coming on. Anders stepped back out into the hallway, raising a hand.

"No problem, B-level. Drink some water. It'll make tomorrow better, trust me." As soon as Anders stepped out and the door closed again, he dropped from the bed and crawled across the floor, barely making it to the toilet in time.

The next morning he couldn't rush through breakfast like he usually did. The lights were far too bright as he stumbled into the canteen and up to the automat. He picked miserably at his porridge before giving up and taking a thermos of green tea with him down to The Engine Room.

Bjørn was sitting on the table in the office when he arrived, waiting for him, fresh oranges in hand.

"I bribed the canteen worker Runa coordinates with from The Gardens. Figured you'd need a little something extra after last night." Lysander nodded his thanks.

"Nice of you not to send any messages this morning for me to read on the way down." The floor was still spinning and he hadn't slept much in between the bouts of retching.

"Not like you would've read them even if I had!" Bjørn laughed. "I didn't think you had that much to drink?" he continued as Lysander massaged his temples.

"Ned definitely slipped something in there," he replied, his eyes closed.

"I guess you weren't drinking homemade brew in the barn at fourteen like the rest of us down in D, huh?" Bjørn slapped him on the back lightly and hopped off the desk.

"No," he groaned, following Bjørn out of the roaring room and down the stairs. "I was starting university at fourteen."

"That actually answers a lot of my questions about you." Bjørn threw him a cheeky grin. "You ready to get to work?"

When his band alerted him that the workday was over, he went to dinner and ate alone in B. The atmosphere in the canteen was no comparison to the night before, people eating in hushed voices on the concrete furniture, dispassionate and fully unaware of the festivities happening miles beneath their feet.

He watched the families coming and going for some time, their polite and reserved conversations littered with overuse of the 'Mimir's bough' greeting in hushed tones that made him yearn for the abandon he had felt in D. If this half-life in the upper levels was how the Norse were to survive, what kind of survival was it? Compliance.

When he was finished, he bussed his dishes, obediently separated out his various waste products, and headed back down in the direction of D. Ned had messaged him to meet at the doors leading to the canteen and he was eager to talk to the old Celt. His feet fell lightly on the steps as he hurried past C and down towards the entrance to D. It felt like coming home.

"Oi. Over here." Lysander heard Ned's gravelly voice and turned to see the old man's wiry hair already weaving down the hallway. He glanced back every so often, eyes glancing up at the blind spots in the surveillance and Ned guided him through the maze of open doors, so as not to raise any suspicion on the cameras.

He followed Ned along the cramped hallways, getting yelled at by a few elderly women for running into their laundry lines and tripping over a chair leg once. After snaking through several hallways, they reached a dead-end where the lightbulbs needed to be replaced. Two burly men greeted Lysander with a friendly "*góðan dag*" and Lysander was reminded that Ned lived down with the Icelanders. There was a flash of green and a door gushed open ahead of him. He followed Ned inside a darkly lit room, the door shutting behind him with an ominous hiss.

At first glance, Ned's bunk looked cramped and filthy. Every available surface was covered with knickknacks and junk, making it tricky to know where to move. He tried to adjust and bumped into an ornately decorated horn that fell from its perch. Ned reacted instantaneously, with the agility of a far younger man, catching the horn midair and replacing it on the shelf so delicately you would have thought it was explosive. He grunted, disapprovingly.

"Sorry," Lysander apologized with a sheepish grin and gave the room a deeper look, noticing there wasn't a spot of dust anywhere. None of it was junk. The objects around him were placed with care and purpose and they were picked up and admired often. He certainly didn't seem like he was trying to forget The Time Before, as Magdelena had implied. Everything in the room was precious to Ned.

He walked slowly along the shelves reading the names of the books - the ones he could understand anyhow - running his fingers across their peeling leather spines. On the shelf above, he reached out and touched a row of strangely formed rocks, each one slightly different than the next, some sparkling in the dim light, gleaming jagged and dangerous. Others were smooth and dark, glassy to the touch. Scattered around were small artifacts and pieces of pottery from civilizations long forgotten, some things Lysander vaguely remembered learning about when he was a child, but most of them painted and formed into shapes and patterns he didn't recognize.

Pictures leaned against the wall behind the bits of rock and pottery. Faded, folded, and worn but deeply, deeply cherished. He could see on each picture where the color had started to fade away from Ned's fingers - picking them up in the same spot every time he looked at them. He followed the pictures, of cliffs and mountains from The Time Before, volcanoes the old man had visited with strangers Lysander would never meet until he came to the grungy mirror hanging above the sink. Speckles of toothpaste splattered the mirror and it smelled vaguely like whiskey, which made Lysander's stomach start to turn. But, it was the photo he had taped to the mirror which caught his attention. He recognized the long, blonde plait of the woman Ned had his arm draped around.

Reaching up, he ran his finger up to her faded face.

"That was the day she told me she was pregnant with the little one." Ned's voice was throaty and when Lysander looked again he saw that Magdelena was wearing the silver dress she had described to him.

"There is not a day that goes by I don't wish things had turned out differently for her." He lowered his head as he spoke.

"How do you mean?" Lysander asked and Ned raised his head again, looking Lysander in the eyes with a terrible intensity.

"I shouldn't have let Helgi stay there on the island. That little girl deserved to have two parents, and Magdelena, she shouldn't have had to deal with everything alone. With *Ragnarök*." His dark, trusting eyes rolled as he enunciated the last word.

"She wasn't alone though." Lysander felt himself bristling. "You haven't seen Magdelena in a long time. She's not the person you used to know."

"No." Ned pulled out a chair and sat down. He picked up a dirty glass off the floor and spit in it, rubbing around the edge with a grubby finger. He poured himself a glass of whiskey and looked up at Lysander. "You want one?" Lysander shook his head, trying to hide his repulsion.

"No, thanks." He unfolded the other chair in the room, sat down, and leaned back against the open door of the closet. Ned had finished the first glass in silence and poured himself another.

"No, she is not the same."

"What did she say to you when she came to see you that day?" he asked and Ned sighed, pausing.

"She told me about you, laddie."

"What?" He didn't understand.

"She talked about how you had stuck with them all these years, been like a brother to her little girl, done what you could to protect them and feed them. She told me about your parents, about the shipwreck. She told me everything."

"She didn't ask about Helgi?"

"I mean, she did, of course. The last time we saw each other, Helgi and I were headed to Svalbard. But, it was like she wanted me to know about you. She wanted to make sure that we found each other."

"But why?"

"She didn't explain, but that woman rarely explains things." He shook his head and lowered it, turning his whiskey glass in his hands.

"Well, unless it's about plants. Then she carries on for hours," Lysander said and Ned snickered.

Well that's because -"

"- plants are easier than people." Lysander finished the sentence with Ned, having heard Magdelena say it so many times over the years. They both let out a huff of amusement. "But, you know?" Lysander continued, "For someone who claimed not to know people well, she can read people pretty damn good."

"Exactly," Ned agreed, pointing at Lysander. He downed his second whiskey and slammed the glass back on the concrete floor. "Did she ever tell you about her parents?" Ned fiddled with the whiskey bottle, peeling at the corner of the label with his long, dirty fingernails. Lysander shook his head.

"Not really. Just that they lived in Old Oslo and they didn't get along so well," he replied.

"That's an understatement," Ned scoffed and took a swig straight from the bottle. Lysander wondered why the old Celt had even bothered with the glass in the first place. "She was supposed to be this big débutante, brushing arms with politicians and big business. Her parents were socialites who made their money by destroying the environment." He could hear the distaste in Ned's mouth. "She was supposed to marry well and serve the family." Lysander shifted in his chair. So this was why she had wanted to leave all that in the past. "But Magdelena, she broke with them. She spent her teenage years going to anti-fossil fuel rallies and protests against her parent's company and then when she was eighteen she left and put herself through school to be a biologist."

"Is that where she met Helgi?" he asked Ned, but the old Celt shook his head.

"No, no, she met him much later. They were working in a lab together and Helgi, he just carries himself with this charisma that enchants everyone he meets. This adventurous, son-of-Thor hippie that lives his principles even if it kills him. And all that, wrapped around this wicked smart science-brain. It was enough to make every person in the lab weak in the knees. So, when she fell for him, she fell hard."

"And you were working there? In the same lab, I mean," Lysander asked.

"I knew her father. I worked for her parent's company long before we worked together in the lab, as a geological consultant for drilling. I was -" he took another gulp of whiskey - "young and stupid." Lysander saw the shame on his face. "I thought somehow that by working with them we could figure out a way to drill that wouldn't kill the planet." He shook his head. "I recognized her family name when she joined the lab, so I went over and introduced myself. You know, families like that, they held onto surnames longer than the rest. She remembered me from when she was a child. She was interning when we met, but she got a permanent position pretty quickly after that. She's probably the smartest person I've ever met - even smarter than Helgi - she sees things others don't think to look at. She cares. It really was a shame."

"A shame about what?"

"Well, when she got together with Helgi, they wanted to start a family and he said the stress of the job was making it impossible for them to conceive. They fought about it all the time, even at the lab, until she agreed to give up work. More and more, it became about Helgi's work and how Helgi was going to save the world. And Magdelena was supposed to play the docile housewife role she had worked so hard to get away from."

"But then," Lysander shook his head, processing everything Ned was telling him, "why would she still want to go after him now, after all that?" he asked and Ned sighed.

"Hell if I know." He shrugged, leaning back, his chair creaking. "You said it, the woman I once knew is gone. She doesn't need Helgi anymore, not like she did then."

"It sounds like she never really did need him," Lysander grunted.

"I'll toast to that," Ned growled, throwing back some more whiskey. "I mean, don't misunderstand me, Helgi's heart was always in the right place. He loved her, in his way. But he had a savior complex. He thought it was his job to save her and everyone else in the world and I think, for a while, she believed him."

Lysander was quiet for a few minutes. Even though his stomach was still turning a little from the night before, he grabbed the bottle from Ned's hands and took a gulp. It burned and the smoky flavor made him gag a little.

"That's disgusting," he coughed as he handed Ned the bottle back.

"Laddie, that's the good stuff," Ned replied, letting out a laugh that showed off his chipped teeth from under his bushy, red mustache.

"The only reason I can see for her to go after Helgi is for Linnaea's sake," Lysander concluded.

"Not every kid needs a father," Ned countered and Lysander nodded in agreement. It wasn't as if he'd had much of a father figure either - being shipped off to school at ten years old, only allowed home on holidays.

"I don't think this is about Linnaea needing a father figure in her life," Lysander paused, "so much as about knowing who her father really is. About knowing who she is."

"I hope I live to find out," Ned said, standing up and going to the sink to splash some water on his face.

"Hey, Ned?" he asked while the old Celt dabbed his face with a towel.

"Hm?"

"Why did you come to Mimameid, instead of going to the Celts?" Lysander asked and the old man sighed.

"Everyone always wants to know that," he replied, rubbing the water from his mustache.

"Well, is it really so much better here?" Lysander wanted to know just how much of the truth about Mimameid Ned would be willing to tell him.

"Mimameid has a kind of peace, even if it's a fragile, temporary peace. After what my people did to one another, the genocide they committed..." his voice broke a little as it trailed off. Lysander wondered what Ned couldn't bring himself to say. "I don't think there will ever be peace again among the Celts."

"So, it's just about survival, then?" he asked and the old man's mustache twitched.

"Isn't it always just about survival?"

An unexpected beep from his band jolted him awake the following morning. He sat up in bed and looked around at the mess his room was starting to become and took a deep breath. But, when he read off what the beep indicated, he ran his fingers through his tangled hair and pinched the bridge of his nose with a puffed exhale. A meeting had been scheduled for him first thing after breakfast on the top level with Sigrid.

His initial reaction was that he was in trouble for visiting Ned or breaking the beer limit in D, but from what he had learned about Mimameid so far, those infractions seemed a little below Sigrid's pay grade. Nevertheless, he would relish the chance to ask Sigrid a few lingering questions head-on.

He rushed through breakfast and sent a quick message to Bjørn, telling him he'd be late, before climbing up to Sigrid's office. It felt odd to be climbing up toward the glass roof instead of away from it.

The rusty old elevator happened to arrive just as he stepped off the staircase, Yvonne ushering a group of people that looked like they came from D down a hallway off to the right. She flipped her long hair over her shoulder and threw him an impossibly bright smile without breaking step or ceasing in her chatter to the people behind her, her tablet clutched to her chest. Silently grateful that he no longer had to ride in the rusty, old machine, he nodded to Yvonne in greeting, turned down the hall, and knocked on Sigrid's office door. The wheel lock in the center clicked and Lysander could hear Sigrid's silver voice echo from the other side.

"Come in." As he entered, the window out to the fjord behind her desk displayed a particularly active day today as a school of fish ebbed and flowed with the current, dodging a predator that nipped lazily at them. "In the boughs of Mimir's tree, Lysander," Sigrid greeted him as she looked up from her wide, concrete desk. "Come, have a seat."

Feigning a pleasant smile, he pulled out a chair across from her and crossed his legs.

"Tell me, is it customary for Mimameid community members to have such frequent personal contact with you? I thought that's what the monitoring devices were for." He held up his band provocatively. Sigrid's eyes sparkled a clear quartz grey at his combative tone, a small smile twitching on her lips.

"Anyone would think we were spying on you." Her voice was full of false dismay as she took a seat. "And no. I reserve this kind of personal contact for particularly," she paused, searching for the right word, "*valuable* community members."

"You need me." His directness didn't seem to faze her.

"I wanted to check in with you," she corrected him, calmly. "See how you were settling in, getting on with work duties, if you had any questions for me. See if there's anything I can get you to make your time here more comfortable. That sort of thing." She leaned back in her chair and Lysander watched the fish swirling around behind her head.

"I see," he replied, crossing his arms.

"Of course, if you think it's unnecessary, then you must find everything satisfactory and that's that. No need to waste anyone's time." She uncrossed her legs, folding her hands and setting them on the edge of her desk, daring him. His mind raced, calculating every wrinkle in her placid face, the angle of her head. He unfurled his arms and rapped the armrest of the chair twice with his knuckles.

"No, no. Let's talk. I do actually have a few questions for you."

"Excellent. How can I help?"

"Let's start with Petra." Her eyes narrowed. He had taken her by surprise. It wasn't the name Sigrid had been expecting to come out of his mouth.

"What about the lieutenant?" she replied, coolly.

"Where is she?" he asked.

"I don't understand." She was deciding to play dumb, it seemed. Lysander took a deep breath in. Well, he could play dumb, too.

"I had arranged some self-defense lessons with her and since then I haven't heard anything," he offered, a small half-truth. Lysander saw her resist the urge to roll her eyes at him. But her shoulders had visibly relaxed. Confused as she was, she was following him into his trap.

"What the lieutenant does with her free time is hardly my concern," Sigrid said dryly.

"Hardly," Lysander agreed, equally dryly. "That would, undoubtedly, be beneath you." He plied her and like a good interrogator, she continued on with him. She gave him a wry smile.

"No one in Mimameid is beneath me, Lysander. Every single person here is in my care and I take that responsibility very seriously."

"And yet," Lysander began, done playing games with her, "Petra is somehow unaccounted for." Her lips tightened again.

"Did you try checking in with her commanding officer?" Sigrid offered.

"Did you?" He turned the question back around at her and saw something like offense flicker across her face.

"I'm sorry?" she asked and he couldn't contain himself any longer.

"Did you think she would just disappear and no one would notice?" He struggled to keep his tone even, but a quiver of rage broke through.

"Lysander, though it is touching, there is no need for concern." Her voice was even-tempered, smooth, "The lieutenant must have her reasons for not contacting you, but I assure you, she is perfectly safe." How easily the lie slipped off her tongue. He raised a pointed finger at her,

"I know she was sent on another Above Ground mission and I want to know where she is," He demanded and he could see as the words left his mouth that he knew something he shouldn't. Quickly, she arranged her face to mask her surprise.

"I don't know what you heard, but that is simply not true." This lie came out less practiced, more indignant.

"I heard it from Petra." There was a pause. A sigh.

"As much as I would like to disclose to you her whereabouts, that information is, unfortunately, confidential." At last, some honesty.

"But you must know," he challenged her. "And I am, as you have already stated, a valuable member of this community. Just how *valuable* am I?" Her eyes narrowed at his threat. And then in a moment, she was all maternal grace and dignity again.

"Valuable enough to upgrade to A," She said warmly. She had regained her footing and was pivoting, trying to distract him. "Think of that - relaxed working hours, the best of the food, no need to wear the uniform, the in-house Finnish sauna, unlimited access to the VR studio. Imagine being able to go Above Ground every day without ever leaving the comfort of your bed." She paused to let it all sink in. "I have the power to give you access to any part of Engineering you want, blueprints, histories of this place, the original building plans hand drawn by the architects themselves."

She gestured around the office at a wall of transparent cabinets stacked high and thick with bursting leather binders and large rolls of paper.

"You could hand-pick apprentices to train under you and develop your own department. You could bring them and their families up to B or even A. Think of all the people you could help. Think of all the good you could do." Lysander was ashamed to admit he was tempted. Appalled that this was how she was trying to buy him, but tempted, nonetheless. He remained silent, his face not even twitching at her brashness, so she continued.

"But, the information you are asking for could put the entire Mimameid community in danger. I am not prepared to take that risk," her voice was clear, unmovable, "Not for anyone. No matter how valuable."

"There are other ways for me to find out, you know," Lysander told her spitefully. He hated how childish he sounded, but he couldn't stop himself.

"If you are referring to your friends down in D-" She began, quickly.

"Yes, let's do talk about D." He leaned forward, spreading his big hands out onto her desk and looming towards her in a way he hadn't intended.

"I don't need to tell you, I control their fates as much as anyone else's here." Her voice had become dark and tinny.

"No, you don't." Lysander bit back saying something more, hoping she would incriminate herself.

"Your friend Bjørn, for example." She raised an eyebrow at him, menacingly. "He has a daughter about to be chosen for her work assignment, no?" He felt his heart drop into his stomach. He would never forgive himself if his actions cost her her shot at a better life here.

"You wouldn't."

"Don't try to tell me what I would or wouldn't do, Lysander." Sigrid's voice was almost a hiss, ribboning in the air like an eel in the water. He bit his lip, thinking. There had to be someone untouchable. Someone Sigrid couldn't afford to lose.

"And what about Ned?" The words twisted their way out of him.

"Ned Wallace is loyal to Mimameid." The sentence tumbled out of her mouth in a moment of desperation. Like a hiccup. And he immediately saw that she wanted to take the words and put them back in. It was the first crack he had seen in her façade.

"Ned is only harmless as long as you keep him pacified." He felt sick using the old man this way, but he needed her to know, "Tell me, is that why you don't challenge the illegal booze trade or persecute the beer-limit infractions?" He had pushed himself onto his feet, his voice growing louder, shaking as his anger threatened to boil over. "Are all those special rules only to keep Ned complacent or is it just easier to let the entirety of D succumb to alcoholism and poverty so they aren't a problem for you anymore?"

Sigrid stood up, matching him and eyes narrowing. He had succeeded in drawing her out. Her mouth was thin with rage.

"How dare you come in here and try to tell me how to run this community. Me, who has kept all these people alive for all these years. You know nothing of what it is to be a leader. You know nothing of the sacrifice. You know nothing about what we have had to endure." Her voice was icy cold.

"I know nothing of sacrifice? Of what you have had to endure?" He was livid, his words foaming like poison on his tongue. "Tell me *leader*, when was the last time you were face to face with the Celts? When was the last time you worried about not freezing through the night?" She ignored him, and the fish behind her head jerked, panicking as the predator narrowly missed.

"You want to know why we allow them to carry on? Thinking they are fooling us? Why people like *you* are allowed to go down there and drink your pain away for one night? Those are little fail-safes built into the system, regulated and protected. Because people must be allowed the *feeling* of rebellion, they must have the *illusion* of freedom or else they will suffocate."

Her voice was so smug, he wondered when was the last time she had been down in C and D.

"They are already suffocating!" He shouted, slamming his fists down onto the concrete desk and wincing. It was cold and painful.

"The rules exist to keep them safe from exactly that which you are implying - the Celts, the dying world - and so they must be maintained, even if the rules they are following are not the whole truth. Even if the rules aren't the same for everyone." Even with her eyes narrowed, she kept her anger in check and her face rigid. Behind her, the jaws of the predator outside came down around one of the other fish, blood seeping out the side of its mouth into the fjord.

"The people deserve to know the truth," He replied simply.

"The truth about what exactly, Lysander? What are you going to go back and tell them, that their life down here is a sham? That they are the lifeblood that supports A and B? That they would be better off in a world that has been burned to the ground? That *they* burned to the ground?" He raised his eyebrows.

"You're a fan of our stories, right? Of our epics? You know the one thing I always remembered about Ragnarök?" Sigrid crossed her arms and he backed away from her desk, towards the door. "When the fire stopped burning and the waters receded, the people came back out. And lived."

14
PETRA

THE LIGHT WAS BLINDING.

She closed her eyes again, but she could still feel the heat of it on her eyelids and she thought for a second maybe she had died. Maybe she had died and gone to Valhalla, forever feasting in the light of the midnight sun, in a world unspoiled by those who had destroyed Midgard. But as the searing pain crept up into her veins and made her hiss, she accepted that she couldn't be in that much pain and also be dead. So, she must still be alive.

She tried to reach up to cover her eyes from the light, but she couldn't move her arms. They were bound to something - attached somehow - and that something was reaching inside her.

Turning her head to the right, she squinted in the brightness, trying to focus on what exactly she was attached to. Though her head ached against the light and she felt like there was a brick pressing on her forehead, she narrowed her eyes and managed to concentrate long enough to take in her surroundings. There, along her arm and torso, were row after row of evenly spaced tubes filled with a luminescent, blue liquid flowing in and out of her body, all the way down the side of her leg. Her left side had the same tubes in identical spots. Taped to her chest and stomach were several monitoring wires.

She tried to lift her head and felt a throbbing pain in her belly as she realized the needles were injected directly into her stomach, streaming down her torso over the sides of her rib cage. She felt panic begin to rise and tried to steady her breathing so she could think. She felt her heartbeat in the aching pressure behind her eyes, and though it was an almost unbearable pain, she forced herself to focus on it and use the pain to orient herself. Whatever this was, she could handle it. Help would be on the way. Arthur, if he could. And if it was too risky for him, she could count on Benjáme and Maike. She felt her heartbeat slowing back down and noticed the light above her flickering with the growl of wavering electricity. It was a good sign. It meant she had to still be in one of the Celtic camps, they didn't have electricity that flickered in the wind anywhere else.

Now that she knew where she was, she searched for what had happened to her - how she had gotten there. The last thing she could remember seeing was Arthur's face, those midnight blue eyes alight with pride. Pride. It was a strange expression to have seen on his normally easygoing face. The word sent her mind whirring, hearing Maike's words of warning in her ears. Was it possible she had let her guard down too quickly and he'd used her? That this was part of the plan since they'd met in the village? Her heartbeat shot up erratically at the thought, drumming in her ears, panic rising in her chest, blinding pain in her forehead. She wanted to rip the tubes out of her stomach and arms and run, but she felt heavy, drowsy. The more she fought it, the heavier she felt until her body went limp and she was drifting in a weightless, white sea.

When she awoke again, a man was standing over her. At first glance, he looked more dead than alive, pale skin and sallow, dark eyes sunken into the sockets above his cheekbones. She wanted to recoil, but when Petra looked deeper, she saw a glimmer of warmth in his beady, black eyes that made her speak.

"Help," she croaked, quietly. The man pushed his oily, dark hair from his brow, looking briefly away from her and then back down. He placed his palm on her cheek and nodded, the understanding in his eyes giving her hope, like starlight on the blackest of nights.

Petra felt herself sinking, caught in a cool, black ocean. She was suspended inside the dark of his eyes and looking up at a night littered with stars she had never seen before. They were strewn across the canvas in streaks of purple and gold that throbbed like a heartbeat.

She felt a sense of peace as she watched the lights twinkling above and as her own heartbeat synchronized with the pulsating of the stars. There was no sense of time as she lay there, but when she felt herself being pulled back to the room with the wires and the tubes, she cried out for the ocean of starlight.

A woman's face was there to greet her when she came to for the second time. The light in the room had been turned on again, but it wasn't so bright as to wash out the woman's features.

She had milk-white skin with a few faded freckles shaken across her cheekbones. Her silky raven hair was plaited over her shoulder so that it shimmered around her face and highlighted her flame-blue eyes. She looked more spirit than human.

But, it was the eyes that made Petra's stomach turn - not because of how they glowed like the hottest part of a fire, no - but because she had seen them before.

She had seen them on the face of the Celt she'd fought in the village after the explosion. The girl that had sliced open her leg, cut Lysander's face. The girl that had brought Arthur to them.

"Hello, Petra." Her name dripped off the woman's tongue like acid, evaporating into the air with a sizzle.

She squirmed uncomfortably, feeling the needles tugging beneath her skin as she did. She was completely trapped. "I just wanted to welcome you, personally," the woman continued. "I heard you were asking about me."

Petra stopped at the second statement and look straight into the woman's eyes. They were laughing at her, the bright blue dancing with heat. *She* had been asking about her? Petra had to think for a moment before she could comprehend what the strange woman was saying. Could it be? "Yes, that's right," the woman interpreted as Petra's racing heartbeat lit up the monitors and, "I'm Siobhan." She nodded and shows of light caught her cheekbones.

Siobhan's face broke out into a predatory smile as she stood up, towering over Petra, while simultaneously giving her an idea of how high she was off the ground. Petra felt an involuntary tear escape the corner of her eye as she looked into Siobhan's hypnotic face.

"You took quite a tumble there in our clinic," Siobhan went on, examining nails that, though they looked clipped and cared for, Petra noticed were blackened at the tips, as though the woman had dipped them in soot. "But don't worry, we've got an excellent doctor. Though I think you've already met." There was a touch of something Petra couldn't quite name, something akin to sarcasm or maybe disdain. She felt Siobhan lay her hand on her leg, exactly where the Celtic girl had cut her open. Where the "T" was burned into her flesh.

The hand seared against her like the hot knife Arthur had pressed to her wound. "He's going to take care of you." She turned swiftly on her heel, and although Petra couldn't see where the exit was from her place on the examination table, she heard the open and close of a tent flap.

She tried to ignore the light humming above her, but the more she tried to block it out, the louder it rang, trembling in its circuit until her head pounded and she ached to jump up and claw the wiring out of the walls with her bare hands. It wasn't normal, this hypersensitivity to sound and light; she glowered down again at the tubes and a thought started to form.

The tent flap rustled again, strong enough that it tore through the humming and into her thoughts. She tensed. But, when his face finally came into view above her, Petra felt her breath leave her body.

His blonde locks hung around his face, crusted with blood, his lips purple and scabbed over. The laughing, midnight blue of his eyes barely visible beneath the swelling from where he'd been beaten. His shoulders were hunched and his fingers trembled ever so slightly as he raised them. His sleeves were rolled up to work and she could see welts on his forearms, fresh and blistered. She tried to search his face for something, anything, but it was clouded with fear. They locked eyes and she saw under the bruising and blood, the familiar twinkle in his irises. Though the hope was veiled, he hadn't given in.

"Arthur." Her voice came out like a scratch and he looked at her as she spoke, his lips twitching. He shook his head, pursing his purpled lips together tightly. "What happened to you?" She wanted to reach for him.

He extended out his hand and lifted her head, where she, for the first time, realized the throbbing was coming from. "Who did this to you?" she begged to know, defiantly. As his hands touched her, however tender, it sent a shooting pain around the sides of her skull, so white-hot she had to close her eyes.

He lowered it again and she felt the towel he had placed beneath her head. When the pain had subsided enough, she opened her eyes again, searching his battered face, but he remained stoic. She saw the fresh blood from her head on his hands and she let out an involuntary whimper.

"What's wrong with me?" she pleaded, her voice ragged. There was a flicker of something in his eyes like he wanted to reach out to her, but he resisted. "Won't you say something?" Instead of speaking, he picked up one of her many bubbling, blue tubes and tapped it. She felt the lurch of some new medicine entering her bloodstream. She'd been right. They were lacing her with something. "What...?" she tried to ask, but Arthur finally spoke to her.

"Sleep," he commanded, and her eyes fluttered shut.

The medicine burned in her veins as if the Celtic fire itself had been liquefied and pushed through her. It made her want to scratch off every inch of her skin, peel it away, so her blood could breathe again. She writhed in the fitful sleep, the needles pumping more and more of the drug into her. How could Arthur have done this to her?

When the burning finally subsided, Arthur's expressionless face reappeared, administering the drug while Siobhan leaned over his shoulder and whispered in his ear what a good boy he was. He turned to kiss her raven hair, hands clawing at the woman's milky throat until he had kissed the color away, leaving the strands of hair dull. Petra felt her stomach turn over and tried to close her eyes, but they wouldn't obey. She looked at the face of the woman Arthur was now seated beside, following the silver strands up to a steely face she was all too familiar with. Sigrid bent down slowly, using one long finger to pull back the bloodied, blonde hair from his ear and whisper what a good job he had done.

Petra felt a wild scream erupt from her battered body as the people melted away before her eyes. Back with a surge was the burning in her veins - unquenchable pain that pulsed through her over and over - and when she thought she could take no more, the dreams returned. She counted the resurgences three, four, five until in the white-hot of it all, she lost count.

When she came around, she was wet, drenched in sweat and the taste of blood in her mouth, as though she had bit her tongue sometime during the process. The dark-eyed man was holding her hand, his face full of understanding.

"How are you feeling?" he asked her, his voice gravelly and worn. Petra couldn't speak but a small sob escaped her. He lifted a cup of water to her mouth. She drank deeply and though it tasted rusty, it was cool in comparison to the burning of the blue liquid. He set the cup down and picked up a damp cloth, patting her sweaty brow gently. "Your fever broke in the night. The treatment worked." He spoke kindly, but she was confused. *The treatment?* They were drugging her with something, not treating her. She had seen Arthur do it, felt it in her veins. If it was medicine for something, Arthur would have explained what was going on step by step - just as he had done in the village and the med tent - just as he always did. He would not hide behind his bruised face for fear of his life. Petra narrowed her eyes at the man, trying to shake the damp cloth from her forehead. It was obscuring her view and she needed to find Arthur. Suddenly, there was a rustle of the tent flap opening and the dark-haired man jumped to his feet. Someone else had entered the room and he bent low, practically cowering at whoever it was, his oily hair falling in front of his sallow face.

Siobhan's face appeared above her, the man fading back into the shadows. Her face was ablaze as she peered down at Petra.

"Did you believe the little sob story he told you about his parents?" she sneered. Her eyes flashed, a surge of electric blue, like a bolt of lightning across a purple sky. Petra set her jaw, protective of her time with Arthur. What did they know about it? What did she know about him? Only what he wanted them to know. "Did you think he was falling in love with you?" Petra glared at Siobhan, challenging her, but still not speaking. The poeticism of the Celtic language spilling from Siobhan's mouth had her both captivated and confused. Was this what Anja and Maike had been warning her about? How sneaky, how intentionally misleading the language could be? "How do you think it is we found you in the med tent, anyhow?"

"Why did you have him beaten, if none of it is true?" she spat back, her voice coming out hoarse and cracked.

"Do you actually believe he wasn't doing exactly as he was instructed the entire time?" She felt a flicker of apprehension race across her face, knowing she had already had the thought herself. "Don't pretend you didn't know that we sent him to do all of it - stay behind to help you in the forest, come to the rescue when you snuck out of camp, offer to help feed information to Sigrid and the Norse." *How did she know Sigrid's name?* She'd only mentioned it to Arthur. Had he really betrayed her? Had he given her up and all that she had told him? "It was all part of the act, dear Petra." Siobhan pulled out a long fingernail and traced the line of Petra's jaw. Petra's head throbbed at Siobhan's touch and she had to close her eyes to concentrate. "We'll give you another treatment, see how you're doing after that." Siobhan looked up at someone else - not the dark-haired man, but a third person, out of view - as she spoke. "You see, *we* are a magnanimous people." She touched her heart as she spoke, her gaze returning to Petra. "We will do more than you Norse have done to us and will at least nurse you back to health before we decide what your fate will be."

Petra furrowed her brow, confused about what Siobhan could be referring to. But the woman had already turned to leave, the dark-haired man following apologetically behind her. The third person in the room moved into her view, lifting the tubes she was attached to inject her yet again with the 'treatment.'

Just before the pain set in and she was blinded by the burning once more, she saw the flash of Arthur's haggard eyes.

She was alone when she woke next. The first thing she felt was the relief of the treatment subsiding. Her body jolted as the last of the burning left her bloodstream.

The feeling slowly crept back into her arms and she remembered Arthur's eyes. She tried to focus on them - what had they been twinkling with? Hope? Pity? Deception? The tent flap rustled and in a panic she attempted to look where the noise was coming from, but the pain shot back into her head and she had to squeeze her eyes closed for a moment.

As she opened them again, the dark-eyed man sat down next to her, his face clouded, lips sour. He took her hand gently in his own, caressing around where the needles were injected.

"I'm sorry for Siobhan's manner. She means well, truly. She just wants to help you, sometimes she just gets in her own way, if you understand what I mean?" Petra wanted to, but the burning and the dreams, they had taken her will from her, washed her veins clean of it.

It seemed that maybe by indulging this strange, sad man the treatments would stop, so she decided to play along. She nodded her head slowly and watched the man's face break into a soft smile, crooked teeth lining his mouth. "I knew you would understand. She said that you might not be so forgiving, but I knew that you would be," he sighed. "We haven't been properly introduced yet. I'm Ciarán." His eyes shone like obsidian as he said his name and she had the sense that he didn't get to say who he was out loud very much.

It was an odd thing to revel in, one's own name, but Petra felt a twang of sympathy for him. She knew the power of speaking yourself back into being. The months she had wandered alone in the north before Sigrid had found her, she had had to remind herself who she was every day. She tried to smile up at Ciarán, but the throbbing pain in the back of her head returned and she winced.

"I'm Petra," she told him, hoping she could trust their connection.

"Yes, I know." Chuckling a bit, he added, "It's a pleasure to meet you." And shook her hand down by her side, the tubes moving with her.

"You too, Ciarán." And she felt him glow when she said his name. This was it, this was her way out. If she could connect with him, and get him to connect with her, then she could get him to stop the treatments. She took a deep breath.

"It's a good name," she commented.

"Sorry?" He asked.

Ciarán, I mean," she said, "It's a good name."

"Oh." He was clearly surprised. "Thank you." He stood up and busied himself checking her incision sites.

"Are you named for someone?" She wanted to press him but needed to know how far was too far to go, so she focused on the power his name had given him.

"There were plenty of Ciarans in my family before," he explained, "but it was my idea to change my name to Ciarán." He emphasized the difference proudly.

"Why did you?" Petra asked, tentatively. His shining eyes pierced her. She couldn't read him, whether she had taken it too far.

"To reclaim the name as my own." He was wringing his hands. Here Petra sensed a tremor in him.

"It should have always been Ciarán," she said stiffly. "To honor the Celtic path." She saw a smile curl onto Ciarán's lips. After a pause, he spoke, again.

"You don't have to pretend with me, you know." His voice was oily.

"Pretend what?" she asked, trying to ignore the drumming in her head.

"That you burn for the Celtic cause," he said, casually. "There are many here who do not." She felt herself start to panic. Did he know something about Arthur she didn't want him to? Had they been observed? A chill sent goosebumps rippling down her arms. Ciarán continued, "It makes them no less welcome. Nor you. We take those who the others have cast out, gladly," He told her, "Our only goal is security for those brave enough to have survived this long." Petra felt herself biting down on her cracked, dry bottom lip, running her tongue over it, desperately.

"Do you know where Arthur is?" she asked Ciarán and almost instantaneously his face darkened. She withdrew at the reaction.

"Why do you need to see Arthur?" His tone was sharp, jealous even.

"I, I just wanted to know if he is okay," she said, keenly aware that his hand had moved up her arm, towards the tubes. As if to remind her that he was the one who had the power here.

"Even after he betrayed you?" Ciarán tilted his head as he spoke, as if he couldn't understand.

"I don't think -" Petra started to say, but the words fell apart before she could get them out. It was too dangerous to have an opinion, so it died in her throat. Mercifully, Ciarán ignored her, deciding to change the subject.

"Well, the good news is, the treatments are working. You are on the mend, so with a few more rounds, you'll be healed and ready to go." His voice was softer again, maybe even something reminiscent of cheerful.

"What happened to me, exactly?" She was having difficulty remembering. She had thought they had discovered her, beat her like Arthur, and brought her here to drug her and pump her for information. It was the only thing that would make sense, given she'd been sneaking around, so why didn't she remember it like that?

"Oh my dear, you fainted in the clinic and hit your head. Badly, I might add. You would have bled out in minutes if we hadn't been there." It was fuzzy, her memory of the time between going black in the clinic and waking up in the room with the needles in her. But if she concentrated she thought she could see Arthur's face above her, or maybe it was Ciarán's?

"And the treatments?" she asked him, her head starting to pound.

"What about them, dear?" he asked her, seeing her in pain and checking her tubes.

"What do they do, exactly?"

"Why, they heal you, of course." His voice was as tender as freshly butchered reindeer meat as she drifted to sleep.

The burning returned and she saw that *Baba* was there, bustling about in the kitchen, telling her about how kind a hooded stranger had been to her in the street on the way home from the commissary on the base back in Old Finland. She turned around and opened the door to let the stranger in - still hooded - and he stepped into their house.

The house was decorated oddly though, not as Petra had remembered, but lit with glowing candles everywhere. As the stranger took off his hood, the candles all tipped over at once and the house was engulfed in flames around them. Petra's feet were glued to the floor. She was helpless as she watched her grandmother ignite and turn to ash before her eyes, the stranger's face still hidden in the shadows. She felt a wail erupt from her lungs so ragged it tore through her very chest, ripping muscles apart, and snapping ribs in half. She screamed until her throat was raw and she spit up blood and her body ached.

When the house had burned it was only her and the stranger among the charred remains. She fell to the ground and felt pine needles pressing into the palms of her hands, the weight of someone on top of her, pressing the breath out of her. She looked up in the swirling ash at the stranger who had burned them to the ground, his eyes shining like obsidian.

Coming around after the latest treatment, she turned and spat warm blood over her shoulder.

Breathing heavily, she saw that Siobhan was sitting beside her. Unlike Ciarán, she did not reach out to hold her hand but instead watched with a stony gaze as the spasms of the treatment left Petra's body. As Siobhan's face became clearer above her, she could also make out Ciarán behind her, his face subdued. She felt rage rising in her at him, even though she knew it had been a dream. Her grandmother hadn't died warm, she had died cold.

"Hello, Petra." Siobhan's voice was strained. Whatever she was about to say, she didn't want to. "I believe I owe you an apology." Petra blinked, now unsure if she was still dreaming.

"I'm sorry?" she replied, still tasting blood in her mouth, feeling a trickle run down the side of her cheek.

"No, I'm sorry," Siobhan repeated, though she didn't look sorry. "I forget sometimes that you all come to us a little bit brainwashed and it isn't fair for me to blame that on you." She reached out and wiped the trail of blood from Petra's face with the edge of her sleeve and leaned back.

"I'm sorry?" Still confused by the apology. She tried to sit up, forgetting that she was still connected to tubes and wires. They caught and pulled at her and she winced.

"Oh no," Siobhan said and pushed her, rather forcefully, back against the table, her head landing on the matted, crusty towel under her head. "I wouldn't recommend that just at this moment. Ciarán?" The man stepped forward and eased her into a more comfortable position, but her head still throbbed.

"You are mending, but you aren't quite ready to stand yet. Just relax," he cooed, and when Petra stopped resisting, he retreated behind Siobhan.

"So, Petra. I want to explain myself," the woman began, "because you have been told certain lies about us and I want to set the record straight." Siobhan laced her sooty fingers together. "Is that alright with you?" Petra nodded, her head heavy, unable to fight the woman.

"I believe I am right in assuming that the person you answer to is a woman named Sigrid?" Petra hesitated, wary of giving too much away. But they already knew Sigrid's name. "That's okay." Siobhan held up her hand. "You don't have to say anything." She adjusted herself in her chair. "Once upon a time the woman called Sigrid and I knew one another." Petra turned her head to face Siobhan.

"What?" She didn't even know that Sigrid knew Siobhan's name. She'd assumed Siobhan only knew Sigrid's name because of her, because of Arthur.

"Yes." Siobhan's folded hands were squeezed so tight the knuckles were white. Petra couldn't help herself, this was the moment she had waited for. A chance to finally get some answers.

"How?"

"How did we know one another?" Siobhan asked and Petra nodded. Siobhan's face twitched, remembering something fondly.

"We had an agreement," she replied simply. But her face remained amused, or maybe reminiscent. "We set sail for these shores all those years ago because we had been promised safe haven here. Sigrid told us her people had been planning and preparing for 'Ragnarök' and that they would offer us refuge from the impending cataclysmic events." Petra tried to keep her face in check as Siobhan explained, but her mind was racing. The words sounded so strange, coming from Siobhan's mouth. She stopped for a moment and fidgeted with her jacket.

"So we accepted the offer, gratefully. We had little choice, as our islands had all but disappeared." She adjusted and crossed her legs in her chair. "Sigrid's control of the government meant we were granted refugee status and with that, we set sail. But, when we arrived here, we were immediately met with," the woman paused to choose her words carefully, "military force." The look on Siobhan's face was one Petra knew. The woman was reliving her memories of that day - the haunting screams, the panic in the crowd as they realized what was happening. The ringing after the explosions and the sound of shells hitting the ground. Petra had her own day like that - a day she'd rather forget.

"So, it was a trap," Petra concluded, and Siobhan pursed her lips, brushing a strand of raven hair from her face. She exchanged a glance with Ciarán, who encouraged her to continue. Petra watched the interaction with curiosity, enraptured by what Siobhan was saying, but equally so by the body language between the two people before her. Siobhan was so clearly in charge, but she in turn needed Ciarán's permission, his approval. Petra wrinkled her forehead.

"It was a trap," the woman confirmed. "I think she needed to eliminate the competition." There was a pause. "It's normal to be confused," Siobhan said when Petra didn't react.

"No, it's not that," Petra started to say and stumbled. "It actually makes sense," she admitted.

There was more honesty in this conversation than anything she had ever heard from Sigrid.

Finally, she was starting to understand the truth. Why Mimameid - why Sigrid - was so afraid of the outside world. Why she kept everyone in check, like the children in D with too-small shoes on their feet but still grateful to have shoes at all, or soldiers in C with dashed hopes of one day achieving glory for Mimameid, A and B levels pacified in a faded virtual reality - everything balanced so as to remain in her control. So no one would go Above Ground or know what she'd done. But Petra had met a Celt - she was a flaw, a weakness in the armor of Mimameid.

"I prefer to think that Sigrid had a change of heart and that no ill will was initially intended," Siobhan paused. "In any case, before she reneged on our deal and bombed us halfway to Sunday, she did impart on me that their secret to survival was a massive bunker, built to last decades - maybe even centuries - if the population could be culled." Petra winced, knowing how medicines were handed out by level, and food was distributed based on social class. Siobhan looked down at her, expectant. "Oh, her choice of words - not mine." Siobhan's eyes flashed like gunpowder thrown in a fire. "She informed us that if her plan was successful with the culling of the population and we were able to survive Ragnarök on the surface, that the remaining Norse would need people to breed with. Only the strongest of us - the ones who made it - would be of use." So the Celts were meant to be breeding cattle? Petra was struck silent. "And she sent us on our way. To survive until we were useful to her. With no homeland to go back to, we voted as a collective to stay and search for the bunker, to try to scratch a living out of this dying planet as best we could. Until we could end this."

"So you burned Scandinavia to the ground? Your quarrel isn't with the Norse, it's with Sigrid." Petra knew what Siobhan was saying was true, but it didn't excuse the many Norse brothers and sisters that the Celts had slaughtered over the years. As the words left her mouth she felt a surge of medicine being pushed into her veins, a soft burning creeping back into her limbs. Siobhan looked at her, lips trembling with anger at Petra's defiance.

"We know there is a bunker and we are simply looking for the entrance. The entrance we were promised. My people deserve that much." After all, how many of them had Petra killed in return? She tried not to see their faces.

"What about the people you burned?" Petra wasn't sure if in that moment she meant the English or the Norse, but the treatment surged in her, making her voice quiver.

"You mean the people that Sigrid left to die? The people she decided were unworthy of living in her new world?" She paused, her words ringing in the silence. "We were left behind in the ashes of a dead world. I do not pretend that every decision we have made has been perfect, but we have done what we must to survive." She was breathing heavily. "Sigrid is the one who betrayed us all, Petra," she seethed. "How many people - both Celt and Norse - have burned because of her? And how many more will she leave behind, helpless against the rising night, because they do not fit her vision of a perfect world, post-Ragnarök?" Ciarán reached out and put a hand on Siobhan's shoulder, steadying her temper. The medicine receded and Petra swallowed, breathing deeply.

She knew that Siobhan was right. She had even suspected some dark secret when they left Mimameid. Benjáme had known it too, and even now, that no one had come to her rescue, she knew it in her heart. Sigrid had sent her to her death rather than expose herself and her secret.

"My apologies," Siobhan said, her voice once again steady. "You are not yet well enough. We will speak again soon." She rose to leave.

"What did Sigrid get in return?" Petra asked Siobhan's back.

"I'm sorry?" She turned back around to look Petra in the face.

"In your deal. What did Sigrid get, for offering you all refuge in the bunker?" Siobhan just looked at her, her eyes blazing, a sneer playing on her lips.

"You should ask your doctor friend," she replied and turned to leave.

Ciarán looked sympathetically down at her as he took the seat that Siobhan had vacated.

"You did very well," he assured her. "Now, I think perhaps one more treatment. Sleep, and I will see you when you wake." He tapped her tubes gently as sleep overcame her, her protests dying in her throat.

Arthur plagued her dreams as she watched him tied to a chair, beaten in wave after wave of treatments. Only at the very end did he turn to her, blood dripping from the edge of his mouth and eyes obscured by purple bruises, smile and say, "She'll believe anything I say." Then out of the corner of the room - from utter darkness - a huge, lumbering bear came bounding towards him and Petra sucked in her breath.

Ciarán was waiting for her when the burning subsided and her eyes fluttered open.

Ciarán?" she asked, coming out of the haze of the medicine.

"Yes, Petra?" he replied, reaching out for her hand.

"Did the treatment work?" She held her breath in waiting for the answer. Her body felt hollowed out, weary beyond understanding and her head heavy, but she trusted him.

"We will have to see, but I am optimistic," he told her tenderly. She tensed at his reply, however gentle. It wasn't a yes, but it also wasn't a no. She could think of nothing else but preventing the next treatment. "You have a visitor if you are feeling up to it." She nodded, in spite of the pain radiating in her body, the throbbing in her heart and in her head. She wasn't sure if she was ready to face Arthur after the dreams. Who had the 'she' been that he'd spoken of in her dream - her or Siobhan?

But, the tent flap rustled open and closed and when she looked over, it was Siobhan who took a seat beside her, not Arthur. In what looked like a great effort, she raised her arm and took a hold of Petra's hand.

"I hear that your treatments are going well and that you may be able to join us on the outside soon," she began.

"Outside? Is that true?" Petra asked, looking to Ciarán, who nodded.

"I think that depends on some tests they need to run," Siobhan continued, "but first I have a few questions for you. Are you feeling up for that?" Petra wanted to be on the outside again, she wanted the treatments to end, and she wanted Ciarán to get the recognition he deserved for taking care of her, so she nodded. If she did what Siobhan wanted, Ciarán would be rewarded and she would be released. "I'm very glad," the woman said and let go of Petra's hand, leaning back in her chair and flexing her fingers - her blackened fingernails shining in the overhead light. "Do you feel like you can trust us, Petra?" She looked from Ciarán to Siobhan as she considered.

She'd been so focused on the dreams and the treatments she had forgotten to think about it. But by talking to them, she found so many of the answers she'd been searching for. And they had healed her, hadn't they? Though she had infiltrated their camp and spied on them, they had treated her and now they had said she could go outside and join them, without any repercussions. She never had to go back to Sigrid even, nor the injustices of Mimameid. She could be as free as Darcy or Gwenna or Siobhan.

"I think I do."

"I need to be sure I can trust you, you see. For the safety of our people," Siobhan paused, leaning forward and resting her chin on her fist. " I need you to prove it."

"How can I prove myself to you?" The little girl inside of her who had been trapped under the weight of thirsty men all those years ago could almost taste the freedom.

"I need to know what information you passed onto Sigrid, so I can protect you and so I can protect my people. Think of anything you can that would protect Arthur." Petra tried to think, but her brain felt foggy. What had she told them? She furrowed her brow and felt her heart rate jump.

Siobhan watched her carefully, looking from Ciarán back down to her with a touch of fire rising in her eyes. "It's alright," she said after a minute. "You don't have to tell me today. This will be my reciprocation, how I prove myself to you. I will let you go today, but when I call upon you, I will need you to protect us from Sigrid." Petra felt the words reverberate inside her. That was something she could do. That was something she had been trained to do. Protect people. "Do you think you can do that?" Siobhan asked her and she looked deep into her blue eyes and answered honestly.

"Yes."

"Swear it."

"I swear," she promised, eyes searching, but Siobhan shook her head.

"No, I need you to swear it on the gods." Petra didn't know what she meant, but Ciarán stepped forward, holding out a small stone in his hand. Petra saw how it shone in the bright lights, like black glass. He reached his hand down to hers and pressed the stone into the palm of her hand.

"You will speak your oath into the stone," Siobhan instructed her.

"Repeat after me," Ciarán beckoned her and her fingers closed around the small stone. He stood up straighter.

"I swear by the gods, by whom my people swear," he said, eyes gleaming.

"I swear by the gods, by whom my people swear," Petra repeated, her voice cracking.

"If I break my oath, may the land open to swallow me, the sea rise to drown me, and the sky fall upon me." Petra's breath caught as she heard him speak the words. It was Ragnarök. He was describing Ragnarök. Her voice was small when she spoke again,

"If I break my oath, may the land open to swallow me," she repeated, "the sea rise to drown me, and the sky fall upon me." There was a silence and Ciarán removed his hand from hers, the stone warm in her palm.

"How can I be sure you will keep this oath?" Siobhan raised an eyebrow, "what can you offer me in return for this trust?" Petra searched inside herself, she was so close.

"The bunker is called Mimameid," she said and Siobhan turned her face away, shaking her head.

"I'm afraid that you aren't the first person to give us that information." She started to stand up, turning to Ciaran. "Perhaps one more treat-" she started to say, but Petra raised her voice. She couldn't handle another. She would do anything to keep the dreams at bay, the burning. To not see her grandmother or Arthur in pain again.

"It's in the fjord. It's underwater," she interrupted them.

"What?" Siobhan turned to her, full attention captured. At last, some information she could trade with.

"I said," Petra breathed heavily as she spoke, "Mimameid is underwater."

15
LYSANDER

IN THE DAYS THAT followed, he spent as little time as possible in B, working from the early mornings with Bjørn until long after the older man had cleaned his glasses and left for the night.

He would join Bjørn and his family in D for dinner as often as possible, losing himself in merriment until he was feeling silly enough to let the girls try and teach him their traditional dances. It was a kind of kinship he had never experienced before, having always been younger than his peers. He started making friends with Bjørn's neighbors, offering to help fix a fisherman's leaky faucet or oil the rollers on a pull-out bed of a young couple so it didn't wake their baby in the middle of the night. When Heiká told him at dinner one night about a seamstress whose daughter had developed some sort of chronic lung disease since coming to Mimameid, he asked Bjørn why they didn't just go up to The Infirmary.

"Oh, she's in line for the medicine, but they have to make sure A and B won't be using it first," Bjørn explained and Lysander tried to find the hint of irony in his voice, but there was none. "Once it gets closer to its expiration date, they will send it down to us." He exchanged a glance with Heiká that told Lysander there was more to the story. Something they had lived through that he had not. Hastily, Bjørn changed the subject. "Did I tell you Tuva's been given her work assignment?" he asked as they bussed their dishes in D, summoning the girls with a wave to leave the canteen.

"No, you didn't. *Lykke til*, Tuva!" The girl's cheeks flushed and she threw her dad an embarrassed glare. Runa and Åsa giggled happily.

"He keeps telling people," Tuva complained, but a smile was dancing on her cheeks.

"That's because I'm proud!" Bjørn said, putting his arm around his oldest daughter's shoulders and squeezing her encouragingly.

"Well, where are you being placed?" Lysander asked.

"Accounting," she replied confidently, "I start my induction in two days."

"Accounting?" Lysander wasn't quite sure what she meant. No one was paid a salary in 'egalitarian' Mimameid.

"It's up in A," Tuva explained and suddenly Lysander understood why the family was so proud of her. She had earned an elite position - they were moving up in the world of Mimameid. "We monitor data collected from around Mimameid in order to make the entire system run more efficiently. Keep accounts of everything." Did she mean what he thought she meant?

"Data?" he probed her further.

"Yeah, you know, from the bands, medical data, food waste, numbers of people going to The Infirmary or The Closet," she explained, "any kind of pattern we can find that can help us adapt to make Mimameid better." Lysander wondered if he was the only one that found it suspicious they were monitoring things so closely, but he didn't say anything more, not wanting to spoil the family's good news. They had arrived at the base of the staircase anyways, where he parted ways with them and climbed up to his bunk. Waving goodbye, he began the long trek.

The extra work kept him busy and it kept him distracted. That is until he would have to climb the lonely staircase back up to B, returning to the company of his own mind, lost somewhere between wanting to stay and help the people here and wanting to go find Magdelena and Linnaea.

Tonight, he didn't even remember if he took his shoes off before falling into bed.

In a blur, he was floating up and up in the blue-green of the fjord. He fought against seaweed restraints and when they broke, he felt the little green ribbons release and watched them fall into the mouths of his friends in D. But he kept swimming up, a greedy feeling bubbling up inside of him as he reached for the sunbeams that cut through the surface of the water.

When his head broke through, he gulped down a deep breath of salty air. He looked up to see the beams of light he had been chasing weren't sunbeams at all, but moonbeams. The pearly streams of light were so thick, he felt like he could reach out and touch them. The moon was bigger and brighter than he could remember from The Time Before. Had it always taken up so much space in the sky?

He looked around him, searching for land, but felt a tugging at his ankle. When he looked down he saw Magdelena's watery face, her blonde hair luminescent in the water. She pulled him back down beneath the surface and started swimming toward a dark shadow.

He felt the need to warn her, not to let her go. He tried to reach out and stop her, but when he opened his mouth to speak it filled with water and he couldn't breathe. She swam farther and farther beyond his reach and he began to sink again as the water filled up his lungs, burning.

Suddenly, a hand shot down into the water, skin as fair and iridescent as the pearly moonbeams had been. He reached up to grab hold.

The hand clasped onto him, heaving him up onto a grassy bank. He looked back at the water he had been pulled from and he saw it was a small pool of water fed by a spring at the base of a massive tree. Silver moss crawled up the side, its branches hanging low, twisted with age. From the gnarled branches, in place of leaves, hung strips of glittering cloth, swaying gently in the soundless breeze. He had never been one for believing in the myths of old, but if he had to guess where he was, he would have said the World Tree.

The pearly hand offered to help him up, and when he was standing he could see the person it belonged to. Inky, black hair that shone in the moonlight, wild curls framing a face of milk-white skin. Her eyes were the color of blue flame.

He felt his heart stop.

She turned away and he saw a small etching on the back of the girl's milky neck. A small Celtic rune - a 'T' shape - glowing in the moonbeams. She looked back at him, playfully and beckoned him to follow her down a path that led around the tree. Unsure of whether it was safe to follow, he hesitated. The girl, sensing his hesitation, turned to him and raised her arm to place a cool hand on his cheek. A jolt of calm washed over him. He felt her take his hand gently and bewitched, he followed her down the path.

Fireflies flickered around them as they walked. The grass was wet on their bare feet and the air had a scent to it that reminded him of midsummer in the hills. From a distance, he heard Runa's voice calling to him, calling him back to the mountains, but the girl led him onwards, unconcerned by the sound of the song. They walked for a long while, Lysander watching as the girl let her fingers weave through the tall grasses.

She turned to him, coming close enough to cover his eyes with her hands. The sweet scent of pine branches burning filled his nostrils and he could feel the heat of a fire up ahead warming his skin.

When she took away her hands, they stood in the middle of a circle of Celts, a bonfire blazing in front of them, spiraling into a night sky that twinkled with starlight. The girl opened up her hands like a butterfly opening its wings and inside was a stone, carved into a runic compass.

He cupped his hands, looking into her flame-blue eyes as she place it onto his open palms. He felt the weight of it, the coolness of it. As he lifted his head to the circle of people gathered, he spotted, through the blazing firelight, a flame-headed girl, eyes flashing tawny gold.

He took a step forward towards her and the earth gave way, Lysander falling into blackness.

He awoke tangled in his sleeping bag, drenched in sweat. The lights were still out in his room, but his internal clock told him it was just before the artificial Mimameid dawn.

Reaching under his pillow, his hand closed around the hilt of the Celtic knife. The mysterious girl in his dream had made him feel so safe, and yet he'd awoke with the urge to check that it was still there, secure under his pillow.

He pulled the knife out and held it up in the darkness, examining the graceful curve of the blade and the soft, worn leather wrapped around the grip. How the oils had warped the shape of it to fit the Celtic girl's hand perfectly. In the beams of eerie light that shone through his small window out into the fjord, he caught a glimmer of a small etching on the blade closest to the hilt. A tiny, runic 'T' carved crudely into the steel. Just like in his dream.

He tapped his band into the port beside the door and saw that his heartbeat had been erratic for the last half an hour, while he'd been dreaming. That would certainly raise some red flags in Accounting.

Sighing, he stood up, grabbed a glass off the shelf, and headed over to the sink to pour himself some water. He took a sip, but it tasted metallic and he spit it back out into the sink. He closed his eyes and leaned forward against the basin, feeling the coolness of the metal on his forehead, and tried to steady himself. Even now, as he closed his eyes, he couldn't shake the familiarity in the girl's touch.

He shook his head. It was clear he'd been listening to too many of the Liddie's stories down in D, to be this affected by a figment of his imagination. But, this had felt different. Who was the mystery girl and why had his subconscious landed on her, of all people?

The way her hair had fallen, the weight of her hand in his, and the coolness of her skin, hard and smooth like moonstone, it had all felt more like a memory than a dream.

Under ordinary circumstances, he would have chalked it all up to something bad he'd had for dinner, but he knew how respected the old seer lady was down in D, and he did feel like he needed advice. So, he decided silently to talk to Liddie, or at the very least Runa, about the dream at dinner tonight after he and Bjørn finally had a look at the old valve today.

Just then, the hum of gentle birdsong and music that was his alarm lifted into the air and the lights slowly lit up in his room, warm and inviting. At first, he'd enjoyed that he could personalize his alarm and escape in the pleasure that the bird's singing used to bring him. But, now it was just a grim reminder that those birds would never be alive again. He raised his head and looked into the mirror at his own deep, brown eyes and willed himself not to see the Celtic girl's, but it was too late, he'd been branded by the flame-blue.

Splashing some of the metallic water on his face, he stepped into his Mimameid jumpsuit. Before zipping it up, he tucked the Celtic knife into his waistband for good measure. Somehow, it felt like the right thing to do after the dream. He took a good look at himself in the mirror over the sink, tucking his wild hair behind his ears and straightening his collar before heading over to the canteen for breakfast.

He was running late now, distracted still from his odd dream, so by the time he arrived in The Engine Room, Bjørn had already worked up a layer of sweat on his brow. He wiped his hairline with the back of his hand and waved good morning.

"Some big A-level is all brassed off because her floor started cracking," he said as Lysander descended to the floor. "So, you know me - the morning is gold in the mouth - so I get up to figure out why. I've got Selby up there now sealing the floor back up with a hybrid polymer we cooked up down in D for patching leaks when work orders take too long to get approved," Bjørn explained to Lysander, sounding less annoyed about the whole situation than Lysander felt he would have been. But then, Bjørn's ability to appreciate an opportunity for problem-solving was unparalleled. The old construction worker with the long scraggly beard, Selby, on the other hand, would be less than pleased. "The upper levels aren't going happy to be about it, but it sounds like we got ourselves a leaky pipe. We'll have to go into the raceway to fix it. Probably have to shut the whole system down while we figure out what's going on, or risk flooding the whole bunker."

"What do you need me to do?" Lysander replied, welcoming the distraction.

"Oh this isn't something you need to bother with," Bjørn assured him. "Go focus your energy on whatever you had planned for the day. I can manage this."

"No. No, it's fine." Not wanting to admit that he was seriously considering talking to the seer about his dream and needed to divert his thoughts away from it, he straightened up. "I want to help," Lysander told him. "Where's the raceway we need to get into?" Bjørn let out a sigh, a rush of relief washing over the lines of his face.

"Well, I can't say I like heights, so, if you're offering-" He ran his hand through his hair and smiled up gratefully.

"I'm offering," Lysander promised him.

"There's an access point between A and B, near the entrance to The Gardens. You have to climb up to A and see what the issue is. There are several floodgates you have to pass through to get up there, but if there's a crack in the concrete, then the water has been sitting for some time and it won't be difficult to spot." Bjørn went silent for a minute, thinking. "You ever welded before?" Lysander laughed, glad Bjørn had come to the same conclusion he had.

"Wouldn't that have been a good question to ask before you agreed to give me the job?" he joked, lightheartedly. Bjørn winked at him and pushed his glasses up the bridge of his nose.

"I knew I could count on you," he said and stood up, clapping Lysander on the back. He sauntered across the room to the utility room where they kept most of their equipment. The portable stuff, anyway.

From beyond the door, Lysander heard clatters and bangs as Bjørn continued talking. "Here we are. And yes, okay. That should do it." The equipment scraped the floor as Bjørn pushed it over the threshold and dragged it towards Lysander.

"So, we got your gloves and mask," he said, using the bulky metal gloves to point down at the mask. "We got your copper for the pipe, we got your mounted gas tanks," he pointed at the two pressurized containers configured onto a contraption that looked like a jetpack, "and of course, we got your welder."

He helped Lysander into the getup before picking up the gloves and mask and leading the way back up the stairs. They exited The Engine Room and into the ebb and flow of the crowded D hallways.

Unlike A and B, down here people walked as if the weight of the upper levels were balanced squarely on their shoulders. They trudged to their long shifts of manual labor work assignments, or wearily back from the night shift with rumpled jumpsuits and too-worn boots. Bustling parents were herding their unruly kids off to the Mimameid school, shouting orders into the chaotic crowds at their offspring. Lysander and Bjørn exchanged an apologetic look at the grumblings from the people about how much space they were taking up and how slow they were moving.

"Let's take the elevator today!" Bjørn shouted over the chatter and reluctantly, Lysander nodded. Much as he distrusted the elevator, he fancied it over being gawked at as they lugged the equipment halfway across Mimameid. "Little more discrete, don't you think?" Bjørn concluded in a more reasonable tone as they boarded and the gate slammed shut. Lysander nodded, his stomach turning. The elevator gave a lurch as it kicked into action and Lysander grabbed onto the handrail, knuckles white.

"You okay there? You look a little er...green," Bjørn added and Lysander sucked in his breath, feeling his grip on the railing tighten.

"I'm fine. I just don't much like the elevators," he replied, trying to ignore the crunching of the cables as they continued to climb.

"Yeah, it isn't much to go on about, is it?" Bjørn admitted, with an apologetic look on his face. He stayed quiet for the remainder of the ride.

When they had disembarked, Lysander felt his chest relax and he began to breathe normally again.

"So I'll go with you up to the access door and then you'll make the climb yourself," Bjørn told him as he led the way down the hall towards The Gardens. "But we'll be in contact through the bands the entire time, in case you have questions," he promised as his wrist beeped against an inconspicuous door, swinging open in front of them.

It was little more than a utility closet, and hot from lack of ventilation, with shelving piled from floor to ceiling piled in loose wires, cables, and dusty old machines that seemed to sag under the weight and lean towards the center of the room. On the far end of the wall was a large hexagonal plate in the wall with a keypad embedded beside it.

"Is that our way in?" he asked Bjørn, taking off the welding pack to inspect the door more closely. He held up his band and it blinked red. No access.

"It is, indeed," the older man replied, brushing back a mess of wires and pulling a dusty old laptop off the shelf to the left of them.

"What's that for?" Lysander asked, running his finger along the edge and leaving a trail in the dust.

"Oh, these older locks, they can be finicky if they haven't been used regularly," Bjørn told him. "Just a precaution." He blew the rest of the dust off, then rubbed his nose when the dust blew back in his face.

"You have access, I hope?" Lysander confirmed and Bjørn sneezed, then chuckled.

"Yes, of course. That uppity girl who works for the boss forget to give you access?" It took Lysander a second to realize he must be referring to Yvonne. Bjørn reached out his hand and the pad lit up green, the pieces of hexagon retracted into the wall, revealing an unlit, plated metal passage. "In you get." Bjørn pounded on the floor of the tunnel twice with his fist, the sound warbling against the metal, distorting in Lysander's ears. He let out an exhale.

He bent down and pulled the welding pack back up over his shoulders, so the gas canisters were flat against his back. He clipped the waist belt shut and adjusted it around his slim figure. The welder slid into a loop on the belt securely and the heavy-duty welding gloves clipped onto the back straps, left and right, respectively.

Bjørn faced him as he placed the welding mask on his head and adjusted it for size. Lysander tested the weight, shifting from one leg to the other, feeling like a boxer. Between the gas canisters and the gloves, it was more than he'd been expecting to climb with. Bjørn stepped back and Lysander lifted the visor of the mask to look at him.

"Will I even still fit in the crawl space in all this gear?" he joked, nervously.

"Better you than me!" Bjørn laughed without answering. "At the end of the tunnel there's a manual wheel lock and that will take you out into the raceway. From there you'll have to climb until you find the leak."

"And if I can't find it?"

"It should be pretty obvious. But if not, then you come back out and we'll figure out another plan. Maybe another access point." The older man seemed unperturbed, so Lysander tried not to let it bother him either. He hoisted himself into the crawl space and moved forward in the dark.

The metal was cool to the touch here, for which he was grateful, as it was not too long before he was dripping with sweat from the sheer weight of what he was carrying.

With a relieved sigh, he felt the clang of the visor hitting something in front of him and he reached out to feel for the wheel lock. He wrapped his fingers around and gave a tug. Clearly, it wasn't only the electronic lock that had grown finicky with disuse. He struggled with the wheel, his grunts echoing back down the corridor and mixing with Bjørn's voice.

"Everything okay?" the older man asked.

"The wheel is sticking. Don't worry about it, just give me a minute," Lysander responded, twisting his arms around and leaning into it with his full body weight. With a lurch, the wheel broke loose and Lysander's body flung forward with a thunk.

"Still okay?" Bjorn called out into the echo.

"Yeah, all good," Lysander shouted back and continued to rotate the lock, the sound of metal scraping against itself bellowing back along the passage as he did.

After a minute, the wheel thudded to a halt. Lysander heaved on the door, pushing it open.

He didn't know what he had been expecting, but it hadn't been this. He was inside what appeared to be one of the hexagonal columns - a smaller utility one instead of one outfitted for living - that rose vertically from the base of the fjord. Automatic lights flickered on in rows, clicking one after the other until Lysander could see the floodgate doors several floors both above and below him.

The sound inside the hollow raceway hit him like a wall, a roar of water that made him curious about Mimameid's wave generator, which he knew from the blueprints was down below. Bjørn hadn't ever given him more detail about it besides his initial tour - maybe because he didn't fully understand it himself - but Lysander was intrigued now that he heard the rush of power it had.

He turned to look up and located the rungs of the ladder along the wall which he was meant to climb, high enough to take him to the first set of floodgate doors above that Bjørn had described.

Over the roar of the water below, the hum of the lights, and the pounding of creaking sheet metal, he heard Bjørn's voice come through his band.

"You ready?" the voice asked, tentatively.

"Yeah, all good to go," Lysander huffed, gripping the first rung of the metal ladder and pulling himself out of the crawl space.

"You should already see the first set of doors above you," Bjørn instructed as he climbed.

"The band will open them, right?" Lysander asked, pausing in his climb.

"Theoretically, yes, but if you didn't have access to the tunnel..." His voice trailed off and Lysander heard what sounded like a keyboard tapping as he tried not to look down. The floodgate above him wasn't so far away, but it was a long fall down to the next one.

"I'll just try it and see. Can you override it with the computer if it doesn't work?" Lysander asked, hoping he had retained something from when they had reprogrammed the air filtration system together.

"One...second..." Bjørn replied and more keys tapped away. "There are like a hundred different security codes to get through to the utility servers," he complained.

Lysander had reached the door, so he took the chance and stuck his hand out, hoping he'd been cleared for access. No such luck. The door responded with a disheartening red beep. Lysander heard a grunt of frustration from Bjørn. He shifted his weight on the ladder and tried not to focus on the growing fatigue in his arms. This was far more upper body work than he was used and the mask, welding gloves and gas added an extra forty pounds, at least.

"Got it!" There was an exclamation from the other end of the band and the floodgate above him twisted open with a rush of salty air.

"Nice!" Lysander said, hearing Bjørn whooping laughter through the band. "Okay, I'm headed through the floodgate." He felt a rush of adrenaline at their success as he resumed climbing.

"There should just be just one more floodgate before you will start to see where the problem is." Bjørn was talking as Lysander crossed the threshold into the next chamber of the raceway and stepped onto a wobbly catwalk that ran the perimeter of the raceway. He looked up at the long climb to the next level and shook out his arms.

"Okay," Lysander replied, "just catching my breath for a second."

"Ready when you -" The floodgate beneath him twisted shut and as the metal sealed off, Bjørn's voice cut out.

"Bjørn? Are you there?" he paused, hoping to hear something, but all he heard was static. "Bjørn?" He reached down to see if his band would open the door from this side, but it beeped a disappointing red again. He was on his own.

Briefly, he considered if it was even worth the climb - if his band wouldn't open the door anyways - but he'd already come this far and he was trapped until Bjørn could open the lower door again. If the doors were notoriously finicky, then maybe the other two doors had nothing to do with his access and just weren't working properly. He had to at least give it a try.

Heaving himself up, he went along slowly and carefully, pausing every few minutes to catch his breath, until he reached the next floodgate. His muscles ached.

"Here goes nothing," he muttered to himself as he raised a shaky arm and put his band up to the pad. It flashed green and he felt his stomach flip.

There was only a moment of revelry before the doors above began twisting open and a stream of water exploded through the hole in the door. He sputtered and gasped, the moving waterfall continuing to wash over him, as the floodgate retracted into the walls.

Not wanting to fall back down to the lower floodgate, he tried to focus on his grip on the ladder. He pushed off to one side, pressing himself flat against the wall to avoid being pounded by the water.

Glancing down at his left and right, he made sure the gloves were still attached and adjusted the welding mask, which had shifted slightly on his face. He let out a deep, steadying breath, shook the water from his ears, and leaned his head back against the wall, waiting and listening to the rush of water around him.

So the compartment above was partially flooded, he reasoned. At least he had found the source of the leak. The water below beat against the lower floodgate with a thunderous bellow, rising quickly towards his boots.

When the doors had completely twisted open into the walls of the raceway, he turned back to face the slippery ladder and pulled himself up the final rungs into the upper chamber. He gripped the grated platform of the next catwalk and heaved himself up onto it with a clatter. Using the railing to pull himself to standing, he panted as he looked around the raceway, dripping with saltwater.

Though the visor had kept his hair mostly in place, he pushed a few loose, wet strands back behind his ears and scanned the walls, squinting his eyes. He tracked along the catwalk and then up across the sprawling lines of piping that crawled up the sides of the raceway, looking for any water that was bigger than a drip.

The walls look corroded with salt and age and he tried to focus on the task before him, but the brackish, wild smell of the fjord ignited something in him. It made him think of his dream with Magdelena and the Celt. It made him think of the surface above. The light that had cut through the water calling to him.

Then he spotted it, on the other side of the raceway, a spray of water coming from one of the more corroded-looking pipes. He took a tentative step onto the creaky, old catwalk, whose integrity was most definitely compromised from prolonged exposure to the salt water. He felt it give under his weight and creak as he took a step forward.

If it was a choice between this rickety catwalk and the elevator they had just ridden on, Lysander would choose the elevator every time. There, at least, the damage was secondary and due to old age. Here, the rusty bolts holding the metal frame up had wiggled loose and the salt water had started to eat away at the edge of the catwalk. This was a disaster waiting to happen.

Attempting to be as cat-like as possible, he sucked in his breath and scrambled across the path with about as much grace as a bear, his footfalls echoing throughout the raceway. Halfway across, he fumbled, then hurried until he thunked against the wall. His heart pounded in his ears as the catwalk trembled precariously behind him.

Safely on the other side, he knelt down before the spray coming from the pipe, trying to determine where the valve was which would cut off the flow for repairs. It was too dark here to work as the automatic lighting in this long-since flooded section of the raceway had short-circuited. He tapped his band to use as a flashlight.

Guided by the faint glow, Lysander followed the pipe along the wall, snaking around the sides of the room until it disappeared beneath the catwalk. He bent over and stuck his band out, submerging the light in the water below and finally it illuminated something which looked like it could be the valve.

Using his arm to brace against the wall, he tried to pull back the valve operator and seal off this section of the pipe. It was stubborn and though his arms were still tired from the climb, he mustered one last heave, strong-arming it shut.

He stood up and wiped his brow, damp with sweat and saltwater. Finally, he'd be able to fix the problem Bjørn had sent him up there for in the first place. He reached over his shoulder and unhooked the welder. Hugging the tool to his chest, he reached around with his other hand to the top of the gas canister, turning the peg that would start the flow of air.

The last of the seawater was spitting out of the exposed crack as the pipe finished draining. He pulled on his gloves and began; the sizzle of the sparks as they hit the water below him gave him a satisfying sense of accomplishment.

The heat of the copper through the face shield felt like the glow of a real fire on his face. He'd made innumerable fires Above Ground, the rhythm he'd had with Magdelena and Linnaea on who collected what and how to stack and feed the fire was muscle memory to him. But even with the bittersweetness of the memory, his mind returned to the question of the Celtic fire he had seen at the end of his dream and he felt the weight of the knife tucked into his waistband, the question of what the "T" could mean, rising again.

The copper seam in the pipe glowed hot and fresh as Lysander reached back over his head and turned the gas tank back off. It cooled and Lysander couldn't help but smile at the shiny, new ribbon, gleaming in an otherwise dank and brackish raceway.

He hooked the welder back onto his backpack and the gloves back onto his waist, ready to test the integrity of the pipe. He leaned all his weight on the handle of the valve and it ground back to the open position. Holding his breath, he waited for the water to begin flowing again, pushing out against the lovely, shiny copper vein, but it didn't budge.

He turned his attention to the problem of getting back. The chamber below was almost completely flooded now, so the only solution he could see was to swim down and try to get the doors to open. Or wait to be rescued.

Carefully, he lumbered back across the precarious catwalk and to the ladder. Bracing for the cold water, he took a deep breath and pushed down, sinking into the stinging salt water.

He flipped in the water and swam, propelling himself towards the floodgate. He tried not to think of the waves after the boat wreck, but instead to imagine he was back swimming laps in the Olympic-sized pool that had been at his university. It had been his routine to get up before sunrise and be in the water before anyone else was there. They had always looked at him with the same judgmental expressions - too scrawny, too foreign, and far too young to be there, but it had cleared his mind from his worries about Judit back home and about not measuring up to the expectations of the professors. Silly worries, he accepted now, considering what had come to pass.

In the end, it wasn't the swimming that had made him stronger, although he had been grateful that he'd practiced when the refugee boat did go down.

No, he realized now that of everyone who had been at the university with him, he was probably one of the few that had survived because he'd been deported and gotten away from the continent. And in surviving all the years after the eruptions, he'd felt his body harden and shape from the constant trekking, physical labor of working the refugee camps, and irregular meals. He was certainly not the same skinny kid who had thought those laps in the pool would somehow make him grow up.

He came to the door and in a futile effort, reached out to test the pad. Maybe they had thought far enough ahead to waterproof them? But no, the circuit was dead, no light reacted - red or green - to his band. Grunting in frustration, he punched the wall of the raceway.

Feeling the reverberations in the water gave him an idea. He straightened up. Gripping the ladder as an anchor, he lifted his feet and slammed them into the door. Hopefully, the sound would echo enough into the chamber below to get Bjørn's attention. He repeated the motion, banging over and over on the door until his vision started to blur, and he knew he needed to resurface for air. Pushing off again from the ladder, he ascended.

He broke through the surface and gasped, holding onto the rungs of the ladder to steady himself as he gulped down air. As pleased as he was to see the gleam of his repair to the pipe holding, he felt uneasy, not knowing when or if the door might decide to close on its own and cut off his last little bit of extra air supply. He readied himself for a second dive. His eyes were more acclimated to the saltwater now and he could see more clearly as he swam toward the door.

Again, he managed to pound on the door four times before he ran out of air and had to go back up to the surface.

On his third descent, he could feel the lack of oxygen getting to him, but steadied his grip on the ladder nonetheless. Lifting off, he prepared to pound the door again when suddenly the panels on the door began to recede and the water pulled him down, threatening to suck him through the gap and into the empty chamber below.

He heard the bellowing of the wave generator and his vision blurring, moving faster than his brain could process. The suction was pulling him down and his fingers were slipping, grasping for the rungs.

Clasping his hand tighter, he felt the cold metal of the ladder against the palm of his hand. His fingernails dug into the rung, in desperation. He grunted as the force of the water pulled on his shoulder - probably tearing something - and swung his other hand up.

Panting, he found his footing. He waited, impatient, as the doors twisted back into the walls and the water drained into the lower chamber. Mercifully, the opening to the crawl space was only a few meters below him and this chamber appeared to be deeper because the water level was below the access tunnel.

"Lysander?" a voice called out, despairingly.

"Bjørn!" he called back, realizing that his voice had come out a little hoarse. Shoulder aching, he climbed gingerly down the ladder and found Bjørn's bespectacled, blue eyes waiting for him at the mouth of the crawlspace.

"Oh thank the gods," the older man said, wiggling his way back into the tunnel to make space for Lysander. He followed him in, slamming the wheel lock back into position, and together they went back through to the antechamber surrounded by the sounds of water pouring into the raceway and the aluminum sheet metal warping under their weight.

Bjørn offered Lysander his hand, stumbling back as he helped him clamber back into the room.

"Sorry about that!" Bjørn started to apologize. "Good thing you taught me how to override the air ventilation system," he grinned. "Once I got inside, this one wasn't quite as complicated." Lysander looked around at the laptop setup and he was able to take in Bjørn's frazzled hair. At least he had anticipated Lysander needing help getting back once their communications had cut off.

"Phew." Lysander dropped the gas backpack onto the floor and felt his knees give out. He raised his hand to massage where he had pulled his shoulder stopping his fall down through the final floodgate and found himself grinning up at Bjørn. "Good thing."

"You want to tell me what happened?" Bjørn asked tentatively, taking his glasses off to polish them on the rolled-up sleeve of his jumpsuit.

"How about over a drink?" Lysander offered, even though it was still early.

He was so filthy after the expedition in the raceway that Bjørn gave him the rest of the day off and told him to go for a real swim. Once the workday was done, they agreed to meet up for a drink down in D. It had been a long time since he'd even thought about the drysuit he'd been issued, so when Bjørn suggested it, he felt a lightness come over him. A taste of freedom, like he might be able to discover something about his dream out there.

"You just take your suit back up to the split level in between B and C. It's a little tucked out of the way, but there's The Back Door-" *Could it be the same Back Door that Petra had been referring to when they first arrived?* "and that *sjef*,

Hafthor, will get you all set up," Bjørn explained to him. "It's like taking a walk in the backyard. You can get out there to swim in the seaweed farms."

His interest piqued, he smiled his thanks to Bjørn and made his way to the door of The Engine Room. With an airiness to his step, he found that he was actually happy to leave the worries of D behind him for the first time in a while.

A and B never wanted for anything, they got the medicine their children needed right away, they worked when they turned eighteen and not a day earlier. Their heating never turned off, and when energy was in short supply or when they had a problem, someone from D came to fix it within the hour. They didn't need to come up with creative solutions to the problems of their slowly aging bunker because the part of the bunker where they lived was intentionally built to be problem-free.

It wasn't inherently wrong, to want a problem-free or at least a life with fewer problems, but the problem that Mimameid had created was that it came at the expense of those in C and D. A and B only flourished because C and D were diminished. It reminded him too much of the way people had treated one another in The Time Before. How he had been treated when he was too green, too foreign, too naive - an outsider in the continent. That was before people started to value his engineering, language skills, and ability to adapt - all skills that ironically came from being an outsider in the first place.

With a flash of green, he was in and out of his bunk, headed back down to the so-called Back Door with his diving suit in tow.

Turning off the staircase at the split level as he had been instructed, he passed the unassuming room they'd been in earlier for repairs and followed along a darker corridor until he came to a steel door with a spinning lock. He tapped his band against the keypad outside and watched the lock click and spin as the door retracted into the wall ushering him into an airlock chamber.

The rush of air beckoned him forward. The door snapped closed and a row of calming blue lights flickered on, illuminating hooks where several other people's personal belongings were already hanging.

He stepped out of his boots and unzipped his jumpsuit, leaving them on the hook farthest away from the others. Pulling up his drysuit, he picked up his fins and helmet. He felt the cold floor through his footed bottoms and wiggled his toes, feeling a swell of curiosity rise up into him, as if he'd absorbed it through the pads of his feet. He went to the next door - this one manual - and heaved the spinning lock open himself.

The room before him was like an old airport hangar from The Time Before. Easily twice as tall as The Engine Room, the walls were bare except for a few windows in the base of the exterior wall. When he looked closer, he realized was one giant door to the fjord outside - 'The Back Door' he presumed. There were a handful of pods lining the far wall Lysander recognized from their initial arrival at Mimameid. A light off to his right caught his attention as a man stepped out of a windowed booth.

"In the boughs of Mimir's tree. Here for a swim?" A stranger's bellowing voice greeted him customarily, but he looked like anything but a Mimameid believer. Lysander took measure of him, brawny with a bushy, fair beard and dressed differently than anyone else he had met since coming to the bunker.

The man wore a pair of old fishing dungarees emblazoned with Mimameid's crest over a thick *lopapeysa* and rubber boots on his massive feet. The differences in the uniform were perhaps only nominal in nature - different coveralls, different boots - but when everyone else was dressed identically, the smallest details made the man stand out.

"Yeah," Lysander replied. "Is this the right place?" he asked, still bewildered by his surroundings. The room groaned and creaked around them, like a giant metal belly of a great whale digesting a healthy amount of krill. Not that he had ever seen a live whale or krill for that matter. He'd only read about them in books; they were long since extinct. He looked back at the man, his face shadowed as he approach Lysander.

"Welcome to The Back Door. I'm Hafthor." Hafthor's face broke out into a wide smile as he answered. A smile that suggested he'd been in his fair share of fistfights, but the divots in his cheeks were that of a man who laughed deeply, and often. "Follow me." He gestured for Lysander to come into the booth. The windowpanes were thick, fogged from what he guessed was exposure to salt water, and heavily scratched.

"How does it work?" Lysander asked tentatively, as Hafthor closed the door to the booth, rotating a lever up to seal them in. He felt himself tense up a bit as being closed in and shook his shoulder out where he had pulled it earlier.

"Is this your first time swimming in Mimameid?" Hafthor gave him a questioning, sideways look. "How long have you been down here and haven't gone for a swim yet?" His brows furrowed at Lysander.

"Too long," Lysander answered him honestly, although he suspected they had different definitions of 'too long'.

"Well, it's definitely the raisin at the end of the sausage," Hafthor chuckled and Lysander responded in kind, though he didn't know exactly what the man was trying to say with his odd turn of phrase. "Since you're the only one here though, it's pretty straightforward," Hafthor continued explaining, "You'll just go into the airlock chamber, hold tight to the safety railing and wait for it to fill with water." He walked Lysander through it as though he was talking to a child, which he found oddly reassuring, given what had happened in the raceway. "The doors will open and you can follow the illuminated markers out to the seaweed farm for a little 'forest swim,' if you will. It's definitely an experience if you've never been out there," the man assured him. "When you want to come back in, just follow the lights back and tap in with your band." Hafthor put his enormous hands in his dungaree pockets, "The doors will open. And don't worry," the man pulled one of his hands back out and tapped a mounted tablet screen on his console with one finger, "I'll be watching the whole time, so if you have any problems, just give us a shout." Hafthor gestured along the console to a further series of screens connected to cameras placed along the path. He saw the pixelated figures of other swimmers and felt his ears heat at the thought of being watched. But then, he reminded himself, all of Mimameid was being watched. Linnea had figured that much out.

"Good to know. Thanks," Lysander replied as he dropped his fins to the ground and stepped into them.

"Keep an eye on your band, it'll alert you every half an hour, so if you want to pace yourself, you can." He nodded and Hafthor put his giant hand on the door, spinning open the door to the airlock with impressive ease.

Clumsily stepping over the threshold, he could already feel a sense of excitement washing over him. He slipped his helmet over his head, felt the seal lock into place, and clicked on the light in the visor. The door lowered with an anticipatory thud and Hafthor took a seat at the console, giving Lysander the go-ahead with a thumbs up.

Water started pouring into the room and Lysander felt himself rise, instantly weightless. There was no pull or panic like the water this morning in the raceway, just peace. He grabbed ahold of the safety rail and allowed himself to sink beneath the surface.

When the door to the airlock opened, he felt the rush of the wild come inside. He was tempted to let go of the railing, his arms still aching from his climb, and let the current take him away, but his hand stayed put and he waited for the suction to subside.

Turning to issue a hasty wave of thanks to Hafthor, he swam out into the open fjord.

The silence that overcame him was profound. Left alone with only the thud of his heartbeat and the ease of his breath, the world seemed to stand still. The bright blue-green of the water was so much stronger here than through the glass ceiling of Mimameid.

He reached his arms out to his sides, letting the water take him, floating effortlessly. He closed his eyes and hovered, feeling his mind leave his body behind.

This was no lap pool in the early mornings. No struggling through the rough water of the coastline to shore as the refugee boat sank. This was the summers of his early childhood in mountain lakes. This was before he understood what famine had meant, or occupation, or deportation. This was when the world had been simple - before even Judit was born - when it had just been him and his parents, city people soaking up every ray of the sunshine they could in the Swedish countryside. Abruptly, he felt something brush his leg and with a jolt, opened his eyes.

A school of silver, spotted fish glistened past him, giving way as he swam down towards the first glint of the lighted path. He followed the thin stripes of light, swimming parallel along the edge of Mimameid and making note of the cameras. Along the outside of the bunker were an array of candy-colored starfish, walking drunkenly through the gentle rays of light that had cut deep enough into the fjord to hit the deep exterior, crusted with barnacles, here so far from the surface. Lysander thought he saw one settling over the lens of one of the cameras and felt a smirk creep onto his face.

As he approached the outer edge of the farm, he put his hands out to feel the thick brush of plants that lined the pathway into the thicket of seaweed forest. The plugs of seaweed were implanted onto scaffolding in straight, manufactured rows - orderly and precise, except for the soft ripple of the ribbons in the unfettered current. He reached a cold hand out in the water and let the smooth pieces run through his fingers.

Among the plants, he felt hidden away and protected. He was aware, of course, that there were other divers out there with him, and probably people in The Observation Deck too, but it didn't matter.

He looked up and he could see the distant quivering surface of the fjord, far above. He could taste how close freedom was, biting his lip, as he debated his next move. He had left the Celtic knife tucked into the folds of his jumpsuit, hanging on a hook, but the glinting of the water reminded him of how free the Celtic girl had seemed to be in his dream, how untethered she had been. He pushed up, out of the farm and into open water, his arms reaching.

From the top, he could look down and see how vast the farms spread, the sheer amount of seaweed that was actually being produced to feed the people of Mimameid and he had to admit, it left him awestruck.

As he continued to rise, the farm growing smaller beneath him, he thought of the 'T' on the blade of the knife and how it had pressed into Petra. He thought of the firelight as they had sat in that old, earthen barn, the blade glowing orange against the hot stones. He thought of the enigmatic blue of the Celtic woman's eyes and the warmth of his blood as it had dripped from his ear.

His heart jumped for a second, as movement caught his eye in the seaweed forest below. He followed the shadow through the water, his heartbeat racing, and then, with a lighthearted twirl a creature burst through the canopy.

A seal, with beautiful, shimmering rings speckled across its back glided through the water towards him. Big, black eyes full of marvel bore into him as it circled, beckoning him to come and play, to swim. It darted and twirled with surprising gracefulness, while he was left unable to move for fear of scaring the magnificent creature off. How it had even found its way down to their seaweed farms was anyone's guess, but by the way it twirled around him, Lysander inferred it was a place the seal was quite familiar with and felt safe being there.

His band turned red and the light startled the inquisitive little creature enough that he squealed and bolted away, up and into the current. Looking down, he saw with shock that thirty minutes had somehow already passed. He let out an audible sigh that fogged up his visor for a moment. Wistfully, he looked up at where the playful seal had been, already carried off by the current.

Not wanting to keep Bjørn waiting on that drink - especially now, to thank him for the swim - he turned to head back along the lighted path towards the Back Door. The little sea creatures wiggled and squirmed beneath him as if to say farewell. He tapped his way back into the bunker, feeling like the swim had been a salve.

"So, how was it, your first swim?" Hafthor asked enthusiastically, when Lysander was safely back inside the booth, dripping onto the floor, with a grin on his face he hadn't used in ages. He lifted his helmet up over his head.

"Exactly what I needed," he replied, pulling off his fins, one by one.

"Took a little free swim, huh?" Hafthor tapped the screen and Lysander felt his ears heat again, at being caught.

"Don't worry, *vinur*," the man tapped his mustached nose, knowingly, "I'm not telling anyone." He flicked a switch on the console and threw Lysander an earnest look. "The cameras were probably just glitching, anyways," Hafthor added with a playful wink and Lysander felt his shoulders relax. But, of course, this guy didn't mind bending the rules a little bit. If he was anything like the Icelanders Bjørn and Ned had talked about - if he was anything like Anders, for that matter - he wanted to stay out of politics as much as Lysander did. Lysander watched the man lean back in his slightly too-small, squeaking swivel chair and stroke his beard, before stretching his arms up and lacing his finger behind his head. Lysander set his helmet down on the console. The man looked over at him.

"Can I ask a question?"

"Sure," he unclasped his hands, "ask away."

"How does all this work? Being so far away from the mainframe?" Lysander hadn't been able to figure it all out, being so far from Mimameid's power source. There was a sneaky twist in Hafthor's mustache before he grinned.

"You must work in Engineering," he replied and Lysander dipped his chin into a small nod.

"I can always tell." The man's deep creases had reappeared with his smile. He pushed his chair back, sliding across the room to a nondescript panel on the wall. "There's a second unit here - a secondary central server." He pushed gently against the wall and it popped open to reveal a dark, discreet room blinking with small red and green lights. Lysander took a step forward, but Hafthor, with a raised, bushy eyebrow, pushed the panel back closed and wheeled his chair back towards the panel. Lysander hesitated but followed him back.

"That makes sense, given the size of this place." He gestured through the windowpane. "What's a big hangar like this used for anyways?"

"That's a good question. Most people came in on a vessel, so they know The Back Door, but it sounds like you came later on." Lysander was visibly confused and a smile crept back onto Hafthor's bearded face. "In the beginning, Mimameid had three huge submarines to deliver people to the bunker, back when survivors were still coming in by the hundreds. There are still a handful of smaller subs they use when they need to transport something, but the big vessels, they were all lost."

"What happened to them?"

"It was during Ragnarök, or so I'm told. That was before my time as watchman down here. The tremors washed them away. Took them right out into the current as well as whatever people were on them at the time."

"And they never found them again?" Lysander ran a hand through his hair, trying to shake out some of the water that had dripped in.

"Nope. Not the ships nor the people. But I reckon not very many people know about that part. I only know it by coincidence myself." Hafthor stroked his beard again and fiddled with a dial on the console.

"What do you mean?"

"Well, my work duties are here, so I know we don't have them, anymore. And I also know why we don't have them. The guys I took over for made sure I knew all about it. But as I said, most of the people in Mimameid were brought here in the subs. I think it's safe to assume, that they think when it's time for life Above Ground again, we'll all leave the same way."

"But you don't think so?" Now, Lysander was really interested. Hafthor looked at him, big hands stuck again into the pockets of his dungarees.

"I think if they were planning on us ever leaving, they'd be a lot more interested in finding out what happened to those ships."

16
PETRA

When Siobhan had left, Ciarán fiddled around her with the tubes. Each time his long, slender fingers lifted another one up, Petra held her breath, nervous she would be sent back to sleep for a treatment. But after a few minutes, he turned to her, a cunning, satisfied smile on his lips.

"Good news," he said, pulling his oily hair back from his face. "You passed the tests."

"So, I can go?" she asked, tentatively.

"Oh, more than that," Ciarán promised, his eyes alight. He let go of the tube in his hand and she heard the tent flap rip open, another person entering, wordlessly. With a reassuring squeeze of her shoulder, Ciarán left, and the person who had entered moved into view.

His eyes were no longer swollen, the traces of the bruising barely visible. There was no blood in his hair and his lips were healed. His sleeves were rolled down, covering where the welts had been. If she didn't look too closely, she could imagine that she had made up the image of him being beaten in her head.

"Arthur," she breathed his name. He locked eyes with her as she said it, their fair twinkle sparking only for a brief moment in time.

They held each other's gaze and she felt his breath steady. She had thought she would be hesitant to see him, after the nightmares, but she saw something in his eyes - something defeated - and she wanted to reach out to him. A rustle outside broke his gaze and he blinked, sniffing and busying himself by hastily ripping off the wires attached to her one by one.

"Let's get you out of here," he said, trying to mask the wavering in his voice with confidence as he moved onto the needles, gently pulling them out. She winced to see how big they were. Arthur looked at her, apologetically. "I'm so sorry," he whispered to her and she cocked her head sideways. Being able to stretch at long last felt good.

"Sorry for what?" She tried to laugh, but her ribs were sore, almost unbearably so. She cringed in anticipation of the treatment and the burning in her veins, but Arthur had finished removing the needles.

They were out. She was free. She tried to be somber about it, grateful for their medicine, but her obvious relief was visible to anyone who might be watching and she didn't have the strength to hide it.

She turned around and took in the scene of the cold, hard of the table she'd been lying on, shining under the stark, white light above. The towel Arthur had placed under her head was stained with a rust-red splotch of dried blood. And now that the light wasn't blinding her, she could see how small the tent actually was.

On the chair lay fresh clothes of black wool that were warm, really warm. The little *Imbolc* charm she'd been wearing since she arrived lay on top, the string carefully arranged in a swirl. Arthur helped her get dressed, her body aching from the many needle pricks. She first had wrapped the new, deep blue tartan around her matted hair, then stepped into the pair of sheepskin lined boots and laced them up. Arthur took her hand to lead her to the exit. She felt her heart thundering in her chest. She licked her lips, eager to leave the treatments behind.

"You ready?" he asked and she nodded, not entirely sure what she was agreeing to, but too weary to give any other answer and too eager to leave the tent behind her.

It was night outside, blustery and snowing. Arthur led her to the door of a Humvee like the one the Norse used for Above Ground missions. The door resisted against the wind as Arthur pried it open and she climbed in. When the door slammed shut, she was left alone for a moment with the dampened sound of the blizzard beating against the armored vehicle. Snow swept inside the car again as he tumbled into the driver's side and they crunched into gear. They rode through the camp without speaking, Petra still bobbing in and out of the reality that the treatments were over, until she realized that they weren't in the camp she knew. She raised her chin to the frozen window.

It would have been nearly impossible to tell the difference, but their paths were carved out slightly differently and the outer defense vehicles were fewer than she recalled. Arthur paused at the edge of camp and lifted a metal-plated keycard with cryptic runes punched into it through the window at a guard.

Apparently, it wasn't enough because he had to open the door and converse in Gaelic for a minute, although Petra could barely understand the conversation over the howling of the storm and the aching in her head. The car door slammed shut again and she flinched as the car jerked back into motion.

They continued across what in the dim headlights looked like a frigid wasteland. The wind continued to rock the car back and forth, but Arthur kept his hand steady on the wheel, glancing now and then over at her and giving her a small smile. She tried to smile back, but for the doubts in her that the treatments had brought to the surface.

She wasn't sure how long they drove before they made it back to their camp, but after another checkpoint, they were ushered into a parking location and Arthur ran around to get the door for her again. She groaned as she fell out of the side of the Humvee. She used the freezing side of the car to steady herself and then turned into the wind.

Fat flakes of snow stuck to her eyelashes and melted on her cheeks as they trudged through camp. She pulled the woolen tartan closer around her face with one hand and let Arthur lead her onwards with the other.

There was no bonfire tonight and no torches lit, not in this blizzard. Petra could see that very few people were outside their homes, all bent low against the wind and the snow. They trudged through the snowbanks, rising like sand dunes in the storm, towards what she quickly figured out was Arthur's camper van.

Only when he had slammed the camper van door shut behind them, blocking out the wind and snow with a grunt, and turned the dim lights on inside, did she lower her tartan.

"Here, let me get that," he said and took the now soaking-wet tartan, hanging it over a line strung up in the front seat. She ran her fingers through her hair, trying to comb out the matted knots with her fingers. "How are your arms and legs?" Arthur asked her, hesitantly. There was a strange energy coming from Arthur. She was confused about where this, docile, neutered version of him was coming from.

"They're okay," she told him, honestly, unsure of how much he wanted to know. She wasn't sure what he could handle in the state he was in. He was feeling guilty about something and she had to ask why. She had to ask the question that burned in her as hot as the treatments had.

"Petra I -" he stopped.

"Were you using me?" she interjected, twisting her hair over one shoulder. Her voice was soft, but she needed to know. He sucked in his breath. "To trade for information? For protection?" she continued, but he couldn't bring his eyes to meet hers. He slumped down, holding his head in his hands, and in the pause, she feared the worst. She tried not to let her temper rise, but she could feel the remnants of the treatment still fizzling in her veins. "Was any of it real?" she asked him, finally. He looked up, shaken by her words.

"Real?" The word slipped out of him.

"Uh-huh," she said.

"Of course it was." His eyebrows furrowed, like a wounded animal. "At least, for my part it was." Petra studied his face, her eyes darting back and forth, trying to read the truth from it.

"And you think it wasn't real for me?" she retorted, feeling the burning in her veins from the treatment fluctuate and rise.

"You were using me, weren't you?" he replied and she felt a pang of guilt in her chest. He was right, of course. She had been, from the very beginning.

"Not by choice," she confessed, feeling the shame slip down her throat and hit her belly like a rock.

"No." There was a pause. "Me neither. They - well, they did what they always do to get what they want," Arthur said without elaborating, but reaching out to her hands. "But, I did put you in danger." She felt his pleading with her to absolve him of his transgression. "And I'll never be able to forgive myself for that."

"If you didn't turn me in, do you know who did?" she asked, sensing he was holding back.

"I think so." He paused, unsure of how she might react.

"Yes?"

"Ugh. Iain is going to kill me," he sighed and pulled his hands away, rubbing his weary face. "I think it was Gwenna." He spoke sideways, as if he wished the words would float right out the window of the van and get carried off in the howling wind.

"What? Why?" She looked away from him, mind racing. Had she done something to them? To Aeron? To offend Gwenna? Had something she'd said tipped them off? She wasn't exactly the most experienced at undercover work, but she also wasn't dumb enough to get caught. Or so she'd thought, anyways.

"You never have to go back there if you don't want to." His voice was apologetic, more than apologetic. He was mortified. "Gwenna, she," he tripped over his words, "she's Welsh. She married the English. She's tired of being at the bottom of the barrel. I think maybe she thought they might reward her for it. Some misplaced sense of loyalty." Petra sighed, helplessly.

325

She knew that feeling, of being at the bottom. She knew it all too well and she didn't know if she could be mad at Gwenna for trying to improve her situation.

No more taking whatever was leftover of baby formula, instead of the good stuff she knew Domnall's stomach could handle. No more slurs being hurled at her across the common area as she waited for the weekly rations drop-off. For Gwenna to rise, someone had to fall and this time, that had been Petra. But the thought would have to wait; she had other questions for Arthur. She pocketed the information for now and looked back up at him, hesitantly.

"They did beat you, right? I didn't imagine that?" It was a question, even though it had come out as a whisper. She reached up to touch the healed cut by his eye, the only visible remains of the beating. He leaned into her touch, closing his eyes.

"No, you didn't imagine it."

"Why? Why did they do it?" His eyes opened, a deep blue flashing in them.

"To remind me that I belong to them." She didn't understand.

"Belong to them, how?"

"That anything I do here, I do only by their grace." She was confused. Ciarán and Siobhan had been good to her, generous even. They were different than Sigrid. They were honest.

"Is it so bad here?" she asked him and he shrugged. "At least they tell you the truth. They take care of you. It's more than they do in Mimameid." The words fell bitterly out of her mouth, the truth about Mimameid and the woman she had long thought of as her family still a fresh wound, burning like the needles. Arthur bore into Petra's eyes, searching. But she wasn't sure for what.

"They made me do it," he told her. "You know that, right?"

"Made you do what?" She was confused again.

"They told me that I had to treat you."

"Well, of course. I mean, I hit my head. You're the doctor." Of course, he was going to treat her. What did he mean by "had to"? She felt her hand reach up and feel where her skull had been sewn back together, the scar tissue beginning to form.

"No," Arthur was shaking his head. "They did that. They stormed the clinic and knocked you unconscious. They threatened to let you bleed out unless I helped with the interrogation." He wasn't making any sense. The burning in her veins came back with a surge that made her bite down hard to keep from screaming.

"What interrogation? They were just treating me-" She reached out and pulled his hands close to her, searching for his grasp as though it would keep her grounded in reality. "And confirming my suspicions about Sigrid." She forced herself to finish.

He hung his head, shaking it. "Oh, I know you are stronger than this, Petra." It made her angry to hear him talk like this. "Most people can't even remember what happened during the treatments - the pain is all they know, but you, you aren't like other people." He lifted her hands to his face, pressing them against his cheek, the rough stubble scratching lightly against her, and the burning subsided.

"They aren't better than your Sigrid," he said and she felt a powerful need to contradict him rise up in her, but she pushed back at it this time. "They tell just as many lies and keep just as many secrets to stay in power. They bend the truth. And they used the treatments to bend you to their truths, too." Petra felt the hot distaste at his words continue bubbling inside of her. She looked at him, her eyes burning, and then turned and vomited over the side of the bed. She spat the same neon blue the medicine had been, a bitter taste on her tongue. She felt Arthur's hand rubbing her back, gently. "I'm so sorry. It's a side effect of the drugs." When she was done, her anger at him had subsided somewhat and she sighed. He filled up a cup of water for her and she settled back against the side of the van, resting her eyes.

"So then what did they do to me, exactly?" she asked, her eyes still closed.

"Counter-conditioning. The drugs loosen your willpower, make you susceptible to suggestion and then they destabilize what you know to be true and embed what they want you to think in place, reinforced over and over by the dreams, the pain." She shuddered and thought of how her distrust of him had grown. Was he right? Had they done that? But they had known things that only he could have told them.

"How did they know about you helping us in the village?" She opened her eyes and looked at him, her eyes narrowed.

"I had to tell them about it. I had to account for why certain parts of my supplies were missing after the mission." The bandage he had given her. Of course.

Arthur shifted on the bed. "Before they decided to use me in the interrogation, they made me pay for helping the enemy." He reached down and rolled up the sleeve of his sweater, peeling back a bandage and revealing a patch of raw skin, twisted and pink where he had been branded with some sort of rune. She lifted her hand up to the wound and he flinched at her touch. "Better being branded though than something happening to my family," Arthur said indignantly, and Petra swallowed at the thought of Aeron or Domnall being used as leverage.

"But Siobhan said that had always been the plan, for you to stay behind and help us. Those were your orders." She wanted to believe Arthur, but she had to admit Siobhan's logic made sense. After all, why would a Celt help a Norse?

"Does this look like someone who followed orders?" he asked her gently, raising his arm. The blisters weren't healing well, he obviously wasn't taking very good care of the wound. She stayed quiet. "I didn't plan anything. I reacted when I saw your man there gasping for breath. I'm a doctor, that's what I do." His voice had raised a little, there was a passion behind it. "Besides, you said it yourself that day in the village. We didn't even know one another would be there, so how could Siobhan have known that?" Petra bit her lower lip as she considered it, the sensation of the treatment in her veins hummed beneath her skin. According to him, Siobhan had said those things with the intent to plant seeds of doubt in her against Arthur. Could he be right? And if he was, could Siobhan have been lying about other things?

"And about me passing information back to Mimameid?" Her eyes narrowed and he deflated under her gaze, but she wasn't sure why. "Why did they know about that?" He sighed and nodded.

"I did say that and I'm sorry for it. And I have no excuse, but the way I stay alive here is to make sure Siobhan trusts me. Keep her on my side." He struggled as he said it, tripping over the syllables. "I'm English - the lowest of the low here - and I have family to protect. From everyone, Celt and Norse alike."

"Who's side are you actually on, then?" she asked him, trying not to sound accusatory, but it came out anyway. Arthur's face fell.

"Don't be so naive, Petra." His words stung. She had gone through too much to be called naive. "The world isn't so black and white." Arthur's voice was deep. "I'm not on anyone's side. I'm just doing what I can for me and mine to survive." So, he was choosing his family over her.

"And that includes betraying my confidence?" His face fell at the sharpness in her voice. His voice lowered.

"I didn't know what they were going to do with the information I gave them, but I would do anything to keep you safe," he said. "And they know that. It wasn't Iain or Aeron they threatened to hurt if I didn't comply. It was you."

"What do you mean?" she asked, her voice suddenly quiet, matching his tone.

"I thought that by talking to them I was keeping you out of harm's way. But that's why they made me treat you. As a punishment. They want me to suffer more than they want you to." His words fell like rocks against her chest. He had recoiled against the back of the chairs, she realized, making himself small in a way she had never seen before. "I'm a Celt and I have to understand who is in power here, that's why I have to be punished. Put in my place." A part of her wanted to reach out to him, but another part of her held back. He sat up now straighter, as he worked through his thoughts. His eyes traced the pattern of the bedsheets up to her leg, then followed her body up to her eyes. "But I understand it now," he continued, "you are a tool for them, a means to an end, to be sharpened and refined. Not punished. Although, I don't know what their play with you is yet."

"Ciarán wouldn't do that," she said reflexively. Her arm gave a shudder as the burning pulsed for a moment in her veins. She didn't even know exactly why she had said it. She saw Arthur's face flicker with pity.

"Maybe not," he sighed, "but Siobhan would." She didn't answer him, instead taking a long drink of water from the bottom of the cup. Arthur picked at a fraying thread on the end of his pant leg. They sat there in the silence, listening to the wind howl and beat on the outside of the van.

"I don't know who to trust anymore, Arthur," she said after a long while, feeling defeated and exhausted. She drummed her fingernails on the side of the cup. "Sigrid lied to me and left me for dead. You say Ciarán and Siobhan are lying too, but you were informing on me the whole time. You told them everything. How am I supposed to know what was real and what wasn't."

"I didn't tell them everything," he said quietly, pulling something from his jacket pocket. "I *couldn't* tell them everything." He opened up his hand and in his palm lay the love knot. She let out a breath. She hadn't even thought about it. It was supposed to be in her jacket. A jacket she didn't have anymore.

"Where did you get that?" She reached for it.

"I didn't want them to find it, so I took it from your pocket."

"Why?" He looked at her, his eyes burning hot.

"You know why."

She felt herself fighting against trusting him, the burning from the treatments somehow warning her against it, but when she closed her eyes she could see the reeling stars above through the damaged roof of the earthen house, feel his cool hands on her forehead and she did know. She sighed.

"Petra." Her name was so bittersweet on his tongue, as though it were the last time he would be able to say it. "I don't -" he began, reaching out and placing the love knot in the palm of her outstretched hand, putting his hand over hers and closing her fingers around it, "I don't deserve your forgiveness. I don't deserve another chance," he paused, his usual carefree tone completely replaced with aching sincerity, "but I'm hoping you'll give me one. I never should have kept things from you. You were so honest with me and I thought-" She waited for him to find the words as he searched the air. "I thought I was protecting you."

Arthur raised his face to her, the blue of his eyes shadowed with worry. Worry for her, she realized and she felt something break in her, crumble to the ground. She pocketed the love knot and reached a hand up to his face.

"You don't have to protect me," she whispered to him, her voice quieter, softer than falling snow.

"No. I know that, now." He shuddered against her hand and she wrapped her arms around him, holding him. "I've spent so long protecting the people I love by giving them what they want, I thought this was the only way to keep you safe. Please, please say that you forgive me."

"Arthur," she told him, her voice still tender. She knew the feeling all too well, "there is nothing to forgive." She felt a stifled sob escape him in her arms. "But next time, we do it together, yeah?" He raised his face to her again, his cheeks red with salt water. She pulled down the blue tartan from the cord it was hanging on behind his head and wiped the tears from his face.

"*Mar pleg*," he said, the Cornish slipping off his tongue like a promise.

"What does that mean?" she asked in a whisper.

"Please," he replied.

He stayed the night with her so that when she finally did nod off to sleep, there was someone there to hold her when the dreams returned.

Swirls of Russian lullabies and calls for Mimir's tree pounded in her head while continuous bombs exploded over the old base where she grew up. She was trapped, unable to move as the snow drifts piled up around her.

Arthur said it was another side effect of the drugs, but she didn't care what was causing it, only that she didn't have to face them alone this time. Every time she awoke screaming, he pulled her close and held her in the dark until the terror passed.

The morning finally came, and the snow that had stormed through in the night subsided. When Arthur shoved open the van door, the snow banks glistened with the faint morning air. Somewhere on the other side of the ashen clouds above, the sun was shining.

"There's another bonfire tonight," Arthur told her, closing up the door again. She pondered vaguely how she should tell Benjáme and the others, but she didn't have her charcoal anymore - as if that mattered. She sat up in the bed, groggily. Her head ached and she was sore where the needles had been.

Arthur mixed up an instant coffee and passed it over to her outstretched hand. "I'm guessing Ciarán will be there. He and Siobhan lead them most of the time." Petra rubbed her eyes and tried to tame her hair by pulling it back into a ponytail. She thought about the torches, she could use the ash from them to communicate with her men perhaps. But did she really want Sigrid to get any more information about the Celts? Maybe she could feed them something false about the bonfire? After she knew what Siobhan and Ciarán were doing at this one, that is.

"What's the deal with the two of them? Siobhan and Ciarán?" She yawned and took a sip of the tepid coffee. Though she was tired, she was glad the night was over.

"How do you mean, like, romantically?" Arthur asked her with a curious look. It was an absentminded thought, but even through the haze of the treatments, she'd picked up on - what to call it - a dynamic.

"Yeah," she nodded.

"They're married, if you can believe it." Arthur leaned back against the driver's seat headrest, cupping his own mug of coffee with both hands. "They have a grown daughter, set to take over when her parents can't anymore." Petra's heart stopped for a second, her leg throbbed and she almost spit out her coffee.

"The Celt in the village." Those blue eyes burned in her memory.

"What?" Confusion played on his face.

"The girl who cut my leg. The girl who shot Lasse. She was with you in the village that day."

"Oh, yeah," he paused, "she was on that mission with me." Arthur started nodding, realizing. "That's her. Ciarán and Siobhan's daughter." Now that Petra's interest had been piqued, she tipped the last of her coffee into her mouth. This was something she might be able to use against Sigrid.

"We should definitely go to the bonfire tonight," she said and Arthur smiled at her decision.

"I had a feeling you might want to investigate."

She waited until the last possible moment before the bonfire to check and see if her charcoal signal on the van had been acknowledged, but it remained as it had been all day long, untouched.

Petra turned her eyes up to the ridge line, scanning. Her team had done a good job hiding their campsite. You couldn't tell from below that they were watching, so she didn't expect to see anything now. But they had also never left a mark unacknowledged for this long.

For reference, she had asked Arthur how long she was in treatments, but he wasn't completely sure himself as he'd blacked out after the beatings. So, she didn't know for sure how long it had been since the team had heard from her.

The more she went over the top of the ridge, however, the more she got the feeling they had pulled out and returned to Mimameid. She didn't know what to make of it. Had Benjáme been so quick to abandon her? Had Maike given up hope?

Her faith in the Norse, already shaken by Siobhan, dwindled further at the thought that they had abandoned her at the first sign of exposure - content to, at best, let her rot as a prisoner and at worst, become a ritualistic sacrifice. But perhaps the worst thought of all was that had been the plan all along, to dump her with the Celts and let them deal with her.

Her eyes stung with unshed tears as she considered whether Benjáme had simply been playing a part. Intended to rile her up, make her sloppy. She hoped not. Desperately, she clung to the bond that they shared and prayed he'd only left because he had no other choice. But at that moment, she couldn't be sure.

She wiped the water from her eyes, soaking the few salty droplets into the dark blue tartan draped over her head. Turning and heading back across the threshold to camp, she raised a hand to Angus, who - although he let her pass without trouble - she saw narrow his eyes at her. She wasn't with Arthur now, who had been her shield, her immunity. Now, she was just the flame-headed Norse girl who was making a new start with them. Someone who had to earn everyone's trust.

The news of her presence had made its way around camp swiftly, prompting some reactions more strongly than others. Derogatory graffiti had mysteriously appeared on the side of Arthur's van after lunch one day, but Iain and Darcy had used some alcohol from the clinic to scrub it off. Their rallying behind her was a gesture she hadn't expected but welcomed all the same.

Many had commended her for her bravery, in escaping the Norse, and some had even thanked her for being able to help them combat the enemy and protect their families. The warmth was foreign to her, soft. When she had joined Mimameid, it had been a question of strength, of what she could provide to help the greater good. Here, the greater good would be served by nurturing her, so she, in turn, could then nurture.

But then there were the rest, the ones who saw her as less than. Her presence was a threat, and she couldn't be trusted. She knew, in a way, they were not wrong. She did compromise them, for as long as she was there, they were a target in Sigrid's eyes. And the news of her being alive would not stay hidden forever. But Mimameid would have to wait. There was no investigation into the graffiti, there was no time to waste resources on that.

Still, the rift her presence had made in the tribe grew with every sideways glance in the street and every huff in the line for rations. She felt like the people's stares and silence should bother her now, but it was nothing new. She had spent her entire life being an outsider, a Rus among the Finns, a Sámi among the soldiers, a woman among the men. And this was no different.

So she kept her head down and headed back towards Arthur's van to make her debut among them as a Norse among the Celts.

They decided to arrive at the bonfire separately, to try to set the field for whatever game Siobhan was playing on their terms, not play openly just yet. Arthur wanted to assess what the general gossip was about them, what kind of information Siobhan had been circulating.

Petra, who ordinarily would be seeking out that kind of proactive mission and purpose, was grateful that tonight all she had to do was be present. She was still exhausted from the treatments and simply being there at the bonfire was enough of a distraction to allow Arthur to move through the crowd, ale in hand, and undetected. Petra allowed all eyes to fall on her, seated at the edge of the fire, keeping her gaze directed forwards, enraptured by the rising of the flickering flames.

She felt naked and exposed. Observed. Though her red hair made it easier for her to fit in, she had no illusions about the whispers of a Norse among them. Someone behind her hissed '*póg mo thóin*' under their breath. She'd heard it more than once now and Arthur had told her it translated roughly to 'kiss my ass.'

She sipped her ale slowly, letting the alcohol numb her sore body, and watched the smoke spiral into the night. The buzz washed over her and she let herself be taken by it, by the whispers of the Gaelic ringing in the air.

"What are we celebrating tonight?" She leaned over and asked a bent, old woman sitting beside her on the bench with long grey locks. The woman gave her a gummy smile so bright and friendly, there was no way she could have known she was talking to the Norse girl.

"The first of the cloudberries have been found in the hills," the woman replied with wonder, and Petra realized this was the same old woman who had served her on that first night in camp at the bonfire. *Cloudberries*. She'd used to collect the small amber fruits as a child, always popping three in her mouth for everyone she dropped into her bucket, under *Baba*'s approving eye. It was her wisdom that the berries tasted best the moment they left the bush. But, what did it mean now? Why were they celebrating the cloudberries?

"I'm sorry?" she asked and the woman reached out a gnarled hand, holding tightly to Petra's fingers.

"*Ostara* is finally upon us. The Long Winter has ended," the woman said as Petra searched for meaning in what she was saying. The Long Winter. The cloudberries. The moss in the moor. What had Magdelena said all that time ago? That the plants had begun to heal. She turned to the woman, her face illuminated by the firelight.

"Springtime?" she asked and the woman nodded gleefully.

"Yes! *Ostara*!" The woman leaped up from the bench as if she were a new bride on her wedding night and joined in the dance, the steps coming as naturally to her as the smile on her face. Petra watched the people swirling around the fire. She saw Iain pass her, dancing with Aeron, whose laughter lifted into the night as bright as the full moon shining through the silver clouds above. Petra scanned the crowd until she found Gwenna, seated with the baby Domnall bouncing on her lap. When she saw Petra staring, Gwenna quickly averted her eyes, busying herself with the baby.

She didn't know if Gwenna's snitching had had the desired effect of elevating her status, Arthur hadn't mentioned anything so far. Petra felt her eyes instinctively narrow but stopped herself when a group of women crossed in front of Gwenna, one of them intentionally knocking into her legs and another laughing at the provocation. Petra saw the baby's fat bottom lip jut out as Domnall let out a whimper on his mother's knee. It was a moment Petra wished she hadn't witnessed. She wished she could stay mad at Gwenna. She bit her lip and took a sip of her ale.

The bonfire raged into the smoky night and the drumbeats grew wilder around her as Petra's breath escaped out into the crisp air.

Though Ciarán was nowhere to be seen, Siobhan's gaze was on her, all intention hitting her like an electric pulse. But there was another pair of eyes lingering on her as well.

She turned her head away from Siobhan, drawn through the rippling heat of the flames, where she saw that roguish, midnight blue. His chin was jutted forward in amusement and his head cocked to the side with an arrogance she found herself wild for. He was with a group of Celts not far away from Gwenna. Iain, with Aeron on his shoulders, had come up and clapped his brother on his back, shoving a bowl of ale into his cold, red hands.

He raised his bowl to her, toasting her silently, bidding her to return the toast. His eyes glowed with motive - this was something he wanted Siobhan to see. Petra tilted her own bowl back at him and brought the edge to her lips. She watched him drink and then look back at her, his fair hair falling across his face, shadows playing against his jawline, his lips. She felt the flush rising into her freckled cheeks like the flames before her.

For a moment she slipped away from her perch there, observed by Siobhan, distrusting everyone. For a moment, she was only with Arthur, the blaze from the fire lifting into that starry night they had had so long ago when he whispered his name gently into her ear. And she was his Guinevere.

A tap on her shoulder jolted her back to the bonfire. Ciarán had finally, it seemed, made his appearance. His hand was extended out to her and his dark eyes were shining. She could see the glances being passed around and the whispers, hissing like smoke from the end of a piece of kindling.

"Would you like to join in the dance?" The last time she had danced was so long ago her grandmother had still been alive. She wasn't much of a dancer, but a glance in his obsidian eyes made it seem like refusal wasn't an option. Ciarán, it seemed, could sense her apprehension and tried to ease it. "There is no expectation. I only thought you might enjoy it." His eyes burned like the edge of a volcano in the firelight, his twisted smile curling like a river of lava down the mountainside.

This hadn't been a part of their plan, but as her eyes darted over to Arthur, she saw a mischievous grin had crept onto his face. A trace of boldness caught in her throat, she threw him a sideways look, took Ciarán's hands, and plunged into the heat of the dance.

She felt the drums reverberate down into her bones and the flutes and the fiddle lift into the air like the smoke rising from the bonfire. She followed Ciarán's lead, guided around and around in the dizzying dance. Arthur's gaze followed her the entire time, that unadulterated laughter shining in the lines of his face.

After several rotations around the fire, Ciarán stopped her abruptly, extending her hand out to someone. Her head still spinning, she steadied herself for her new partner. The crook of his smile grounded her immediately and with a carefree wink, Arthur pulled her back into the frenzy.

They twirled until Petra was wound up in his embrace and then in one wild release she leaned her head back and laughed into the blackened night. His hand was firm on the small of her back. His eyelashes brushed her cheeks with the softness of the wind. She relaxed in his arms, the feeling of the untamed North - of home - creeping back up into her stomach and out into her limbs.

She felt what the Celts had to offer her. Warm, moonlit nights dancing, family meals spent bickering, the freedom of the North Country laid before her feet. She felt what she had before her fall in the clinic. That this existence here was a good one with good people, full of hope and joy and celebration at the possibility of a new life in the ashes of The Time Before. And here in Arthur's arms, she felt that life was hers for the taking.

"Ready to give them a show?" Arthur's breath was hot on her ear as he whispered. She looked at his face, the fuel from the fire dancing in his eyes. She wasn't sure she followed what he meant, but he took her hand in his and led her towards Siobhan, who was deep in conversation.

Just before they reached her, they were intercepted. Ciarán stepped out, his arm around a girl near Petra's age, with a mess of raven curls and those flame-blue eyes, she knew so well.

"Petra, I have someone I'd like you to meet. This is my daughter, Briony." He pushed the girl forward, her pale face thoroughly unamused.

"Yes, I know. We've met." The words slipped out of Petra's mouth before she could catch herself. The girl's pale eyes flashed dangerously.

"Oh, you have! I didn't know that." Ciarán said, his words dripping with falsehood, but the girl rolled her eyes as though she had anticipated the lie. This girl, this Briony, she didn't play the game the same way her parents did. Arthur extended his hand.

"Briony. Nice to see you again. It's been a little while since our last mission together."

"Yeah, I lost a rather nice knife on that mission," Briony replied snidely to Arthur, ignoring his handshake. "Your Norse wagon doesn't happen to have it, does she?" She turned to Petra, the fire in her eyes raging. She certainly had more of Siobhan in her than she did Ciarán.

"Now, now," Ciaran soothed and Briony backed down, "I thought maybe the two of you could train with one another," he continued. "Maybe you'd learn a thing or two from one another if you sparred together. Petra, you must have all kinds of knowledge to impart on such a fresh, young fighter like Briony." He looked from Briony's narrowed eyes over to Petra. "When you're feeling well enough again, of course," he added, a little provocatively. Briony was so riled up she looked like she was ready to spit on Petra. She felt her pride growl inside of her. This was a fight she would gladly take on.

"I'd love to," Petra said through gritted teeth, keeping her voice as steady as possible. Arthur's grip on her hand tightened. "Shall we say tomorrow?"

"Excellent!" Ciarán said gleefully, clapping his hands together. Briony glared at her father.

"Do you need anything else from me, or am I allowed to go socialize with *our* people again?" Petra raised her eyebrows at Arthur at the snide tone in Briony's voice. And then, as if she'd been called over by name, Siobhan appeared beside her daughter.

"Arthur and Petra are our people now, Briony," she said, her voice harsh and syrupy sweet. "Both important members of our community and they deserve our respect." Petra saw the girl recoil ever so slightly at her mother's touch, but she didn't say anything else snide about Petra. In fact, she was silent for the remainder of the conversation.

They mingled long enough with warm bowls of ale in their hands until eventually the fire died down. When Aeron was asleep from dancing over and over with Petra, and Iain had stopped speaking any kind of intelligible Gaelic, Arthur put a hand around Petra's waist and pulled her close. His breath was warm and sweet.

"Will you come somewhere with me?" he asked her gently. His voice was far too gentle for the rough, cold air around them, littered with drunk Celts and snow-covered ashes. It took her aback. She tilted her head sideways to where Ciarán and Siobhan were still talking across the way, their faces huddled close together, illuminated by the glowing embers.

"Will we be missed?" she asked him.

"I think they will be happy to see that we've successfully 'bonded'," he said playfully, though the word struck her in the chest. "Come on." He took the chipped bowl of ale from her hands, set it in the snow, and offered his arm dramatically with a sweeping motion. Joining in with his ridiculous charade, she snickered in the dark and accepted. They side-stepped over a drunk who had fallen asleep against the bench, and together they wandered out into the darkness.

Arthur pulled her forward, deeper into the woods behind camp, his fingers intertwined in her own. Petra felt her heart pounding against her ribs as the moonbeams illuminated the snowy path before them. Pools of white spotted the North Country trail into the forest of ancient trees, thick and heavy. A breeze caught the back of her neck, spiraling up into the trees and making the branches shiver snow off into the night air.

Arthur turned back to her, a small smile playing on his lips.

"Where are we going? Won't we get caught?" she asked and Arthur paused.

"I want to show you something. We're almost there," he whispered as he guided her around an enormous oak tree into a small clearing lined by the giant roots of the twisted trees. The moonlight here was naked, the clouds having parted, a pure white-blue against the night sky. It shone down on a spring of water, bubbling up from under the roots of the biggest tree in the clearing with silver moss climbing up its bark. Around the edge of the water were stones frosted with snow, placed carefully to form a pool.

She stepped into the clearing and let the moonlight wash over her.

Petra's feet crunched in the snow as she walked forward and knelt at the edge of the water, placing one finger on the surface. The ripples glistened, dancing. She looked back at Arthur's face, bathed in the soft moonlight, and he nodded. Slowly and intentionally, she dipped both of her hands into the water and cupped them, bringing the spring water to her lips. It was cool and fresh, no trace of ash. She pressed her wet hands to her skin, the cold water calming the warm blush of her cheeks. She closed her eyes and sighed, feeling the magic of the North Country wash over her. When she opened them, Arthur had his hand offered out to her. She took it and rose to him. He pulled her close, wrapping his arms around her waist. Petra felt her heart rate surge. Their faces were close enough that only the moonbeams could shine through.

Arthur let out a steadying exhale. His arms fell from her waist and he retreated, studying her carefully. His eyes were still soft and kind, but there was something else, something more. After a moment, he looked away. Petra followed his gaze to the edge of the clearing.

She gasped when she saw it.

On the trees all around them, instead of leaves hung thousands of pieces of cloth, tied in knots along the branches. They swayed in the light breeze - all different - brightly colored family tartans, delicate pieces of embroidery, torn pieces of shirt or skirt, even feathery pieces of organza. Some looked weather-worn and faded, others freshly knotted.

She turned in a circle, taking it in as a whole. The wind beckoned her forward. She reached out an arm, running her fingers through the many hanging colors while she walked the perimeter of the small grove. It reminded her of the laundry lines she and *Baba* had hung in the wind back on the base. As she walked, she felt Arthur watching her.

"Do you like it?" he asked her tentatively.

"What is it?" she asked in awe.

"It's a symbol. A promise."

"A promise of what?"

"Well, I may not like everything about the Celts, but they have this tradition when you find your mate." Petra's heart fluttered at the word.

"Yes?"

"To promise yourself to that person, you tie a knot together here, at the clootie well."

"So all these knots - they're all people who have promised themselves to one another."

"Every knot. A joining of hearts." In that moment, he really did sound like the poet king of old. "Some people choose the color of their clan, some just use what they have on them at the time. All that matters is that the promise is true."

"I've never seen anything like it," she replied. And she hadn't. The snowy military base she grew up on and then Mimameid never had sentimental places. The closest thing she could think of was The Observation Deck back on Mimameid. But standing here now, she realized that The Observation Deck had been a place to silence everything around her, to muffle the voices and the memories that resided in her, whereas here, there was a freedom. She could speak and be heard for all she was and all she could be. Arthur made room for her to be exactly who she wanted to be, he had found the parts of her with his kind, laughing eyes that she had long since tucked away. There were no expectations for her here. No judgment. She could simply be and he would be there to take her hand.

Her hand fell from the cloth back to her side. She had lapped the clearing back to him. The wind whispered to her, lifting her hands into the air and she placed one shaking palm on his cheek. He closed his eyes and leaned into the touch, his skin warm against her cool fingertips.

Her head fell forward towards him so their cheeks were touching, her fingers tracing the vertebrae at the base of his neck, soft locks of hair rustling. She felt the up-and-down of his chest.

She wasn't quite sure when it changed, but when their breath had synced, his lips were on hers, warm and gentle. Despite all that was happening, there was no sense of urgency, as they savored the moment of absolute peace, drinking one another in.

Petra caught her breath after what seemed to be an endless moment. She raised her fingers to her lips, warm and wet, and took one step back from Arthur, those same kind eyes still steady in their gaze. Though she was surprised herself, she looked at him and stepped back into his arms. Pressing her cheek against his chest as he held onto her tightly, the feeling of safety there in his arms rose in her like a wave.

17
LYSANDER

SINCE HIS SWIM, LYSANDER had intentionally sharpened his gaze at the goings-on of Mimameid, watching the small inequities and unspoken transactions amongst the folk, taking note of anything that made his gut turn over uneasily. Anything that could point to what Sigrid was hiding.

The activity proved useful to him in that it gave him a sense of purpose. Even Bjørn commented on how his productivity at work had increased. At the dinners they shared in D his dancing with Åsa was also progressing, although the little girl proved to be a demanding teacher. And although he loved dancing with the little girl, he increasingly valued the time when Tuva eagerly told them all about her new post in Accounting, when she wasn't with her new boyfriend, that is.

A series of induction tests intended to identify her strengths and weaknesses had placed her in inventory for The Closet. It wasn't the most glamorous position, she admitted, but it had relatively low consequences if she made a mistake, which made it the ideal training spot.

"At least I didn't get stuck monitoring people's bowel movements," Tuva shuddered. Lysander was more shocked by the comment than disgusted.

"Wait, they do that?" he asked. She nodded with a grimace that crawled all the way up her hairline.

"For fertilizer," she admitted in a whisper, "but don't *ever* tell anyone I said that." She wiggled herself around uncomfortably and went back to talking about her new post.

The Closet meant that she was in close communication with the team who monitored the seamstresses and cobblers in Mimameid. Tuva's eyes were bright as she detailed a scandal on her first day with huge, animated gestures. They'd caught someone who they'd been watching for months who had been sneaking socks in and out for repair from C without going through the proper channels and waiting in line.

"We have rules for a reason, you know?" The young woman leaned back and crossed her arms. "The military can't just go around thinking they are above everyone else." Tuva rolled her eyes, incredulously. Lysander didn't like how much the words coming from her mouth sounded like Sigrid, but he valued the insight immensely.

All in all, he tried to use his observations to occupy himself as he bided his time waiting for Magdelena and Linnea to return from Svalbard. He thought of the wave generator he'd seen. He'd ask Bjørn about it later that week, once they'd repaired the valve. Maybe he could learn something useful from it, something they could use once they were Above Ground again.

But, one thing in particular still pressed on in the back of his mind: Petra. Why had Sigrid been so quick to deny him any information concerning her whereabouts? And why had it been her there, at the end of his strange Celtic dream? He couldn't make any sense of it. He missed her acerbic nature, her bluntness. He was grateful for his budding friendship with Bjørn and his family, but he missed being able to talk to someone about the world above the surface of the water.

He made up his mind to find Liddie down in D during dinner that night and ask her about his dream. He could hardly believe himself for considering it, but he couldn't explain why he could still feel the Celtic girl's hand in his own - days later, even - not scientifically anyway. As much as he had never believed in the stories of old or destiny or whatever, he did want answers, and wasn't that what a seer was for?

When he arrived at dinner, Åsa was bouncing at the door to greet him and let him in, her ash-blonde hair swaying to the music like her mother's had when she'd sang.

"Tuva's been spending so much time with her *hjärtat*," Åsa complained as she took Lysander's hand and led him into the canteen. Lysander smiled at Åsa's little crush on him. "It's getting really boring to talk to her. She's trying to be so *adult*."

"So your *pappa* approved of, what's his name again?" Lysander asked her.

"Heiká." She rolled her eyes dramatically, tucking a lock of hair behind her ear.

"Heiká, right. So your *pappa* approved of Heiká?" His heart jumped for a second - sure he'd heard that name before somewhere, and unease about whether it indicated friend or foe.

"Yeah, but they are only allowed to see each other when someone else is around," she explained as they waited in line for the automats, the soft lilt of the folk music blending melodically with the chatter.

"What, he doesn't trust this Heiká guy?" Åsa threw him a cutting look that only a girl on the cusp of adolescence could.

"Heiká? No, he's a moron and *Pappa* knows that. It's Tuva he doesn't trust." She smiled wickedly, saying such nasty things about her sister out loud, but Lysander could see the laughter in her eyes, so he winked at her playfully and they stepped forward to get their food. "How do you sign *moron*?" Åsa asked him as they made their way to the table. He smiled. So she hadn't given up on learning sign language yet either.

"It's a good one to know," Lysander chuckled and demonstrated the motion for her.

When they were seated - Åsa beside him and the two of them across from Bjørn and Runa - he unrolled the paper bag around his fish, releasing the steam into the air. He breathed it in, the warm, honied salmon and the potatoes, salted and served today with a small portion of mushrooms. The mushrooms Lysander knew Runa had grown herself in an unsanctioned closet near The Engine Room where they siphoned off the excess steam generated by the reactor. Lysander himself had helped Bjørn check to make sure the mushrooms weren't radioactive. But otherwise, D wouldn't have gotten a portion of vegetables this week since the seaweed yield was lower than usual.

The music from the accordion lulled in the background with a drum beat thumping along. Lysander grinned over at Bjørn, who was unintentionally glaring across the room to where Tuva and Heiká were cuddled up.

Tuva was seated on her boyfriend's lap and had her arm resting on his shoulders. She was chatting away with a group standing around them, playing absentmindedly with the boy's locks of hair. He was the only one among the group of friends who had a girlfriend draped over him and his face showed it. The boyfriend balanced an inner disbelief with an outward attempt at coolness. Of all the options available, Tuva had chosen him - gawky and awkward as he was- and he was trying hard to be the man he had not yet grown into being. He was desperately aware of how lucky he was and simultaneously terrified that she would discover at any second that he wasn't cool and dump him. But, it was endearing and he seemed to have a good heart. He felt for the kid, sweating under the pressure of being observed by his girlfriend's father. He looked back at Bjørn with a smirk and then back at the boyfriend.

"Are you warming to your new son-in-law then?" Lysander teased and it shook Bjørn from his reverie.

"Ha! That'll be the day," he said, adjusting his arm around Runa's shoulders and kissing her cheek. "She's doing it just because she knows it annoys me," he reassured Lysander, although he could tell Bjørn didn't really believe it himself.

"There now, he's not so bad," Runa cooed at her husband.

"Yes, but a soldier?" he asked, looking back at her.

Then, Lysander recognized him. The boyfriend was one of the people he'd met up in C among Petra's men. But he was so young, Lysander thought, he couldn't have been a soldier long.

"He's making a plan for the future, way I see it. And he wants to move up in the world, what's so wrong with that?" Runa replied, pushing a lock of Bjørn's blonde hair behind his ear.

"Is he a soldier already then? He looks a little green," Lysander interjected. Bjørn sighed a little and looked at him, a raised eyebrow creeping up at Lysander's own age.

"He's training to be. Started about six months ago when he got his work assignment. Fancies it'll get him out of D, that he'll get to move up to C." He leaned back in the chair and folded his arms across his chest.

"They are still young," Runa soothed. "Many things could change." She had a twinkle in her eye. She unfolded her husband's arms from his chest and took his hands in her own, pressing them to her cheeks.

"Let's hope so." Bjørn softened at her touch and she let his hands fall away. He adjusted, turning to Lysander and Åsa, who had nearly cleaned her tray.

"Do you know, is Liddie telling stories later?" Lysander asked Åsa innocently. The girl was usually the first to sit down with the old woman for story time, eating up every delicious detail of the epics. Even when she had spent the night dancing instead of listening, she would go to the old woman's room after dinner and ask about what she'd missed. They were neighbors with her, so Åsa generally knew where to find her.

"I don't think she's coming tonight," Åsa replied, distracted.

"No?" He tried again not to sound overly interested.

"No," she told him and hopped up from her seat to buss her tray. "You'll dance with me tonight?" she asked him, blushing slightly as she demonstrated the sign for dancing.

"I promise," he signed back and inclined his head as she bobbed away to find her friends. Lysander turned back around to his food and Bjørn raised an eyebrow at him as Runa sat down beside them, delivering two beers.

"What do you want to see Liddie for?" he asked, slurping the foam off the top of his drink. "That's not exactly your usual company, is it?" He wiped the excess foam from his upper lip. "In fact, haven't I heard you being a little critical of the fact that she was filling the children's heads with nonsense?" Lysander scrambled, debating whether to be honest with Bjørn or not. He wasn't sure where Bjørn stood on the whole 'logic versus legend' thing, being an engineer. And he certainly couldn't deny what Bjørn was saying. He conceded, sighing.

"You're going to laugh." He hushed his voice and Bjørn leaned forward to hear him, fists balled with excitement.

"Try me," the older man prodded and Lysander shrugged.

"Remember a little while back, when I had to climb up the raceway?" Bjørn nodded. "Well, the night before, I had a weird dream." He waited for Bjørn to ridicule him, to scoff or something but nothing came, so he continued. "When I woke up it felt like more than a dream. Different than anything I've ever felt." He searched for the words. "Visceral. Exposed."

"What happened in the dream?" Bjørn asked, still listening, and Lysander paused before answering him.

"I saw, well, someone I didn't know I remembered." He wasn't sure even now, what to call the Celtic girl. He inadvertently raised his hand to where the knife had cut his ear.

"Well, that's not so unusual." Bjørn crossed his arms over his chest. "That happens to me all the time, my subconscious playing tricks on me." As he leaned back Lysander saw a charm shaped like Thor's hammer peaking out from Bjørn's neckline. Maybe he was more of a believer than Lysander had thought. Beside them, Runa was listening closely, quietly.

"No, this was different. When she touched me, it felt like something familiar, more like a memory than a dream." Runa reached out to Lysander, squeezing his hands reassuringly, her gentle touch was maternal, calming.

"You're right to go to Liddie," she told him. "She will know what to do," the woman promised him. "But she's staying in tonight on account of some pain in her back. We were going to bring her something to eat, later." Lysander rose to his feet without thinking, his mind already spinning with questions for the seer.

But Runa pointed and he turned to see Åsa gesturing at him to join her on the dance floor. Looking back at Runa, he saw her face was slightly apologetic but full of gratitude for his friendship with her daughter.

The melody from the *nyckelharpa* and the drums swelled. He heard the sounds of the ancestors beckoning him forth. He downed the last of his beer and looked around at the people of D, bright colors of traditional garb swirling around each other, plants fat with leaves pouring from every free space on the wall. He fixated on a mandala-like drawing etched onto the far wall - a Runic Compass - and inclined his head to Åsa, accepting her outstretched hands as they plunged into the dance together.

It was late when Lysander tore himself away from the dancing to bring some supper to the old seer woman. Once he'd started, he'd been persuaded to remain dance after dance, and now that the night was in full swing he'd be able to slip out, unnoticed. The hallway lights had been dimmed some time ago - for the dual purpose of conserving electricity in D and simulating a normal circadian pattern - so he stumbled through the hallways of D until he found the door Runa had instructed him to.

Most people on Bjørn's corridor left their doors propped open with various knick-knacks - an old reindeer antler or a faded shoe with too many holes to be useful - so neighbors could come and go well into the late hours of the evening, but Liddie was one of the few who kept hers closed. He knocked on the door, listening through the door to the rhythmic sounds of her making her way to the pad to let him in.

It opened with the familiar whoosh and the woman looked up at him with a critical eye.

She had wispy curls streaked with hints of the sunshine yellow it must have been in her younger years. Her eyes shone like glassy orbs of cornflower, still sharp and clear. She moved slowly, but with a grace he would have attributed to a much younger person. All he knew was that she was over one hundred, but not a single person he'd met knew by just how much.

When he watched her tell stories, he had always found it easy to imagine how striking she must have been in her youth and how easily she must have ensnared people with her captivating words. Bjørn had told him more than one rumor about the many lovers she'd had when she was younger - politicians and royals who had run completely mad for her. But to see her looking him up and down the only thing he felt was intimidated.

"You aren't Runa," she said dejectedly and turned to usher him inside, rubbing her lower back irritatedly as she hobbled back towards the bed. The room smelled heavily of incense, although he couldn't tell what kind - sage or maybe frankincense - but something illegal, expensive and that made his head spin. The smoke from the incense was rising from the shelf above her bed, which was open into the room, making it hard to walk around in the narrow space. He skirted the bed as deftly as he could, bumping into a charm hanging from the ceiling that clanked together, sounding like driftwood and old bones. He set her dinner down on a makeshift table pulled up to the bed, made from old pieces of piping from the garden hydro-planters and some scrap metal. It certainly wasn't standard Mimameid issue, probably patched together by Bjørn and Runa by the looks of it.

"No, sorry. I'm Lysander, I work with Bjørn down in engineering," he apologized as she sat down on the tattered mattress and pulled a thick, reindeer-fur blanket over her lap.

"I've seen you around with the family. You're the one from B." She raised an eyebrow and unrolled the bag covering her food, a little puff of steam escaping as she pulled the tray of food out.

"Yeah," he'd gotten used to people down here referring to him like that, "yeah, that's me." She picked up a fork and dug it into her salmon.

"Well, sit down," she told him and he hastened to the fold-out chair that was open. "The girls usually sit and talk with me while I eat anyway. So, what can I do for you, young man?" she asked him.

"Um." He didn't want her to think he'd only come to ask her for something, rather than just to be neighborly. But she was the Seer after all, so wouldn't she already know why he was there?

"Don't be shy. It's not as if I haven't had my eye on you. I can feel when someone enters Mimameid - energy like yours. It's hard to miss," she told him as she ate, voice still matter-of-fact, fork sifting through the food.

"What energy is that, exactly?" He pulled open the chair she had gestured to and sat down.

"You reek of serendipity." The words came out rough and final. He furrowed his brow and crossed his arms.

"What, like fate?" he asked and she shrugged.

"If you believe in such things." She paused and looked up at him, one eyebrow poised above her cornflower eyes.

"What does that mean?"

"Well, do you?" the woman asked.

"Do I what?"

"Believe in fate. Destiny. The gods. The nine worlds."

"You mean like Sigrid." The words tasted foul on his tongue.

"No. No, not like Sigrid." Liddie's face softened as she looked at him, but then hardened again as her gaze traveled upwards. "Sigrid uses these things to control. To manipulate. But she is an empty vessel. She seeks only power over others. Without respect for the things that were, so very long ago. Things bigger than she or you or I will ever know. To believe, truly believe, is something different." There was a silence.

"Different how?" Lysander asked her slowly.

"Like children," the old woman explained.

"How?"

"They can see the most trivial moment and recognize the mystical power in it - the sprouting of a sapling, the ripple of the seaweed, looking into the eyes of another creature and seeing its sentience stare back into you." Lysander thought of Linnaea and of Åsa, and he felt something in him settle. Like a knot had been undone.

"Then tell me," he asked, "what is this serendipity you see for me?"

"It's not your destiny that I sense, but the role you must play in everyone around you. You are the conduit through which the connections must be made. The copper wiring which must be carefully placed or we all fail." He thought back to the house where he'd nearly blown them all up.

"So you're saying my destiny is...to help other people achieve their destinies?" He stood up. If his job was to bring people together, then what had his dream been about? All the people he had managed to lose? As much as he appreciated the colorful metaphor, this had clearly been a waste of time. "Thanks." He headed for the door.

"Tell me about your dream," Liddie commanded him, softly. Stopping, he pivoted back around to face her. She set down her fork and folded the top back over the remainder of her meal, pushing the leftovers aside and folding her hands in her lap.

"How do you know about my dream?" he asked quietly.

"Tell me, please. I have been waiting for it." Very slowly, he moved and sat back down in the chair, taking in this woman who was clearly something more than a storyteller. But what exactly, he couldn't say. Seer, yes, but did that mean more than he realized?

"The woman in the dream," he began and Liddie nodded.

"You have seen her before."

"I think so, but I don't know where." He shook his head, confused. "How can I know so much - *sense* so much about her - if I've never actually met her?"

"In dreams, time is twisted and bent. They are the feelings of a time that has not yet come to pass. That is the touch of *Skuld*."

"The touch of what?" He felt like maybe he should have paid closer attention when she spoke to the youngsters in D.

"Not a what, a who," she corrected him. "*Skuld*. You were visited by three women, yes?" she asked and his heart dropped into his stomach. Wordlessly, he nodded.

"One was a woman of your past?"

Magdelena.

"One was this other woman you speak of?"

"Yes," he breathed.

"She lies still before you. The future." *So, he would see the girl, again.* Lysander let out a breath.

"And the other woman?" he asked, Petra's red hair flashing across the Celtic fire burned in his mind, just out of reach.

"You tell me, what is missing?" she urged him onwards.

"My present," he said, hope in his voice. So, Petra was not lost.

"You were visited by the Norns, Lysander," Liddie told him softly, and though he wanted to deny it, he knew she spoke the truth. "The women who spin, weave, and cut our fates together from the mouth of Yggdrasil," she continued in reply to his furrowed brow.

"They wear the faces of those we trust so the news they bring will not be discarded. *Urðr*, she has already cut the thread to your past, bidding you to say farewell, as the purpose of the gods has been served. *Verðandi*, she wore the face of the task at hand. The message to be delivered. And *Skuld*, she wore the face of your future, so you will recognize your path when the time is right."

"But what message am I supposed to deliver? How will I know when the time is right?"

"I cannot know such things," Liddie told him. "Only you will have those answers." He wanted to be angry at her, but he felt a sense of peace washing over him. Like the moment the girl had touched his cheek in the dream. She watched the resolve on his face and smiled, encouragingly. "You have nothing to fear. The Norns do not come to deliver bad tidings."

"How do I figure out what they want me to say?" He wanted to understand. "Is there something I can read, some story I can study?" Her face broke into a wide, gracious smile as he spoke, pretty even, under her cornflower eyes.

"Always trying to learn," Liddie laughed brightly, as though they had known each other for years. "Their message will reveal itself in time. It is enough, for now, that you listened." She reached out, placing her hand on top of his, her papery skin and delicate veins squeezing his rough hand, reassuringly. Glancing across the table at her, he wondered fleetingly, if this was what a grandmother had been like. If perhaps Liddie had been a grandmother. Could seers have families? He felt his thoughts unraveling.

"It is time." Liddie stopped him before his thoughts got too far and pushed the little makeshift table away. Lysander wanted to stay, to ask more questions, but he could tell she was tired. "Some water, I think, and then, bed," she said as she started to push the blanket from her lap.

"Oh, let me," Lysander said, hopping from his chair to fill a glass at the sink. He lifted the handle, but no water came out.

"Oh, they shut it off at night down here if you're over ninety years old," Liddie explained and pointed a long finger to a thirty-liter jug in the shower that was half drained. Something else he presumed came from The Gardens or was siphoned off somewhere in The Engine Room.

"Why's that?" he asked, trying to be nonchalant, fearing the answer.

"All in the name of preserving the tribe," Liddie said. "We old people, we have nothing left to give, you see." She flashed him a cheeky, sarcastic smile. "We only cost resources."

"I think that's rather a matter of perspective," Lysander replied as he handed her the glass of water, a bubble of rage rising in him at yet another injustice tied to Sigrid.

"Thank you," she replied and he bowed his head. She drank deeply.

"Thank *you*." He took the empty glass from her hand and set it on the shelf beside the incense. Liddie rolled her knuckles over her neck, massaging the aches and pains with a strained expression. "I'll be at the next story time," he promised her, minding to leave the leftovers of her dinner on the table where she had placed them.

He saw her lean back in her bed as the door slid closed before turning and walking straight into a clothesline that he could swear hadn't been there when he'd entered Liddie's room.

Wringing his hand, he climbed the stairs up to B, only one sadness remaining - stuck in his throat - unsaid. He would never see Magdelena again.

He heard voices as he passed the landing to C and as they rounded the corner, he recognized the group he had met on the steps the last time he had stayed in D too long.

"Great," Aksel said when he saw Lysander. "Not you, again." And Lysander couldn't help but break into a small grin.

"Fair enough. I deserved that."

"Ah, look at that. The engineer can go a whole night without getting pissed!" Aksel replied, his voice snarky, and Milla threw him a disdainful look.

"I swear, you guys have no idea how to be discrete, do you?" she growled at him. "Excuse us," she said dismissively to Lysander and tried to move around him. He made brief eye contact with Lasse, who seemed stiff and reluctant, but didn't resist Milla's directness.

He'd wondered at the time if it had just been because he'd been drunk that Lasse had seemed strange, but he could see now that this wasn't the same jovial, friendly guy he had met Above Ground. He wasn't even the guy that had come and warned them about the bands. Something had changed.

Aksel bobbed behind Lasse and Anders, who looked apologetic as he passed. He was followed closely by a short man who caught Lysander by surprise. He was a man Lysander hadn't seen, he now realized, since he'd seen Petra.

"Benjáme!" he exclaimed and immediately pulled him into an embrace. "Hey, *Opp*." Benjáme swung his long ponytail over his shoulder and grinned at Lysander. He was leading a dark-haired woman who, by the way she carried herself, was also from C.

"Good to see you." Lysander returned the smile, and the man reached out to Lysander's shoulder, affectionately. He exchanged a look with his companion and Lysander could see him trying to formulate his next words carefully. *A message*, Lysander thought - perhaps the task Liddie had spoken of.

"We need to get going," Milla interjected before another thought could surface.

"Wait," Lysander said without really knowing what he wanted to say next, only that he was feeling emboldened from his conversation with the seer. "Petra…" he began but stopped with a cutting look from Milla. He bit his lip and decided to try another angle to get to the message Benjáme was hiding. "Where are you guys going?"

The question was everything other than the discretion that Milla wanted. She scoffed and rolled her eyes, turning back again to the next step. But Anders' face had shifted to determination.

"Guys," he said in a hushed voice, "I heard this guy totally went off on Sigrid not too long ago." He looked from Benjáme to the dark-haired girl, saying something Lysander couldn't understand with his eyes. "It was about Petra." Lasse and Benjáme both raised their heads and exchanged glances at their Lieutenant's name. "I think we should show him," Anders said cryptically, and Milla sighed, exasperated.

Lysander noticed her shift her body ever so slightly away from where he knew the cameras were mounted in this part of the stairwell, so they wouldn't be able to read her lips. The others followed suit, a little too obviously, Lysander thought. But then, he'd been on alert for oddities lately.

"Who'd you hear that from, anyway? Your little girlfriend?" The others looked around at one another.

"He could be useful," Benjáme offered, giving Lysander a hopeful smile. "He works in The Engine Room." His voice tapered off at the end of the sentence to a whisper.

"And he lives in B," Anders added quietly out the side of his mouth.

"So what, you want to bring him with us, just like that?" Milla crossed her arms as Benjáme and Anders looked at each other and nodded. "Without any scrutiny?" she sighed at their silence. "You guys really don't think he's a mole?" she asked, and Lysander opened his mouth to protest, but Anders raised a hand.

"He hasn't been here long enough to be." Even Milla couldn't disagree with that, though she tapped her foot up and down for a few moments before agreeing.

"Fine," she conceded, pursing her lips and uncrossing her arms. Abruptly, she ascended back up the stairs towards him and narrowed her eyes. Lysander had to lean back to avoid getting poked by her finger as she pointed at him, her hazel eyes like a hot, green flame.

"If you tell anyone anything, I will find you," she said, the words slipping through her teeth like venom. He nodded and she spun around, leading the way back down the steps. Anders clapped him on the back, grinning.

"Nice," he said to Lysander and followed after Aksel down the stairs. Benjáme gave him a sideways smile and gestured for Lysander to fall into step with him, the dark-haired woman flanking his other side.

Milla used her band to get all of them through the doors and into the canteen, which was, to Lysander's surprise, still full, until he remembered the night shift for the unskilled laborers that worked down in D. Bleary-eyed men and women sat at their tables in threadbare jumpsuits, their hands raw from chemicals or coughing from whatever their job exposed them to without proper air filters. Their food looked like it had been cooked at the same time as Lysander's, the fat from the fish congealed and cold, no steam rising from their potatoes. They passed through the canteen, slipping out through the thinly-stocked kitchens in waves, moving in and out of the dancing, letting the music cover their voices. He followed behind Anders closely until it dawned on him where they were headed.

It was a roundabout way to get there, certainly harder to track than the way he knew, but he was unmistakably on his way to The Engine Room.

When the door finally opened to the familiar hum of the reactor, Lysander peered over into the hull of the room, trying to reckon with what exactly he was walking into.

Gathered on the floor of The Engine Room were close to fifty people, shoulder to shoulder, huddled around the carbonium reactor, stuffed between the tanks and pressed up against the wall of turbines. They were packed tightly, sweating and chattering, their faces were glistening with hope.

He descended the staircase, scanning the crowd for any faces he recognized. To his surprise, he saw a few men from The Engine Room: the construction worker, Selby, and the twins, as well as the boy that Tuva was seeing, Heiká, among the crowd. As he continued scanning he saw the massive figure of Hafthor, the gatekeeper at the Back Door who he'd met the other day. Anders herded him alongside Lasse, Benjáme, and the new girl off into the group, while Milla and Aksel broke off, staying on the last steps, so they could look out into the sea of people.

"Thanks for coming," Milla began. "And thanks again for your cooperation in staggering who comes to the meetings. Obviously, we can't afford to attract unwanted attention." He felt her gaze linger upon him as she said the last bit. "But, of course, it does mean that you need to spread the information you receive tonight, on behalf of all of us. And to those of you whose first meeting this is: we welcome you to the Resistance." Lysander sucked in his breath. She finished with a short, professional smile, then turned to Aksel. His dark face was full of fire as he stepped forward.

"We all are here because we have had enough of the lies that the leaders of our little utopia here have tried to feed us."

There were shouts of agreement that bolstered his confidence. "We all know that while we toil to keep the fires of Mimameid burning, our compatriots live a life of luxury. We work the long hours, so they can lounge as they please. It is our children who are denied medicine so that their children can live. It is our water that is cut off so that their systems won't overload. It is our air system which pumps out poisons so they can breathe easier."

"They have told us we are the lucky ones because we were welcomed here to survive Ragnarök, but the truth is, we have been brought here to serve as slaves to the upper levels. It is on our backs that Mimameid is borne. Our lives are the price that allows them to thrive. But we are captive to the boughs of Mimir's tree no more!" He held his hand against his heart and said it again. "No more!" There was a roar of approval among the crowd. Hafthor threw a fist into the air.

"We called you all here tonight because one of our operatives in the military has returned with valuable insights. Benjáme, would you join us." Milla took over as Askel's chest rose and fell from his impassioned speech.

More hesitantly than Lysander remembered Benjáme being, he made his way to the platform. In an effort to steady his hands, Lysander watched Benjáme roll up the sleeves of his jumpsuit, revealing burly forearms and tattoos wrapped around both wrists - bands of the bright Sámi colors.

"You all will remember that after my last mission, I was able to confirm that the first of the ice had begun to thaw. The Long Winter - the ice age that Ragnarök caused - is coming to an end." This caught Lysander's attention. Benjáme had learned from Magdelena and Linnaea.

"Now I can also confirm that there is a path heading into the North Country that we can take to get away from Sigrid, away from Mimameid." There was scattered applause and a few gasps of relief throughout the crowd. Benjáme took a deep breath and let it out again before he continued, "There is no easy way to say this, but it will not be without its challenges to get there. There is little by way of food Above Ground." Lysander straightened himself up. Here was something he knew he could help with. He was, after all, as much of an expert on how to survive Above Ground as there was in Mimameid. "The game we once hunted are all but extinct, the plants are only barely beginning to peek through the permafrost, and," He glanced over at the dark-haired woman in the crowd "the path to our new home goes directly by the Celtic camp." Immediately, trepidation surged through the gathering, for Benjáme had spoken of the unmentionable. The monster that had no face to anyone down here anymore: the Celts.

Lysander could see that they were like a ghost story to the people of Mimameid. Whispers of someone who had been burned alive in ritual sacrifice, another strung up in the street and stripped of their clothes as The Long Winter had made its way across Old Scandinavia, families forced to watch one another burn and how the charred bones were collected after to ward off evil spirits. Horror stories that, while Lysander knew some of it to be true, were undoubtedly inflated and circulated by Sigrid and her circle to maintain order by fear in Mimameid. Milla waved her hands to quiet the crowd.

"We, as a group, must decide what to do. So please, talk amongst yourselves. We will address any concerns you might have individually and after we have been able to inform the other members of The Resistance as well, it will be put to a vote."

At Milla's words, the group dispersed, and Lysander watched the leaders making their rounds, to speak to all. People stood up a little straighter when they came over, something Lysander enjoyed seeing, knowing Milla and Aksel in the roles of cook and foot soldier that they maintained in the world of Mimameid. Here, Milla played the part of the cool-headed and rational rebel, while Aksel spoke with his entire body, electric. They were a powerful team. Lysander, hardly believing it, pulled himself back against the wall, leaning against the backdrop of his beloved Engine Room in awe and humility.

Here he had been, egotistically thinking he was the only one disquieted by the injustices of Mimameid, but really, he had only just arrived. He had no idea how long this 'Resistance' had been building, but if these fifty-odd people were only a portion of their members, then it had to be long enough.

Questions were coalescing in his mind - to find out what their plan was to stop Sigrid and her followers, how could he help them, how long had they been looking for a way out - but he hung back, watching. He felt a pair of eyes on him and turned to see Anders coming over to him.

"What do you think?" he asked, his voice as transparent as ever.

"I had no idea," Lysander replied, honestly.

"Milla's father, the sub captain, was one of the first people to start the group, right after they lost the submarines. When he passed away, she took over," he explained.

"That makes a lot of sense. How many of you guys are there?" Anders eyed him.

"I think we're up to about three hundred or so people."

"Not bad," Lysander told him earnestly.

"What do you think? Will you help us?" Anders asked him. Lysander was again silently grateful for Anders' candor. A smile twitched on his lips.

"Help you?" He chuckled a little. "When do I start?" Anders laughed. Lysander spotted Benjáme across the room with the dark-haired woman and decided to ask Anders.

"Do you know who that woman is with Benjáme?"

"Well she's new here, so I haven't met her properly yet, but I know her face from the canteen in C. I think her name's Onni." He waved over to Benjáme and Onni and they made their way over toward Anders and Lysander. Anders and Benjáme embraced and Onni stuck out her hand to them as she introduced herself.

"Heya *Opp*," Benjáme laughed as he embraced Lysander. He couldn't help but smile.

"Nice to see you, too! Where have you guys been?" Lysander replied, and Benjáme's face twitched, amused that Lysander had wizened up since he'd last seen him. He waved a finger at him.

"I think you already know, *ustit*, but we got sent back Above Ground," Lysander noted how Benjáme had changed his name for him from *opp* to *friend*. The young Sámi continued, "We got back about a week and a half ago and we've been debriefing like mad. Honestly, I'm amazed they even let us back in here at all." Exchanging a look with Onni, he carried on. "We got sent north, obviously, to find the Celts." It was as Lysander had suspected, but it made him unsure of what to expect from his next question. Especially after what had transpired in the stairwell.

"Is Petra back too, then?" Benjáme's face twisted up and Lysander felt his stomach turn. There was something very wrong.

"Um, no." What could Benjáme mean by that? She was his 'present', Liddie had said so. Could the Norns have been wrong? Or was he just a moron to have entertained such a dream to begin with? "Petra was taken," Benjáme continued somberly and Anders' face hardened. It was clearly new information for him, too.

"How do you mean *taken*? Petra?" the Icelander asked, gravely.

"The Celts got her. Who knows what that means, if she's dead or alive." Lysander could hear the helplessness in Benjáme's voice. Onni put a hand on her companion's shoulder. Lysander remembered how Benjáme felt about the Celts and after seeing the reaction from the crowd tonight, he wasn't surprised when Anders sucked in his breath. No doubt thinking of the stories of ritual sacrifice and charred bones as protection charms. But, Lysander reminded himself that Anders was no stranger to the Celts' brutality and he had the scars to prove it. "I wanted to go after her - we - wanted to go after her." Benjáme looked up at Onni. "But the orders came from Sigrid-on-high and the Captain wouldn't let us."

"Maike and Anja, they don't understand." Onni shook her head, talking about people Anders clearly knew, even if Lysander didn't. "They've never been down in D. They don't know what it's like down here. They would do anything for the dream of Mimameid, even if it's just a fantasy." The woman's big, dark eyes were full of heartbreak.

"So what, Sigrid just left her there, to be killed by the Celts?" Lysander felt like the purpose of his dream was getting clearer. But he was torn, if he went to rescue Petra, what would happen when Magdelena and Linnaea returned only to find him gone?

"She's been compromised," Benjáme told them and Lysander thought immediately of the Celt Petra had mentioned before she left - the doctor, "so, Sigrid decided to cut her loose." Had that really had something to do with it?

"Compromised how?" Anders asked. The connection the doctor and Petra had shared that night - it was more than just their arguing and the pain of her wound.

"She knows too much, she's seen too much. Sigrid considers her a liability," Benjáme replied. And then it dawned on Lysander - he had seen the look in her eyes when she had spoken to him of the Celtic doctor. And for all Sigrid's deception, she was no simpleton. Why else would she send Petra on a dangerous mission while her leg was still healing, so quickly after returning to Mimameid? Petra was already primed for the taking. Sigrid had simply arranged the players on the board in the way which best suited her motives.

"So, instead of killing her herself, Sigrid let the Celts do her dirty work," Lysander concluded, feeling sick.

"Exactly," Benjáme confirmed, jaw clenched. They were all silent for a second. Lysander felt his hands ball into fists.

To change the subject, Benjáme looked up at Anders and asked, "Hey, did something happen with Lasse? He seems...different." Lysander was glad Benjáme asked since he had been wondering himself. The Lasse he had known Above Ground hadn't been this sullen, reluctant person that he knew down here. He'd been warm and kind. He'd tried learning sign language for Linnaea. But he also had only known Lasse a short time, so he wasn't sure if his observations had any merit. Anders shrugged.

"I don't know what he said in The Infirmary that made them so nervous, but he hasn't been the same since. He keeps going back for regular 'therapies,'" the Icelander explained, "but none of us really believe that's actually what's happening."

"He was fine when we got back from the mission. A little beat up, but not like this. I talked to him right before I left." Benjáme looked puzzled.

"So did I," Lysander told them and they all looked at him, curiosity burning in their faces. He decided to indulge them, he felt like he was in good company here. "He came to my room, right before Magdelena and Linnaea left. Said something about the armbands and then the doctors knocked him out." Anders raised an eyebrow.

"Very interesting." They were quiet for a moment before Anders continued. "Well, they're clearly doing something to him in there, even though he won't talk about it and he won't stop going. He defends Sigrid and Mimameid, he doesn't want to come to The Resistance anymore." They all watched Lasse standing beside Milla, their arms interlocked, his face blank. "And Milla," he sighed, "she pretends like it doesn't bother her - like they just had a fight or something - but she's scared, she can feel him slipping away, the Lasse she knew." The giant Icelander sighed, disheartened. "First him, and now Petra."

When the meeting had died down and all but a few people had left for their bunks, Lysander excused himself, slipping out the door of The Engine Room quietly.

He was exhausted. Between talking with Liddie, learning there was, in fact, a Resistance, and hearing about what happened to Petra, he felt the strain of the day and already dreaded having to wake up for work tomorrow. As he approached the stairs, preparing himself mentally for the climb back up to B, a hand grabbed his shoulder, forcing him around.

It was Ned, smelling strongly of whiskey, but his eyes were as clear as a morning at sea.

"I've had a message," he said and Lysander felt his heart leap up into his throat.

Maybe Liddie had been wrong. Maybe Magdelena wasn't in his past after all.

18

PETRA

They walked back to Iain's trailer in the wee hours of morning, hand in hand. The darkness was starting to give way above the hillside, casting flitting shadows across the melting snowbanks.

"You know, we have a tree, too," Petra said, her voice hushed in the stillness.

"Oh, yeah?" Arthur replied, rubbing his nose in the frosty air. "We don't learn much about the Norse here." He looked at her sideways, "Only that they can't be trusted." His cheeks were rosy with amusement as he caressed her hand with his thumb.

"Oh?" she asked, feeling herself grow hot at his touch.

"Tell me about the tree. I want to learn about your people." *Her* people. If they were that. Maybe she would tell him about the Sámi someday, or her Russian grandmother. But of course, they weren't hers either. She shrugged.

"Well, it's more of a metaphorical tree," she started, wishing she had something with the Mimameid insignia on it to show him. "We call it Mimameid," she told him.

"And people hang cloth from its branches, too?" he asked, giving her hand a playful squeeze.

"No, no," she laughed a little, feeling his fingers in between her own, frozen, but she didn't want to let go. "It's a giant ash tree with a spring at the bottom, and its branches and its roots connect the worlds." Arthur's eyes twinkled.

"There's more than one world?" He turned to face her and she couldn't help but laugh again at his curiosity. "How many worlds are there?" She felt buoyant in the soft dark of morning and his questions, while simple, made her feel a sense of freedom. To talk about where she came from, who she was.

"Nine," she told him, remembering how Sigrid had taught them to her. Though her name left a sour taste on Petra's tongue, she couldn't help but smile at the memory of those long days they had spent training together, as she'd learned the lore and what it meant to her Norse people. A life dedicated to honor, a death worthy of Valhalla, and a legacy that would survive generations.

"Tell me," Arthur beckoned and he raised her hand to his lips. She felt his kiss ripple through her.

"Well, fruit from the tree supposedly brings you safe childbirth - which is important when you're trying to repopulate the earth after Ragnarök," she explained, "but most people want to drink from the water in the Mimir well, beneath one of the three roots of the tree."

"Why do they want to do that?" Arthur asked and she was keenly aware of how close he was to her now, as they continued to walk.

"It gives you wisdom. But you have to leave something behind for the guardian of the well," she continued.

"Like what kind of thing?" His jaw was set and square in the darkness.

"Odin left an eye. Heimdall, an ear," she told him.

"That's a steep price to pay for wisdom, I'd say." He raised an eyebrow, curiously.

"It's a sacrifice you have to choose to make on your own. That's how the gods work." She felt Sigrid laced in the words, even though they were still her own.

"Would you do it, do you think? Leave something of yourself behind for wisdom?" Arthur puzzled her with the question. She paused. She'd never considered it. Never thought of herself as worthy of the gods' favor, their wisdom.

"Isn't that what people do at the clootie well?" she finally replied, a cunning smile creeping onto her lips. He raised his arm to drape it over her shoulders. It made her heart jump and beat against her ribcage.

"Well, in a manner of speaking, you're right," he admitted, but she barely heard the words for the sound of her heartbeat in her ears.

"I guess I don't know anyone who would call "love" wise, though." She tried to speak of something else, but the word was already there, on her tongue.

"A lot of people would agree with you, I think, but if you had seen my parents in love," he paused before continuing, "Being in love is born of wisdom." She felt a twinge. Her own parents had sometimes felt like strangers to her. She knew they had loved her, loved her so much they had done everything in their power to keep her safe. But when she looked in her past for an act of love, it always brought her back to her *baba*. Had it been wise, though? Her love had gotten her killed.

"How do you mean?" Petra asked him and he let out a deep breath.

"My Pa was a wild creature - dangerous and powerful as the waves on the beach, always reaching for something more than he had, full of dreams. My Ma, she was calm and steadfast as the sand the waves beat against. She kept him here, grounded to his greatest achievement - his family, and he kept her wild, pulling her over and over into the sea - after adventure." He was a warrior-poet king of old as he spoke of them. "Each without the other would never have been complete, but together, they could take on anything because they had not only the courage of one another but the wisdom." He looked down at her and seemed to remember himself. "You got me all on a tangent." He winked and her heart fluttered.

"I like to hear you talk about your family," she admitted.

"I like hearing you talk about your people," he replied and she cast her eyes down, kicking at the snow. "So, there are nine worlds. And which one is ours, then?" he prompted her, gratefully changing the subject. They stopped for a moment in the snow and she lifted her eyes back up to him. He raised a hand to her warm cheek, placing a cool finger against it.

"Midgard. Right in the middle," she whispered and in one swift motion he wrapped his arms around her waist and pulled her in for another kiss. Unabashed, right in the middle of it all, in the darkness of the early dawn.

Gwenna shook her awake with a scowl that reminded Petra that maybe she wasn't entirely thrilled with how her arrest had gone. Maybe Arthur was right, maybe she had been the one to turn her in.

"There's someone here for you." Gwenna's voice was impatient, the lilt of her Welsh accent grating rather than the usually charming. Petra closed her eyes again. She'd only slept a few hours, but the day had arrived just the same. Groaning, she rose, pulled her hair up out of her face into a ponytail, and stumbled to the door in her long underwear, bumping her shin on the pull-out countertop that stuck out when it was stowed. She swung open the door.

Light poured into the trailer alongside the blast of frigid morning air and it took a second for her eyes to adjust. When they did, she was confronted by Briony's frosty expression beneath a rigid brow.

"Unbelievable," the dark-haired girl said, stepping back to examine Petra's haphazard appearance, her hands on her hips. "And they actually think I might learn something from you?" Petra groaned. *Perkele*. Training.

"One second." She scrambled around the trailer, hopping into her pants one leg at a time and stomping into her boots, her socks bunching uncomfortably at her heels. She wiggled into an oversized, cream-colored wool sweater of Arthur's, folding the sleeves up to her wrists. It felt good inside and it smelled like him. Gwenna rolled her eyes as she fed baby Domnall breakfast at the table. Petra shimmied into a thick leather jacket and tucked the corners of the bedding into the cushions just like she had on her bed back in Mimameid.

"I'm not waiting all day, yer lazy hole," Briony called, and Gwenna adjusted her tartan on her shoulders against the cold pushing in through the open door.

"Coming!" Petra yelled back, shoving the love knot into her back pocket and jumping out the door. She tried not to imagine Gwenna's scoffing.

She trudged through the snow behind Briony, her body still aching slightly from her treatments. Rubbing her sore neck, she tried to ignore the pounding in her head, rolling her shoulders up and down, shaking herself loose. Briony led Petra past the med tent to a small training arena that she hadn't noticed before blocked off by a wooden railing. When she turned around, she realized that at night they pulled out the benches and tables and the ring became the pub. Maybe that was why she'd never noticed them training here.

There was already a small group pressed up around the perimeter of the sparring ring and Briony greeted several of them as they passed through the crowd. They clapped her on the shoulder, wishing her luck, or muttering something obscene about teaching the Norse dog a lesson. Petra saw at the edge of the crowd the glowing eyes of a few younger Celts, perhaps only seven or eight, who looked like they were just beginning their combat training.

Briony lunged swiftly under the rail with a grace and ease that Petra felt compelled to match. She followed the girl under, but her muscles were heavy with the toll of the last few weeks. She let out a deep breath as she glanced around at the spectators. Most of the people gathered around the ring had strips of tartan tied around their biceps, flurries of green, red, blue, and yellow. Their family colors she presumed, or maybe a way to divide them up for sparring. She recognized the deep green one she had stolen from the van that first night wrapped around the arm of a stringy young boy and averted her eyes, embarrassed. She saw the colors she was wearing now tied to the arms of Darcy's two oldest children, Orlaith and Fergus, and realized where her new tartan had come from - a donation from the sympathetic nurse to help her blend in. Her breath smoked in the cool air, thin with anticipation.

Briony turned to face her, throwing her fur-lined jacket over the rail and putting her hands up, displaying the red and green tartan that was hanging from her own arm. There was a roar of approval from the spectators as she did so. Feeding off the energy of the crowd, she raised her head and howled like a wolf into the morning air. The muscles in her neck rippled and the sound made Petra jump. It was so...animal. But then Briony lowered her chin again and narrowed her gaze at Petra. The Celt blew out a breath and whispered something just for herself.

"Danger is sweet."

Petra shrugged off her own jacket and bent to lace up her boots. Standing, they paced around the perimeter of the ring momentarily, then Petra cracked her neck right and left and mirrored Briony's stance.

She beckoned the girl to come forward to throw the first punch. With a tilt of her chin, she dared her opponent to try, knowing Briony wouldn't be able to refuse.

Across the ring, Briony danced, her energy electric, but she responded to Petra and dove, jabbing Petra in the ribs and the jaw. The punches stung, especially the ribs where the needles had bruised her. But she ground her teeth and didn't let herself flinch. She needed to get Briony riled up, but her movements were so foreign to Petra, almost reckless.

This was where Petra was strongest. This was what she did best back in Mimameid, put wild little children in their place. Only, of course, because she had been one. She knew she could defeat Briony because she had been Briony. Her ego would be her downfall and Petra could make sure of it.

She watched how Briony beat her breast and shook herself loose across the ring. She noticed the way her boots slid in the sludge as she set herself up again. The slight hum of the girl's breath in the air told her maybe her lungs were compromised from living Above Ground for so long; perhaps it wouldn't take as long to wear her out.

The Celt girl dove again and Petra averted with a block and a sidestep. Briony's breath came out as hot steam from a kettle. The crowd groaned and Briony growled low. She was annoyed at Petra, already. She dove again like a mad bull, punching Petra repeatedly in the stomach until she had her against the rail. When Briony finally let up and the crowd cheered for her, and some of the youngsters threw their fists up triumphantly. She backed up to the opposite side of the ring with a smug look on her face as she spit into the snowy ring.

Petra steadied her breathing, trying to get oxygen to the places she had taken hits. Although her opponent was trying to hide it, she could see Briony heaving. The last attack had been fueled by adrenaline and it had taken the wind out of her. That was good.

Petra stepped forward like she was going to attack before Briony had enough time to catch her breath. She threw a feint and in the space of Briony's reaction, she came at her from behind, punching her straight in the kidney, hard. The girl let out a moan of pain and then massaged her back, huffing at Petra.

Briony's attack lacked strategy - Petra suspected that was because everyone else was afraid of her - except maybe Siobhan. It was clear to her that Briony had never needed strategy before to win, but if she did learn it she'd easily be able to outlast Petra in the state that she was in.

"You have to control your anger, Briony," Petra said calmly, spitting over her shoulder. The girl's face flashed with rage. "Otherwise you'll never understand your opponent." Briony charged at her, but Petra sidestepped again, knocking the girl's feet out from under her. She went down with a crack, scraping her cheek on the icy snow.

"Just shut up and fight me, Nordic spy," she hissed as she sprang back up to her feet. Behind her, Petra saw Ciarán had floated into the crowd.

"You don't get it," Petra said, dodging another punch from Briony, "I am fighting you." She grabbed Briony's exposed arm and twisted it around holding her down. They backed up together until the girl let out a cry and Petra released her. Briony glared at her as she made her way back across the ring. She had made a fool of her, in front of Ciarán no less, and she could see it in Briony's eyes: she was going to pay.

Briony charged, but in her anger, she had started to slow down. Petra was able to get underneath her and drive her back into the corner with punch after punch to her gut.

"What's the matter?" Petra jeered as she backed off. "They didn't teach you how to lose 'cause your the boss's kid?" Briony growled at her, spitting out blood into the crowd and the spectators hushed. But when Petra looked over, Ciarán's face had changed. He smiled. Something wasn't right. This wasn't normal for them, Briony losing, so why was he happy about it?

The girl was heaving, out of breath, but when she came at Petra this time, she had found her pacing again. She dealt a blow that split open Petra's eyebrow. She went for a second punch and Petra tried to duck, but Briony was faster, clocking her in the jaw and kneeing her in the stomach.

"I got you the last time we fought and I will get you every time after," Briony taunted her as she fell to her knees. Her eye started to throb and she rose to her feet as she saw Briony going over to her jacket. From her jacket pocket, she drew a blade. So, practice was over.

Petra's heartbeat quickened. Her face must have flinched because Briony started to smile. "Not so high and mighty anymore, are you?" she sneered, the blood coming from her mouth crystallizing to her lips as she spoke.

She lunged at Petra, spinning around and managing to slice open the side of her ribs. It wasn't a deep cut, but Petra could feel the blood warming her shirt. She coughed, wiping blood on her hands. Briony's entourage let out a barrage of approval.

From off to her right, amidst the cheering, she heard a voice she recognized shout some indiscernible profanity into the wind. Out of the corner of her eye, she saw that Arthur had appeared at the edge of the ring and she tried to refocus as Briony lunged at her and she dodged it, again. She needed to get the upper hand back. Briony snarled and Petra's eyes narrowed. The girl was getting impatient with her evasive maneuvers, but she was also running out of breath. Now was the time.

Petra relaxed her body, in an attempt to throw off Briony's offensive. Her face glowing triumphantly, the girl took the bait, attacking Petra, the blade raised in her hand.

In one swift motion, Petra lunged, punching her in the solar plexus, and while Briony choked for air she swung around and slammed the girl down onto the flat of her back. The blade slipped from her fingers and Petra snatched it up, pinning Briony down with her knees, knife edge pressed against her milk-white throat. The girl's face was blind with fury. She stayed on top of her as the crowd's roaring died down, scattered applause littering the air, cautiously.

"Do it, then," Briony coughed. "Teach me how to lose." Her flame-blue eyes dared Petra to try to touch the daughter of the Celts. She gritted her teeth and eased up, tossing the weapon aside. The girl was right. She was untouchable. Petra stood, offering a hand to help Briony up.

With a razor-sharp look, Briony spat on Petra's outstretched hand, blood and spittle, and rose to her feet, massaging her back where she had landed.

Stalking past Petra, she bumped her shoulder, hard enough to make her turn. Over her shoulder, Petra could see Ciarán, practically gleeful beside Siobhan, the woman's piercing blue eyes following after her defeated daughter and dripping with disappointment.

She sat on a cot in the med tent, her legs dangling over the side as Arthur nursed her swollen eyebrow. She winced as he tapped at the cut with disinfectant.

"You shouldn't have provoked her so much," he chided. Her eye was swelling, making it hard for her to throw him a look in response.

"I can handle a spoiled little brat; everyone else lets her win," she said smugly and Arthur smirked.

"Yes. From your face, I can see how you handled it," he teased and she winced again as he pressed the disinfectant into the wound.

"All part of my strategy," she assured him as he pulled the plastic off of a bandage and taped up the cut.

"Sure, sure. Lift up your shirt, please," he directed and she eased herself out of her shirt, turning to show him where the knife had sliced open her side. He ran his fingers over it and then below, where she knew she had a birthmark splashed across her ribcage. The same place as her *baba* had had, the same splash of color across that cage around her heart. His fingers felt tender on it as if he was trying to trace it, memorize it. It wasn't the first time he had seen it, of course, he would have seen it when she got her treatments, but the marks of the treatments were fading and her birthmark remained bright.

She looked over at him, allowing the moment to linger before he found her eyes and was broken from his reverie.

"Sorry," he apologized and picked up the bottle of disinfectant. She hissed as he poured it over the knife wound. "Look, Briony has more influence than you might think. You don't want to get on her bad side."

"It was Ciarán's idea to put us in the ring together. What was the reason, if not to teach her a little humility?" Petra reasoned.

"Ciarán and I disagree on the method chosen to teach that particular lesson," Arthur said decidedly as he placed a larger bandage over her ribs. "I think your body would thank you for a little rest, at least for the next couple of days. But that is just my opinion as a medical professional. How does your jaw feel?" He asked her.

"A little sore, but I think it will be okay," she replied.

"Good. Let me take a look at the bruising on your other side then. Can you lie back?" She swung her legs up and leaned back on the cot, his cold, gloved hands touching her belly and causing her to start. She grimaced a little when he pressed on her stomach. "Bad?" he asked and she tried to smile through gritted teeth. "It's a little tender, maybe we should try an ultrasound, make sure there's no bleeding?" He walked towards the other end of the med tent to roll the ultrasound machine over just as two figures entered.

"Siobhan and Ciarán have asked to speak with you," the taller one with cropped, orange hair said.

"Yes, okay. Just give me a minute," Arthur said, starting to take off his gloves. "Darcy, can you take over -" The shorter man interrupted him, his voice stiff with a deep, Scottish accent,

"I was talking to the girl," he said stiffly.

"Sorry?" Arthur asked.

"The Norse girl. They asked to speak to the Norse girl," he repeated.

"Ah. I see," Arthur said and stopped fiddling with his gloves. "As her doctor, I wouldn't recommend -" But this time it was Petra who interrupted him. There could be no excuse for looking weak in front of Siobhan; she knew this from Sigrid and she knew Arthur wouldn't understand.

"No problem," she told the two men, lowering her shirt and sitting up on the cot. She slid down into her boots and started putting her jacket on with a wince before Arthur could protest. He rushed over to help her into it.

"At least take some ice for your eye," he said, handing her a snow-compress from Darcy's outstretched hand. She nodded.

"Okay, okay." She walked over to the two Celts, turning back to him. "It'll be fine," she said, trying to look reassuring through the swelling in her face at his concerned expression. She put the compress on her face to demonstrate she would follow his instructions.

"Come right back when you're finished," he insisted, following her out into the cold. "We still need to do that ultrasound." She nodded as the men herded her away.

The two men led her across the camp, beyond the sparring ring, where a few of the younger Celts were now paired off and practicing drills. They stopped and watched her as she passed by, unsure whether they had expressions of awe or fear on their faces as they looked at her. The men led her to a smaller, unassuming tent that she never would have guessed was the Celtic strategic headquarters. The orange-haired Celt held the tent flap open for her while the Scot led the way inside.

"Here's the Norse girl," he announced, gruffly. She turned to him before he exited the tent.

"Petra. My name is Petra," she told him, her jaw clenched.

It was plain enough inside, but it was also clear to her that this was the commander's quarters. There were furs draped over the furniture and lining the floor. A space heater hummed in the corner, and the sound of a generator could be heard outside. A cot was set up in the corner near the heater as well as a small table with a mug of ale, and a half-finished meal of what looked to be a meat pie.

While the tent at first glance looked like it was decorated very finely, she could see that the furs were in a grubby state and that the meat pie was some reclaimed frozen dinner from a raid of an old freezer - the gods only knew how old it was. The bedding on the cot was a threadbare tartan flannel so worn the colors had faded. She walked over and ran her hand across it.

There was nothing glamorous about living like lost souls in a land that was supposed to be home. Food and resources were redistributed among the people after raids, Petra knew this already, but from her experiences in Mimameid, she had just assumed that the best of the raids automatically went to Siobhan and Ciarán.

This place, this *home* of theirs told a different story. Ciarán and Siobhan only took from what was left after all the other people had had their pick of the spoils. It was definitely not what she had expected.

Petra's eyes found a large table in the center of the tent with a map spread across it that, as she approached, she could see was of Old Scandinavia.

Ciarán looked up from the table as she approached, his dark eyes glimmering gleefully at her appearance. He opened his mouth into a smile. She caught herself on the edge of the table and let out a breath. She hadn't noticed him, still as he had been sitting.

"Welcome, come in. Have a seat." He offered her a chair draped in a matted sheep pelt at the large table and she sat obediently. "Your fight was," he paused and raised his hand out, examining her bruised jawline and swelling eye socket, "productive. To say the least."

The flap to the tent brushed open abruptly and Siobhan and Briony entered, in step. Ciarán released Petra's face, rose, and gave both his wife and daughter a modest bow, stepping to the side and allowing them to sit down around the table before he took his seat again.

Briony's face shone viciously under a smug brow line across the table from Petra, blood still crusted on her lips. She was clearly proud of the number she had done on Petra's face, even as her own cuts and bruises healed, but her smugness seemed to be radiating from something more. Petra shifted uncomfortably under her gaze and adjusted herself in the chair, angling towards Siobhan and Ciarán.

Siobhan cleared her throat and put her hands on the table, fingers folded neatly together. She leaned forward.

"Petra, you will remember that I said there would come a time when I would call upon you for help." So, they weren't here to talk about the fight. Petra leaned back in her seat, away from the three of them, back against the sheep pelt, nodding. It was only a few days ago, so she certainly remembered. "There has been a change in circumstances and an opportunity has presented itself - sooner than I had expected, I admit - but, if you would be brave enough to help us...it could change everything."

"What happened, what change in circumstance?" Petra asked, folding her arms across her chest, eyes darting between them.

"That is not important right now." Siobhan waved her hand around, dismissively. "But what is important , is that you will be able to do something for us. Help us get justice for the people that Sigrid left to starvation and slaughter. For the ones she continues to sacrifice." Siobhan let the word stand in the air. Let them settle like dust.

Of course, Petra wanted to fight back against Sigrid, but Arthur had planted a seed of doubt in her mind about Siobhan's true motivations. That she didn't want to help anyone at all, that she was only after revenge. Petra looked to Ciarán for some sort of clarity. His face was blank, neutral, almost intentionally so, as he looked across at her. It sent a chill down her spine she hadn't been anticipating. Briony beside him looked like she was ready to cackle with delight, reclined in her seat with her arms splayed on the armrests.

"I want to help," Petra said finally, after a pause. After all, how could someone who takes the last of the bounty from the raids not want to help? "But, I think the more information I have, the more useful I can be. What change in circumstances are you referring to?" She saw Siobhan purse her lips at her refusal to be ignored - her defiance - and watched the woman calculate her next move. Briony leaned forward, curious to see how her mother would handle the negotiation Petra had laid down on the table.

"You will get all the information you need to do the job at hand. Just like your doctor friend." The words were laced with something slimy, something threatening. "No more, no less." Petra felt small, outnumbered. Maybe he was right about Siobhan, and she couldn't protect him if she wasn't here. Siobhan softened her face, but it was deliberate and didn't have the effect she had undoubtedly been hoping for. If Petra's band had been calibrated it would have shown a spike in her heart rate.

"A project we have been working on for a long time has come to fruition," Siobhan began tactfully. Petra waited for her to continue. "What we would need you to do - for starters - is get back into your bunker, into Mimameid. Do you think you could do that?" Petra knew that she could. She didn't know how welcome her reception would be, though. She nodded. "Good," Siobhan confirmed.

"But I won't be able to stay - Sigrid will be too suspicious." She felt a little piece of her twinge at this small betrayal. It was strange, even after everything Sigrid had done to her, she still had a sense of loyalty she couldn't shake.

"That's alright," Siobhan promised. "You won't be there long, anyways." Her face dripping in mirth.

The words Siobhan had said to her as she left the tent rang in her ears like the icy winds sweeping through camp.

"The doctor stays."

It had been Siobhan's final card to play. The last piece of leverage she could wield to bring Petra into submission.

She had seen past Petra's armor, as Sigrid had all those years ago. But Sigrid had used that insight to call upon her hate, her rage. Siobhan called upon an even deeper part of her. She'd seen what Petra hadn't even known until that moment. That her love was a far more powerful force than her hate. And far more destructive.

She reached the van, winded. Her side ached and her eye was throbbing in the cold. Something didn't feel right. She rapped her bruised knuckles on the door of Arthur's camper van. He swung the door open abruptly, his face darkened with worry.

"What happened?" he asked wildly, looking her up and down. He reached his hand out to her shoulders and she felt she could have melted into them. He grabbed hold of her and helped her into the van. They sat down in silence opposite each other while she caught her breath.

Siobhan was right. Everything she held onto from her grandmother and her parents, the soldiers who had trained her, even her men, Milla and Lysander - their kindness, strength, goodness - all the things she didn't have, Arthur did. And the love that had built up inside of her over all the years - the little happinesses she had squirreled away - they were all for him now.

It was just that he made her feel safe to face whatever it was she was feeling, without judgment. "You were gone for so long, I wasn't sure. I waited for you at the med tent, but it got to be so late," he continued and she looked up at him, eyes swimming, from the pain or what she had to tell him, she couldn't be certain. Siobhan had made her feel vulnerable, she'd found the chink in her armor that Petra didn't know she had. But at least here, with Arthur, she didn't feel so afraid of that vulnerability. "What happened?" he repeated the words and she rested her cheek on his chest, avoiding his gaze. His hand went instinctively to her head, holding her close.

"I've been given a mission," she told him.

"What?" His voice incredulous, breaking away.

"They have a mission for me. It's time," she repeated, but couldn't bring herself to look him square in the face.

"But it's so soon. It's too soon." He tried to take her face in his hands, and she sucked her breath in from the pain. "Sorry," he apologized, taking her by the hands, "Maybe I can talk to Siobhan, maybe I can change her mind."

"No," Petra shook her head, "you can't."

"Why, where are they sending you?" he asked.

"I have to go back to Mimameid. They didn't tell me everything," she said, softly. "But, they think that the bruises will help sell the story that I escaped being imprisoned."

"At least now we know why they put you in the ring with Briony," he said bitterly and pulled her into another embrace, rubbing her back gently. Even that hurt somewhere inside her. "At least let me come with you." He spoke the words as if either of them had a choice in the matter, but Petra's heart broke at his small hope.

"You and I both know that's far too risky. Everyone knows everyone there. You can't come to Mimameid." She hated every word she was saying. "Anyway, I won't be there long." She repeated Siobhan's words with bitter remorse on her tongue, trying to hide their true meaning. "Look, we don't have much time. I have to leave just before dawn," she told him. And it was as if a light turned on in his head, his eyes glowing with their familiar, warm blue.

"Then there's something we have to do."

When they were beneath the branches of the ancient oak tree, snow melt still scattered around them, Arthur let go of her hands and reached into his pocket.

"I couldn't get my hands on any extra cloth, but I did manage to steal something from the clinic." His eyes were full of laughter as he handed her the rolled-up bandage he'd swiped.

She unfolded it in her hands, feeling some unusually tiny twists and knots between her fingers. She looked down at it and recognized the stitches of a delicate, handmade lace, just like her own grandmother used to do, sitting at their rickety, old kitchen table.

"And what's this?" she asked him, fingering the lace, ever so gently. It was a fragility she hadn't felt in her since she became a soldier, save for the one piece of red yarn that had been left for her in the wilderness.

His cheeks reddened a little as he opened his mouth. "Well, as you know, I grew up in Old Cornwall, son of a miner, grandson of a miner, great-grandson of a miner." He waved his hands around in the night air as he explained, his voice heavy. "But my mum, she was an Irish girl, Isolde was her name. She was left in a convent when she was young, so when she was growing up she learned how to make the finest Irish lace from the nuns." He put his hands in his pockets, bashfully. "It's all I have left of her now."

It was unlike him, to be so self-conscious. But Petra found it endearing. No, it was more than that - she felt privileged he could be this naked with his feelings around her. Petra looked up at all the knots swaying in the trees and pressed the lace to her heart. "I think she would've wanted me to give it to someone I truly cared about."

So, that was how Arthur had known how to weave the love knot for her. Now she knew what the act of weaving it had truly meant to him.

"Thank you." Her breath spiraled up into the sky as she spoke. Arthur looked at the bandage in her hand and up into her eyes.

"Would you like to tie a knot, then?" Arthur asked, his voice still sheepish. That was what he wanted. To be joined with her. To promise himself to her.

A warmth spread from her chest and she smiled through her bruised and beaten face. She didn't have the words to reply, but this was something so sacred to him and to the Celts. She buried her face in her hands, hardly believing it. "Is that a yes?" he asked, tentatively and found her voice.

"Yes. Yes."

Tenderly, he took the pieces of cloth from her hands and moved toward the edge of the clearing.

"Where shall we go?" Petra looked past him to a small space opposite the pool of water. The pieces of cloth hung there were old, and they hung long, like a curtain against the outside world, keeping all the magic of the clootie well contained.

"Here," she gestured to the branch, "but -" she took the bundle of bandages from his hands, "just the bandage. I think we should save the lace." The word *we* tasted so sweet on her lips.

Arthur nodded, a blush creeping up from his neck onto his cheeks. "Very well. Agreed. Just the bandage."

He bent down and dipped the white cloth in the pool of water, wrapping it around their bonded hands. The water was freezing, but it felt good against her swollen knuckles. Petra looked up at him.

"I promise you my heart. Now and forever." Petra watched the words leave his lips, barely hearing them as her heartbeat pounded in her eardrums.

"And I promise you my heart, now and forever." She wrapped the bandage one more time around their hands as she spoke the words back to him.

He tucked one small, wild lock of hair behind her ear and their lips met in the darkness - cautious, but peaceful.

Together they slid the bandage off their hands, securing the first two knots. They then tied it to the branch, letting the ends of the bandage disappear discretely into the folds of the other, larger pieces of cloth.

Arthur wrapped his arms around her as they watched their knot dance in the light breeze, starkly white against the inky drape of night. He rested his chin on her shoulder and whispered.

"If you ever need help - if there is ever a time when you need me, come here. Meet me at the clootie well. Nothing can touch us here, *meurgerys*."

It was the first time he had called to her in his native Cornish tongue.

They walked back to camp together, hand in hand, the silence between them like a long breath before a storm. They didn't sleep, instead holding one another, Petra memorizing every line on his face and every ribbon of color in his irises.

She wanted to hold onto his musky scent, to carry it with her on the journey ahead. The curve of his arms, the way his hair fell around his face. He held her tenderly, stroking the bruises that had formed where the needles had been and kissing her bloodied hands, softly.

When it looked like dawn was approaching, she took off her Imbolc charm and put on a small pack for the journey. As she filled it with water and provisions for the multi-day trek back to Mimameid, she realized the tenderness in her stomach was getting worse. She wanted to say something, but the swelling in her eyes was already shocking enough and she didn't want to worry Arthur. He had too much going on here without having to worry about her, too.

Together, they walked to the edge of camp. He kissed her in the rising light, pressing the lace ribbon into her hand, something desperate about his lips as they touched hers. With a bittersweet smile, she reached into her pocket and pulled out the love knot, handing it to him, their fingers lingering.

Heavy with reluctance, she pulled herself away, trudging up the path that lead out of the valley. When she turned to look back she saw him, still standing on the edge of camp. How long would he wait there? A few paces behind him, parked beside the nearest vehicle, was a woman with long, raven hair and a pair of flame-blue eyes, her arms folded across her chest.

19

LYSANDER

"Boat acquired. Departure imminent. See you both on the other side."

It was the 'both' that had told Ned she wanted Lysander to know as well. Or Lysander to tell Ned, depending on who got the message first. It had only been a glitch in the system which had allowed her message through in the first place. Ned had no idea when the message was first sent or how long it had been broadcasting.

He repeated Magdelena's short message over and over in his mind. She was okay. They were both okay and they were on their way to Svalbard.

He wanted to respond to her, but Ned had said it was too risky. To reply Lysander would have to boost his signal far beyond the normal capacity of the bands, and that would surely raise suspicion in Accounting. Through their conversations with Tuva, he had learned that the people who monitor communications - both internal and external - had extremely high-security clearances. Their offices were in a different part of the department with what - at least as far as Tuva knew - was a private entrance to Sigrid's office.

"But that could have just been gossip. Yvonne doesn't like anyone having more access to Sigrid than she does, so sometimes she says things." Tuva rolled her eyes as she referred to the peppy girl Lysander remembered from his first day there.

"Yvonne works in Accounting, too?" he asked, trying to sound casual. Tuva, having just put a piece of potato in her mouth shook her head and swallowed before answering.

"No, she just works *with* Accounting. She knows everyone, though." She stabbed another potato and shoveled it into her mouth, eager to finish and join Héika, who had just arrived down from C.

Now, given what he knew about the life Ned had lived, Lysander found his advice about returning Magdelena's message to be abundantly cautious, too cautious even. Perhaps it was that very fact that made him so cautious. He considered if maybe Ned was a part of The Resistance and that's why he was trying to fly under the radar, but he didn't dare try to ask him.

He pushed the thought from his mind and thought instead about the familiar faces he had seen at the meeting the other night. He was still mulling over whether or not to tell Bjørn about Heiká as he opened the door to the roaring sound of the reactor.

Bjørn, face and arms up to his elbows already covered in grease, grinned up at him from where he was working on the floor of The Engine Room, his hair pulled back behind his ears by a pair of massive, noise-protection ear muffs. He had a section of the grated floor pulled up and it looked like he was searching inside for something.

Lysander had other work to attend to in the back room today, so he simply raised his hand to the older man today before heading off to the room where they had worked on the auxiliary air ventilation system all that time ago.

He tapped his band against the door and it rushed open with the familiar flow of air on his face. He let it wash over him as he took a deep breath in. The whirring of the parallel ventilation systems made him smile in a way that only a machine he had repaired could. But, as the steam dissipated from the warmer room into the colder, his smile faded into confusion.

A mane of hair the color of copper stood before the interface, hands pressed against the walls. No one was supposed to be down here, least of all some random civilian.

"Can I help you?" he asked, and the woman jumped at the sound of his voice, turning around, slowly. The face was swollen and bruised, marks like fingers around her throat, but the eyes were unmistakable - a deep, tawny brown alight with golden flame. It shouldn't be. It couldn't be. She was with the Celts. He was supposed to be planning a way to find her if he hadn't been so distracted by Magdelena's message. "Petra?" Lysander felt her name leave his lips and she gazed at him for a second, confused, her brow furrowing as she looked around the room.

"Lysander? Her voice sounded odd, detached.

"What are you doing here?" It felt like the wrong thing to say, that he should ask her how she was, comfort her somehow. He wanted to hug her, as they had the last time they had seen each other, but she backed away from him when he took a step towards her.

"What are you doing here?" she echoed as if she had forgotten where she was.

"It's The Engine Room, where else would I be?" he asked and she started to sway, unsteady on her feet. He reached out to help but she put her hand up and steadied herself against the wall.

"But you're here," she continued, "in Mimameid. You shouldn't be here." So she knew she was in Mimameid. That was good, but her expression worried him.

"Where else should I be?" he asked her, gently now, looking her up and down, seeing that the bruises weren't just on her face but on her neck and forearms as well.

"I -" she started to say, but she stumbled again, this time her eyes rolled back in her head and Lysander caught her just before her body dropped to the floor.

He lay her head tenderly on the metal floor and checked for a pulse. Her heart was still beating, but her lungs had stopped breathing. He stood up, opening the door behind him back up with his band.

"Bjørn!" he shouted, panic rising in his voice. He didn't wait for a reply. "Bjørn, we need medical assistance!" He heard a metal clattering as Bjørn leaped to his feet.

"Are you alright?" His heavy boots pounded across the floor of The Engine Room towards them - thump, thump, thumping. He dropped to his knees in front of her and lifted her chin, so as to push air into her.

"Yes! Yes, it's a friend. She was back here when I arrived. I don't know how-" he said. Bjørn had his ear muffs around his neck when he arrived at the door to the back room and the sentence died in Lysander's mouth.

Above them, the doors to The Engine Room burst open, fresh air gushing into the steam rising from the engine core. Two people with red-marked sleeves - medics - emerged from the steam carrying a stretcher, and utility belts with all manner of medications and devices strapped around their waists. Lysander and Bjørn exchanged a look as if to ask one another who had called them in the split second that had passed. Panicked and confused, Lysander looked down and saw Petra's band glowing a faint red. Of course, how could he have not thought of it? They would have known the second she was back within a certain radius of Mimameid.

The medics pushed past them, ripping open the black jumper Petra was wearing and exposing the extent of the bruising along her ribs and stomach while they tried to administer CPR. Lysander cringed at the sight of it, the sickening yellows and greens snaking alongside one another - intentional and systematic bruising mixing with darker purple and blue bruises and swelling from blows that looked more recent to him, although he wasn't exactly an expert.

One of the medics loaded her onto the stretcher - feet first and then head and body - while the other kept a hand on the pocket mask pumping air into her bruised and battered lungs. They paused only once to let her turn her head and vomit blood over the side of the stretcher.

Lysander watched, completely paralyzed, as Bjørn stepped in to help carry Petra out of The Engine Room. He watched them go, still repeating the questions over and over again to himself - what had Petra been doing here, to begin with? How long had she been back in Mimameid? And what in Odin's name had happened to her?

When he finally felt his feet move, it was like they were wading through water. He tried to race up the stairs after Bjørn and the medics, but the drag made it feel like he was moving in slow motion, fighting some unseen current. After what seemed like an eternity, he did catch up with them, even following them into the rusty old elevator.

Once the elevator began moving upwards, the medics questioned him about what had transpired in The Engine Room. He tried his best to answer them, but his brain still racing.

"How long was she conscious for?"

"I don't know, 60, maybe 90 seconds?" He was confused. *Wouldn't they know that information from her band?*

"Did you speak to the patient?"

"Yes." *How was that relevant to what had happened to her?*

"Did she seem coherent?"

"I mean, she knew my name. But I don't know, something was off." The medics exchanged a hard glance. *Had he said something wrong?*

"Off, how?"

"She didn't understand why I was there. Maybe she didn't know exactly where she was?" He scrambled for words.

"Are you certain about that?" They carried her out of the elevator, away from him.

"No, I mean. I don't know. Everything happened so fast. Is any of this relevant?"

They had arrived at The Infirmary and were passing over the threshold.

"Thank you for your help," the one medic said. "It could be quite a long time." His voice was harsh, but he gestured to the group of chairs where people sat, grim expressions on their faces.

Lysander parked himself in a chair far from anyone else, but close to where he might see what was going on inside. The chair felt oddly sticky and cold. He adjusted himself, crossing and uncrossing his legs over and over again. It had all happened so quickly, he wasn't even sure if he had imagined the whole thing. He jumped up from the seat when he heard a nurse shouting and the chair scraped against the floor.

He decided after a few anxious minutes that sitting was no use, so he stood up and began pacing up and down the ward, much to the disgust of the people working there.

"Could you please take a seat, sir?" A tall nurse with grey-blue eyes approached him, his voice cordial, but face as sharp as a razor blade. "You are making the patients nervous."

"I'm sorry, it's just my friend is in the back, and I just -" Lysander began and Bjørn emerged from the far end of The Infirmary, making his way up the rows.

"Hi, yeah, um. I think you should check who you're talking to." Bjørn held up Lysander's wrist for the nurse to scan. The nurse's expression melted almost immediately into buttery softness.

"Why don't you come with me and we can find somewhere private for you to wait for your friend," the nurse replied calmly, placing his hand on Lysander's arm. He understood. He was a B-level, so he didn't have to wait with the others. The nurse guided Lysander away from Bjørn and the sitting area, past an older man muttering to himself in Danish as an exposed bone pushed out of his skin, into the room. A little girl beside the man was curled up on her mother's lap, her hands clutching her stomach, her face white as a sheet as her mother sang a soft lullaby.

Lysander wanted to say something, to point out that The Infirmary's beds and care should be put to better use for the patients who had gotten there first, but these people were most likely there from C and D. A stern look from the nurse told him his protests would have been in vain. In the end, he wouldn't get to see Petra and the people waiting wouldn't be better off, they might even receive infractions for his behavior. The nurse came to an empty bed, the privacy screens on either side drawn.

"Why don't you see if you can lie down and relax for a little bit? I will come and update you as soon as I can about your friend." The nurse's voice was clear and calm, but he spoke with a steady authority that made Lysander certain he didn't want to cross him. He nodded obediently, sat, and put his feet up on the bed, leaning back against the pillows, trying to think about something, anything other than Petra. He felt his chest still heaving.

"Do you want anything to help calm you? We have a few mild draughts I can give you, anti-anxiety medication, or a poppy tincture if you're more for the natural stuff," the nurse offered, eyebrow raised.

"No, thank you," he replied quickly, placing his hand over his eyes.

What had the Celts done to Petra? Had Sigrid known what she'd condemned Petra to when he'd confronted her?

He was spiraling, trying to figure out what to do. He had already decided to send a message to Magdelena, after all, so now he needed to make a plan so he could warn the two of them not to come back to Mimameid. He would find a way to get up to the surface to them - he'd bring Petra with him if he had to - but he couldn't let them come back here. Not if Sigrid was willing to sacrifice people - his people - to the Celts. He sat up, swinging his feet onto the floor just as there was a rustling from the bed to his left.

The privacy screen came ripping down in a fury, as the patient stumbled from his bed and into the center of The Infirmary. His eyes were wide with hysteria, or maybe clarity, as he looked around at the people surrounding him. His arms were wrapped in bandages and he was dressed in nothing but a starched and stiff hospital gown. Lysander met his gaze and recognized him as a Resistance member from the meeting - a particularly vocal one if he recalled correctly. He nodded discreetly to the man and the man nodded back, knowingly.

The dark-eyed nurse that turned on her heel and marched toward the Resistance member was the same as when Lasse had come to his room all that time ago. She waved her hands, trying to herd the man back to his spot, but he jogged down the aisle, pulling privacy curtains down as he went.

"Back to bed please, you shouldn't be on your feet." The nurse attempted to grab and guide the man back, but he ducked clumsily and took off, his bare feet sticking to the cement floor of The Infirmary as he ran down the ward.

"No, no! Not until I've done what needs to be done!" The man laughed a little as he ran and waggled a finger chidingly at the nurse "You don't fool me. I know you all are part of Sigrid's plan!" The commotion reminded him of how Lasse had been: the smell of disinfectant in the air, the wild man in a hospital gown, and the dark-eyed nurse chasing after him.

The other patients were aghast at the commotion, trying to get out of bed, and the people in the sitting area had gotten to their feet, peering around the corner into the ward. Lysander wasn't sure what point the man was trying to make by running around aimlessly, but another nurse came at him.

Then, he ran down the other side of the aisle stopping to rip out the IV of a boy Lysander knew from the B Canteen and knock over a cart filled with medicine, a rainbow of pills rolling across the floor as the man danced on top of them. Lysander stood up, unsure whether to run to the boy, but concerned for the others' safety.

The wild man dodged the second nurse - the man from earlier - doubling back around until he was in front of his own vacant bed.

"You are being lied to! The only thing Sigrid wants is control!" The man's voice shook, triumphantly. "But today, I'm going to open your eyes." He put his hand on his wrist with purpose and ripped his band off, lifting it over his head in victory.

It was shockingly instantaneous. A thick, black liquid dripped from his mouth and he fell to his knees, laughing and choking. He turned his face back to Lysander, eyes glistening with joy as the liquid leaked from his tear ducts. It was so strange to see the elation across the man's face - whether at his freedom from Mimameid or at knowing he had been right all along - Lysander couldn't say.

The man convulsed long enough for the nurses to reach him and try to stop the poison from taking effect, but it was too late. He lay on the floor of The Infirmary, a final few convulsions rippling through his body, his band falling to the ground from his outstretched palm.

The Infirmary had become quiet, the patients who had seen what had happened exchanging glances, nervously. Lysander followed the wave that was sweeping across the room, terror washing over the faces of everyone present. Lysander realized that in the panic a doctor had knocked over a bottle of sanitizing chemicals that were starting to mix and smell particularly noxious. The child who had been asleep in the waiting area was wailing, her mother's arms wrapped around her. The old Danish man looked like he was going to be sick. The poor B kid who had his IV ripped out was pale with fright as the mother of the wailing child eyed his bed, greedily.

Lysander was overcome with the urge to leave while fighting his instinct to stay and help. He needed to make a plan for how to escape this nightmare, but first, he needed to contact Magdelena and Linnaea. Fast.

The disheartened nurses, though more used to dealing with blood and death than others, looked wildly overwhelmed by the body of the man in front of them. Lysander rose from where he was sitting and offered quietly to give the dark-eyed nurse a hand. Disingenuous, but help nonetheless. Even if it was just to cover his escape from The Infirmary.

"Do you want me to help carry the body somewhere?" he asked, tentatively as the nurse attempted to mop up the black blood that the man had spewed from his body with her smock. Her male colleague beside her had fixated on a groove in the concrete and was wiping it over and over again with an already black-soaked towel. The woman looked up at Lysander, dark eyes full of fear that she was trying to keep at bay. He wondered if they had known what would happen when he removed his band. If there was actually anything the nurses could have done to save him.

"Oh no. No, that's okay," she looked right through him as she spoke, "thank you, though. Everything's under control." Her voice was shaking in a way that told him everything was clearly not under control. No, Lysander decided, she didn't know what was going on and she didn't understand what had just happened. Reflexively, he tried to comfort the nurse by putting a hand on her shoulder, but she shuddered away from it.

Rising to his feet, he slowly backed away, away from where the dead man lay. He watched the patients, who had slowly slunk from their beds and made their way toward the man's body, engulf the scene in front of him. His heart thumped in his ears and he ran his hands through his hair, nervously. He needed to find Anders, or Aksel, or Milla. He turned and left the uncertainty of The Infirmary behind him.

He could not wait any longer to get out of here. And he needed to take as many people as he could, Petra, Bjørn, Åsa - anyone else who was willing to leave - with him when he left.

He was at the entrance to C waiting for someone to let him through the door when Heiká walked out. He glanced around, pulling up his collar and shrinking his neck down to hide what Lysander thought looked like a hickey when he stopped and looked Lysander full in the face as if trying to place where he had seen him before. Lysander took his chance. He wasn't Anders or Milla, but this was an emergency, so he would do.

"Hey! Heiká, right?" The young man nodded in response, stuffing his gawky arms into the pockets of his jumpsuit. "I'm a friend of Bjørn's," Lysander clarified and though Heiká looked a little less nervous, he was still visibly uncomfortable. Perhaps he worried Lysander was there on behalf of Bjørn to talk about Tuva. "Listen, I saw you at the meeting the other night. I need your help." The young man looked surprised. This obviously wasn't what he had been expecting.

"What do you mean?"

"The meeting down in D." Lysander was aware his voice was too loud to be talking about The Resistance but his adrenaline was running so high he couldn't control himself right now. Heiká's eyes shifted, nervously.

"I don't know what you're talking about." The young man slumped his shoulder and tried to push past Lysander, but he didn't have time for this.

"How do you organize one of those? Those meetings?" he persisted, huffing. Heiká sighed and leaned in towards him. He lowered his gaze and angled himself away from what Lysander realized was a mounted camera observing the entrance to C from above.

"Look, usually the leaders put out word a few hours before," he whispered cautiously, "Why?" The young soldier looked left and right at the people passing by them.

"Can you get in touch with whoever it is that organizes them? Milla? Or Aksel?"

"I could try, I mean, I have temporary access to C," he admitted and Lysander ran his hands through his hair absentmindedly while he thought.

"Okay, that's good, good."

"What's the problem?" he asked. "What should I ask them?" Heiká looked at him, still a little hesitant. He pulled his collar up again around the hickey, anxiously.

"There needs to be a meeting. I need to call a meeting," he replied without looking at at the young soldier.

"I don't know if it works like that, B-level," he shrugged, "but okay, I'll tell them." Lysander wanted to grab this kid by the shoulders and shake him, tell him what he had just seen. He tried to calm himself down instead. To not think about the black blood.

"Okay, then, thank you," Lysander grimaced. "And tell them I saw what happened in The Infirmary." The words felt bitter on his tongue.

"Why? What happened in The Infirmary?" the young man asked him, interest piqued.

"Just tell them," Lysander said, putting a hand on Heiká's shoulder and the young man's eyes darted back and forth between Lysander's own. After a second, he nodded and turned back to go into C. Lysander watched him go, his chest rising and falling, heartbeat still drumming in his ears.

He wasn't sure where to go now, whether to go back to work or his bunk. He wanted to be there beside Petra when she woke up, but he just wasn't sure he could go back to The Infirmary at the moment.

Instead, he found himself wandering down in the direction of The Observation Deck. The door whooshed open and he felt the immediate calm of the soft, blue light from the piezo crystals envelope him. The aquamarine of the fjord pressed in on him, muffling the sounds of the man choking on black blood and laughing as he died. Lysander closed his eyes and leaned against the cool, cement wall, listening to the sound of nothingness. He felt his breath start to steady as he let out a long, deep exhale.

All of a sudden, there was a small hand on his arm. He started, opening his eyes and he saw Åsa, her big blue eyes staring up at him, quizzically.

"Are you okay?" she asked him, quietly.

"Åsa? What are you doing here?" He tried to wipe the worry from his face and make his voice sound normal. "Shouldn't you be in school?" The distraction seemed to have worked. The girl rolled her eyes, leaning back against the cement wall beside him and sighing.

"I skipped. I'm no good at school, not like Tuva anyways. What's the point, when I can come here and watched the fjord and write." He thought he probably should scold her for skipping, but just at that moment, he happened to agree with her. What was the point of all this anyways?

"What are you writing?" he asked her, unaware that she wrote anything. She pulled a notebook out of her pocket that was rolled together. It was made of cheaply recycled materials, the burgundy cover worn with folds from constantly being rolled up and shoved into the girl's bag, the binding peeling back at the corners. In the center was a World Tree stamp, telling him this was a school-issued notebook Åsa had commandeered.

"I like to write songs. And if I come here when everyone else is in school, then I'm alone and the acoustics are really good," she said matter-of-factly, still not looking at Lysander, but out into the fjord. He'd had no idea.

"What kind of songs do you write?" He watched her fingering the notebook, running the pads of her fingers over the folds, habitually.

"I don't know. Whatever inspires me." She shrugged, unapologetically. "Down here, I'm just singing for the fish and the seals. You know, like my mom used to sing to her cows. So, it doesn't really matter what I'm singing."

"Would you -" he stopped and Åsa looked at him.

"Wait, why are you here?" she asked him, suddenly curiously.

"I guess," he clenched his jaw; she didn't need to know every detail, "I needed to get away from it all. You know, *Mimameid*," he replied and she nodded knowingly with all the wisdom of a child. Just like Liddie had said.

"I get that," the girl sighed and turned her face out towards the fish. "I don't remember much about life before we came to Mimameid. But I know that *mamma* and *pappa* were scared a lot. And I know it's better here," she looked up at him, "but sometimes I just *wonder*. What is it like up there? You know?"

He looked down at the optimism on her face and it reminded him so much of Linnaea. How could he tell her about what life was really like, with Petra beaten within an inch of her life above the surface? The countless nights he had spent so cold, he didn't think he would survive. The truth about Mimameid and Sigrid? He found himself wondering if it wasn't better just to keep his mouth shut, and let them go on living as they were.

Maybe it wasn't so bad down here, safe at least. Away from the Celts. How could he have been so quick to forget what dangers awaited them Above Ground?

Maybe they'd gotten it wrong and it was worth paying the small price of their freedom in order to keep them from harm's way, these children who had so much ahead of them.

"Would you sing me one of your songs?" He looked over at Åsa, pleading for the distraction. But he needn't have bothered. The girl was her mother's daughter and had seen the pain in his eyes the moment he'd entered the room. She wanted nothing more than to ease his pain. Standing up straight, she started walking slowly towards the middle of the room, the little song journal rolled up in her hands, thrumming against her leg as she tapped herself in.

Her song started softly, echoing off the glass like a drop of water. Her voice was deeper than he had expected but clear as a bell. She started vocalizing like her mother taught her and her eyes closed. He did the same, letting the song carry him off. The melody had a strange darkness to it as if she was questioning something or maybe longing for something that she had never known. His heart ached for her, a girl who so dearly wanted to put her hands into the soil and feel the pulse of the earth beneath it. To look up and see the white-tipped peaks of mountains stark across the horizon.

When Åsa's voice had faded he opened his eyes to see her smiling at him. She didn't have the gall to ask him if he had enjoyed it, but it didn't need to be said. His gratitude was plain across his face. He took her by the hand and squeezed it. Then they turned to head down to Bjørn in The Engine Room and with the clarity of the song still ringing in his ears, he said to her.

"Who needs school anyway?"

20
PETRA

When she awoke on a cot, the first thing she thought was that she was back in the Celtic camp getting treatments. Her heart raced, she had to get out, she was doing what they wanted and she couldn't survive the dreams another time. But she couldn't hear the hum of the generator heating the tent, and the smell of the bonfire wasn't wafting in the air. Frantically, she looked down at her arms, but there was only one IV going out of her hand attached to a clear tube. As her eyes adjusted to the light, she reached for the lace on her bedside table, pressing the pattern into the palm of her hand as her memories started flooding back. Leaving Arthur in the camp, coming back to Mimameid, seeing Lysander. She shook her head as if trying to rid herself of water and a face appeared around the corner of her privacy curtain.

An older nurse with dark, fearful eyes, and frazzled, greying hair, stepped inside as Petra pushed herself up to sit, feeling how sore her stomach was.

"Welcome back, how are you feeling?" Her voice was practiced, and calm, but her manner suggested something was making her nervous like she knew something she shouldn't. She reached out to take Petra's pulse from her band readings. "May I?" she asked before touching her and Petra nodded.

"I feel okay, I guess," she replied. "What happened?"

"You collapsed in The Engine Room. We had to perform an emergency partial splenectomy." Petra nodded, trying to put the pieces of the story back together in her head. "Do you remember how you got back on board Mimameid?" the nurse asked as she peered over onto Petra's stomach at her wounds from the surgery and made a note in the tablet in her hands.

Of course, she knew. She'd come in The Back Door. But Petra shook her head. The nurse's face fell slightly at her, dusted with a hint of disappointment. Maybe Sigrid had promised her family safety if she extracted information from Petra, maybe she'd been promised the chance to move up to the higher levels of the bunker. Not A of course, the people up there had paid good money to make sure they wouldn't have to interact with anyone as low as this nurse, but perhaps she had hoped she could get her family into B, better schooling groups, medicine first. Those kinds of things.

"I'm sorry, what kind of surgery did you say I had?" she asked the nurse.

"Partial splenectomy. We had to remove a section of your spleen, it was bleeding into your abdominal cavity. Do you remember what could have caused it?" Petra pretended to think about it for a second, but she knew, of course: Briony. Arthur had wanted to do an ultrasound before she left camp but they hadn't had the time. "It looked like it had been bleeding for some time," the nurse continued, her face lowered timidly.

"I um..." Petra prepared for the lie, "I escaped the Celts," she said and the nurse's face shriveled up in horror.

"Oh, you poor dear. They said there was a soldier that had been taken by the Celts, I had no idea. Did they-" she looked around warily and leaned in to whisper her question, "were you going to be sacrificed for one of their rituals?" Petra tried to hold back at the ridiculousness of her comment.

"No, no. They wouldn't- they don't- never mind, I'm fine. I just. It was pretty traumatizing." She decided her safest choice was to try to get as much sympathy from the nurse as she could, so she tried to sell her story. "I had to walk for a couple of days to get back here, you know. Alone. In the cold. Hoping the Celts weren't trying to recapture me. And then, of course, there was the torture."

She watched the nurse's face carefully, as she gestured to her bruised eye and bruising up and down her body from the treatments. When she raised her hand to it, she noticed that the swelling in her eyes had gone down. Whatever Arthur had done before she left, it was healing faster than she had anticipated. But it was as if the nurse had completely forgotten what life was like Above Ground, she would believe anything Mimameid told her. Petra tried to look pitiful and the nurse seemed to buy it.

"Well you seem to be healing nicely from your surgery, so that's some good news at least," the old nurse told Petra, patting her on the hand, maternally. "So, I think I'll leave you to get some rest. You deserve it." Petra inclined her head as to say thanks, and leaned back to close her eyes. She needed to keep herself composed and keep her plan straight, but her head was feeling a little fuzzy from whatever drugs they had given her for the operation.

No sooner had she closed her eyes, than a familiar voice spoke up.

"Petra?" It was Lysander. She opened her eyes and gave him half a smile, recalling the last time they had seen one another, hugged one another.

"Hey," she said. He looked ragged compared to the last time she had seen him, his eyes ringed with dark circles and his hair long and unruly. He needed a haircut, or rather, he needed to be shorn.

"How are you doing?" He approached her cautiously and he sat down on the edge of her bed. She tried to get a sense of where his apprehension was coming from, but then she caught him analyzing the various bruises and scrapes on her arms and it relaxed her a little. Siobhan had been right about that at least, the battered state of her body sold the story pretty well.

"They say I'll be fine. I'm sure I'll be up and at it in no time." She winced as she adjusted herself on the bed.

"What happened? Do you remember?" She felt like the lines on his face had deepened since she last saw him, his eyes a little wilder as he spoke.

"My spleen. Must have happened when I was escaping." The lie slipped from her tongue so easily, she felt bad. He trusted her far more than she deserved, he always had. She'd pointed a gun at him the first time they'd met, for god's sake, and he'd still gone with her. When this was all over, she would owe him an apology.

"No, I mean," he leaned in and whispered, "why were you in The Engine Room to begin with? What happened to you?" His big, bear eyes shifted back and forth as he spoke. She was so grateful that he had developed a healthy level of skepticism during his time in Mimameid; she almost told him everything. But, as much as it pained her not to be open with him, she swallowed her words and bit back her short-lived happiness.

"I don't remember much, they tortured me, so everything is a bit jumbled up," she explained, keeping her voice steady and her heart rate down so as not to raise any suspicion in her band data. She kept her lie vague, so there was still a vein of truth to it.

"Petra, so much has happened since you left. I can't tell you everything here..." His voice trailed off. "Magdelena and Linnaea, they left." She watched his face as the words slipped out and she had the sense that it might be the first time he had spoken them aloud. That it was real now.

Suddenly, his band lit up and he looked down at it, pausing. "Milla has leftovers in C, what?" he muttered and then, "Oh.." when the true meaning of the message dawned on him. She watched, curiously. What had Lysander gotten himself into? She wanted to ask, wanted to know, but she had to focus on her mission. Arthur's life depended on it. And so did everyone else's in Mimameid.

"Do you need to get going?" she asked and he looked around, anxiously, torn between staying and going.

"I'm so sorry," he apologized and stood up, abruptly.

"It's okay," she told him. She needed the time to prepare, to plan. And she needed to get this godforsaken IV out of her arm so she could think straight.

"I'll come back after to catch you up. I -" he paused as he pulled the privacy curtain aside and Petra followed his gaze to a man in the bed beside her - still and cold with death - his lips tinted with black blood, "Petra. I'm so glad you're back." His voice was so clear, so honest, her face broke into a genuine smile.

"I missed you, too, engineer," she told him and she prayed to Freyja, to the Akka, and to anyone else she could think of that he would be okay.

Not long after Lysander left, she fell asleep, exhausted from her operation. She floated in the darkness she remembered from the treatments and somehow, it felt peaceful. Arthur's voice whispered out to her in the inky blackness, to remain vigilant and focused. That she knew who she was. Starlight of wild purple and gold began to swirl above her she saw only the purple of his irises. When she awoke, she was being shaken by the dark-eyed nurse.

"There's someone here to see you," she told Petra, a hint of apology in her voice. Rubbing the sleep from her face, she could see that The Infirmary lights had been dimmed to a pleasant glow for night.

"Okay," Petra told her, but she could see the nurse had brought a wheelchair around. So this meeting couldn't be public, couldn't have witnesses. Well, there was only one person in Mimameid who had that kind of authority. Sigrid was here.

Petra slid her legs around the side of the bed, pushing the wheelchair aside. If Sigrid was here, she would walk. Let the woman see what her handiwork had done to Petra. Let her see how long it would take for Petra to get to her.

The nurse looked over, face shining with concern, but she took hold of Petra's arm to steady her and together they walked down the long ward to the processing room where Sigrid was waiting for her. The last time she had been in this room, Magdelena and Linnaea had still been in Mimameid.

Sigrid's eyes were downcast as Petra shuffled in, wearing only her medical gown and socks, embroidered with the Mimameid insignia.

The nurse left her momentarily hanging onto the edge of the counter while she wheeled the chair in and Petra was able to sit down. She groaned as she did, the incisions still raw and the stitches pulling on her skin. She wished for one fleeting moment that Arthur had been the one to perform the surgery. *He probably wouldn't have done such a hack job*, she thought bitterly.

When the nurse had helped Petra settle into the chair, Sigrid raised her glittering eyes and wordlessly dismissed the nurse. Only then did she look at Petra.

Her silver eyes shone in the dim, blue light of the artificial night.

"In the boughs of Mimir's tree, Petra." Her voice was cool, removed. It was not the motherly tone she usually used with Petra, there was some unmistakable undertone warning Petra that Sigrid had not expected to see her again. And she certainly didn't trust her.

"Sigrid," Petra replied, matching the coolness in her voice, but refusing to repeat the standard greeting. There was no need to hide her true feelings here. Sigrid knew her far too well for that.

"I heard you escaped from the Celts," she began. "We're so glad you made it back to us safely." Her voice was tinny with falsehood.

"I'm glad to be back safely. I'm glad that your rescue efforts were not in vain," she replied, her sarcasm like a steam in the air.

"We could not risk the men for a rescue mission, as I am sure you are aware. We sent you in with our top Celtic specialists and if all of you had been lost any advantage we had over the enemy would have vanished. Surely you can understand that." Sigrid examined her fingernails as she spoke, cleaning out one of her long talons, disinterested in Petra's reaction.

"I understand. Of course," Petra replied, stiffly. There was a silence and then Sigrid cleared her throat uncomfortably and looked back up.

"I hope your time in captivity was fruitful." She narrowed her eyes at Petra, evaluating her as she rapped her long fingernails on the table edge she was leaning on, over and over again, rhythmically.

"It certainly was," Petra replied, short.

"Then you should have valuable information to share with us on how we can overpower our enemy and defeat them once and for all. You must agree, they have no place here." How had Petra never noticed before how much like the dictators of The Time Before Sigrid sounded?

"Yes. I do have information." She looked Sigrid directly in her shining eyes as she answered. She wanted her to know and fear exactly what she said. Sigrid appeared to back down from the confrontation.

"Well, when you are feeling better, we will look forward to a more complete debrief, but is there anything you feel comfortable sharing with me now? *Oh, the things I could tell you.* Petra wanted to say, but she kept her face expressionless in the dim light.

"I am still wrestling with the memories of my capture and torture myself. I'm still sorting through what is fact and what is fiction," she spoke, softly and tactfully, "but I will surely look forward to debriefing with you after my recovery." Sigrid rose, and Petra noticed her body language morph. Having not extracted anything useful from her, she was pivoting strategy.

"I'm so sorry about how they treated you. You must have felt so utterly abandoned by us." She moved closer to her in the dark room, lifting her hands out to Petra's cheek. But the illusion had been shattered for Petra. She no longer needed nor craved Sigrid's approval. And empathy was not Sigrid's strong suit. Petra grabbed Sigrid's wrist, stopping her hand in midair. The woman flinched. Her fingers flexed, instinctively, as though she was going to slap her for her disrespect, her insolence.

"I have been abandoned before and grown stronger for it. I am no stranger to disappointment in other people," Petra growled.

"Are you disappointed in me, Petra?" Sigrid sank to the floor before Petra's wheelchair as she spoke, her wrist still in Petra's firm grasp. "Because that would be understandable, you know." Carefully, she raised her chin back up. "I have failed you." Petra knew this piety at her feet was a show but felt how much she wanted it, she wanted to know what it felt like to have Sigrid kneeling before her, begging for forgiveness. "I have not protected you as I promised you I would, all those years ago, when I saved you in the woods."

"No."

"I left you to the wolves, to be consumed by the fires that ravage our land."

"You did."

"I am sorry," Sigrid said simply to her, taking hold of both of her hands. It sent a shock through her body and she felt her grip loosen as this woman she had regarded for so many years, as highly as her *baba*, reached out for her. "I hope you can forgive me." They were the words Petra wanted to hear, but they were so hollow, so empty, that Petra could tell Sigrid herself didn't even believe them.

The silver-haired woman stood up, letting her hands fall to her side. Petra's eyes remained where they had been, looking at the emptiness between her hands and the bruising up her arms.

The hollow lie was enough to make Petra jump from her chair and wrap her hands around Sigrid's long, thin neck. But she had a larger game to play, and she needed Sigrid to think that she wasn't a threat. "We will speak again, soon," Sigrid concluded, straightening herself up and smoothing her hair down.

Without looking at Petra, she spoke into the darkness. "Never forget who you are, Petra. Or where you come from," she said, her voice was cool again and her eyes as bright as the moon had been in the night sky.

She walked out of the room without another glance and left Petra alone in the dark.

She was released from The Infirmary the next morning after they confirmed she was healing properly from her surgery.

When she finally did make it back to her quarters, she tapped in with her band and the door gushed open. She saw her bed was made and her clothes were hung in the closet, but none of it was how she had left it. They had obviously cleared out her half of the room, not expecting her to return. It was a wonder her things had not already been redistributed among the community members. Milla's side of the room, on the other hand, looked just as messy as usual, her hydroponic plants still high in the corner underneath the jerry-rigged grow lights, bottles of hooch rattling at the slightest nudge. Clothes were strewn across the half-stowed bed and Petra had to be careful not to trip on the pile of boots Milla was mending for some families down in D.

She walked over to the mirror and popped open the sink from the wall. There, lying beside the tap, just as she had left it, was a faded picture of a woman with long, shock-white hair clutching a young, flame-headed child. She sighed. At least Milla had been able to protect that little trinket for her.

She picked up the photo and pressed it to her chest, closing her eyes for just a brief moment, thinking about what her *baba*'s hair had smelled like, what her laugh had sounded like, but she couldn't recall. It only now occurred to her how fabricated and synthetic her grandmother's voice had been in the dreams, not actually real memories. A little melancholy at the thought, she turned her mind instead to what *Baba* would have made of Arthur, pinching the lace in her jumpsuit pocket as she did. Her heavily accented voice sang in Petra's ear, "A doctor in the family, very well done. Good with his hands, I presume!" She'd always been rather blunt and a little brash and Petra held onto that piece of her with everything she had. She wished she had inherited that boldness. She hoped *Baba* would forgive her for what she had to do.

Exhausted from the descent down into C from The Infirmary, she rolled out her bed and sat down on the edge of it, staring around the room, blankly. Her stomach let out an enormous growl and she realized for the first time since she'd been back that she was hungry. That had to be a good sign. Satisfied that all her things were still in order in her bunk, she heaved herself back onto her feet and headed down to Canteen C.

When the double doors opened with a flash of green, she was hit with the wave of noise in C. She'd forgotten how busy it always was and how rowdy the soldiers could become when they weren't given enough recreation or training.

Heading slowly towards the automat, she tried to make herself small, avoiding the larger groups of people moving through the space, especially the ones with runic tattoos. When she ordered food, she noticed that she was allowed a slightly larger portion of fish and potatoes, the algorithm accommodating her recovery period.

She turned to survey the layout of the canteen. Scanning across the room, she saw that her usual table was intact, still occupied by her men, Benjáme and Lasse among them, along with Anders. Even Onni was sitting with them, though she threw her glance towards a sour-looking Maike and Anja - both sat together far removed from the action. Petra started towards the table, but a voice called out from behind her.

"Petra?" She turned and saw Milla's dark head popping out from the kitchen.

"Milla," Petra replied and walked over to her slowly, setting her tray down on the counter so she could steady herself. Although neither Milla nor Petra were big huggers, they reached for one another's hands and Petra felt Milla give her a reassuring squeeze.

"Everything okay?" Petra was getting a little tired of that question. Of course, it wasn't okay. She was being blackmailed into betraying the people who had made her feel like family. But of course, she couldn't tell them any of that. If Siobhan sniffed one thing out of order with her plan, she'd harm Arthur and his family. And besides, Sigrid deserved what was coming to her.

Milla's hazel eyes shifted back and forth, uncertainty clouding her gaze. It reminded her of how Lysander had looked in The Infirmary. "I just heard you were back and you had surgery or something?"

"Who'd you hear that from?" Petra was pretty sure she hadn't been seen by too many people since returning. Sigrid would have kept her return under wraps until she was sure she could control Petra.

"Oh, sorry. Lysander told me. I hope that's okay that he did?" Petra felt her face grow hot with flush, but she tried not to let it upset her.

"Of course it is," she said, forcing part of a smile onto her face for one of her oldest friends.

"You know, I've got your back," Milla whispered reassuringly to her, and Petra felt her heart flip flop as she wished she could confide in her friend. She was accustomed to keeping certain parts of herself hidden away from most people, but seeing the faces of her family back here in Mimameid made her wish she could warn them of what was coming.

"I was taken prisoner by the Celts Above Ground," she told Milla, trying to believe the lies herself. "I don't completely remember how I got back, but I'm lucky to be alive."

"Well, I'm glad to see you back. I missed you." Milla wasn't usually so soft and it left Petra curious what had happened since she'd been away.

"I missed you, too." She gave her friend's hand another reassuring squeeze and then pulled her fingers back and shoved them into her pocket, feeling the lace.

"Let me know if there's anything I can do, yeah?" Milla said and Petra nodded, smiling a little back at her and tucking a lock of wild hair behind her ear, anxiously. "You going over to the guys?" Milla asked, looking over at the usual table where Petra's men sat sprawled out.

"Yeah, I haven't seen them yet." Petra made a face, taking a deep, nervous breath in.

"Don't worry about it," Milla assured her, "they've missed you, too. A lot. More than they will admit. Tell Lasse *hej* for me, yeah?" she asked, eyeing him weirdly while busying her hands with a dishtowel on the countertop. Petra raised an eyebrow.

"Something going on between you guys? You get in a fight?" she asked, invasively, she knew, but she hoped it would distract from how odd she was being. Milla paused her cleaning.

"He's just been - a little off lately." She scrunched up her nose. "Keep an eye on him for me, won't ya?" She resumed the absentminded polishing of the countertop. There was obviously more to it, but Milla didn't seem to want to talk about it right now. "I have to get back to work. It's so good to see you." She smiled warmly and turned, running back into the kitchen after what Petra could see was a little bit of smoke she hadn't smelled until just now.

She picked up her tray, butterflies in her stomach, and headed over to her table across the room.

They saw her before she arrived. They jumped up from their mismatched and odd assortment of chairs, bumping into everything around them and knocking things over, huge smiles plastered across their faces as they waded over to her.

"Lieutenant!" Anders rose to his massive height and opened up his arms to welcome her back. Lasse and Benjáme, both smaller than Anders, though not by much, wrapped her in hugs before she was able to finally take a seat. Benjáme held on for a long time before passing her over to Onni for a quick hug. The woman gave her a shy smile that told her there was nothing to fear. Anders kicked out a chair for her and she eased herself down, setting down the tray of food.

"Welcome back, sir." Anders grinned at her. "Benjáme was telling us a little bit about your exploits. Did it really cost you a kidney?"

"Spleen," she said lightheartedly, lifted by the mood at the table. They laughed, as though she had made a joke.

"Unbelievable that you escaped," Anders said, leaning back in his chair and crossing his scarred arms behind his head, clearly impressed.

"Even more unbelievable that you lived with them for so long before you got caught," Aksel added to his right. His eyes were glowing with admiration, something restless and fiery about them.

"Well, I don't know what Benjáme told you, but I had some help," Petra said, meaning Arthur, but they all took it to mean Benjáme and it was better that they did.

He looked pleased with himself as they patted him on his back. She exchanged a grateful look with Benjáme, his dark eyes shining at her with a little something that reminded her of Ciarán's. Was it pity, was it trust? She turned her face to Lasse. "I'm glad you're back on your feet, too," she told him. Lasse smiled half a smile at her and Petra saw what Milla had meant. Though his eyes were still kind, Lasse's jaw clench uncomfortably. The easiness of his manner was gone, the openness. "I wouldn't be here without you, Lieutenant," he told her, voice steady and truthful, but nothing more.

"And I wouldn't be here without my men," Petra told them, but Benjáme lowered his eyes, dissatisfied.

"I'm sorry, for my part," he said solemnly and Onni leaned forward on the table, her face full of apology as she spoke.

"We would have done more if we could. We would have stormed the camp, just the two of us if -" Petra saw her gaze shoot across the canteen to where Maike and Anja were eating, faces still sour, like the food they were eating had gone bad. Maike's eyes caught Petra's for a split second and she saw the slightest inclination of a nod.

"No explanation necessary," Petra told Benjáme and Onni, her eyes still lingering on Maike. "I know where orders come from here. And I know the price for disobeying." Anders started clapping, slowly.

"Bravo!" he laughed. "Take her to the bakery!" Petra bit back an amused smile at both his enthusiasm and the Old Icelandic idiom. "I hope they heard that." Anders raised his voice as he waved his hands around, indicating to the cameras and microphones that they all knew were hidden in the walls and the ceilings. She winked at him.

"They did," she reassured him.

Petra knew her men weren't used to her disregarding the higher-ups, and that she had a reputation for being Sigrid's pet - it's what made her so ideal to Siobhan. So, she wasn't surprised to see a couple of them trying to mask their shock at her words. It was risky, to let her guard down like that, but among her fellow soldiers she felt herself relaxing, getting sloppy.

"Had a little chat with Her-Royal-Highness, did you?" Anders asked her, slyly. She had always known Anders to be cheeky and insubordinate, to act untouchable, but something more seemed to have emboldened him even more since she'd been away.

"You could call it that," she replied, trying to rein herself back in, or give away that anything had changed.

Suddenly, around the table, their bands started all going off, one right after the other. Anders, Aksel, Onni, Benjáme and Lasse. They all looked down with furrowed brows before looking up again and exchanging telling glances. Lasse was the first to stand up, his lips tight and jaw flexing nervously.

"I told Milla I'd meet her," he said, but based on the conversation she had just had with Milla, that seemed rather unlikely. Nevertheless, he turned and headed off toward the kitchens. Onni and Benjáme were the next to stand up, coming around the table to say their excuses, Aksel close behind them, fidgeting and flighty.

"We've got a training session down in D. But we'll catch up at dinner?" Benjáme explained. *Down in D?* That was weird, the only sessions in D were for new recruits. "It's good to have you back, Lieutenant." He paused, putting a warm hand on her shoulder and Petra felt in the energy of his touch that something had shifted in him. He wasn't the young firebrand she had left behind in the North Country. But what had happened? What had changed him?

Only Anders stayed seated, sipping his tea and lounging in his chair, unperturbed. Petra raised an eyebrow, bemused.

"Aren't you going to go join them, doing whatever it is you guys are up to?" she asked and he grinned at her.

"They're all terribly discrete, aren't they?" he chuckled. "I'll be there in a bit, no one will miss me if I'm a little late." He leaned forward and stole a potato off her tray.

21
LYSANDER

He had opted to stay late after work to prepare for The Resistance meeting. He decided to spend the extra time trying to figure out why Petra had been in The Engine Room. Stressed as he was, he was happy to see her and glad that he had been able to take a good look at her haggard face in The Infirmary, and see for a fact that she was back and still herself. But what bothered him was he didn't know if she was being truthful with him about her memory of captivity.

Everyone he knew had gone through some kind of trauma in the years since Ragnarök, and patience had always been a effective way for him to deal with it, to let Magdelena and Linnaea open up to him in their own time, for example. He just didn't know if whatever Petra was holding back was dangerous or not, and that scared him. Could she have been down there to betray them - certainly not the Petra he had known - the one with unwavering loyalty to Mimameid and Sigrid. But what if she hadn't been there to betray the people, but rather the system itself? Then whatever she was up to wasn't unlike what The Resistance was trying to accomplish.

Once everyone had left for the day, including Selby, Arne, and Bo, who he knew would be back later for the meeting, Lysander began his search. He started in the back room where he had found Petra, feeling his way along the walls, centimeter by centimeter, looking for any spot out of place, anything that might flag what Petra's true purpose in The Engine Room had been - nefarious or otherwise.

It wasn't that he didn't trust her, but she had told him everything was jumbled up in her brain. He couldn't ignore the possibility that the Celts may have planted some subconscious, hidden trigger inside of her. And when everything became un-jumbled, she would be activated, or whatever sleeper spies do. Or maybe he had just been living in Mimameid long enough that he was starting to see treachery wherever he went.

By the time he had gone over every surface in the back room and returned to the main space, the first members of The Resistance had started to trickle in, as they had before, in waves.

The people who were coming in had circles under their impassioned eyes, bone-tired from mending or gardening, smelling of fish or algae. Their faces were sweaty and glistening from a full day of hard labor, their hands blistered or rubbed raw from fertilizing chemicals and soap. More people than he had realized wore threadbare Mimameid jumpsuits, patches on the elbows and knees, or with outright holes. They weren't even allowed to have a needle and thread down here without the leaders' approval, and most of them were last on the lists for things like clothing replacement, medicine, or mechanical repair. There was certainly no one among them whom he recognized from B with their white-collar jobs in 'management'. When the young woman who'd stomped out that first day he'd arrived, Ingrid, he thought her name was, walked through the doors, her hair pulled up out of her face and a smudge of something black over her right eyebrow from wiping sweat from her face, Lysander wasn't surprised.

As more people arrived, Lysander continued his analysis of The Engine Room as discretely as possible. That is, until Benjáme and Onni entered and veered over to him.

"Hey Lysander, we just saw the Lieutenant upstairs," Benjáme told him, excitedly. "Did you know she made it back from the Celts, alive?" He was beaming so widely at the news that his commanding officer was back, Lysander didn't have the heart to tell him about how and in what state he had found Petra. He decided to play dumb.

"That's great news. How did she seem?" he asked, trying not to sound distracted since he hadn't been able to finish combing the walls.

"Fired up. She might have to be the next member we recruit for The Resistance," he said tossing his long ponytail over his shoulder. "And boy, could we use her."

"You think so?" Lysander asked, with a nervous half-smile playing on his lips. Maybe he was wrong to question Petra's intentions - Benjáme saw the same change in her, but in it, he saw the potential.

The room quieted and they all looked up as Milla and Aksel entered. Excusing himself from Benjáme and Onni, Lysander raced up to greet them on the steps, reaching out to Milla first, her face lined with its customary skepticism of him, and then to Aksel, fiery and expectant. This was, after all, the meeting he had called.

He looked down from the platform that the last steps of the stairs afforded him, down onto the faces of his colleagues and friends, of strangers he shared common ground with. The Resistance was rooted deeply within the unsatisfactory walls of Mimameid and he could feel its roaring energy filling the room. The gentle throbbing of the reactor in the center of the room fed its energy as a beating heart.

Heiká raised his hand in greeting from the crowd. As Lysander returned the gesture, he saw that Heiká had brought Tuva with him tonight and he wondered if Bjørn knew what the two of them were up to or if they had told Bjørn that Lysander was involved. Tuva was looking around uneasily at the patchwork of different people gathered there. She would be one of the few employed in A here, maybe the only one, and based on her expression, this was her first time.

Milla put a hand on Lysander's shoulder as he steadied his breath. When he turned to her, her face had softened into something resembling kindness, and faith in him.

"Friends, we have called this emergency meeting because yesterday one of our members, Darri," Lysander saw an older woman in the crowd let out a sob at his name and thought it must be Darri's mother, a man with broad shoulders stood beside her, rubbing her back "took his own life," Milla finished boldly as scattered gasps shivered through the crowd. She didn't let it stop her.

"In his opinion, this was how he could make the biggest impact," she continued. "He chose to take his life in the crowded Infirmary, full of people from all levels of Mimameid, all different walks of life, to expose the treachery and lies we have been told. He wanted it to be known that the leaders of Mimameid are liars, so he removed his band, knowing what would the result would be."

There was a cheer from someone that encouraged more shouts of approval.

"May we all be so brave!" The man with broad shoulders raised his fist and a few others joined in.

"Yes. He was brave." Milla's voice was soft, heartbroken for them as she raised her hand to subdue them. "But now we don't have that bravery anymore. And this rebellion needs fire." There was a silence, bubbling with anger and grief. Milla continued, tenderly, "We have never and will never condone this as an appropriate form of resistance. Humanity has suffered enough losses and our numbers are few. Even fewer are those who know the truth and who believe in the possibility of something better than the life we have here in Mimameid. Protect your families, protect one another. We are all we have."

There was a wave of approval throughout the crowd, knowing nods and hearty grunts of agreement. Lysander was amazed at how Milla was able to take such a horrific event and spin it into something that felt motivating.

"Your life is precious. Please, don't throw it away, needlessly. We celebrate the people whose eyes our brother's sacrifice may have opened, but we do not encourage any of you to follow in his footsteps. Do not remove your bands. *Never* remove your bands." Lysander fingered in his pocket the bio-implant he had removed from the man's body when he had visited Petra in The Infirmary earlier. A quick slice to open his wrist with his Celtic knife to root around the cold, hard tendons. It sent a chill down his spine. He felt his eyes go foggy in the memory before a hand on his shoulder shook him back.

Milla was ready for him. She stepped aside and he cleared his throat as if to rid himself of the memory.

"Some of you already know me," Lysander started, lifting his hand out to the crowd, the implant balanced in his palm as he scanned over the faces he was familiar with. "For those of you who don't, I'm Lysander and I work down here in The Engine Room." His eyes met Selby's and slid to the twins, their arms crossed and their faces glowing, impassioned. "My training in The Time Before was in robotics and I have had a chance to look at the devices they implanted into us when we all arrived here in Mimameid." The crowd murmured, some people instinctively reached for their wrists in surprise. Maybe they hadn't even considered before, that the thing inside them could be harmful.

He rolled the bio-implant in his hand to his fingertips, stained black from the poison, holding it up higher for them to see it. "This is the bio-implant I took from inside Darri's body in The Infirmary. Inside every one of us, the leaders of Mimameid have planted an identical device. And we let them," He sighed as murmurs rippled through the crowd. "They told us that it was for our own good - that it would help us become more efficient members of our community and that it would allow us to remain here in safety longer. What they did not tell us was that alongside the device they inserted a kill-switch designed to silence those who chose to no longer comply with their rules," Lysander felt a knot tighten in his stomach and wished he could reach for Judit's charm, "or an easy way to dispose of those who are no longer efficient enough members of Mimameid - the old, the sick." He swallowed and thought of the people he'd seen outside waiting in The Infirmary - the young girl, the Danish man. Saying out loud for the first time, he found himself at a loss for words at the betrayal. And the crowd below him was starting to get angry, the volume rising, the people pushing their way toward him to get a better look at the device in his hand. Steam hissed from the generators, the core whirred and he felt sweat slipping down his neck between his shoulders. His ears warbled and muffled, as though he had water in them and the protests continued.

"I knew it! Sigrid has been lying to us from the start!"

"Enough is enough!"

"That can't be true! How do we even know we can trust this B-level?"

"Hey! Just because he's from B-level doesn't mean he's not trying to help!" It was Ingrid's voice.

Lysander felt his face getting hot, unable to respond, but Milla stepped in.

"Listen, I know that you are angry. I am, too," she intercepted, "but, there are other ways to defy the leaders of Mimameid. Better ways. Our best revenge is our survival." Lysander watched in awe as she managed the crowd. "We have begun steps towards a way for those of us who want to leave, to leave. Hafthor -" she pointed down to the gatekeeper, "has established a team of people who are interested in searching for the lost submarines, so we can get our old and our sick out of Mimameid. Those of you interested in helping, don't hesitate to contact him, but *be careful,*" she said, sternly. "This is only the beginning of a long process to get us to safety." There was hesitant applause among the group, a whisper of hope. But not everyone was so convinced.

"It's not enough!" protested a disgruntled-looking Selby, and a few people chimed in with agreement. "It's not enough!" he repeated. Beside him, Bo gave him a hearty shove, encouragingly.

"It's better than doing nothing at all." Arne's face was dour as he spoke, but Lysander knew that it was only his way. Although Bo was the optimistic one of the two, Arne agreed with his brother.

"And what about the Celts?" Came a shout from someone else in the crowd and the dissidents raised their voices again.

"Onni and Benjáme," she pointed now down the steps towards the two of them, "are making preparations for the journey past the Celts. We are in good hands."

"But how can you be sure we will be safe?" another voice asked, and this time Lysander saw who had spoken: Tuva. She continued, flanked by Heiká, "The Celts can't have changed so very much in the time since we were last

Above Ground. The only difference will be that there is even *less* food and *less* shelter than there was before." Spoken like someone who was in Accounting, and as much as Lysander wanted to disagree, she was right.

What she didn't know and he did was that he had met a Celt Above Ground, out on the road, and he hadn't seemed as bad as they had been led to believe. Maybe even good. And maybe there were more like him out there.

"We cannot be certain about any of this," Milla agreed. "We are in completely uncharted waters, but we have been in uncharted waters before. We all survived Ragnarök. The choice belongs to you - and you alone know if this is a path you want to follow," Milla replied. Tuva twisted her mouth, looking unconvinced, but nodding her thanks nonetheless.

When the meeting had died down, Lysander found Milla again. She mingled her way through the crowd, reassuring people that they would bring them extra medicine, or arrange help for someone, much like what Runa had been doing for Liddie.

Everyone trusted Milla and she had the kind of generous authority that made each individual feel special, attended to. She wasn't overly friendly, that wasn't who Milla had ever been, but she moved through the room like the sun, warm and bringing hope to each despair. He wondered why he had never noticed it before, but he understood why she and Lasse were a couple. The Lasse he had known on the road Above Ground had also been that kind of open and hopeful. When Milla finally approached him he spoke first.

"I had no idea you guys were working on a plan," he began and she smirked. It was the first gesture, besides her encouragement on the platform, that she had shown him which wasn't at least partially made up of annoyance. Maybe she was warming up to him.

"I had no idea you could be such a useful ally," she replied, her eyes searching his face. "Not bad, for your first time."

"Thanks." She was completely different down here, in her element. "Friends?" he asked her and stuck out his hand as if to shake on a deal.

"I think we should stick with allies," she said, putting her hands on her hips and smirking as she considered. "Don't want to get ahead of ourselves." But, she reached out and shook anyways.

He woke the next morning with a lightness in his chest.

The Resistance meeting the night before had left him feeling more cautiously optimistic than he had in a long time that by the time Magdelena and Linnaea returned, he would have a way for them to take off their bands and escape Mimameid for good. As good as it had seemed at the beginning - the semblance of life from The Time Before that still existed - it wasn't how he wanted to live. Good only meant good for some people, never for everyone.

The renewed sense of purpose had awoken him earlier than usual, even earlier than Bjørn, so he decided to go and head down to The Engine Room. He had made up his mind during the night that, because he knew now there was an escape plan in the works, he could risk sending a reply to Magdelena. Even if he were caught, he would be able to buy enough time to escape and meet up with them on the road to the North Country. Taking advantage of the early morning meant that he might even be able to boost the signal and get the message sent out before Bjørn arrived for the day.

Lysander zipped up his jumpsuit and tucked the Celtic knife into his waistband - carrying it had become something of a habit now - before splashing some water on his face and heading down the hall to the canteen. It was so early that B was still relatively empty. He found the stillness of it pleasant enough to sit down rather than take breakfast to-go like he usually did to avoid the irritatingly mindless chatter of the upper levels.

He ate his porridge with honey and sipped his green tea, trying to ignore the pang of guilt he felt at being so at ease with the warm meals here in Mimameid. It was such a weight off his shoulders, not having to worry about running out of gas for a camping stove or fresh, drinkable water. He finally had time to entertain more leisurely thoughts again, like learning how the wave generator worked or going for a swim to clear his mind. Abruptly, he felt his food turn in his stomach, remembering the gaunt face of the Danish man in The Infirmary, the sick little girl, and Darri's still face, streaked with black blood - the genuine cost of that security, that luxury.

He spit the mouthful of porridge he had been eating out back into the bowl as the urge to be sick rose. He stood up and bussed his tray, avoiding other people's glances as he left the canteen to head down the stairs towards The Engine Room. With a quick glance up at the glass ceiling of the stairwell, he watched the water of the fjord glimmer for a second and promised himself that sooner rather than later, he would get back up there, to the surface.

When he had made it down to D, he raised his wrist to the door and opened it with the familiar whoosh that was quickly overpowered by the sound of rushing water. *That can't be good.* Lysander leaped over the threshold, tripping on the door frame as his heart jumped into his throat, and nearly face-planted on the grated catwalk. He caught himself on the railing and peered over into The Engine Room.

From the top of the stairs, he could see the room was already under three feet of water.

One of the turbines had been knocked over by the force and was crackling dangerously in the water that was pouring into the bunker. The turbines were slowing with a wretched, dragging noise as the water bubbled. And the reactor, well the reactor was dead quiet in the center of the room. They must be operating on reserve power for the time being or whatever the wave generator could manage to sustain alone.

The water level was rising fast and the bubbling and gurgling coming from across the room made him think maybe the source of the leak might already be underwater.

Hurrying down the grated steps, he waded into the freezing water, frantically searching. He took a deep breath and sank beneath the surface.

It was icy, hitting his lungs like a slap, knocking the breath out of him. His eyes went dark for a second before he was able to refocus. And then, in a moment, it dawned on him, nothing had hit or attacked The Engine Room, but rather something was missing. Something he should have noticed when he was combing the walls last night, before The Resistance meeting.

Although blurry in the brackish underwater, he could see the force of water coming in where the makeshift valve on the far wall had been. He pushed towards the current, fighting against the swirl of pressure until he was able to grab onto the wall where the paneling had come off.

His knuckles were white as he gripped the wall and pushed up to the surface. *Skit,* he thought, trying to assess how quickly he could repair the damage. He took another gulp of air and submerged again, trying to get a look at the inside of the pump, but there was no way to see what was happening through the raging waters.

He forced his arm inside the wall and fumbled around where the valve would have been.

It felt as though the valve itself had ripped right off and had been carried away when the water rushed in. But Bjørn would never have let a patch like that get so far beyond repair. Feeling carefully along the edge he realized the water was pouring directly from the fjord outside straight into The Engine Room.

He stood back up and looked around, calculating in his head just how much the water level had risen just since he'd arrived when he heard Bjørn's voice call out above him.

"Holy mother of Thor. What happened?" he shouted at Lysander, ripping his glasses from his face and leaning over the railing.

"That old valve burst!" Lysander cupped his hands around his mouth as he shouted over the sound of the water.

"What valve?" Bjørn's eyebrows furrowed and Lysander looked at him, incredulously. Maybe Bjørn had been a little distracted.

"The one that has been barely hanging on for months!" The realization hit Bjørn like a wall of concrete.

"There's so much that's just been patched up and held together for so long, I completely forgot." The older man closed his eyes and rubbed the bridge of his nose, trying to think.

"Should we try to go in from the outside and contain it?" Lysander shouted quickly. The water was up to his waist and the drag was pulling him every which way so he started to move towards the stairs.

"The water in here is rising too fast," Bjørn replied and Lysander could see he was stuck in a desperate loop, unable to find a solution.

Half swimming, half walking, Lysander dragged himself out of the water and clambered up the stairs towards Bjørn, his jumpsuit heavy from the water.

"How many systems are controlled from down here?" he asked the man as he shook the water from his hair and rang out his sleeves.

"All of it. It's all down here," Bjørn said, the look he gave Lysander was grave.

"All of it? What, there's no backup anywhere?" He was aghast. He'd never heard of someone being so egotistical as to design a structure that had no backup, let alone one underwater.

"If there is, they never shared that information with me," Bjørn said plainly, staring a bewildered hole through Lysander.

"Okay," Lysander began. "We get out, seal the doors, repair it from the outside, and drain The Engine Room, so we can get back in there and get the power back on." He laid it out, hoping the plan would jump-start Bjørn back to life.

"It gets worse," the older man continued.

"Gets worse, how?" he asked, starting to shake from the cold.

"The air filtration system." Bjørn's voice was thin, his cheeks ashen grey with dread.

"Yes?" Lysander was getting impatient.

"The door jammed yesterday. It's stuck open. I wasn't able to repair it before dinner, so it's been sitting open all night." Lysander hadn't been paying attention when he arrived, too occupied by the flooding. He leaned over the railing and saw the door still wide open.

"Okay?" Lysander tried to figure out what Bjørn was trying to say.

"The air filtration system doesn't have a failsafe built in. If the water gets into the vents, there will be nothing to stop it from flooding the entire bunker."

"What?" Lysander's mouth dropped open. "We have to fix it. Now!" He was so annoyed at Bjørn, annoyed at how slow his brain seemed to be moving, meanwhile water was still pouring in below them. Not that it would make any difference, now.

"We can't," Bjørn said. "The electrics are fried, there's no way to keep the area dry while we work. We only have one option." The gears had begun to turn in Bjørn's head again as he spoke, "We have to evacuate."

For a split second, Lysander felt a revelation - this was Sigrid's downfall, this was the end of the oppression of Mimameid - before he remembered how many people would die if they couldn't evacuate in time.

"The security system should kick in soon and shut the bulkhead doors to The Engine Room." As the words left Bjørn's mouth an off-pitch alarm started blaring above them and the red emergency lights clicked on.

"Time to go!" Bjørn shouted, grabbing Lysander by the arm and pulling him towards the door that was lowering as they ran, the metal clanking with age. Bjørn ducked under the closing door, Lysander sliding in narrowly behind him. He turned to Bjørn and felt cold beads of sweat form along his hairline as the door shut behind them with a deep, clanking groan. They crossed the length of the decontamination chamber and sealed the manual hatch behind themselves.

"The doors to The Engine Room are watertight, right?" Lysander asked and Bjørn turned, his face grim.

"I mean, they were at one point, but this is the oldest part of Mimameid, remember?" Bjørn's face soured apologetically as water started to seep through the bottom of the door.

"At one point?" Lysander looked at Bjørn, baffled. This was unbelievable - first, no backup, and now, the door to The Engine Room of an *underwater* bunker wasn't *waterproof*? "We have to at least try to stop the leak from the outside, while everyone is evacuating." Bjørn nodded in agreement and they turned in the red-lit conference room to exit the other side.

This was the room he had been in when he met his other colleagues and toured The Engine Room for the first time. The tattered chairs that sagged where his colleagues had sat in them over the years - Selby stroking his beard and the twin's identical looks of disapproval. The table with a myriad of scratches etched into it. Lysander had imagined the head engineers and architects digging into the surface during long brainstorming sessions and coming up with brilliant solutions to the multitude of problems they inevitably encountered during the build. In the red glow of the emergency light, he could almost see their ghosts in the room with them, glaring at him for what he would do to their creation. The water slithered across the floor, towards the furniture. Soon it would all be underwater.

Bjørn clambered past the table and chairs to tap them out of the room on the keypad with his band, but nothing happened. He tried again then turned to Lysander.

"Maybe it's just a fluke, let me try," Lysander offered, trying not to let the small bubble of dread rising in him slip into his voice. He tapped his band against the pad, but the doors remained still and the reality of their situation sunk in, cold as the icy water rising at their feet.

The bulkhead doors had been lowered. They were trapped. There was no way for them to get out and the room was filling with water.

Bjørn looked at Lysander, his face flush with hysteria and Lysander could see that Bjørn was spiraling, unable to think straight.

"Let me see what I can do," Lysander said calmly, and they traded places. He pulled the Celtic knife from his waistband and used it to pry the pad off the wall. Throwing the cover aside and stowing the knife between his teeth, he ripped out the different wires to see how he could bypass the system and override the lock to open the door.

"If all our doors have been locked," Bjørn's blue eyes were moving fast as he riddled it out. "Then that means all the doors in all of Mimameid have locked."

"Grab those cable rippers for me," he instructed Bjørn, who passed them to him from the tabletop. Lucky he had them at all. Lucky he'd scavenged them from the wreckage of that old house Above Ground.

"No, you don't get it. *All* the doors are locked," Bjørn repeated.

"Well, at least that should mean the door to the air ventilation system closed, right?" Lysander asked, trying to remain optimistic about their situation. Of the wires to connect before him, there were eight options to choose from. He tested the blue output wire against a purple one, nothing. Then against yellow. Nothing.

"Frigga protect us." He turned around at the sound of Bjørn's voice. They watched the vent cover fall off the shaft and land in the rising water. It floated to the surface of the water and bobbed in the undertow.

"Obviously not," Lysander said, looking candidly at Bjørn.

"You have to get that door open," Bjørn growled and he splashed over towards Lysander, his legs caught in the drag of the rising water.

"I'm trying," he chewed his lip, biting back his fears, "nothing's working!" He touched the output wire against an orange one, still nothing.

"Get us out of here!" Bjørn bellowed, the water rushing in from the vent was making the water level rise even faster. It was already up to their calves.

He felt the electric jolt when the blue wire touched the red and his heart jumped when the door lifted open. The water rushed out with them, into the red-lit hallway, disseminating in either direction. Besides the water, it was empty.

Bjørn was right. The alarm system had shut everything down and all the doors were closed.

"We have to get outside and repair the leak!" Lysander said and Bjørn shook his head. Whatever had been blocking Bjørn's judgment before seemed to have passed through him. His face was alight and terrified, his blue eyes determined.

"There's no time for that anymore. By the time we get a suit and get out to The Back Door to do the repairs, the entirety of D will be underwater. All the doors are closed, do you understand?" He looked wild, but Lysander was confused. "Understand?" The desperate man grabbed Lysander by the shoulders as he spoke and as if Bjørn had knocked it into him, Lysander suddenly did understand.

Runa, Tuva, and Åsa were trapped behind closed doors in D, water rising from the bottom of Mimameid, and air running out. And they were three of hundreds trapped in D.

The entirety of Mimameid was now imprisoned behind closed doors, with water pouring in through their air vents, but D would be the first to go under. The water would keep rising, up and up, without any regard for the well-thought-out class system Sigrid had worked so hard to protect.

"We have to get them out," Bjørn said simply, wading forward to the next door and ripping off the panel.

"Okay. *How* do we get everyone out?" Lysander asked. They certainly wouldn't all fit out the top where he had first come in. Not in time, at least.

"We have to get to The Back Door," Bjørn told him. "That's the closest exit and the biggest."

"What about the people who can't leave? Liddie? Ned?" Lysander asked, thinking not only of them but of the seamstress who had never gotten the medication for her daughter's condition. The old Danish man in The Infirmary with the broken arm. There were so many. Bjørn looked at him, confused.

"The submarines, of course. We prioritize the old and the sick for the ships and everyone else can swim to the surface. Everyone has been issued a suit." Lysander sucked in a breath, but he didn't have time to be gentle with Bjørn as they approached the next door. He hesitated as he ripped off the panel and Bjørn leaned over to watch him and see which wires he was connecting. The door lifted and they continued on, turning the corner that would lead up the staircase and take them to the canteen.

"I hate to break it to you, but the subs aren't there." Bjørn tripped as Lysander said it, his glasses sliding down his nose, but he tried not to show his shock.

"What do you mean, where are they?" he asked, as he pushed his glasses back up the bridge of his nose.

"Hafthor told me the other day when I went swimming. They haven't been there in years. He's never even seen them. All that's left are the little 8-seater transports." Bjørn set his jaw, this was so very clearly news to him, he couldn't possibly be a part of the Resistance.

"They always just told me they were out being used, whenever I'd ask." Bjørn adjusted his glasses. Lysander put a hand on his friend's shoulder.

"I'm sorry," he said.

"Then they have to swim. We have to get as many people out as possible. They have to swim." Bjørn was determined and Lysander nodded in agreement as they approached the doors to the canteen.

The vents behind them were pouring water out into the halls as they arrived. On the other side, in the canteen, people were panicking in the red glow of the emergency lights.

Lysander could see through the windows that the people inside who had been eating breakfast were putting their children on tables as the water started to reach their shins. Selby was among them, having been at breakfast before his shift down in The Engine Room. Åsa's playmates, the twins with the big ears were there, too, dark eyes wide with fear. The Danish man stood beside them, his broken arm now bandaged up, the other holding the hand of one of the twins.

Ripping the panel off the wall, Lysander tapped the wires together and the doors opened with a gush, the water in both rooms meeting with a crash. Screams burst out at the noise and the rising water.

"Everybody, stay calm!" Lysander shouted over them. Bjørn continued wading towards the people, searching for his family as he helped pick the children up off the tables and get the elderly to their feet. "Listen, we have to evacuate, the entire bunker is flooding. I need everyone to get their drysuit from their bunk and then we will head up to The Back Door. Can you all do that?" The canteen had quieted and he tried not to let the gentle sobs of a smaller girl hugging a stuffed reindeer distract him as he looked around at their panicked faces. He saw the frightened face of Ingrid. He reached out for her.

"Ingrid, right?" She nodded. "Can you help me make sure everyone heard that and knows what to do?" Her face was full of panic, but she bit her cheek and nodded again, turning around to repeat what he had said. He noticed Bjørn getting Selby up to speed and explaining how to rig the wires and the doors to him.

"Okay," Lysander rounded on Bjørn when he was done explaining. "Go, find your family." He and Selby exchanged a look and then like that, Bjørn was gone, wading back out the door, and down the hall. He didn't need to be told twice.

Lysander led everyone forward as the water level rose in the halls around them. There was one more bulkhead before they arrived at the first hallway of living quarters. He ripped off the panel and in trying to touch the blue to the red, his hand slipped and touched the green. He felt the electricity of it as all the doors in the hallway opened simultaneously. *Good,* he thought. That would save time. He turned to Selby, who nodded and stroked his beard, having seen what he'd done. He stepped aside so the people who had been trapped could file out into the hallway.

"Remember, come to The Back Door when you have your equipment!" he repeated to them. "If your quarters are further along, follow me."

Around the next corner, they ran into Bo and Arne, who had also been on their way to work. They had never really given him the impression that they liked him that much, but the alarm on their faces as they trudged through the water melted their disdain for him. Lysander explained the situation briefly and showed them how to rewire the doors safely. With resolute expressions, they set back off down the hallway with Selby to get a head start on the rest of D still locked in their work stations.

The remaining people waded with Lysander through the hall until they reached the next panel - the one that led down to Ned's bunk and the Icelanders. He coupled up the wires and the doors gushed open, water spilling out into the hallway from their individual bunks, people stumbling out in the darkness, gasping for air, drenched and confused.

Along with the rest of the group, Lysander splashed through the water, directing everyone to get their drysuits and start the climb upstairs. No one complained or asked questions, these were the people who had seen the most, the Icelanders. They had faced extinction before, so what was new about this time?

At the very end of the hall, the red light flickering from the bad circuit, Lysander entered Ned's room to see the old man gathering his photographs and knick-knacks together, shoving them into every nook and cranny of his jumpsuit. He looked up at Lysander as he entered, his face wild in the red glow.

"Don't you come in here and tell me I have to leave them behind," he growled at him. Lysander put his hands up in surrender.

"I'm not here to tell you anything except to bring a drysuit. The only way out is to swim," he said, gesturing through the bunker and to the surface. Ned scowled and shoved the bundle of photographs into the breast pocket of his jumpsuit. Lysander handed him his drysuit and helmet from the hook next to the closet. He followed Ned out the door and back down to the main hallway.

"Come on, everyone!" he yelled over his shoulder and led them onwards through the rising water, finally making it to Bjørn's hallway where the older man had just turned the corner flanked by Runa and Åsa.

"The girls were already outside, they got out as soon as they saw the water in the vent. We went back in and got some provisions." He indicated a bag as he shouted down the hall at Lysander. Theirs were the closest living quarters to The Engine Room, so it didn't surprise him that the water had gotten here so fast, "But Tuva isn't here!" Bjørn continued shouting over the rush of water.

"She went to breakfast with Heiká early this morning." Runa's eyes were wide and anxious, her hair sopping wet as it hung around her panicked face, water running down her cheeks, whether tears or fjord water, he couldn't tell. It rocked Lysander to see her sense of calm so completely absent. "We haven't seen her since."

Lysander turned and shouted into the crowd, "Tuva!" but Runa touched his arm, voice trembling dangerously, "She's not here. They will have gone up to C." He nodded curtly, his mind racing, calculating how he was going to get all these people out. The Danish man and his grandsons were still there, shivering in the near-freezing water. Ingrid was huffing as she helped someone who appeared to be injured, her drysuit shoved under her other arm. Tuva would have to hold on a little longer. She was, at least, with Heiká and probably Anders and Aksel, too.

"Then, she's safe for now," he replied, uncoupling the wires that Bjørn had tapped together.

"It hasn't flooded up there?" Runa asked, hopeful. He shook his head.

"No, not yet," Lysander replied, "but it will." Runa nodded solemnly and glanced down at Åsa, who was clutching her notebook in her hand, her trusting eyes watching Lysander's every move in the red-lit hallway.

"I know, Bjørn told me," Runa replied.

"What are you doing?" Bjørn leaned over and asked as Lysander tapped the blue against the green so that all the doors in the hallways opened like the other side had. "Brilliant." Bjørn shifted a backpack on his back and adjusted his glasses as if to say he understood, this was how they could free the people of Mimameid in time.

Water rushed out of the other rooms before the people could, meeting the water in the hallway with a splash so that it rose above their knees. "We have to get everyone to the upper levels," Bjørn told Lysander and he nodded, turning to lead the people onwards. Bjørn doubled back to check that everyone spilling out into the hallway knew to bring their drysuits with them.

With the doors all open and D emptied, Lysander led the charge splashing toward the stairwell, where he opened another bulkhead door so they could start the climb up to level C.

As people started filling up the staircase, packed like animals being led to the slaughter, there was a crackling and an explosion from above their heads. Lysander looked up in time to see the nearest elevator speeding towards them from above, the metal cables snapping and unwinding as if a giant serpent waking from a long slumber. He turned around and shouted down the staircase.

"Take cover!" The elevator sped passed them, the cable whipping around in the air. Lysander threw his arm in front of his face to protect himself as it crashed into the flooded shaft. The crowd on the stairs stood back up, cautiously. Below, the electricity continued crackling as he watched the coils of metal sink below the surface. *Good riddance,* he thought grimly.

Because the stairwell hadn't started flooding yet, they moved faster once they were on the steps. A second elevator crashed down on the other side of the column as they climbed and Lysander watched it go from his perch up the staircase.

Much to his surprise, they arrived to see the doors to C already opened. Anders was hunched over, fiddling with the wires while, even more surprisingly, Yvonne was leaning over him, helping with the coupling. Anders had his weapon slung over one shoulder and a backpack on the other.

"Hey! Anders!" Lysander shouted over the sounds of the people behind him and the Viking man turned, grinning at him.

"Oh hey, engineer! There must be a system failure somewhere in C. I'm trying to rig it so all the doors will open at once, but the systems aren't connected," he explained to him, frustrated. He shrugged off the backpack and handed it to Yvonne.

"Where did you learn how to do that?" Lysander asked Anders and the man threw him a brazen smirk.

"All military recruits learn how to bypass the doors at one point or another. How else are we going to get into the booze supply after hours?" he laughed and Yvonne rolled her eyes. Anders eyed the mass of people building up behind them.

"And what are you doing down here?" Lysander asked Yvonne, a little skeptical that the upper levels would have been able to get help down there faster than he and Bjørn had made it up.

"How do you think Anders knew about your little outburst in Sigrid's office the other day?" She raised an eyebrow at him. "Every good resistance group needs a mole." She winked at him and he found a wave of admiration for her rising up. He should have known. "So, what's with all the people?" she asked him as the stairwell started to fill. Lysander nodded gratefully at her question - D was filling too fast to waste time.

"Listen, we gotta get out of here," he explained to them. "The reason the doors are down is because a pipe burst and the bunker is flooding from the bottom up. The Engine Room is already underwater. We need to evacuate everyone." Anders nodded standing up.

"Evacuate - as in - leave Mimameid?" Yvonne asked, going pale. She tossed her long hair over her shoulder as the news sank in.

"As in get to the surface," Lysander confirmed and Yvonne's mouth hardened. Maybe it had never occurred to her before, the reality of living life Above Ground. Anders stopped tinkering and turned around to look Lysander full in the face.

"*Skít*. It's that bad?"

"Yeah." Lysander's face fell.

"How?" Yvonne asked as someone pushed forward, knocking into Lysander. She was considering something, maybe even something helpful, but he was acutely aware of the people being pushed up the stairs to get away from the rising water so he just shook his head in response.

"No time to explain," he replied and she nodded, curtly, pursing her lips together. Just then the doors burst open ahead of them and Benjáme, Aksel, Milla, and Lasse burst through. They were at the head of a large group of soldiers and stumbling out from behind them was Heiká, hand clasped tightly around Tuva's.

Bjørn rushed forward, wrapping his daughter up in his arms and Runa let out a gasp of relief, a couple of tears escaping her eyes.

"I told you all the military recruits would be fine." Anders winked at Lysander, and Bjørn released Tuva.

"Hey, guys!" Benjáme greeted them cheerfully just as a series of cries started to ripple up the steps. The water was starting to rise up the stairwell. Benjáme exchanged a confused look with Aksel, while Milla and Lasse reached for one another's hands.

"Lysander, it's coming!" He recognized Selby's voice over the screams from below.

"We gotta move!" Lysander instructed, gesturing up the stairs as he looked around at his friends on the threshold of C. "Listen, make sure everyone has a drysuit and then head to The Back Door, yeah?" Lysander said, and Yvonne's face broke out into a smile. She hit Anders on the arm, triumphantly.

"That's perfect. There's a central server in there. You can rewire the entire system from The Back Door. Get the doors back open for all of Mimameid!" She exclaimed.

"Good. Good. That will save time," Bjørn answered for them all. "Then, the upper levels will have time to evacuate, too."

Lysander turned to the people on the steps behind him, guiding them. "Everyone who can keep going up to The Back Door. Get your suits on and swim up to the surface as fast as you can!" He watched Ingrid turn to one of the twins and start passing the message down the line to climb the stairs.

Bjørn forced his way out of the mass of people to grab at Lysander's arm. "Promise me something? If I lose them in the crowd, you look after my family, you hear?"

Lysander nodded and took a hold of Åsa's hand. Åsa grabbed hold of her mother's hand, tightly. They turned to Bjørn and Tuva as a cacophony of screams from above echoed down. There was a horrific snap as a cable gave way and another elevator - this one with people from the upper levels inside - came crashing down the long shaft into the water below.

22
PETRA

THE FLASHING RED LIGHTS were like a heartbeat thrumming over her head. She was crouched in the dark, waiting for the Icelandic gatekeeper to move away from the jammed door to the control room so she wouldn't have to knock him out. Abruptly above her, water started pouring through the air vent. *The vents were flooding. Then her plan was working, so far.* She gulped, hoping Lysander and the others had already discovered her trap and had begun the evacuations. She was counting on him to lead everyone to safety.

Hafthor abandoned the door, crowbar still in hand, and came lumbering over at the sound of water pouring into the hangar.

"*Hlandbrenndu!*" the man swore when he realized what was happening. He reached for a way to close the vent and keep the water out of the hangar, even though his efforts would be futile. There was no stopping it now that The Engine Room was flooded.

Petra seized her chance while Hafthor was distracted and crept along the wall, toward the control booth before he could notice so she could begin phase two of the plan.

She popped open the panel and touched the blue and red wires together just like they had done as new recruits to sneak into restricted areas after hours. It was how she had first seen The Gardens. It had been Anders' idea, to show her a glimpse of her new home, to give her a sense of just how much there was to fight for down here. If only she still believed that. But she wasn't that little girl anymore. The door to the booth gushed open, the sound masked by the rushing of water.

Once she was in the booth, she scanned the controls, looking for a way to open the hangar door. She went down the row, her eyes flitting over every button and switch. Then, she spotted it. Just as she had placed her hand on the lever that would open the door to the fjord, there was a clank from the booth doorway. Hafthor was there and he'd dropped the crowbar.

"How did you get in here?" he asked, his voice full of something she wasn't sure was shock or accusation. "I was trying to open it, but the doors just lowered themselves and wouldn't open back up."

"Old trick from the military," she told him casually and she saw his shoulders relax. He didn't see her as a threat.

"Good. Then we can use that to help get people out. The doors must be down everywhere," he said, clearly not too panicked. "Do you know why there's water leaking out of the air vent?" he asked and she shook her head, face neutral.

"No idea." She needed to get the door closed again so that when she opened the hangar they didn't get flushed out. She tried to keep talking so that Hafthor wouldn't notice her inching across the room. "But yeah, you just cross the red and the blue wires together and the doors open." She reached the panel and ripped it open, taking the blue wire in her hand. "And if you want them to close again you touch it to the yellow one." She demonstrated and the door closed with a decisive slam. One step closer to accomplishing her goal.

"Okay." Hafthor watched her, discomfort creeping into his voice and she felt his eyes following her as she edged back toward the lever. "What are you -" he started to say, but stopped, trying to work it out himself. She clenched her jaw, hoping he would let her by without a fight. "What exactly are you doing down here? Shouldn't you be-" he asked, and then she lunged for the lever, feeling her stitches pull.

He instinctively dove and blocked her. She sidestepped and Hafthor lost his balance. He was enormous, so she had to be quicker than him to beat him. Hafthor jumped back onto his feet and turned to face her, confused.

"What's going on?" he asked and she used his confusion against him, leaping forward and punching him in the trachea to disorient him, not too hard, but enough to buy herself some time. He gasped for air as she ran around behind him, kicking his feet out from under him and forcing him to his knees. "Aren't you a soldier of Mimameid?" he cried out, gravelly, as he jumped back up to face her. He was massaging his throat, looking confused still, but no longer caught off guard. She had lost the element of surprise. "I don't want to hurt you," the Icelander growled, delivering a blow to her gut that made her hiss in pain. But, she could tell he was holding back. She sucked in her breath and dodged a second punch, sliding behind him again. She reached for the crowbar with her fingertips, raised it as high as her stitches would allow, and hit him over the back of his head. He fell to the floor, unconscious immediately.

Her hands flew to her belly, relieved she wasn't bleeding. Maybe she had managed not to tear her stitches after all. Stepping over Hafthor's body and breathing heavily, she wrapped her fingers around the lever. They would be here by now.

She eased the lever back carefully and the great, iron doors creaked open, the blue-green water spilling in through the floodgate and splashing up against the windows of the booth with such strength she expected it to break. She caught her breath as a crack began to crawl across the glass while the seaweed swirled in front of her, ripped up into the current, but the glass held firm.

When the hangar was filled, she heard the bellowing of the ship she thought she would never see in operation.

The bow of the *Nilfheim* glided into view, its vast, metal belly floating in the fjord as a relic of a time forgotten. She had to admit, even with the scrap metal patches to the hull, it took her breath away.

When the submarine was safely inside, Petra heaved the lever back up to close the iron doors. She pressed the button beside the lever and the grates in the floor opened up, the water draining gradually back out into the fjord while the sub lowered down to the floor. The feet of the sub extended, spewing seawater and seaweed out as they collided with the deck of the hangar.

Then the gangway of the ship lowered with the same familiar hiss of all things Mimameid and in one terrifying second, bullets rang out, shattering the glass window of the booth. Petra slammed into the floor, the glass landing around her as she lay in wait. No more gunfire came, so she raised her head cautiously above the console.

Celtic troops were strutting across the hangar deck, the army riled and ready. The first wave of warriors had leaped from the side of the gangway and were pillaging the six-seater pods parked in the hall, as well as all their maintenance equipment. They seemed to be breathing fire, the coals of revenge burning in their eyes. Ciarán followed in their wake, a black cloak billowing out behind him, as he approached the booth with a smoking gun in hand.

He swung himself gracefully over the windowsill of the booth and reached out to her.

"You've done well, Petra," he purred, his eyes shining deep and black as he touched her cheek, gently.

"The Engine Room is compromised," Petra told him, feeling the electricity of his touch, the burning in his eyes, and how badly he wanted to make the Norse pay for the Celts they had slaughtered. "They will have already started evacuating the lower levels." She pointed to where the water was pouring in from the air vent.

"The air filtration system is flooding," she explained. "Sigrid won't know the extent of the damage yet, so you have a good chance of catching her off guard."

"Very good." His voice was smooth, like a stone.

"She will be in her office on the top level, so it will be easy to find her," she told him, but he looked beyond her, his eyes shining with some higher purpose. "Just like we planned," she added as if to remind him that only Sigrid was to be harmed.

"And what about this man? Did you kill him?" Ciarán asked as he gestured to Hafthor and Petra shook her head.

"He's no threat," she said, calmly. The cloaked man clicked his tongue at one of the massive Celtic warriors behind him. The warrior walked forward and raised their weapon to Hafthor's unconscious body.

The shot rang out in the booth and the blood ran from his head into the grooves of the floor before Petra had even opened her mouth in protest. As she looked down at his dead body, the room began to spin above her.

One of the Icelanders. One of the last of a dying breed and she had brought him to slaughter. She closed her eyes and took several deep breaths before she could speak again.

"Why would you do that?" Her voice was quiet, tears burning behind her eyelids.

"He knew you had betrayed them. He could not be allowed to live." Ciarán had deceived her. He wasn't this shining man with the warm, meek eyes. He stood here now, devoid of all empathy, a cruelty seeping into his voice she hadn't heard before. He had only revenge. Revenge against Sigrid. Revenge against the Norse. And she had helped him. She had condemned her people, her friends, to death.

He gestured for the soldiers to form up, beckoning Petra forward. She came, like a dog to her master, afraid of what he might do if she didn't.

She followed over the windowsill, grabbing where her stitches were ripping.

"You stay here. Stall them so we have time to get to the top," he ordered her and then gestured to the man who had shot Hafthor. She thought he was going to shoot her, but instead, he laid a punch clean across her forehead. She felt her head split and blood trickle down to her cheekbone. "Good, very good," Ciarán said, his eyes gleaming. "They can't know you helped us and now they won't suspect." Without hesitation, he raised a bony finger to the door and commanded her. "Show us how to open the doors."

She was sitting in the hangar as the water pouring in from the vent rose around her knees. Her eyes were closed and she was trying to think where she could get something to wrap around her stitches. The only cloth she could think of was Hafthor's clothing and she just couldn't bring herself to take it from his lifeless body floating in the control room. That, or her lace from Arthur.

"Petra!" A voice rang out, warbling over the sound of the rushing water. "Petra!" She opened her eyes and moved her matted, wet hair from her face to see Lysander wading towards her. "You're alive!" His face was grave and his jaw set as blood from his hairline dripped into his eyebrow below. The knife in his hand was also dripping. Behind him, a group of people nursing similar wounds spilled through the doorway into the hangar.

"Oh my god, what happened?" Petra asked as she stood up, her hand pressed to her stomach, although she was pretty sure she knew what had happened. Her heart, at least, was light at the sight of him leading evacuees.

"The Celts ambushed us in the stairwell. Not too bad, right? Considering I never did get those self-defense lessons? How did they even know where Mimameid was? Let alone get in?" he asked her as they both fell into a hug. She sucked in her teeth as he pressed against her stomach, but it was nearly inaudible over the sounds of the people and the water flooding in.

"How do *you* think they knew where we were?" Lysander asked. Petra, thinking quickly, gestured to Hafthor's lifeless body in the booth.

"He let them in. Opened the door and in rode one of the old submarines." She felt another piece of herself dying off as the cruel lie slipped off her tongue.

"I don't believe it..." Lysander looked up at the *Nilfheim* and over the windowsill at Hafthor.

"He must have been working with them." She cast her eyes down as she spoke, hiding her shame inside her grief.

"Hafthor?" He was shocked. Maybe he didn't believe her.

"I couldn't believe it either," she whispered and pressed on her wound.

"That doesn't make sense, " Lysander trailed off, trying to understand.

"I know. And then he attacked me, I had no choice," she added quickly, trying to make herself sound convincing. But Lysander's gaze had shifted. He was distracted enough not to notice how flat her excuses sounded. How Hafthor had a gunshot wound, but she didn't have a gun. No, instead, he was looking around at all the people as they continued spilling into the hangar, spreading out and climbing into their Mimameid-issued drysuits. She watched his brow fold and his chestnut eyes ignite as an idea formed. What did Lysander have planned?

"We can get them all out," he told her, the light spreading from his eyes across his face. "We can get them all out!" he repeated.

"We can?" Petra asked him.

"Yes. All of them. The old, the wounded. Anyone who can't swim. We can put them on the boat and get them out of here!" He started guiding people towards the gangplank up into the submarine. "Can anyone drive something like this?" he asked first, then turned and raised his voice to the people. "Can anyone pilot this thing?"

"I can!" Milla's voice rang out in the crowd as she pushed forward, Lasse not far behind. "My dad was one of the pilots of these back when we first came. He taught me how." *Of course.* Petra had completely forgotten, it had been so long. She felt something like hope inside of her. Maybe she hadn't doomed them all after all. Maybe she had been the one to bring them their salvation from Sigrid.

"Good, good. Get in there and have a look around at the pilots station," Lysander said. He paused to clasp hands with Milla. She nodded to him, an almost amused smile playing on her lips before she turned to Lasse, and the two of them disappeared up the gangplank, into the sub. A man with a long beard, flanked by two identical adult twins approached them.

"Lysander, we can get in there and help assess the ship's logistics if that would help," one of the twins said and Lysander put his hand on the man's shoulder.

"Great idea. Thank you, Arne. Go see what Milla needs and figure out how many people we can fit in that thing," he instructed. The three men nodded and Lysander turned to the rest of them. "Everybody who can swim, should. Old and injured, onto the boat. Everyone else, put on your suits and grab a helmet."

Lysander pointed to an old man with a long, grey-red beard who, Petra realized when he spoke, was the old Celt that she had heard lived like a hermit down in D.

"Ned, you should get on the boat, there's no need for you to swim if you don't have to," Lysander told him, but the man spoke with the stubbornness of a Celt that Petra had grown rather fond of during her time in their camp.

"Don't be ridiculous. I lived for decades on an island in the middle of the Arctic Circle. I'm swimming and you can't stop me." The old man pulled his foot out of the rising water and stuck a comically thin leg into the pants of his drysuit, while Lysander rolled his eyes, holding the man steady by his arms.

"Fine, but be careful." He moved around to get the old man a helmet and then looked over at Petra. "Are you okay?" he asked her, pointing down to where her fingers were pressed against her body, soaked in watery blood.

"Oh," she exclaimed, looking down at it. She was so paralyzed by all that was happening, she'd completely forgotten. "Yeah, my stitches ripped." She pulled open the side of the jumpsuit and showed him where. He grimaced and shook his head.

"Bjørn!" Lysander waved over a man wearing thick-rimmed glasses, his hair pulled back out of his heavily-lined face. The man looked bone-weary but bounced over to them with an energy that surprised Petra. "Do you have anything to stop the bleeding?" Lysander asked and he nodded, grabbing a bag from a woman beside him with sopping wet hair and soft features, even in the harsh, red light. Bjørn produced a roll of duct tape from it.

"Only this." His face was apologetic. Petra bit her lip. It wasn't the best fix, but it was a fix. Lysander looked over at Petra, his face mirroring Bjørn's apology.

"Do it," she told them and Lysander squeezed her shoulder, gently.

"Bjørn will patch you up, I have to see if I can find a central server around here somewhere. We have to open all the doors so the rest of the people can get out," he explained as she found a small, grateful smile for him. This was the Lysander she had hoped for when she'd made her plan with Siobhan.

"Lysander, over here!" The voice that spoke was, much to Petra's surprise, Yvonne's, who had yelled at him from inside the control booth. Lysander gave Petra one more look and then went to Yvonne.

"Sorry about this in advance," Bjørn told her, ripping off a piece of duct tape with his teeth.

"It's better than nothing," she replied grimly, scanning the people in the hangar as Bjørn started taping her wound closed. There were far more injured than she had expected. The old hobbling around, children wailing as they clutched at their wounds. Had it all happened because of the flooding? She hesitated, unsure if she really wanted to know the answer. "What happened with the Celts in the stairwell?" she asked, slowly. The man adjusted his glasses on the bridge of his nose and the woman beside him knelt to help a younger girl with ash-blonde hair into her drysuit, a fearful look in her eyes.

"I've never seen anyone fight like that. Killing innocent men and women like that. Cutting through the old and the children like they are waves in the water. They fight like they are possessed by some strange evil." Bjørn's words chilled her. "Thank the gods we had C with us. I don't think so many would have made it if they hadn't been there to protect us." His words rang in her ears. "And their leader -" Bjørn stopped himself at a sharp look from the woman beside him as she pulled up the zipper of her daughter's jumpsuit. He looked instead at Petra. "All done," he told her with a grim smile and tossed the duct tape back into the duffel bag. She moved her body left and right to test out the pull. It was uncomfortable, but not overly painful.

Onni and Benjáme broke through the crowd, both of them soaked in blood that didn't appear to be their own. They reached out for her and the three of them hugged, without even thinking.

"Private, where's Aksel?" she asked when they had pulled back, scanning the crowd behind them. Benjáme's face was already grave.

"He didn't make it, sir, I'm sorry." Petra's stomach dropped, picturing the hard-headed Dane. He'd been young, too young. And this was another death she was responsible for.

"Who was it? Did you see?" she asked although she wasn't sure she wanted to know the answer.

"The big one, at the head of the hoard. Aksel held his own against him. And he died a good death, a warrior's death." Petra felt her blood going cold. Ciarán had promised her. He'd promised they were only after Sigrid. But Arthur had been right. "Lieutenant, you need to hear what Onni has to say." Benjáme put an arm out to her as he spoke. She swallowed back her grief and nodded.

"Yes?"

"Sir, this is a classic Celtic strategy. They've been doing this for centuries, guerrilla tactics meant to disorient. By getting inside the bunker, they've already gotten behind enemy lines, but this is clearly a well-planned attack. I wouldn't be surprised if they were somehow behind the malfunction in The Engine Room, too. It's too much of a coincidence not to be."

Petra's stomach dropped again and she felt the blood drain from her face. "The problem now is they are behind enemy lines, but they wouldn't be here unless they had something else up their sleeve," Onni continued. "They are well known for suicide bombing missions. They could have set it off in The Engine Room or they could have another one already planted on Mimameid."

"You think they're behind The Engine Room?" Bjørn asked incredulously. "How?"

"Typically, they operate by planting a mole."

"You don't think-" Bjørn glanced over at Ned, almost comically struggling to get into his drysuit, beard dripping with Celtic blood.

"I don't know anyone *less* sympathetic to the Celts. And neither do you," the soft-featured woman beside him said, skeptically. Bjørn looked guilty for even thinking it.

"You're right," he told her and squeezed her hand.

"It's usually someone less obvious, someone everyone else overlooks," Onni continued, impatiently. "But, we don't have time for this now. You're not listening to me." She was getting frustrated with them. "Something else, some other wave is coming. This isn't over."

"We have to get these people out," Petra agreed, hoping her guilt over being that mole wasn't obvious on her face. She wasn't sure how to help, but was starting to feel lightheaded from the blood loss and had the sinking feeling that Onni was right. She could see from the state of the others around her that the Celts had done much worse to them than to her.

She felt herself reeling with nausea. Would she be caught? Would she be punished for the people whose blood was on her hands? The voice of the old Celtic man stuck out, loud and uncouth among the Nordic lilts, jarring her back.

"I've got it! I've got it!" Ned was yelling as an elderly woman tried to help him with his helmet. "Bugger off!" He swatted her and the woman looked at him, a growl rising on her face.

"Liddie!" Bjørn waved his hand for the woman to come over to where they were standing. "Let me help you get a drysuit on," he offered and she nodded. Bjørn and the little blonde girl beside him each took hold of one of Liddie's arms as she stepped into her suit.

"Are you sure you don't want to ride on the boat? It will be a lot more comfortable. And a lot drier," Bjørn told her.

"You want me to ride on a boat to the Land of Mist? Bjørn, dear, have you not listened to any of the stories I've been telling?" He helped her get her arms in one by one. "No, thank you. I prefer to swim."

Lysander and Yvonne had appeared again, each wearing their drysuits, with one in hand. Yvonne passed it over to Petra.

"That's for you. My mom grabbed as many extras as she could from The Closet before heading down here," she told her. "One of the perks of working upstairs." She smiled and a woman with mousy, brown hair Petra thought she had seen on the upper levels from time to time came up from behind and gave the group a friendly smile.

"Thanks." Petra nodded her gratitude to them both and gingerly stepped into it, one foot at a time. Lysander held out his arm to help steady her. She pulled the zipper up tenderly past her stomach, discreetly tucking the lace into the edge of the duct tape for safekeeping. She bit her lip thinking of Arthur.

Suddenly, Milla came bounding out of the boat, pushing her way through the crowd of people getting on.

"Everybody off!" she shouted. "Everybody off the boat! Get everyone out of here!" Lasse was right behind her, helping turn people around and head back down the gangplank. The three other men who had gone in to help stumbled back toward Lysander, their faces crestfallen, while Milla and Lasse continued herding people off the boat.

"Selby, what's going on?" Lysander dropped Petra's arm and Yvonne caught her.

"They rigged it. They rigged the damn thing!" the bearded man called Selby shouted, he turned to the one twin who had spoken earlier, Arne,

"It's set to self-destruct in less than twenty minutes," Arne confirmed.

"Twenty minutes?" Lysander shouted and Petra gaped. She couldn't believe that Ciarán would do that. But Arthur could believe that. Arthur had seen him for who he was. They were going to blow themselves up along with any Norse who were still inside when it happened. And then she remembered the Celtic car bombs Onni had just taught them about.

"I *told* you guys! It's a suicide mission!" Onni had fire in her eyes and Benjáme drew his weapon.

"We have to get everyone out of here. *Now*." Milla had returned to them and reached over to zip up Petra's drysuit.

"Okay, pass out whatever helmets we have," Lysander instructed, making a plan. Selby, Anders, and Yvonne nodded. "We can start loading people into the antechamber, get as many people out as possible before it blows."

"Lysander," Milla pressed, sternly, "there is no time. We have to get out, now. As far away from the bomb as possible."

But then it was as if a lightbulb had gone off in Lysander's head.

"The Observation Deck," he said. "We break the glass and then we can get out through The Observation Deck. It'll buy us enough time to get away from the bomb and continue the evacuation." Milla nodded curtly, in agreement, but Petra had known her long enough to see that she was still considering something behind her hazel eyes. Something Petra didn't like. She felt her stomach tighten and it had nothing to do with her wound. Milla turned to the crowd and shouted over the chatter,

"Everybody who can, grab a helmet and head to The Observation Deck!"

There were a few groans from the people, so Lysander jumped up onto the gangplank. Petra watched him, in awe that this was the same gawky man she had rescued back in the wilderness. Despite the pain from her belly and the chaos around them, she found herself warmed with a sense of pride for Lysander.

"There is a bomb aboard the ship!" A few screams and gasps rang out, but Lysander raised his hand, quieting them. "We don't have much time, but we can still make it if we get up to The Observation Deck and break through the glass. I want everyone to grab a helmet and start moving upstairs," He pointed to Yvonne, Selby, and the twins. "You guys, help pass them out." Then he gestured to Anders, Onni, and Benjáme, "You three, start leading the people up to the deck. Listen to me. *We are going to get you out.*"

He jumped back down and grabbed a helmet, passing it over to Petra. "Come on!" He took her by the hand and pulled her through the crowd, toward the head of the column.

23

LYSANDER

"Listen, I'm going to stay here and make sure everyone gets out," Milla told him softly, under her breath. The only other person who was close enough to hear was Lasse. Milla's hand gripped Lysander's wrist viciously, her fingernails digging into his skin. She yanked back the sleeve of his jumpsuit and tapped at his band. "I'm setting a timer to go off in twenty minutes." Lysander looked down at her and she swiped frantically left and right. "You have to be clear of the bunker by then, do you understand?" He nodded. Milla's face was hard, "You get them all to safety," she said through gritted teeth. His jaw tightened. What was she going to do? Without blinking, she let go of Lysander and started herding people away, helping them into their drysuits and adjusting their helmets. Suddenly, Lasse grabbed at her hand and pulled her close, enveloping her. He took her face in his hands and leaned his forehead against hers - desperately, privately - the water swirling around them, now up to their thighs. Milla paused and looked up, staring deeply into Lasse's eyes. Lysander saw a smile flit across her face and she whispered, "There you are." They embraced and then turned back to face Lysander.

"Go on," she commanded them both, and then to Lysander, "I'll be right behind you." There was a small, final flicker of something which passed between Lasse and Milla, and then with a soft twitch of her lips, she was gone in the crowd.

Lysander nodded sharply to Lasse and hiked up his helmet under his arm. He turned to Petra, who was watching where Milla had been and was about to call out to her when suddenly the red lights above them started to flash. An auto-announcement played overhead with the chipper female voice - Yvonne's voice. The crowd of people froze to listen. For a split-second everything was still, but for the rushing of water.

"More than fifty percent of the structure has been compromised. Please commence evacuation." He looked over at Yvonne and her eyes rolled.

"Perfect!" she spat sarcastically as the message began from the beginning. "Exactly what I wanted my final memory of Mimameid to be."

Much to Lysander's surprise, instead of inciting more panic, the people simply resumed passing out helmets and grouping together around the remaining soldiers of C, their faces steely. He was impressed by their determination, but, of course, these people had nearly drowned in their bunks and then fought off the Celts. And that was just today. They'd been pushed to the breaking point over and over again by Ragnarök, by Celtic invasion, by Sigrid, and they were still here, still surviving.

"Hey, at least the noise will cover us while we move," Anders pointed out, "and who wouldn't be afraid of such a fearsome voice?" He winked at Yvonne and she stuck out her tongue in reply.

"Come on, guys," Lysander said, glancing nervously down at the countdown on his band. Seventeen minutes. He drew the Celtic knife from his waistband before zipping up his drysuit and flipping it around in his hand. He saw Benjáme standing in front of Selby, Ingrid, and the twins. Benjáme's fingers were white-knuckled around his bone-blade. Anders and Yvonne were beside Heiká, who had a hold of Tuva's hand. Bjørn had Åsa on his back in the rising water, while Runa wore the backpack. When he turned to look behind, he saw Onni carrying one of Åsa's playmates on her hip, flanked by the old Danish man along and his young grandsons, their faces streaked with tears and blood. Petra had gravitated towards Ned, who was still arguing with

Liddie. Lysander smiled to see that they had found themselves someone to protect them. He straightened up.

They waded cautiously, through the door of the hangar, and through the antechamber where he had hung up his gear for swimming. The water rushed up behind Lysander and swept him back out into the dark hallway, where their enemy was waiting.

He approached the first turn, knife shaking in his hand, the squelch of the blade as it entered the Celt he'd injured still ringing in his ears. Anders chambered a round in his gun next to Lysander, but when they turned the corner, the hallway was clear, except for a few floating bodies - whether Norse or Celt, he couldn't tell and he wasn't sure he wanted to know. The Celtic army had already swept through here and moved on. Anders nodded to him to signal it was all clear and Lysander let out a breath he didn't realize he'd been holding. If they had already been here, then they would have taken the main staircase to get to the upper levels. They couldn't risk being that close to the Celts.

"Is there a back way to get to The Observation Deck?" Lysander called out in the darkness to Anders, but it was a voice from behind him - a young, female voice - that responded.

"Yes!" Lysander turned around. It was Åsa who had spoken. She slid from her father's back and pushed her way forward in the hallway. The water was up to her chest. "I know a way," she said. "It's how I used to get there from school without being seen. Cover me?"

The words felt odd to Lysander coming out of this little girl, but then, she had grown up during Ragnarök. Heiká stepped forward to guard her back, letting go of Tuva's hand to steady his hold around the grip of his gun. Lysander glanced over at Bjørn, who managed to mask his worry behind his disheveled hair and askew glasses. Her father was frightened, but Lysander saw in the lines on his face that he trusted Åsa. Lysander tried to look back and see where Petra was, but she had been pushed too far away for him to make her out. Åsa turned them down a hallway in the flashing darkness, then indicated right. Anders and Heiká checked that it was clear before they continued on, Åsa wading behind them.

The initial shock of the attack and the adrenaline from the fight with the Celts had kept Lysander from really feeling the icy water, but as they made their way along, the reality of how cold the fjord was started to creep up his body. He tried to flex his stiff fingers around the handle of the knife, running his other hand through his hair, nervously. He thought of his sister and her charm, far away, protecting Linnaea. He didn't regret giving it to her, but the last time he'd been lost in the icy water, he'd had her charm to hold onto. At least this time he had a drysuit.

They came to the entrance to the back stairwell and Åsa silently pointed upwards. Anders took one cautious step forward before they saw a shadow moving in the red glow on the stairs, followed by shouts in rough Gaelic. Both Heiká and Anders flattened themselves back against the wall. Lysander pressed a finger to his lips and Åsa nodded silently in response. Runa reached out from the other side of Bjørn to press Åsa back with one protective arm, the others behind them quietly falling into the line. The Celtic voices echoed off the concrete, filling the back stairwell with the clanging and rolling of their mother tongue.

They held their breaths and listened to the voices fade down a corridor above - Lysander silently praying to the All-father that it wasn't the same hallway they were headed towards to get to The Observation Deck. The alarm time on his band glowed. Thirteen minutes.

He looked back and saw Liddie hush a guffawing Ned a few paces back. He wondered if anyone else was praying to the gods with him.

When the voices were gone, they tip-toed up the stairs as quickly as possible, up and out of the water until Åsa held up her hand, stopping them. The lights flashed and Yvonne's cheerful voice continued on a loop as Anders and Héika checked the hallway for Celts. Anders nodded.

"It's clear, let's go," Heiká whispered and Lysander started to lead them out of the stairwell. He had just located the door to The Observation Deck ahead of him when a Celt stalked around the corner, his blood-streaked face with teeth bared now between them and their way out.

Shocked, Lysander raised the knife and plunged it deep into the chest of the looming Celt. It came out with a sickening thunk that made Åsa squeal as the body dropped to the floor.

"Not bad, B-level," Anders told him with a pat on the back, but Lysander felt the weight of the blade in his hand as he stepped over the Celt's body. He saw Åsa looking down at the body as she side-stepped around the fallen warrior and he felt ashamed. Her face was a mix of relief and terror - the man's eyes were still opened, glassy and red in the light - as if he might jump back up and grab her around the throat. But, she set her jaw and nodded her thanks to Lysander, tossing her sopping wet hair over her shoulder as if to put the incident behind her. Of the two of them, he definitely felt Åsa was the braver soldier than he.

Åsa was the first to reach the door of The Observation Deck. When Lysander joined her, he looked back down the line at the group of people filling up the hallway, people he had promised to save. He had to think fast about how they were going to be able to breach the glass. His mind was racing and he felt almost ridiculous for asking, "Anyone got any explosives?" It was as if Anders had been waiting for that moment. He reached into his backpack, producing a handful of flares with a grin on his face.

"Will this do?" he asked and Lysander sheathed his knife.

"Bjørn!" he roared, without looking away from Anders. "I'm going to need that duct tape!" Bjørn clambered up the hallway around Åsa and the soldiers, tossing Lysander the roll with a tense grin on his face. Lysander caught it in his free hand. This, this was something he was made for.

"Let's do this." Bjørn needed no explanation to have worked out what Lysander's plan was. "Lucky someone brought something along that was useful," he said, adjusting his glasses and taking the flares from Anders' outstretched arms.

"For it to work though, we have to be able to close the door again," Lysander said, this time it was Petra's voice that rose and answered him from down the hall.

"You just have to rewire the panel again." She hurried towards them, stepping over the dead Celt as she approached. "Connect blue to yellow." Lysander was glad she was with them, even though she looked wretched and feral in the glow of the red light, her wild hair soggy and the cut across her determined brow congealed with blood.

"Okay. Bjørn and I will go in and set the charges, can you prepare the panel so it will close the second we get back?" Lysander put a hand on her shoulder.

"And then?" Petra asked.

"We blow it open. And swim," he said resolutely and she nodded. Her face was pale, but her jaw was set.

"Away from the bomb?" she said skeptically, but the kind of skeptical that could be easily overridden by doing something heroically reckless.

"The Celts are above us, the water is below us. There are twelve minutes left. It's our only choice." He wondered briefly what had happened to her with the Celts back in the hangar or maybe while she had still been their prisoner, but he pulled his thoughts back to the task at hand. "Okay?" he asked and she nodded again, a flicker of fire sparking in her golden eyes.

"Okay," she replied. Lysander gestured to Bjørn, and they ducked through the doorway, the piezo crystals lighting up a brilliant blue as they walked. It was still deafeningly quiet here.

"It's a pity we have to destroy something so elegantly engineered, isn't it?" Lysander reminisced sadly as he watched the blue fade after each of his footsteps.

"Don't worry, Lysander," Bjørn said, "there will be more opportunities to make art again." He looked at him kindly, the blue reflecting in his glasses, "to find beauty and to create." His usually industrious voice had thickened with wisdom, with promise.

In the silence, Lysander could pretend the water wasn't rising and the bomb in the hangar wasn't counting down. He could pretend he was hearing

Åsa's voice bounce off the glass walls. He lifted his hand, long fingers sprawled, placing it on the outer window as iridescent fish flitted away into the beckoning seaweed. A whoosh from the hallway snapped him back to reality. He shook his head as though he was knocking water from his ears.

"Bundle up the flares you have and position them in the right corner between the floor and the ceiling, at the joint where they meet," he instructed Bjørn, but the older man had already started bundling.

"Where it's weakest?" Bjørn pushed his glasses up the bridge of his nose and Lysander nodded in confirmation.

"Exactly. I'll take the left side. Then we can light them up together." They made short work of it and when the flares were taped down, they counted back from three and ignited them together.

The flares lit up with a sparkle in the dark, meanwhile, Bjørn and Lysander turned and made for the door they had come from. Mid-step, Lysander realized the second door to The Observation Deck had been activated when they'd freed the upper levels from the central server at The Back Door. It would need to be closed, or else the explosion would kill everyone in the hallway. Without thinking, he pivoted and dived across the room to get to the other door in time, the piezo crystals lighting his path in the darkness as he slid over the threshold. He could barely make out Bjørn's objections from across the room while Petra coupled up the wires and the door across him slid shut.

His heart was pounding in his ears. Lysander pried off the paneling with his Celtic knife, listening to the sound of the flares burning, bright and hot, and waiting for the sound that meant they had burned down. The glass started to glow, reacting to the heat, and cold sweat broke out across his brow as he yanked out the wiring. What had Petra said? He tried to steady his breathing. Blue to yellow. Blue to yellow. The sound of the flares fizzled into silence and his hands trembled as he touched the two wires together, the door sliding shut, just as the explosion erupted.

The water pounded against the doors with such force, he thought it was a second explosion. And his first thought was that the Celts would have undoubtedly heard the noise. Seven minutes. Their final countdown to getting everyone out into the fjord safely had just begun.

He gestured down the hall at Onni and Benjáme to come towards him. If they used both doors, then they could get people out into the water more quickly. They were going to have to fight against the force of the water pouring into the bunker hallways, but as long as all the doors within the rest of the bunker remained open, they should be able to get everyone out before the hallways filled up completely. He hoped A and B had been able to get out through the dome at the top.

Onni and Benjáme came towards him, people from back down the hallway filing in behind them. He heard Bjørn shout from down the hall.

"Helmets on! Lysander? You ready?"

"Ready!" he replied, securing his own helmet and feeling the hermetic seal close around his neck. He caught his breath and he thought about being tossed in the frigid North Sea waters between Old Denmark and home, fighting to get back to his sister. He let out the air in his lungs slowly. *This time was different,* he reminded himself.

Benjáme and Onni both secured their helmets and the people behind them followed suit. "Brace yourselves!" Lysander shouted back.

He touched the red and blue wires together, grabbing hold of the door frame and flattening himself back, away from the opening.

The door snapped open so fast that the impact didn't cause it to break off, but the water rushed in with such force he thought a hole had been punched clean through his chest. He closed his eyes as the water rushed over him - out of instinct, he thought - and when he took his next breath he was able to open them again to the rushing water.

He heaved himself over the threshold, throwing himself against the wall of what had previously been The Observation Deck. The water was still rushing in, filling the space inside and pressing against him.

With a groan, he flipped over and offered a hand to Onni, pulling her up over the threshold and onto the wall. She nodded once she was secure. She smiled through her helmet, putting her hand over her heart in thanks. He responded in kind, feeling himself soften at the gesture, and then pushed off the wall into the water, fighting his way out of the suction, up and up toward the surface.

Looking briefly back down, he saw that Benjáme had exited and was helping Ingrid through the door. Over to his right, Anders threw Lysander a thumbs up, Yvonne had Åsa's hand, Heiká had Tuva's, and Bjørn had Runa's. Petra was already through, seemingly leading Liddie and Ned, who followed closely behind, away from the bunker.

She was just ahead of Ned, the light of her helmet gleaming in the water. Lysander pushed himself forward in the water to reach her, his head getting light with the effort. He extended a hand out to her foot and she turned, startled. Her golden eyes betrayed some desperation that he wished he could ask her about, but instead he just turned his microphone on.

"Your stomach doing okay?" He gestured to her wound and tried not to sound overly concerned at the blood she had lost. Petra nodded to him, the desperation shadowed with something he thought might be sadness. They didn't have time for more than that now. He nodded in response and saw the reflection of something massive in Petra's helmet. He jerked around and saw a great shadow emerging from the base of Mimameid. The name of the shadow was scrawled on the side of it. *Nilfheim.*

There was only one person who could be driving it. Milla hadn't come up to The Observation Deck with them. She had stayed behind to try and buy them more time. They watched it glide out of the docking hangar, so small against the size of Mimameid itself. Lysander glanced down at his band. 00:00. The countdown was over.

The *Nilfheim* exploded in a burst of force, sending Lysander tumbling through the waves, bubbles spinning before his eyes as he held onto his helmet. His stomach twisted and writhed. The pressure in his ears was pounding. His eyes went black for a moment and he was floating in the Old

North Sea again, gasping for air, trying to figure out what was up and what was down.

A firm hand grabbed hold and steadied him in the fjord. Liddie's eyes were calm as she held onto his helmet with both hands and pressed it against hers. He tried to orient himself. Her grip was surprisingly strong and her cornflower eyes focused him through the terror of the water, as one thought lifted to the surface. Milla was gone.

He glanced down as they both struggled to swim away from the suction of the boat and he saw that the blast had been large enough to tear gaping holes into the bottom of Mimameid. But the *Nilfheim* sank into the darkest part of the water, as if in slow motion, before coming to a crashing halt at the bottom of the fjord, kicking sand and seaweed up into the water in spirals and bursts.

"Come on." Liddie's voice was thin, but powerful in his ears as she released him. He steadied his breathing once again and turned away from Mimameid, trying not to think of the people trapped inside. Enough of them must have made it out. They had to.

There was, after all, a whole horde of people behind them, both already swimming and still pushing their way out of the remains of The Observation Deck below. Mimameid was crumbling, but there were still people who had managed to escape and he was one of them. He squeezed Liddie's hand in thanks.

Rounding the bend where he had met the orcas all that time ago, he passed Onni, Selby, and the twins, then Bjørn and his family, before pushing onwards. They had begun their final ascent in the water outside the coastal village by the time he had caught up to Anders and Petra at the head of the group.

A sense of anticipation rose, as he felt the group ascending to the surface. It was as though he'd been holding his breath since his dream from the Norns and at long last, he would be able to let it out.

He didn't know if he was imagining the light coming through the surface of the water, but he reached for it, and the brightness that awaited him there.

His head broke the surface and with a gasp, he ripped off his helmet and sucked in the air, greedily. There was something familiar about it. He breathed in the scent of smoke and ash, a smell that brought him back to cold nights together with Magdelena and Linnaea in the Scandinavian backcountry, crisp and wild. Then he saw the source of the smell.

The coastal village was ablaze, a cloud of thick, black smoke rising from it like an omen of death. The row houses that had dotted the water's edge with brilliant colors were now a wall of flames, the sounds of the villagers' screams echoing across the surface of the water. The carnage was more than he could stomach.

They had thought that the *Nilfheim* explosion was the only surprise awaiting them, but they had underestimated their enemy.

Lysander paddled toward the flames, past Petra and Anders and Bjørn, in desperation. The screams weren't only the villagers. From the water, he saw piles of bodies stacked along the beach bearing the insignia of Mimameid across the back of their diving suits. His heart sank as he made out one distinctive body in the pile. The small girl from B with the long skinny braids and glasses, now twisted and broken across her round, still face. The citizens from the upper levels had indeed evacuated when the doors of Mimameid had been reopened. They had made it to the surface and there, like lambs at slaughter, they had been cut down.

"Stay away from the shore!" he shouted over his shoulder at the splashing around him. He watched one of the Danish man's boys with the big ears help his grandfather towards the shoreline. Lysander grabbed at the boy, trying to pull him back and his head bobbed under the water before he came back up coughing and sputtering. He brushed Lysander off.

"What are you doing?" Lysander yelled, but the boy ignored him and continued onwards.

Along the edge of the boardwalk, he could see that the Celts were hanging the dead, as if to taunt them, "Come get your dead and see if we can't get you to join them".

The buildings burned, bright with Celtic fire, and the streets were lined with the bodies of their fellow Nordmenn.

Lysander felt his heart drop with panic and realization. Petra looked over at him, her tawny eyes exasperated, savage.

"Where else can we go? We don't have a choice," she told him.

"She's right," Onni agreed, grimly, bobbing as she spoke, "we'll freeze if we stay in here." They paused, hearing the panic ripple through the people as they continued to breach the surface and to see that they were trapped by the mass of Celtic forces forming up on the edge of the water. Even Anders was without words.

"There's a cove." Lasse swam over to them. In the reflection of the Celtic fire on the water, there was more life in Lasse's eyes than Lysander had seen in his eyes since The Infirmary. Lysander looked at him, this Viking man who had once laughed with Linnaea so gently, and saw the mix of pain and resolve quivering in his brow. Whatever Mimameid had tried to manipulate him with was broken now, as splintered as the bunker itself. This was a man who had been reawakened by the explosion, knowing he could not save Milla, but that perhaps he could save the rest of them. He inclined his head to Lysander, determination set in his jaw.

"I know the one!" Yvonne shouted over the noise, "I've seen it on enough reports. They won't think it's passable, which is why we usually used it for supply drops." Lasse nodded in agreement.

"That's the one," he confirmed with a friendly hand on Yvonne's shoulder, "follow me." Lasse turned and started swimming, guiding anyone that would follow, but there seemed to be enough military and Resistance members who trusted him. Gradually, and with some reluctance, the other groups started peeling off towards yet another unknown, giving a final longing look at the burning shoreline.

Lysander held back, directing survivors where to go and. As they splashed in the water around him, he realized that the taste of the fjord on his lips and in the back of his throat had an odd bitterness to it. The stuffed reindeer the small girl had been clutching in her hands down in D floated passed him, the fur sticky and matted. The girl was nowhere to be seen. There was something off, something wrong.

As though it were some epic tale from the sagas, he heard a vicious female voice call out into the thin, smoky air, and a row of bowmen on the shore released a volley of flame-tipped arrows into the darkened sky.

They hit the surface so quickly, he almost didn't believe what was happening until the blue flame ripped across the surface of the water. Shrieks resonated up the cliff sides of the fjord in willowy anguish.

They rang in his ears like a siren call as Lysander dove beneath the surface.

When he came back up for air, an arrow whizzed past his ear, narrowly missing his head. It was the same ear the Celtic girl had nicked with her knife. He felt something like a phantom cut, but when he raised his hand to the spot, there was no blood.

In the chaos, the only person he could make out ahead of him in the water was Petra, so he dove back under and followed her. After a minute, he lost sight of her again amongst the floating bodies. When he came up again, she had heaved herself out of the water on the edge of a cliffside and thrown her helmet aside, her flaming hair caught in a violent coastal wind as she started to scale the rock face. She stumbled and lost her grip, landing on a shelf of rock and clutching where Bjørn had duct taped her stitches closed.

Far off to the left, he saw the trail of people who had followed Lasse around a bend in the coastline and into the aforementioned cove. He saw Selby following Benjáme, and Anders and Yvonne with an arm around Ned and Liddie, respectively. Bjørn's family had been at the front of the group, so he assumed they had already ducked out of view and into safety.

Lysander bobbed for a moment and wondered why Petra wasn't following them. He looked up at her, fair against the dark rocks, and back over at the group he knew he should be following to safety. Was it possible she knew a faster way up the cliff? She'd been on enough missions Above Ground that there could be a chance she knew a shortcut. Still, it was odd.

He waited until she had resumed her climb, then pulled himself out of the water and onto the rock shelf where she had been, a few drops of blood left behind from her wound. He looked out into the fjord, littered with bodies. He spotted Ingrid among them, halfway heaved up onto a piece of wreckage with a flaming arrow stuck into her, her skin pale and cold. He felt a gasp escape him and fought the urge to jump back in the water to retrieve her. Heavily, he tore his gaze away from her lifeless body and instead kept one eye on the group following Lasse into the cove, simultaneously beginning his ascent up the rock face after Petra.

She summited and disappeared over an outcropping of rocks as he pulled himself up, carefully trying to stay hidden enough from the Celts so as not to get shot at by more flaming arrows. He could hear the same malevolent female voice over and over against the echo of the cliffs, a white-hot rage that rang against the pillars of the fjord like organ pipes in an ancient cathedral, as she bellowed her commands below.

By the time he had summited the snowy crag, Petra had shed her drysuit and disappeared from view, but he could still see over into the cove where the others had swam and the rock face they were ascending. Perhaps she really had just taken another route away from the Celts? He didn't see her copper head dotting among the people already scattered along the top of the crag. He shimmied out of his drysuit and scanned further along the ridge line, trying to stay low to the iced ground as he did. The wind was biting cold through his thermal and jumpsuit, and if he stood up, he could see the far edge of the village below. The Celts could see him, too, if they knew where to look.

Even from this distance, he could make out the mass of Celtic troops down in the village. If their commander decided to march them up and out of the north side of town, it wouldn't take long to find the remaining survivors on the crag. They needed to move. Fast.

He pushed off in one movement and sprinted across the ridge as fast as his exhausted legs would take him. Staying bent against the hellacious wind, he watched the Celts down below, the female voice still ringing in the air. The snow here was only a dusting and the air was thin. The sky to his right was thick with black smoke, and the ridge to the left was clouded and grey. The first of the survivors were completing their climb.

Lysander arrived at the crag to see Anders, dangling and tied to Liddie as he heaved the two of them up the rock face. He reached down to give them a last boost up over the edge, trying to suppress a groan as he did. It didn't work. Anders alone was pure muscle, and the little weight Liddie did add was too much for Lysander. Instead, Lysander stretched his arm out to Liddie. They fumbled with each other's fingertips for a desperate moment. He extended his arm down further and felt her strong, bony fingers clamp around his forearm. He pulled with everything he had left.

Anders gasped for breath as he clawed his way over the summit, collapsing, exhausted. Lysander untied Liddie and helped her to her feet. As he helped her, she shed her drysuit layer and took his face in her hands. At first, he thought she was going to kiss him, or thank him, but then he saw her blue eyes were clouded.

"The girl," she said to him, her voice thick as she turned her head towards the village. *Who did she mean?*

"What girl?" He shook his head, confused. "Petra?" Liddie didn't answer but shifted her gaze back and forth on his face. A knot untwisted inside of him. It wasn't Petra she was talking about.

He felt a brief pang, but there was no time to act on it. "Listen," he told Liddie, "we have to get out of here. They aren't far behind and they will come for us. Follow Lasse. Follow the ridge north." He pointed the way to Anders and dropped to his knees to help Benjáme and Onni both summit the crag. Benjáme drew his antler-bone knife as soon as he had stripped his drysuit, while Onni turned to help Selby, whose old arms were shaking, get up. The twins weren't far away, heaving as they pulled off their drysuits.

Lysander tucked his knife into his waistband again to extend a hand to Bjørn, and together they yanked Runa and Åsa over the edge. Heiká had his arm wrapped around Tuva as they both collapsed to the right of them.

"We have to get out of here," Lysander said to everyone. "The Celts are just over the ridge down in the village."

"But what about the people from A and B? Shouldn't we at least try to help them?" Runa asked him, reaching out to hug Åsa, who was shivering in the cold.

"You saw the boardwalk, right? Do you honestly think anyone is still alive?" Benjáme asked her, his face desperate. Runa hung her head and Lysander saw her jaw tighten.

"Not all of them were bad, you know. Some were just children," she replied, her head still bowed, as she fiddled with the zipper on Åsa's drysuit. Åsa, who had already seen the worst of humanity, the worst of Lysander, and still she trusted him.

"We can't sacrifice the few Norse that are left to rescue people who might not even be alive. That's insane," Benjáme pressed, glancing around for support from the others. They avoided his gaze. It was a decision no one wanted to make.

"He's right," Anders admitted, as he approached them, having helped several more from D, including Ned, over the edge, "we'd be walking into a slaughter." He put his hand on Lysander's shoulder and it made Lysander jump.

"What do you say, Lysander?" he asked.

"Me?" he responded, but everyone else around him was quiet, waiting.

"Look, Milla trusted you. That's good enough for me." Anders' voice was calm, final. He had seen what happened to Milla, and Lysander noticed that he squeezed Yvonne's hand as she joined him at his side. She also wore a look of determination as she pulled her long hair up and out of her face into a ponytail.

Lysander ran his fingers through his hair and looked over to the people following after Lasse along the ridge line. Liddie, far ahead, but going slowly, turned around and sternly met his gaze, as though she could hear every word of the conversation.

There they all were, helping each other up over the edge, piling their drysuits high and moving north. Would Milla be proud of them, he wondered, or would she be ashamed they were leaving their kinsmen behind?

"We will try to find anyone we can. Anyone who escaped," Lysander promised Runa with a nod of his head. "But, not right now. Right now we have to run." He pointed at Benjáme and Onni. "You guys know a place we can go, right?"

"Yes." The Sámi's gaze was steely and his tattooed neck flexed, dauntlessly.

"Can you get us there?" Lysander asked him and Benjáme looked around at the people still summiting the cliff - the old, the injured, the young.

"It's sooner than we had planned for and we don't have many of the supplies we'd hope for, but-" he hesitated.

"We will be slow, I know," Lysander accepted, "but can you get us there?" he asked again, this time it was Onni who replied, matching Benjáme's steely expression.

"We can. And we will."

"Good." Lysander gritted his teeth and Benjáme shifted the wet backpack on his shoulders, straightening up and whipping his braided hair over his shoulder.

"We follow the coast north." He pointed ahead, to where Lasse had already begun leading the people away from the explosion, away from their perished loved ones, away from the Celtic army. Onni offered an arm out to the old Danish man as his grandsons ran ahead to catch up to Åsa, whose family was walking with Liddie and Ned. Anders and Yvonne linked hands and began their trudge, Selby and the twins close behind.

Lysander paused. He felt for the Celtic knife in his belt loop and pulled it out, feeling weary for the first time since he'd discovered The Engine Room that morning. He wrapped his fingers around the worn leather grip and thought about what Liddie had said: the girl. The girl from his dream with the long, raven hair and the piercing eyes, a face he had recognized.

He felt the realization hit him like a light in the darkness. She was *his* Celt, just as this was *her* knife. From that first night, in the village. His fingers traced the etching in the blade and he heard the echo of it whizzing past his ear, of Petra's screams as the blade had seared her skin that first night. His hand jumped to the tip of his ear and that phantom cut that lingered. However unintentionally, the girl had saved Petra's leg and maybe her life.

But, Petra wasn't with them now, and she was wounded and freezing, so she wouldn't have run off alone. The next most logical conclusion was that she was with *them*. She was with the Celts.

He wanted to give her the benefit of the doubt, but why run to them? There was no tactical advantage. The Norse were running for their lives. They were running for anywhere they could be safe. He had to conclude that if she had run there, it was because she felt safest with them. Maybe with *him,* Lysander realized.

The thought pooled in him, like a limb filling with blood. She had been in The Engine Room. She had been by The Back Door. She'd known how to open the doors. It made him dizzy, sick.

Was this all Petra's fault? Aksel, Hafthor, Ingrid, and how many others? A and B hanging from the docks of the village? Milla. Could she really have done that to her friends? He didn't know how to answer the questions flooding his mind. He thought he had sensed a kindred spirit in her, but as he watched the plumes of smoke rising over the village, he realized that if she was willing to sacrifice all of them to the Celts, then he really didn't know who she was at all.

He bent over and vomit came out of him, onto the snow, before he could stop himself.

"Are you okay, mister?" a little girl passing him asked in Finnish. The water from the fjord had crystallized in her long strands of auburn hair from the icy wind. Her eyes were wide, full of fear, but also innocence.

He felt his face grow hot, as he straightened himself up and sheathed his knife. He didn't know how to answer her.

24

PETRA

THE PALMS OF HER raw hands burned from scaling the rock face. She bent down and stuck them in a pile of ashen snow. Arthur's lace was knotted around her wrist, soaked and bloody. Gingerly, she brushed her tangled hair from her face and felt a stabbing pain where her stitches had ripped. The duct tape pulled at her skin and she cringed to think what the wound must look like beneath the bandages.

She stood back up again and prayed to the Akka that the Celts wouldn't attack her as she descended into the village. She had no weapons to defend herself and the pain medication she'd been given post-op in The Infirmary had worn off. She'd be useless if they decided to target her. So, she dodged from covering to covering, hiding away in the shadows from the sharpshooters.

Most of the Celtic warriors had witnessed her fight with Briony; its publicity had been an important aspect of it, to make it as public a beating as possible. And if they had been at post and couldn't watch firsthand, then they had at least heard about the flame-headed Norse spy, so they weren't completely unaware of her presence among their ranks. But she didn't know how many of them would be looking for her on the opposite end of the battlefield.

From her slightly elevated position on the sloping hillside, she could see that the majority of the Celtic troops were gathered nearer to the water's edge. They seemed to be focused on the few straggling survivors still coming up from underwater.

Their wicked laughter lifted into the air as they took them out. As if the elderly and families that had fallen behind were pheasants and they were on some royal hunt of old. The flame-tipped arrows sailed through the air at a leisurely pace that made her stomach churn, cutting them down one by one, their cries for mercy short-lived. She could hear Siobhan's voice calling out across the fjord, ripping through the air as leisurely as the arrows, the wind carrying it high and clear.

Sickening as it was, she wasn't there for them. Not for Siobhan, not to check the bodies for Sigrid, not to confront them for Ciarán's cruelty - none of it. She had come back to them for one reason and she knew he wouldn't be out at the front lines. Certainly not shooting arrows at innocents.

She observed the way the Celts had positioned themselves in the remains of the village. Some troops had set up a large table of food before a gallows that now hung in the main square, decorated with charred bodies. It seemed a little overzealous, to be feasting before the burnt bodies of their enemies, but then, so did this entire massacre.

Soldiers patrolled the edge of the water. The port row houses were little more than blackened frames, still crackling and falling bit by bit into the fjord. Petra bit her lip as she thought of Fiske. Was he another ghost who would haunt her for her betrayal today? She pushed the thought away and continued further down into the village, looking for something like triage or any other kind of makeshift med tent.

Some of the Celts gathered at the shoreline weren't participating in the 'hunt', but rather checking the dead as they washed up against the docks. She allowed herself to scan briefly, to see if Sigrid's silver hair would stand out to her. Her wandering eyes stopped after a moment, but it wasn't Sigrid. A tall woman, with long, twisted braids that fell around her shoulders, even now, like the warrior-maiden Lagertha. Though the Captain's face had been stern in life, it was anguished in death. Someone stopped beside Maike's body and dropped to their knees. They signaled for another soldier to join and together they rolled Maike over onto her side, their hands moving over her body.

Petra felt her stomach knot and she turned her face away. She had pegged the Celts for scavengers of the dead before, but even then, it was just out of a need for resources. This was needless vandalism. This was robbing people of their lives and their dignity in death. Robbing someone she admired for that dignity. And it roiled up some defiant flame inside her.

She looked back and with a breath, she realized that they were, in fact, not checking Maike's pockets or salvaging for anything, but checking her injuries, seeing if she could be saved. She felt the fire inside her quiet and she cocked her head curiously. What purpose could Siobhan have for survivors? Or was this order Arthur's doing?

Abruptly, a military vehicle - from the looks of it stolen from Mimameid - pulled up and idled at the edge of the water while the driver received instructions on where to park. One of the Celts on the beach waved them further down.

It stopped at the end of the row of bodies on the beach and the parking brake crunched into place. A few Celtic warriors climbed out, but bringing up the rear was a familiar face, her kind eyes wide as she turned the corner of the vehicle. Darcy's dark head hung as she took in the sight of the bodies. Petra thought she saw a visible sob shake her shoulders.

It was when Petra looked at Darcy's face that she realized the bodies lined up there weren't only Norse, but also mixed together with Celt. *Of course,* Petra thought.

When the *Nilfheim* had exploded, somehow in the rush of it all, she hadn't stopped to think what that meant. But it dawned on her that all the Celts who had boarded Mimameid had all still been in the bunker with no drysuits, no submarines, and no means of escape. A suicide mission. It was exactly what Onni had taught them about the Celts. These soldiers had gone to Mimameid knowing they wouldn't be coming home. She thought of the soldiers at The Back Door and tried to place them in her memory, but they had been nothing more to her than blurs of feral fighters, mad with bloodlust. She couldn't remember a single face or detail. Had Angus been there, or any of the children she had seen practicing in the ring? She couldn't say. Only that, they would remain like that always now: forgotten, sacrificed on the altar of revenge.

Darcy shouted orders at the warriors who had arrived with her, marking and tagging bodies after she had inspected them. There weren't many, but the soldiers followed behind her, loading the designated people into the vehicle, hastily.

That was it, that was her chance. Wherever that car was going, that was where Arthur would be. She dodged around the remains of the buildings, staying hidden in the shadows and smoke as she went.

It took long enough to get there without being seen so that as Petra finally reached the vehicle, they were loading the last of the wounded in. She heard Darcy's lilted Gaelic tell the soldiers to board quickly, that they needed to get the wounded back to the doctor as soon as possible. Petra ducked and rolled under the car, grabbing hold of the frame and lifting herself up with enormous effort. She heard the pump of the clutch as the car tore off and she bit her lip so hard she tasted blood, against the pain in her stomach.

She closed her eyes and concentrated on the sounds of the car and the road to try to distract herself, letting the hum engulf her for a moment. Above her, even over the sounds of the engine, she could hear Darcy's chatty, dominating voice. She could only assume that Darcy was delegating tasks to the soldiers and instructing them on how to proceed when they arrived.

Mercifully, the drive wasn't long. The car shuttered to a halt and Petra heard the parking brake grind into place again before she dropped herself onto the ground. A moan of pain escaped her but was masked by the sounds of a crowd of people, some crying, some moaning, some just talking. She waited patiently while the car doors slammed shut and the soldiers' boots shuffled their way around the edge of the car, unloading the people from the beach. When she heard Darcy's voice again, she considered herself safe enough to be seen. She wiggled out from under the car and grabbed onto the muddy tire with both hands to heave herself up to standing.

As she caught her breath for the first time since, well, since she'd left the Celts, she looked around. They had arrived at a triage station set up in place of their proper medical facilities back at camp. It was a run-down, old house with faded, cherry-red paint peeling from its exterior walls after years of abandonment. There was evidence that there had been a crisply painted white porch with intricately carved awnings on the front of the house at some point, but now there was just a set of stairs, sagging awkwardly off the front door, while the chipped awnings were piled off to the side to be used as kindling.

White smoke puffed out of the chimney, telling her that somewhere inside wood was already burning in the *kaakeliuuni* tile oven, hot and dry, exactly what Petra needed right now. Maybe the building wasn't beautiful like it had been in The Time Before, but it had enough charm left to pull her towards it.

She made her way slowly through the crowd of Celts gathered outside. A few fires were burning, around which various groups had formed. Judging by the tartans, they had naturally separated themselves by clan. They had pulled the furniture, presumably from the house, outside and arranged it around the fires; everything from armchairs to bed frames was being used for seating. Some of the Celts knelt beside their loved ones, their hands smeared with blood, others clutched at less severe wounds, waiting to be seen by Arthur or Darcy. All of them hushed their voices and narrowed their eyes at her as she passed them. She knew what they saw when they looked at her: the traitor with no morals, someone who would betray her own people. But she was used to the looks, it was the same when she had arrived at Mimameid with her flame-red hair, everyone staring at the girl with the muddled, Russian blood. The sins of her forefathers atop her head.

At the base of the stairs, the new arrivals were getting their injuries cataloged and prioritized before being admitted and shown inside. Darcy barked orders at both patient and soldier alike, using her arms to make a path for the soldiers bringing the bodies from the coastline into the house.

Having already seemed to have caught more attention than she preferred, Petra ducked out of sight and slipped around the side of the building, looking for a low window or an unlocked back door. She would rather not parade into the building, demanding to see Arthur, with everyone's prying eyes on her.

She heard raised voices as she turned around the corner to the back side of the house. They were lifting through an open window with the same delicate carvings over the top of it as the front porch awnings.

"She killed him, Arthur. Killed him." The voice was familiar, but she couldn't quite place it.

"I know, I hear you," he replied, his voice focused, concentrating on something. Petra could hear the soft, tinkering of his medical instruments.

"Did you know?" The voice replied with burning accusation. "Did she tell you what she was planning?"

"Of course, I didn't know." Arthur's voice remained calm, collected. "Do you honestly think I could have let hundreds of men and women go down there if I did? Go down there to their deaths?" He paused and the tools clanked as he set them down. "Forget my obligations as a physician to do no harm, I mean me as a person. Do you think I could do that? Do you think I could have let-" he stopped abruptly and the girl cut back in.

"Look, I don't know what you're capable of," the other voice said, "I thought I did, but what with your unnatural love of that Norse-" Arthur interrupted her, but the distaste in her voice had been enough for Petra to finally to figure out who he was speaking to.

"Don't say anything you're going to regret, Briony," he warned her. She paused, and when she spoke again, Petra could hear the agony in her voice.

"Arthur, she sent the only person, the only one who's ever made me feel like I mattered, to his death." There was a sigh.

"I'm sorry," Arthur said and there was a moment when Petra heard boots shuffling around and the tinkling of the instruments being picked back up.

"He was the only one who ever cared about *who* I am, rather than *what* I am."

"That's not exactly fair-" Arthur began, but Briony cut him off.

"Maybe not anymore, but come on Arthur. I'm not naive enough to think you befriended me out of the goodness of your heart." The girl's voice was wry with moxie. She wasn't as slow as Petra had pegged her.

"People change," Arthur replied, "even me." There was another pause and Briony walked over to the opened window. Petra ducked under the rotted back staircase as the young woman leaned out of the window and took a deep breath in. She turned back to Arthur.

"I can't go and face her, not right now," she said as she walked away from the window. Petra crawled back out and stood up.

"I know you don't want to hear it, but she would have told him the plan ahead of time. Even if she didn't tell us." Arthur's response implied something honest, but harsh.

"He wouldn't have chosen to leave me behind. Not with her!" Briony protested. "He wouldn't do that to me." Her voice broke and a door opened inside, followed by receding footfalls.

"Briony, wait -" Arthur tried to say, but it was too late. He sighed and groaned. "*Kyj*," he muttered to himself.

Petra took one steadying deep breath and with her last ounce of energy heaved herself over the open windowsill, into the room.

Arthur gave a start, his hands inside a patient, open on the table.

"Oh my gods!" He was breathing fast, but his face broke out into an impervious grin, his midnight blue eyes alight. "You're alive."

"Hi," she grimaced back the pain as she tried to stand, steadying herself on the open windowsill. The room was warm and a dizziness was creeping over her from that last leap into the room. She a felt woozy smile spread onto her face as she met his gaze and a cockeyed half-smile of fondness greeted her back. Then, she stumbled.

"Are you okay?" He moved to help her, but his hands were already preoccupied. He kept them in the abdomen of his patient.

"Yeah. Yeah, sorry. I had surgery, I had stitches. They, um, ripped on the way out of the bunker." She felt her knees giving out. The swimming, the climb, and the car, it was all catching up to her. Arthur shifted his gaze back and forth between her and his patient, hands working quickly, as she sank to the floor and leaned back against the wall.

"Surgery?" She heard him ask her, although his voice sounded distant, concern clouding his face. He must be trying to keep her talking, she thought, wistfully.

"Yeah. Spleen. They said that it ruptured," she explained, trying to keep her eyes open. They wandered to the sooty tiles of the oven and she concentrated on the various swirls and splatters, trying to figure out how the fire had been burning to make those particular patterns on the white tile.

"I knew we needed to do that ultrasound," he berated to himself.

"It's okay," Petra told him, feeling the sweat beading on her forehead. She closed her eyes, suddenly so tired, and leaned her head back against the wall.

"Stay with me, Petra." Arthur's voice was raised now and trembling. Her eyes snapped open again as she felt his hands clasp her shoulders. Her heart scattered at his touch. How she had missed it. How she had longed for it and she hadn't even realized.

"What about your patient?" she asked faintly, catching her breath as she looked at the operating table.

"He's okay, I'm finished," Arthur told her, his eyes searching her face. "Will you let me look at you?" he asked, cautiously. His voice had become tender and she was conscious enough to notice that he had intentionally asked for her permission. She nodded and accepted his outstretched hand as she got back onto her feet.

Arthur guided her over to a hard, rickety chair in the corner and unzipped her jumpsuit, slowly, watching him. She winced as she ripped open the duct tape and peeled it back from the wound, feeling vulnerable and a little nervous. Without hesitation, he reached across the table to a syringe lying on the table and a glass bottle. Petra extended her arm and stayed his hand.

"Save it for the others," she insisted, the images of the people lined up on the shoreline and those waiting patiently outside to be seen by a doctor burned into her mind, people with far more severe injuries than a few busted stitches. She didn't need the medication more than they did. She certainly didn't deserve it. Arthur nodded,

"Your adrenaline might be enough to stay the pain for now," he reasoned, replacing the syringe on the table and getting a curved needle. He put a hand on her knee as he heated the tip of the needle over a Bunsen burner on the operating table. Her heart leaped again at his touch, followed by embarrassment rising in her. It was so ridiculous, she was bloodied and beaten up, and the foremost thought in her mind was whether or not Arthur had missed her touch as much as she had missed his. She wet her lips, nervously.

She felt the first prick of the needle as it broke her skin and tried to suppress her groan. Arthur's face was apologetic as he continued. Petra, attempting to muscle through the pain, dug her fingernails into the seat of the chair and focused on the musky scent of Arthur's hair, so close to her face as he worked. The smell took her back to that first night at the clootie well, to that last night wrapped up in his arms in the camper van. Over Arthur's shoulder, the door opened with a start and Darcy walked into the room.

"Oh!" She let out an audible sigh when she saw Petra. "Oh, you're back. You're alive." Her face softened. "How lovely." Darcy looked at Arthur, who was poised, ready to make the next stitch into Petra's stomach.

"Hi." Petra managed, weakly. "Thanks for the ride, by the way," she said, and Darcy cocked her head.

"Did you -" she babbled, trying to work the scenario out. "Wait, were you - you know what, never mind!" she concluded, "Welcome back."

"Thanks," Petra croaked, then winced as Arthur pierced her again.

"You're all finished with Leith, yes?" Darcy asked, indicating the patient on the table and Arthur nodded, not looking up from his work on Petra's stomach.

"Yes, and Petra will be done soon as well."

"Excellent." Darcy nodded, even though Arthur couldn't see it as she replied. She looked as though she was stifling the urge to walk over and hug Petra. Instead, she smiled.

"You can prep for the next surgery." Arthur lifted his gaze to Petra's face as Darcy exited the room. "I'd ask you to help, too, but I think it might be better if you rest." He indicated towards her hands and she released her grip on the chair to inspect them, raw from the cliffside and crusted in blood.

"No. I want to help," she said, attempting to push herself up further in the chair and grimacing in pain.

"And what good will you be to me with those hands, anyhow?" He gave her half a smile as he spoke. Now that he had patched her up, he was all ease and lightheartedness. Even now, even after everything that had happened, everything she had done, he could shake the tension from the room. He knotted the thread in her belly and bent down to rip it with his teeth. She jerked a little as she felt the thread pull at her skin. He reached for a bottle of disinfectant and a cloth, turning the bottle upside-down on the cloth. He took her right hand gently in his own and flipped it over to clean.

"I don't want to leave you." The words slipped out of her and she felt the hot embarrassment rising in her again, but Arthur only smiled at them, his eyes warm with kindness.

"Then don't." He raised her hand to his lips and kissed it softly. "Stay here and rest. But please," and he laughed a little as he continued, "try not to get into any more trouble. I feel like I've patched you up more times than any other warrior." She looked up into his midnight blue eyes, searching for some reason to be afraid, but there was nothing there. He wasn't afraid of anything, anymore. He wasn't even afraid of Siobhan.

"But she -"

"She has already tried to take away the one thing I need," he said, raising an eyebrow. "And look how well that turned out for her." He gestured to her. "Besides, she needs me too much to do anything to me," he concluded and he pressed the disinfectant against Petra's scraped hands. She sucked in her breath at the pain in her hands and locked eyes with him. His mind was completely made up; he knew what he wanted. She felt a pang of envy for the clarity in his gaze.

When he had disinfected her hands and wrapped them in bandages, he opened the door to help Darcy wheel in the next patient for surgery.

Half-heartedly, Petra rose to assist, but a warning glance from Arthur had her lowering herself back into the chair. Before she knew it, her eyes grew heavy, lulled by the clinking of the surgery until she gave in completely to exhaustion.

A tender hand touched her shoulder and jolted her awake. Darcy knelt beside her. Even though there was a shadow cast across her face, Petra could see her blood-stained clothes, her rumpled hair, and her desire to get home and hug her children. She smiled at Petra and helped her up from the chair as she spoke, softly.

"We're about ready to head back out. The soldiers are loading the most critically wounded into the trucks and we'll accompany them back to camp." Petra shifted her weight. She was stiff and her back ached, but her stomach already felt better after a few hours of rest.

"What about the Norse wounded?" Petra asked, tightening the bandages on her hands with her teeth, but Darcy shook her head, her lips pursing slightly. She didn't know what Darcy was trying to hide with the expression, but she ignored it, for now.

"They are coming, too." So they weren't going to be killed, but Siobhan must have a purpose for them. She never took anything that the Celts didn't have a use for.

"And those who escaped?"

"They're gone. I heard some of the scouts saying they saw them heading north of the village, but so far there are no orders for them to be followed." *So Lysander and the others were safe, for now.* "We are to stay with the wounded while they are transported back to camp." The words were delivered to Petra as Darcy had received them, as an order and not a suggestion. She was now under Siobhan's protection, which meant she was also Siobhan's to command.

Darcy was clearly uncomfortable being the messenger of such an order, but it was a fleeting discomfort. The woman cleared her throat and returned to her usual kindly self almost immediately. She gestured to a change of clothes on the table. "I figured you'd like to put on something more comfortable."

"Oh, yeah. Thanks," Petra replied. She stretched and felt something in her neck pop as she rolled her shoulders and walked over to the table. She examined the clothes - some thermals, pants, a sweater, socks, a sooty parka, and a crimson tartan.

"It's the best I could do, given the circumstances." Darcy shrugged. "Can't have you sticking out more than you already do." She winked at Petra and turned to leave.

"Darcy," Petra stopped her, "really, thank you." The woman nodded with a satisfied smile and disappeared back out of the room.

Petra slipped into the faded, black base layers and pulled up the rip-stop pants. Judging by the way they hung, they were likely Darcy's own clothes that she'd brought with her for the journey back, having anticipated blood-soaked scrubs. She didn't know Darcy well enough to say whether the act was her own idea or Arthur's, but she was touched by the thoughtfulness, regardless of the circumstances with which they came about.

In addition to Darcy's clothes, there was a leather belt that was entirely too big, which she looped around anyways, fastened at her hips to keep the pants up, and pulled the socks up before slipping into her boots. She shimmied into the oversized, dingy Aran sweater with a fraying collar and a rust-colored stain that Petra didn't want to ask about. She draped the tartan around her head and pulled the parka over her shoulders.

When she had combed through the ends of her tangled hair with her fingers enough to be satisfied, Petra went through the empty hallway and to the top of the crooked front steps of the building. The air still smelled like kindling and the sky looked mysterious and foggy with the brightness of the light grey smoke hanging in it.

At the base of the stairs, she saw Arthur directing which patients would be transported in which vehicles. She watched him for a moment - the confidence with which he conducted himself amongst these fearless creatures of war - and felt her cheeks growing hot. She wished she'd taken more time with her hair in the back room.

When he finally noticed her out of the corner of his eye - as he spoke with one of the commanding officers - she saw a smile sneak onto his face. His eyes twinkled their tantalizing, midnight blue as he finished the conversation, then he reached out his hand to her and she descended the steps, her quivering breath visible in the cold, night air.

"Good to see you up." He took her hand - his fingers lingering for a moment on the lace still knotted around her wrist - and then pulled her into an embrace. His arms were warm around her, strong. "You ready to go?" he asked her in her ear before they released each other.

"Yeah," she nodded, adjusting the tartan around her shoulders. He took a hold of her hand, hesitantly, as though he also wasn't quite sure what to do with himself, although no one else around them would have noticed it. Petra laced her fingers between his and squeezed her bandaged hand gently into his. He tried to suppress a smile by looking at the ground, but Petra caught sight of it and felt her own face lift. Hand in hand, they made their way to the back of the truck they were set to be riding in.

Arthur helped Petra up into the vehicle and then hoisted himself up behind her before turning back to instruct Darcy. Petra sat down on the left-hand side, at the foot of a man hooked up to an IV of some clear liquid.

"Make sure to monitor Leith, yeah? Niamh is about a week from giving birth and will not forgive me if I lose him before he meets the baby," Arthur explained and Darcy nodded,

"You got it," she promised, then closed up the back of the vehicle and slapped the side of it twice.

Arthur found his seat opposite her, at the foot of the other patient, who Petra recognized as the second surgery patient she'd seen earlier that day. He quickly checked both of their pulses, one after the other, while Petra buckled herself in and the truck started with a jolt.

"Are we really headed back to camp?" she asked him over the roar of the engine and Arthur looked up, a little surprised.

"Where else would we be going?" he asked her, cocking his head.

"I mean, the rest of Mimameid, they escaped. Sigrid could be with them," she said tentatively, unsure of whether she really wanted to know whether Siobhan's next plan was to hunt her friends and put them down like dogs. Arthur bit back his bottom lip, debating whether or not to say something.

"Do you wish you were with them?" His shoulders tensed as he asked, a trepidation that maybe she had come to regret her choice to be with him thinly veiled in his voice. She paused before she answered him.

"No," she said, earnestly. Then she sighed and put her head in her hands. "I mean, I can't go back there." The Humvee bounded along around her as she felt the weight of the water closing in around her, the weight of what she had done pushing her down. "Not after what happened. Not after..." She didn't want to think about the bodies floating in the fjord, Maike on the beach, Aksel, Hafthor, Milla. But they were all there, waiting for her when she closed her eyes. Her love for Arthur had done this, and she should be ashamed of herself for it.

Arthur slipped a hand on her leg and it pulled her back from the abyss. She lifted her face to look at him.

"Listen," his eyes were still hooded with a melancholy that she couldn't place, but his voice was full of determination, "Siobhan will have a plan. She always does." His jaw tightened as he said it. "So, the best thing we can do for your friends is keep our heads down and our eyes and ears open." She felt the warmth of sudden sunlight pierce her cheek and she followed Arthur's gaze over her shoulder, out the narrow window of the Humvee. Low in the sky, just under the line of smoke was a deep, red sunset, like nothing she'd ever seen before. Such brilliant hues of plum and garnet and bright scarlet. She watched it as it sank lower and lower into the horizon, the colors growing more vibrant with each passing second.

She turned back to Arthur, now bathed in the ruby glow, and leaned forward to kiss him. He melted at her touch and she felt his hands pull back her tartan, his fingers in her hair. She kissed his jaw, rough and unshaven, down his neck where his scent overwhelmed her, and then their lips met, again - soft, sweet, and sad.

And when they broke apart again, the sunlight was gone.

EPILOGUE

THE FLAME FLICKERED FROM the frigid winds snaking through the caves. Though he was facing away from the water, each time a wave landed against the rock it let out a crack like thunder that made him jump. So he tried to focus on the flame. As though if he concentrated enough he would be able to keep it ignited by looking at it. But the same thing turned over and over in his mind.

Here he was, again. Above Ground, searching for shelter by day, trying not to freeze by night, and every waking moment in between trying to scrounge up food or not get killed by the Celts. There was no end to it. There never was. Mimameid had been a temporary stop on his journey. A fleeting moment in the years he had spent running. And he was tired of it, weary to the bone that he was here, again.

He'd spent most of his life Before alone, sent away to school, too young to fit in and make friends. He'd been okay with it. It wasn't what he'd wanted, but he'd understood the reasons why.

But since Ragnarök, since Lillehammer, he wasn't alone, anymore. And he hadn't wanted that to change, but he'd made the wrong call. He'd split up his family. Linnaea had had a birthday since they'd left, fourteen. She was older now than Judit was when she died. He wished he'd been able to spend those last years with his sister. She was, in his mind, frozen in time as the child she was when he had left for school. But now Petra had abandoned him too, and he was, for the first time, truly alone.

The flame in front of him struggled against the wind. The wood he'd used to feed it now shriveled down to nubs of charcoal. Feet shuffled around him, the feet of the other survivors, trying to find a scrap of warmth for themselves. He adjusted himself to make room and then let his head fall into his hands, splash from the waves hitting the back of his exposed neck.

He felt something cold and hard hit his shoulder and he thought for a split-second the waves had reached him and were there to put out his struggling fire. The last time he'd been here, he'd had Mag and Sprout. And a purpose, a destination. The words Liddie had used floated into his mind - that he was a conduit. A conduit without a current though is nothing. Just a useless wire.

"Lysander," he looked up. The voice belonged to Bjørn. The man's face was weary but warm. His glasses were crooked on his face and foggy from the brackish water. The tips of blonde hair that struck out from under his beanie were frosted with spray from the fjord. He held something in his hand. Something heavy and metal. He tapped Lysander's shoulder with it, again.

"Yes?" Lysander's own voice came out hoarse. He realized how long it had been since he'd spoken. Since the screams, the climb, the trek through a blizzard atop the crag. Since he'd lit the fire and settled into the silence.

"We need an engineer," the man said and Lysander looked closer at what Bjørn had in his hand. His cable rippers. The ones he'd brought to Mimameid, brought to The Engine Room. He lifted his chin.

"Where did you get those?" Bjørn eyes suddenly laughed behind his clouded glasses.

"I brought them with us," his cheeks lifted into a small smile. A smile despite the circumstances. A smile with purpose reflected back onto Lysander's own face. "And good thing too, because someone swiped an old generator from that old village we passed back there, and now," the man held out the cable rippers to him, "we need an engineer."

And then the electrical circuit closed. Lysander felt the current flow into his fingers as they tightened around the handle.

Support me

Your review on Amazon helps future readers discover this book. Share your thoughts with a quick review and spread the love of reading The Mimameid Solution!

amazon.com

Thank you so much for your support!

Language Reference Dictionary

Cornish:
meurgerys – beloved, adored
mar pleg – please
kyj – fuck

Danish:
myseost – sweet brown cheese that is a staple in Scandinavian food culture

Finnish:
ohittaa ruuvimeisselin – pass (bypass) the screwdriver
hitaasti – slowly
saatana – satan
perkele – shit (the devil)
vittu – pussy
pomo – boss/top dog
kaakeliuuni – type of tiled over for heating
korsnäs – traditional red and white Finnish sweater

Gaelic (Irish):
go raibh maith agat – thank you
beannaithe Imbolc – blessed Imbolc
wagon – an obnoxious and annoying woman

póg mo thóin – kiss my ass
dia duit is ainm dom – hello my name is
cá bhfuil an leithreas? – where is the toilet?
cac – shit
dúsachtach – crazy

Icelandic:
pabbi – dad
fíflingur – fool
skít – shit
hlandbrenndu – may you burn from your own urine
vinur – mate (as in buddy)
lopapeysa (lopi for short) – traditional Icelandic wool sweater
góðan dag – good day

Norwegian:
opptenningsved (opps for short) – firewood
tispe – bitch
skatten min – my darling
amma – grandma
afi – grandpa
Fenni – derogatory word for the Finnish/Sami
skit – shit
drittsekk – scumbag
lykke til – good luck
sjef – boss/chief
lusakofte – traditional Norwegian sweater with silver hooks
logr charm – a pendant with a logr rune on it
Hardanger fiddle – traditional instrument from Norway
skol – a toast

Russian:

baba: grandma

pryaniki – russian spiced cookie covered in powdered sugar or a glaze

kolbasa (chocolate) – a chocolate dessert that looks like a roll of salami

Ded Moroz – a Slavic 'Santa Claus' called Grandfather Frost, who visits on New Year's Eve

Sami:

Bergalaga Biru - satan's devil (like goddamit)

ustit – friend

Swedish:

hej - hey

pappa - dad

sötnos - sweetheart/honey/ducky

tjockskalle - nincompoop

skit - shit

fylke – shire

hjärtat – sweetheart

nyckelharpa – the national musical instrument of Sweden, a keyed fiddle

Welsh:

Fy nghariad – my love

cwy - baby

Acknowledgments

There's a lot that goes into making a book.

Not just the sitting down and writing of it - mind you that is quite a feat - but no. The making of a book is research, drafting, time, repetition, back pain, more research, reading, editing, formatting, hiring, video calls, frustration, taking breaks, steaming cups of tea, clenching your jaw, standing up to stretch, proofreading, taking feedback and then doing it all over again.

It takes so much more than one person and their idea to make this happen, so this is for you guys.

Monks - you have been my North Star from the beginning - guiding me through the uncertainty towards this far-off, distant goal that I didn't know I needed. You treated my writing like a job long before it felt like one. This simply wouldn't exist without you on so many levels, but most importantly because you nurtured the faint dream of a little girl who you met long after she had buried that dream. I hold this in my hands because of you.

Mom and Dad - my passion for writing begins with you guys. I look back at writing camp, burying myself in pages of yellow legal pad paper, furiously scribbling, and I see the calling in that little girl. Thank you for allowing her the space to be a creative thinker, for teaching her the discipline needed to do it and for showing her that she is worth supporting.

Xandra - I'm literally a writer and there are still no words to thank you for the amount of time and love you have poured into this book. Thank you for understanding my weird little twists and turns, for falling so deeply in love with my characters and my world. For bringing out their vulnerabilities and their quirks to the surface. For getting lost there with me.

Joe - Joe. You are magic. You truly have made this experience far better than I could have ever imagined. Your passion and the way you always jump when I have a new crazy idea has given life to this project in ways I never hoped for. Anyone reading this who needs a graphics guy for their book project – look no further - this is the guy you've been looking for. And Anna, thank you for sharing him with me.

Sanna, Jonny and Yifei - You guys added layers to the book trailer that made it come to life. Thank you for bringing tears to my eyes.

Alexandria - Your reading of this story has shaped it in small ways and large that I can't wait to implement in the next two books.

To everyone who has supported me (on or off of social media) over the many years that went into the making of this book - you make a girl really feel like she can go out and do this thing of being an author for real. This void doesn't feel so alone knowing there are other moms out there trying to write in-between nap time and dinner prep, that there are other women who love science fiction as much as me, that there are other people making this self-publishing thing work, that there are readers hungry for what I have to say, and that there are friends who want to see me achieve my dreams. Thank you.

And to my little girl – This book began long before you, and you're still too young to know how important you are to this story. But I know that you being here has made all the difference in this book. There are depths to this story that exist only because you taught me how to write them. You, with your giggles and smiles and patience and impatience. You are the heart of me and that makes you the heart of this book. If nothing else ever comes from The Mimameid Trilogy I hope that you grow up seeing and knowing that you can chase your dreams.

Made in the USA
Middletown, DE
11 December 2023

44018746R00293